LEAP OF FAITH

Darbe Ennly

Copyright © 2024 Darbe Ennly

ISBN: 979-832-69236-6-0

All rights reserved. No part of this publication may be reproduced, stored in a retrieval system, or transmitted, in any form or by any means without the prior written permission of the publisher, nor be otherwise circulated in any form of binding or cover other than in which it is published and without similar condition being imposed on the subsequent purchaser. All characters in this publication are fictitious and any resemblance to real persons, living or dead is purely coincidental.

DEDICATION

For Ilona

CHAPTERS

One	1
Two	9
Three	23
Four	44
Five	54
Six	68
Seven	77
Eight	86
Nine	94
Ten	110
Eleven	126
Twelve	138
Thirteen	141
Fourteen	155
Fifteen	168
Sixteen	188
Seventeen	202
Eighteen	217
Nineteen	234
Twenty	252
Twenty-One	262
Twenty-Two	286
Twenty-Three	303
Twenty-Four	317
Twenty-Five	332
Twenty-Six	349
Twenty-Seven	364
Epilogue: One Year Later	384

ACKNOWLEDGMENTS

I would like to thank Heike Sandrock, my beta reader.
Your insights are a source of encouragement,
and your suggestions are invaluable.
And, Julie Forester, my editor:
julieforesterbooks.simdif.com
Thank you for taking me on. I'm learning a lot.

ABOUT THE AUTHOR

Darbe Ennly is a native of California, currently living in Germany with her wife. Her passions include traveling, cycling, and writing stories about life and love. This is her debut novel, the first in a series.

CHAPTER ONE

There is nothing more frightening than the moment you realize you are different in a way that will change your life forever, and not for the better. It's scarier still when you realize there is nothing you can do about it. The only thing remotely comparable to this experience is birth. Too bad you can't remember birth because it definitely presents some interesting parallels to the injustice, uncertainty, and sheer terror of some of life's biggest reveals.

The instant you are born, your parents, your gender, your skin color, and the country you live in determine your worth, your status, your beliefs, and your future. Your entire existence is relegated to a coin toss, the outcome impossible to control, and in my case, landed me smack-dab in the middle of a very religious family and a patriarchal, fundamentalist church. Although not the worst place to end up—given all the possible hostile places a girl could end up in this world—my strange, top-down, archaic lifestyle was by no means a picnic.

The church I was born into promised eternal life in heaven for its members and only its members—no one else was going, just us—insisting that it alone was the one true Christian church. This exclusivity extended to women in the church as well, deeming them less than men in every way while convincing them to be proud of their status. It was remarkable that at such a young age I even developed an opinion about this given how tightly information in my world was controlled, but it basically boiled down to common sense—the Achilles heel of any baseless claim.

Something about the church's exclusivity and apparent dislike of women made no sense to me. It seemed antithetical to its mandate, and the fact that the whole setup oddly resembled a pyramid scheme didn't help either. Nonetheless, I tried my best to understand my place in the church and accept my part in it, even when it became apparent that the only thing required of me was to procreate, effectively making me the key to everything—my very existence and willingness to submit, keeping the pyramid from collapsing in on itself—but because I was a woman, gave me absolutely no say in anything.

Managing this ironic elephant in the room stomping its way through my subconscious as I grew out of adolescence and entered puberty was not easy. It was a confusing time turning fifteen and suddenly growing hips and breasts, getting my first period, going on my first date, and receiving my first kiss from a church guy named Bill. The sudden change in boys' attitudes toward me was baffling. Most of the ones I'd grown up with—including Bill—spent their entire prepubertal lives being mean to me and making fun of my red hair and freckles, generally making it clear that they liked me even less than God did. But that was all water under the bridge now. They wanted to date me. I suddenly had worth.

While grappling with the contradictions of dating, I became aware of a new problem that made the pyramid scheme seem like child's play—no pun intended—further complicating my already complicated life. I was shocked when I noticed it and instinctively knew that if I didn't do something about it, my place in the hereafter could be in serious jeopardy. Given that my entire worth and salvation lay in getting married and having children, an impossible dilemma quickly emerged as my worrying new problem took over my body, making the idea of marriage seem more like a nightmare than a fairytale and the prospect of hell more real than ever.

There was only one thing to do. I dove headfirst into the only thing that was available to me—the belief system that had been ingrained in me since the day I was born. I got with the program, adding to my usual weekly church services every other church meeting and Bible study my schedule would allow, inundating myself with what I needed to believe. I would leave no room inside me for that other thing.

I had to put a stop to it. Failure was not an option. There was too much at stake.

My family didn't just go to church, we lived church. We looked like church people. I had outrageously long, uncut, crazy thick red hair, wore only modest, below-the-knee length dresses and skirts, minimal makeup and jewelry, and only socialized with people in the church. Nothing was left to chance when it came to the parts of me I could control, covering myself from head to toe in the costume of righteousness, hoping that practicing the ways of a proper Christian woman would turn me into one.

My dad was an Elder in the church, and it was a family affair. All of us were touched by the prestige that came with such a position. For me, though, our elevated status just added more pressure to my life and more worries, never letting me forget that if I failed, my dad would fail too. The Bible left no room for debate on the matter; one of the most important requirements for eldership was faithful children. My dad had worked hard for his position, and I didn't want to mess it up for him—like I needed another reason to stay faithful; as if the threat of hell wasn't motivation enough.

I continued to toe the line, trying hard to live a Christian life, while hiding what was inside of me, hoping it would go away. But it didn't go away. So, I tried harder, forcing myself over and over to recommit to the church, getting baptized not once but twice just to make sure. I was all in, doing all the right things, dating all the right men, hanging out with all the right people, and going to all the right church meetings. I read my Bible every night, dreaming of that place called heaven while dealing with the real possibility that this was probably as close as I was ever going to get to it.

* * *

The older I got, the more difficult it became for me to wholeheartedly accept the church's basic premise that, as the weaker sex, women were only qualified to exist as servants. Doubting anything in the church was a problem—a slippery slope, a house of cards—but one I had learned to manage. My new problem, though, was a whole other animal, refusing to be managed and stay in the background, constantly jockeying for position, determined to be my number one problem, making my head a very crowded place. It would not let me loose no matter how hard I tried, claiming ownership of my raging hormones while threatening me with damnation at every turn. It seemed so unfair that I should have such a problem with all the effort I put into being pious. What happened to the promise that God wouldn't give you more problems than you could handle? My new problem was not just in the back of my mind anymore; it was taking over my whole body, making it impossible to ignore.

Education about my condition was nonexistent. There were no role models on TV, and at school, it was rarely spoken of except in the abstract, using insults and a mix of lewd innuendo, cruel language, and slurs. Information in written form was impossible to secure. Where would I keep hidden such information from my parents and siblings? No one in the church would touch this with a ten-foot pole, and I seriously doubted I could count on God for any assistance, or any mercy for that matter, when it turned out that I couldn't handle the problem *he* gave me.

Fresh out of high school, just nineteen years old, I flew solo for the first time from California to Colorado to attend a week-long church meeting. While out with some of the church ladies shopping at the local mall one afternoon, I came upon a Christian bookstore and walked in just to browse, discovering in the back of the store a carousel of pamphlets. Scanning the different subjects—greed, envy, slothfulness—I moved down the carousel and came to obesity, alcoholism, and, to my total shock, homosexuality.

My heart slammed against my rib cage as the room pressed in around me. I reached out and grabbed the carousel, almost knocking it over as I tried to steady myself. I looked around the store, relieved to find it practically deserted, and with stealthy concealment, slipped the homosexuality pamphlet into my hand. I opened it, scanned the first page, then clapped it shut. The words shocked and shamed me, but still, I could not put it down. In my hand was something with the name of what I was on it, and this somehow made me feel empowered. For which side of the conflict I felt this empowerment, I wasn't sure. The message of redemption was clear, but it also provided proof that I was not alone.

It never occurred to me to steal the pamphlet, but the idea of presenting it to the cashier seemed impossible to me, and for a moment, I stood there unable to figure out what to do. Reading it inside the store was an option, but being several pages long, it would take too long to read discretely. What if someone saw me? A brilliant idea entered my mind. I picked out a book, *Mary, the Mother of Jesus and Other Notable Women in the Bible,* and decided to buy both, hoping that such a pious book would distract the cashier's attention away from the pamphlet while also providing the perfect hiding place for the pamphlet later.

The cashier looked at the book, then at my pamphlet, and then at the book again. I swallowed. Was the book having the opposite effect intended? She tilted her head and looked at me over the rim of her glasses. Certain she was about to address the subject similarities, which were suddenly glaringly obvious, I braced for questions about my choice of reading material. Instead, her gaze shifted over my shoulder and darted around the room behind me, landing on something that made her smile.

"Janice?" she called out. "Can you get me a price check on the pamphlets?"

Janice was tucked away in the far corner of the store stocking books. She put down the handful of books she was shelving, walked over to the carousel of pamphlets, and peered at the selection. "Which one is it?" she called back.

I watched in horror as the cashier scrutinized my pamphlet, her lips parting a fraction, primed to reveal the title as she held it up, flapping the evidence in Janice's direction.

"It's okay," I half whispered. "I don't need it." I grabbed

the pamphlet and pulled it and her hand down, hoping to prevent her from saying the name out loud. I couldn't be exposed like this!

She looked at me and hesitated, her brows furrowed in confusion.

Janice hollered across the store. "The pamphlets are two seventy-five."

Holding my breath, I waited to see what the cashier would do.

"Do you still want this?"

Having momentarily lost my ability to speak, I hoped a simple nod would satisfy her. She bagged my purchase, and I slowly exhaled, my pulse racing as I pulled a twenty-dollar bill from my wallet, my hand trembling as I handed it to her. She gave me my change, my bag, and a look that suggested she knew everything about me.

Practically running, desperate to get out of there, I plowed through the door, only to find my companions approaching, asking me what I had bought. In full panic, I grabbed the pamphlet out of my bag, crumbled it up in my fist, and threw it into the trash can next to the door.

So, reading material on the subject was out of the question, and no one in the church gave sermons on the subject. I wasn't comfortable talking privately to anyone in the church—afraid that I would be judged, drawn, and quartered—and the church disapproved of relationships outside the church—friend or otherwise—preventing me from seeking direction on the subject from those who might have insight unrelated to the fire-and-brimstone angle. I was in big trouble. My efforts to exorcise this thing from my body were proving ineffective. It not only remained, it grew stronger, becoming belligerent and brash, constantly tapping me on the shoulder.

* * *

Over the next three years, I must have had a crush on every eligible woman in the church. At the same time, I continued to date men—a lot of them—and no matter how many of them I tried, I could not replicate the physical attraction I had for women and have it for men. It just did not happen. The men I dated were nice enough, but I could barely tolerate all the kissing and petting. Sex before marriage was not allowed in the church, but for some reason, making out in a car for an hour was. With every guy, without exception, after the first couple of dates, making out became an expected part of every date that followed. It was unavoidable, frustrating, and downright disgusting, always ending when I insisted my curfew was approaching and that my dad was waiting for me. That became my go-to line about two minutes into every single make-out session. My dad had clout, and I was not above using it. My boyfriend would drive me home and deliver me to my doorstep with a final goodnight kiss, and I would hurry inside, jump in the shower, and wash the unpleasant evening from my body as I racked my brain for a good excuse to break up with him. Afterward, I would lay in bed until late at night, praying for a miracle.

And just like that, I was twenty-two. It was the middle of spring, and I was between boyfriends. I enjoyed these occasional reprieves and the little bit of freedom they afforded me and used them to catch my breath. At the same time, I worried about running out of men to date. Nearing old maid status would put me in a different category of availability and undoubtedly make dating even more complicated than it already was. It definitely wouldn't make it any easier and would probably increase the pressure on me to get married before I was ready.

When not in church, I went to work—a good job with the state of California. I enjoyed work and was on friendly terms with a few of my colleagues, some of whom would occasionally chat with me about subjects that had nothing to do with the church. But that was all the solace I could glean from the world. Being different and looking different made it difficult for worldly people to approach me. I wasn't exactly sporting your typical eighties fashion—more like fifties fashion—and was seen as weird for some, a curiosity for others, too odd for even the most socially desperate, and all but invisible to those who interested me.

As hard as I tried not to be gay, I kept noticing women at work and even developed a few crushes, but always in secret. I kept my head down and managed my problem the best I could, feeling less pressure about my condition when I was out in the world and taking what comfort I could in that. And then I'd go back to church and feel more like a freak than I did out in the world. Being me was impossible, but I pushed on, trying to balance both sides of me while trying not to think about the inevitable. I would have to marry soon.

CHAPTER TWO

There was one part of my Christian life that I was very passionate about. Cooking. Every good Christian girl learned how to cook, and when Mom first introduced me to the kitchen, I knew I had found my calling. I was a natural and started as a helper, readying everything for Mom the moment she needed it, chopping carrots and onions, mixing batter and stirring sauces, and having the correct spices ready at the right moment for roasts and fried chicken, chili and stews. By the age of thirteen, I was able to prepare five complete meals on my own, and by sixteen, one of my official chores was to prepare our family dinner three times a week. At nineteen, I could put most dishes together by memory, only occasionally needing to consult my binder full of personally perfected recipes.

Compliments on my cooking were not uncommon, especially at church potlucks, which made me proud of myself and helped me forget how miserably I was failing at everything else Christian. When I cooked, I lost myself in the simplicity of it, the challenge of it, and the science of it. Cooking didn't care what I was inside. As long as I treated it with respect, it treated me with respect, reacting perfectly to everything I did to it.

One early Sunday morning, as I stood over the stove putting the last touches on a big pot of chili and carefully watching over two skillets full of fried chicken, Mom walked into the kitchen, still in her house coat and slippers, yawning loudly.

"Good morning, honey. Excuse my yawning."

"Late night?"

"A little. We got in after eleven." She poured herself a cup of coffee and one for Dad. "I know why I'm up so early, Shannon. I can smell that chili all the way down the hallway. It smells delicious."

"Thanks, Mom. These are the easiest dishes for potluck.

If I'm lucky, there won't be any leftovers."

"I'm sure there won't be. You are an excellent cook. Everyone loves your chili." As Mom left the kitchen, she called out to me, "Is potluck at the park this time?"

"Yeah. Are you guys going?"

"Yeah. We'll be there." She continued down the hallway, and a moment later, the bedroom door closed.

I showered, got dressed, and carried my chili and fried chicken out to my truck, carefully arranging them on the bench seat before fastening them in with the seatbelt. Then I drove over to the church for morning services. It was a beautiful day, and I was determined to enjoy it.

* * *

After services, I drove directly to the park and luckily found a parking spot relatively close to the picnic area. I carefully schlepped my chili and fried chicken over to where the potluck tables were set up, and although the tables were already pretty full, managed to find a spot for my chili between a pot of spaghetti and a potato gratin casserole. There was a whole table reserved for meat dishes, so there was no problem finding a spot for my fried chicken. I took a quick peek at some of the other dishes. They all looked delicious, and my stomach growled. I couldn't wait to try them and find out more about what I didn't know about cooking.

As more and more people arrived, I couldn't help but admire what a big group we were. When a couple of hundred Christians go to the park, you notice. The look of us moved me, especially the women. They were beautiful, dressed in summer dresses and sandals, their hair pinned up high or in ponytails. Some wore their hair down like mine, and like me, were probably wishing they had put it up. It was warm for May, even by California standards.

With a good half-hour still before lunch started, I hung my purse on the shoulder of a chair and set out on a stroll, and just like always, before long, my problem began to fill my thoughts. The pressure of being me was too heavy, my situation more and more impossible as I struggled with the secret side of me, the side that was bursting to get out, and the public side of me, the side that was starting to show some cracks, both sides more present than they had ever been before. I grabbed hold of my problem and pushed it away, determined not to let it ruin my day, and instead concentrated on the little pieces of uncomplicated life right in front of me—the sun shining, the grass growing, and the wind in my hair—anything that would keep me from thinking about my problem and the future it threatened to destroy.

"Hey! Shannon!"

I looked up at the sound of my name and saw three young women sitting on the grass underneath a tree. Two of them I knew well: Elena and Vicky. They were sisters. The third I was sure I'd never seen before. I would have remembered. She was striking. I stopped and stared for a moment as Elena introduced her to me, explaining that Jordan had just moved to the area from LA and would be living with her brother, Shawn, Elena's fiancé. Jordan was an unusual name for a girl, but I found it incredibly cool. It suited her very well. I stood there pondering its origin, totally unprepared when she turned and offered me a stunning smile. My breath caught, and I stumbled a bit, my heart slamming into my chest as I attempted to smile back at her.

"Ah… It's nice meeting you," I blurted, realizing they were waiting for me to speak.

Elena began talking about her favorite subject—her recent engagement to Shawn. She asked me what I thought about the color lavender for the bridesmaids' dresses, and when I didn't answer straight away, she continued talking as if she'd never asked me the question. This amused Jordan, and she let out a chuckle, raising her eyebrows as her eyes locked with mine.

I was usually so careful when it came to looking at women, mindful not to dally too long, expertly shifting my gaze the moment they looked back at me. They'd never know

I had been looking at all. But with Jordan, I didn't feel caught, and nothing about her unwavering gaze told me that returning it in equal measure was not welcome. So, I held her gaze, without thought to risk, and the most extraordinary thing happened as the world around me came to a shuddering halt. Something inside me slowly shifted, and the hopelessness that constantly surrounded me evaporated into thin air. This beautiful creature was looking at me. Could she see me?

As the world around me began moving again, a sensation of falling suddenly took hold of me, and I tried to look away from Jordan, fearing that if I didn't, I would fall flat on my face. A conundrum, as her smile, like an unseen force, seemed to be the only thing keeping me upright.

The call to lunch broke the spell, and I managed to get control of my body as the three of them stood up and headed for the potluck tables. I followed, barely able to catch my breath as I grabbed a plate and got in line, stealing glances at Jordan as I filled my plate without a thought to what I was putting on it. I grabbed something to drink at the beverage table and followed them to their seats. I couldn't say what was directing me as I sat down right next to Jordan. I was not usually this forward. I was actually quite shy. It was like being in a trance, unable to act otherwise. Jordan turned and looked at me, and it occurred to me that I might have overstepped. I glanced around for another place to sit, but then she smiled, reassuring me that everything was okay. I sat there and didn't say more than five words the rest of the afternoon. I couldn't take my eyes off Jordan as I listened to the three of them talk, careful to nod when everyone else did, occasionally looking at Elena or Vicky when they spoke, but mostly staring at Jordan. It was a miracle no one noticed.

Around four o'clock, people started cleaning up. The chairs and tables were folded and loaded onto a truck, and people began leaving, heading out to their respective churches for evening services. Elena and Vicky started toward the parking lot, leaving Jordan to wait for me as I grabbed my empty chili pot and fried chicken container. We stood there looking at each other as I balanced everything in my arms, and then Jordan smiled, tucked her hair behind her ear, and stepped forward. I immediately took a step back, thinking... I honestly don't know what I was thinking. It was like my entire being wanted to be close to her, but I was afraid she would notice. Help!

"Here, let me carry some of that," she offered.

"Oh! Okay." I stepped forward, a little too energetically, and shoved my container at her, crashing it into her chest.

"Whoops," she chuckled, stepping back, her hands briefly touching her chest, checking for damage.

"Sorry!" I stepped back at the same time, cringing as I jerked the container away from her, mortified that I'd rammed her in the chest with it.

"That's okay," she said, letting out a snort of amusement as she again reached for the container.

We both stepped forward at the same time, and between her attempt to take the container from me and whatever the heck I was doing, we sent it flying into the air. It jumped around like a volleyball for a second or two as we both hectically attempted to grab it, and then I lost hold of my chili pot and sent it flying as well. As we knelt down to pick everything up off the ground, our knees collided, putting us both off balance, and out of pure reflex, my hand jumped out and grabbed her shoulder. When I realized what I had done, I immediately let go, then practically shoved her away from me.

"Whoa!" she exclaimed, laughing as she reached out and caught hold of my arm, steadying us both.

My face exploded in a hot blush. I had always been a bit uncoordinated, but this was ridiculous! I was a walking catastrophe! I couldn't seem to stop assaulting her! If a hole had mysteriously appeared beside me, I would have gladly jumped in and let it swallow me up.

Jordan helped me to my feet, then gathered everything up off the ground, both of us taking a deep breath before breaking out in nervous laughter.

"Sorry about that," she said.
"No. That was all me."
"Oh, I think I helped a little."
"No. Really, you didn't, but thank you, for...helping." Could I have been any more awkward!

As we walked through the parking lot, Jordan commented on the nice time she'd had at potluck and how good the food was. When we got to my truck and I still hadn't said anything, she teased me about how quiet I was.

"You don't talk much do you?"

"I do talk. Really, I do...despite evidence to the contrary."

This made her laugh, which made me smile. "Okay, then. I look forward to it." She gazed at me a moment before glancing down at my chili pot and fried chicken container still in her arms. "Where do you want me to put this?"

"Oh, yeah. Here, passenger side," I sputtered as I hurried around to unlock the door.

She put everything in on the seat, then left me with a sweet, "See you at church," sprinting off to catch up with Elena and Vicky. I jumped in my truck and turned on the ignition, sitting a moment as I tried to collect myself, wishing I could erase the last five minutes of my life. I looked at my watch, put the truck in gear, and drove out of the parking lot. Church started in fifteen minutes. I was going to be late.

* * *

Pulling into the church parking lot, I couldn't remember a thing about the ride over, so deep in thought was I about what had occurred at potluck. I checked my face in the rearview mirror, then jumped out of the truck, shouldering my purse as I quickly made my way to the entrance of the church building. I was late and tried to enter quietly. Services had already begun, and the first hymn was being sung.

I slipped into the last pew, grabbed a hymn book, and cracked it open, looking over the top of it for Jordan. She was sitting way up front with Elena and Vicky. I stared at the back of her head for much of the service, thinking up clever things to say to her, hoping to make up for my bumbling, mute performance at potluck. Before I knew it, services were over and everyone was standing and greeting each other. I scrambled to my feet and made my way to the foyer, meaning to catch Jordan there, determined to say something remotely intelligible to her.

Jordan entered the foyer a few minutes later, her smile making my knees go weak as she greeted a group of young people eager to make her acquaintance. I took a quick breath and tried to gather myself as she made her way through the crowd toward the front entrance, where I stood greeting members and shaking their hands.

"Wow, there are a lot of people here," Jordan said when she finally turned to me.

She was a little taller than I was, her wavy, dark hair reaching her lower back, her skin light olive and flawless, her eyes brown with long, dark lashes. She was beautiful. She offered me her hand, and as our fingers touched, I quietly gasped as a delicious current ran up my arm and flooded my body, the sexual nature of it undeniable. I looked down at our hands holding, then up at her face and into her eyes, searching for any clue that this was happening to her too.

"It was good to see you again, Shannon," a voice chirped from behind me.

I snatched my hand from Jordan's and turned to find Elena and Vicky standing next to us. I hadn't even heard them approach.

"It was good seeing you too," I returned, then blanched when I realized what this meant.

Jordan was leaving. Our time together was nearly up. This had been the most wonderful day of my life, and Elena was about to put an end to it!

"It was nice meeting you, Shannon. I'll see you later," Jordan said in parting.

"Yeah, likewise," I barely managed before she was out the door, Elena and Vicky behind her. As they made their way through the portico, Jordan glanced back at me before disappearing around the corner of the building.

I stood there another few minutes, mechanically shaking hands and greeting people, still reeling from our day at the park together, hoping I would get another chance to see her and prove to her that I could hold a conversation without assaulting her. I could only imagine what she thought of me after today. Lord, have mercy!

* * *

My Friday evenings were routinely uneventful when I was without a boyfriend, usually spent in solitude recovering from my workweek. Not having many friends and none who were close enough to casually call on me, I was a little surprised when the telephone rang and Mom shouted from the kitchen, "Shannon, it's for you. It's Elena." It was seldom I got a call from Elena, and not one of those calls had ever been to invite me to one of her informal, ladies-only softball games. It was common knowledge that I wasn't very athletic, but she sounded sincere enough when she said she hoped to see me the following morning at eleven o'clock. She had invited some of the other young ladies from church who loved to play softball, and afterward, we were all invited to a barbecue in her backyard. She asked me to bring three bags of chips. There was no need to ask if Jordan would be there. This invite was so rare, it could only have come from Jordan.

The next morning, I woke with Jordan in my thoughts, excited that I would be seeing her again in just a matter of hours. I picked out my best jean skirt and a casual blouse, fixed my hair back so it was out of the way, and did my makeup, careful not to use too much. I didn't want it to look like I'd gotten all dressed up for a softball game, but I did want to look my best for Jordan.

I drove over to the baseball park and parked next to the only baseball field occupied by women wearing skirts. I didn't immediately get out of my truck, nervous as I watched them warm up. These ladies took softball seriously. I was familiar with the game of softball, as most Americans were, and occasionally played when I had to. I was pretty sure I could hold my own as long as nobody threw a ball at me or hit one to me. One could only hope, as I really didn't want to make a fool of myself in front of these ladies, and certainly not in front of one in particular.

Jordan was throwing catch to Elena, and I smiled at how excited and confident she looked. She was obviously an athlete; she certainly moved like one, and she definitely knew how to throw a softball. I deposited my purse in the dugout and walked out onto the field, standing off to the side, trying to stay out of the way, not really knowing what to do with myself as everyone finished warming up.

Elena called us together, then split us up into two teams, and as she went over some of the rules, Jordan threw me a smile and a wave from where she stood with her team. I waved back, returning her smile, slowly morphing into a bashful thirteen-year-old girl right before her eyes as I swayed from side to side, kicking at a stone with the toe of my sneaker and grinning like a complete dork. Jordan stood there staring at me, tilting her head as a look of amusement spread across her face. Oh my God! I was flirting! I snapped to attention, willing my body to stop moving without my permission. Thankfully, my momentary lapse went unnoticed by the others, as Elena had been tossing a coin at the time, tails determining that Jordan's team would bat first. Jordan let me borrow her mitt because, of course, I forgot to bring one, and Elena sent me out into right field—the position best known by the worst player on the team.

The first batter hit a pop fly to left field, which Rebecca caught easily. The second batter hit a grounder to first. Two outs, one to go. Jordan was up to bat next, and Elena, who was pitching, waved to us in the outfield to move back a bit, signaling that Jordan could hit. I moved back several steps as Jordan took a few practice swings. Yeah, she could hit. I could tell by the way she swung that bat that she knew what she was doing.

I took a few more steps back, and the other outfielders did

the same. I hit the pocket of Jordan's mitt with the fist of my right hand, feeling a little breathless as I realized I had something on my hand that she had worn. I shook my head and tried to concentrate, punching the pocket again with a little more force. I was ready! I was feeling it! Nothing was getting by me! Jordan let the first two pitches go, and the third pitch she sent straight to me with a loud *crack*, rocketing the ball high into the air.

I took three or four tentative steps forward, immediately realized I had misjudged, and backtracked several steps before changing my mind and surging forward again. By then, I'd completely lost sight of the ball. Dumbfounded to find tears in my eyes as my vision began to blur, I shuffled backward in a blind panic, hoping for a miracle as I threw my hands into the air in the direction I thought the ball was coming from. The ball managed to make its way through my arms without touching my mitt, slam into my stomach, and knock the wind out of me before falling to the ground, rolling a few feet away, and coming to a stop.

Mouth open, gasping for air, I wrapped my arms around my stomach and slowly bent forward before falling backward onto my butt and toppling over sideways into the dirt. Jordan came to a stop between first and second base and then started toward me, as did several of the other fielders. I knew I had to get up, and fast. I couldn't let her see me like this. Tears were streaming down my face, smearing my makeup, my jean skirt had scooched up to just below my panty line, and I was covered in dirt. Pure humiliation pulled me to my feet, and I ran. "Shannon! Shannon!" someone called out, but I kept running, past the parking lot and down the street, fueled by embarrassment, mortified that Jordan would realize that I was not only a horrible softball player, but a complete doofus.

I ran until my legs started to burn, then stopped, leaned forward, and grabbed my knees, huffing and puffing as I struggled to catch my breath. I gingerly peeked under my shirt and discovered a big bruise forming on my stomach just below my left breast. I dropped my shirt and began walking, hands on my hips, unable to believe what I had just done. I had never been so embarrassed in my life. I would never be able to face her again.

A hand touched my shoulder from behind, and I nearly jumped out of my sneakers. I swung around and there she was. Jordan. She took one look at me and started laughing.

"Are you okay?" she asked. She was out of breath from running after me but somehow managed to continue laughing. I covered my face with my hands and backed away from her. If she couldn't see my face, maybe she wouldn't be able to see what a mess I was. "No! I'm sorry," she said, her laughter fading. She raised her left hand and took a step toward me, crouching a bit, a look of concern on her face as her hand touched my shoulder. "Are you hurt?"

Our eyes locked, and she slowly smiled, her right hand reaching forward and gently pulling my hands away from my face, exposing me. There was nowhere to hide. I looked down at myself, totally embarrassed to be looking the way I did in her presence. I had dirt all over me.

The tips of her fingers touched my chin, and I looked up at her, flinching a little when she touched my cheek. "Are you okay?" she asked softly as she gently wiped the wet smears from my face. "I'm so sorry."

I swear, my heart was trying to beat its way out of my chest. "I feel so stupid, that's all. I'm fine, just very embarrassed."

She let out a small laugh and took a step back, looking down at my stomach. "Let me see," she said as she attempted to lift my shirt.

I pushed my shirt down and her hand away, blurting, "I'm okay!" I quickly smiled to soften my abrupt rebuff. "But I will definitely have a nasty bruise from this."

She laughed and turned, lifting her shirt and showing me a bruise on her lower back. "Elena gave me this yesterday. A hard ground ball, straight at me."

"How did it hit you in the back?"

"It took a nasty bounce, and I turned, trying to get out of

the way. It was either that or take it in the face. There was no way I was going to get a mitt on it."

"Well, I'm glad it didn't hit you in the face. That would have been a real shame." My breath caught and my face turned beet red. I looked down at my sneakers, fighting the urge to cover my face with my hands again. Did I really say that? I swallowed hard and cleared my throat, daring to look back up at her. She was smiling, her eyes gazing into mine. She reached out and touched my arm, and I nearly fainted.

"Why don't you come back? Let's go to the barbecue. It'll be fun. We can take your truck; I'll drive," she said.

It took me a moment to realize what she was suggesting, and I started shaking my head, mortified at the thought of having to go back and explain my strange behavior to everyone. "I can't go back there. I can't face them again today."

"Yes, you can," she said, and I did.

We walked back to the baseball field together, and the softball ladies were still playing, finishing up the first inning without us. We played four more innings, and I had to admit, it was a lot of fun, even with all the teasing. Rebecca gave me a wet nap to clean my face with, and everyone wanted to see my bruise, but I wouldn't show them. Vicky remarked on how I had always been especially body-shy, and my face turned bright red in response, embarrassed that Jordan now knew this small detail about me. Thanks, Vicky. I wanted to clobber her.

We packed up the equipment, then headed for our cars. I assured Jordan that I was recovered enough to drive, but she insisted, so I let her, and while she drove, she told me a little about herself. She wanted to settle in Sacramento and hoped to find a job soon. She had been on two job interviews last week and had several lined up over the next two weeks. She talked about her brother, how crazy it was living with him, and about her parents, who lived in LA.

Her hands lightly gripped the steering wheel, the right one moving back and forth, shifting gears, stopping midair to gesture a point before returning to the steering wheel again. They were brown and strong, her fingers long and elegant, as were her legs, moving effortlessly from brake to gas to clutch, her skirt moving with them. I risked a glance at her breasts and quickly looked away. They were bigger than mine—that was clear. Her voice was lovely. It was mild but melodic and would break sometimes as it rose. It seemed always on the edge of laughter, excited, soft for effect, then strong again. The sound of it made my body tingle in a way that had me grinning like an idiot. It made me happy. I could listen to her talk all day.

When we parked in front of Elena and Vicky's house, I was surprised and disappointed that our drive together was over so soon. I grabbed the grocery bag full of chips, jumped out of the truck, and followed Jordan across the lawn to the front porch. As we walked up the front steps, I experienced a sensation of something exclusively shared when a sudden breeze billowed our blouses and played with our hair. Jordan rolled her eyes at me as she tucked her hair back behind her ears. I adjusted my gawping gaze into an eye roll to match hers, and she offered me a small, knowing smile, charmingly gifting me an intimate moment with her. I couldn't play softball, but I had a bruise just like hers and a head full of hair that was always in danger of being blown in the wrong direction. We had something in common, and I suddenly couldn't wait to know everything about her.

The barbecue was actually very enjoyable. We sat around talking, eating, and just hanging out, Jordan at the center of everything. She was so friendly and always smiling, she loved joking and teasing, and the others enjoyed her attention as much as I did. She would make many friends here, of that I was certain.

At six o'clock on the dot, we were shooed out the door. There was church tomorrow and, as Elena and Vicky's mom put it, young girls like us needed our beauty sleep. Everyone walked out together to get into their cars, Elena, Vicky, and Jordan standing on the front lawn waving goodbye. As I started my truck, Jordan ran over to my passenger-side window. I rolled it down.

"I had fun today. It was great having you out there playing softball with us. I hope I didn't scare you off with that pop fly. I hope you'll come play again."

"No. You didn't scare me off."

"I hope your bruise heals okay."

"My bruise will be fine, and thank you for talking me into coming to the barbecue. I'm glad I came."

"I'm glad you did too. I'll see you later then."

"I'll see you later, Jordan."

I pulled away from the curb, my eyes glued to the rearview mirror as Jordan stood there waving goodbye, again experiencing a total loss of time as I pulled into my driveway twenty minutes later, unable to recall a single thing about the trip except for my thoughts of her. I was severely attracted to her, and it was wonderful.

CHAPTER THREE

In my quest over the years to cram my schedule full to bursting with all things Christian—in an attempt to eradicate all things non-Christian from within me—I had pretty much saturated my life with every possible Christian-related activity known to man. Except for one: the annual church camping trip. A reasonable omission as far as I was concerned, and I assumed I wasn't the only one who felt this way. There were probably lots of Christian women who didn't attend for obvious reasons. Camping was probably fun, but not in a dress. I could not imagine roughing it in a skirt. But still, some women did attend, mostly girls not yet worried about boys seeing them dirty and rumpled, and their mothers, of course. Older women attended too, as did women who were already married, engaged, or had serious boyfriends and had no intention of romping around in the woods anyway. This left one notable group of women glaringly absent from the mix. Me.

But not this year and my parents were surprised when I informed them. They went every year, but just for the first weekend. They arrived on Saturday, spent the night as guests of one of the families, then led church services Sunday morning, heading home as soon as possible afterward to make it back to our congregation in time for evening services. Hearing that Elena and Vicky were going camping, I knew Jordan would be going too. I had to be there. I had to see her.

When Saturday finally arrived, I woke early, eager to get the car loaded and us out on the road. I lugged two boxes of songbooks and a box of Bibles out to the car, then filled two coolers with hotdogs and hamburgers, chicken and steak, a bowl of potato salad, and *my* contributions, chili and coleslaw. I loaded everything into the car, along with four bags of groceries and Mom and Dad's suitcase, then threw in my small backpack stuffed with my jammies, a change of clothes, and some basic toiletry items. We had everything we needed for the two-day trip—and then some. It didn't look like we were setting off on a camping trip, more like a short missionary excursion to convert and feed some gospel music enthusiasts.

I dressed casually, choosing one of my roomier jean skirts and an old blouse that had seen better days. Not owning a T-shirt, I briefly considered buying one but decided against it. Wearing something new that wasn't my style might draw attention, and I feared being accused of *dressing up* for someone. There was no shortage of matchmakers in the church, and the dating rumor mill needed a constant supply of clues about who might be interested in whom.

I brought an old button-down sweater in case it got cool in the evening, one of Dad's baseball caps to keep the sun off my face, and some sneakers and socks for hiking. My impression of camping was pretty narrow, but hiking seemed likely. We were well on our way before I realized I'd forgotten my sleeping bag.

"Charles has to work," Mom informed me. "So, he can only stay for the weekend. But Barbara will be there the whole week. It will be great to see them and their kids." Mom turned in her seat and looked back at me. "Cindy is pregnant again. Her fourth."

Nodding, I tried to look pleased and surprised. No pressure, Mom.

"She and Kevin are coming. And Megan and Peter too. They're due next month, but Megan said she wouldn't dream of missing out on camping. Peter always looks forward to it."

Mom went on and on, naming off everyone who would be there, all of them in some state of being pregnant or actively trying to get pregnant. Mom had seven grandkids herself, so she had plenty to brag about. My brother, Simon, and my sister, Debra, would probably be there with their families, and I began to realize just how humongous this camping trip was going to be. Ugh! But Jordan would be there too, and that was all that mattered to me. I would sleep in the dirt, pee in the bushes, swat at a never-ending supply of mosquitoes, and breathe the filthy smoke of a thousand campfires, all while wearing a skirt, if I could only see her for one second. With the crush of humanity that promised to be there, it looked more likely than not that I could consider myself lucky if I got more time with her than that.

We arrived and all my fears were confirmed. It looked like a small village. I don't know what I was expecting, but not this. There were hundreds of us, and we were serious campers. There were only five tents among us, and they were gigantic. The rest were hard-shell campers, some of them shockingly elaborate, the smallest as big as my bedroom, each with bellowing awnings and clearly staked-out front yards. Each camping place was numbered and had a firepit next to a large stack of wood ready for burning. There were lawn chairs and tables, volleyball nets and horseshoe pits, and there were people everywhere. It would be a miracle if I found Jordan before we left tomorrow.

We managed to find the campsite we were guesting at but not before stopping and talking to everyone we met along the way. My parents were like rock stars, and sometimes it was a burden. It took us half an hour to get to our campsite. We were staying with Boyd and Imogene Cutter, and they had a room all set up for us in their camper. Or should I say, house? The thing was enormous. It had two bedrooms, one bath, a kitchen, and a dining room. It was pretty impressive, except for one thing—there was only one very small bed in Mom and Dad's room, which meant I would be sleeping on the floor. I threw my stuff in the corner and stood there, sticking out like a sore thumb, while Imogene helped Mom get settled in. Imogene hadn't expected me, and she looked a little nervous about not having a place for me to sleep. Mom told her not to worry herself, that I was young and would survive one night sleeping on the floor.

"I'll get the rest of the stuff," I mumbled, squeezing myself past them as they stood there laughing and talking, reminiscing about when they'd gone camping as kids and slept under the stars, apparently before campers and tents were invented.

I hurried out the door, relieved to be out of there, eager to get started on my search for Jordan. It took me three minutes to get back to the car. I grabbed a box of songbooks and one of the coolers out of the trunk, and as I emerged from behind the car, I walked right into Jordan. My hands were full, and there was no way to soften the impact as the entire front part of me smashed into her, including my face, my forehead bumping hers with a light *thunk*. She umphed in surprise as I gasped and stumbled backward, dropping the box of books and the cooler as I fell on my butt.

I sat there in the dirt, my heart pounding, my forehead tingling, and my face burning, unable to do anything but look at her as she knelt down beside me.

"Are you okay?" she asked as she reached out and touched my shoulder, sending a rush of warmth through my body.

I quickly licked my lips and gulped loudly. Jordan's eyes bounced from my eyes to my mouth and back to my eyes again, and a wave of embarrassment washed over me. Crap! Do I have something on my mouth! Mortified, I swiped my hand across my mouth, then turned, grabbed ahold of the car, and attempted to pull myself up. Jordan's hand grabbed my side, her other hand my arm, and she helped me to my feet, lingering a few seconds before letting me go. I held onto the car, feeling her standing behind me, wishing she would touch me again.

"Yes, I'm fine. Thank you," I said, trying to catch my breath.

Shaken and a bit queasy from our very intimate forehead bump, I managed to turn and watch her gather the songbooks and put them back in the box.

She looked up at me and smiled, then righted the cooler and looked inside. "The potato salad spilled a little, but other than that, everything else looks okay... Hey! Is that coleslaw? I love coleslaw!"

She loves my coleslaw! I beamed as she finished arranging the contents of the cooler.

"You need some help carrying this stuff?" she asked as she stood up.

"No. You don't have to."

She leaned to the side and peered into the open trunk at all the stuff we brought. "You're going to make me watch you carry all this stuff to your campsite?"

"No! Of course not." I let out a small groan. "I mean... Yes. Thank you. It's nice of you to offer."

"What? To help you, or to watch you?"

What was it about that sentence? Maybe it was the tone of her voice or the very cute smirk on her face, but I blushed. She licked her lips, and I nearly collapsed. "I meant, yes, could you please help me?" I corrected, but she was already pulling stuff out of the trunk, so I grabbed the box of songbooks and the cooler and hurried after her.

We walked back to my campsite, dropped everything off, and returned to the car for the rest. She talked the whole time—and I let her, happy to listen to her, determined to keep my foot out of my mouth—filling me in on her job search, regaling me with stories about life with her brother, and listing off all the activities she had planned for the week. She asked me how long I was staying and seemed disappointed that I would be leaving the next day. And then she asked me if I would like to go canoeing with her.

"Canoeing?"

"Yeah, there's a lake about a mile from here. It has a small island in the middle of it, and I want to explore it. Do you know how to swim?"

"Yes. I know how to swim."

"Great. Whaddaya say? You want to go on an adventure with me?"

"Yes! I do!" I practically gasped. She smiled, pleased. I was woefully inept at keeping up my side of the conversation, but short, breathy replies were all I could manage, glad that I'd been able to get the most important part out without sounding like a desperate, incoherent naiv. Because I was desperate and would do anything she wanted as long as she let me hang out with her, including canoeing, something I knew nothing about.

"Meet me down at the end of this road in one hour. There's a path on the right that will take us down to the lake."

"Okay. I'll be there. Thank you for inviting me."

"I can't think of anyone I would rather have in my canoe, Shannon."

A blush covered my face at this possible double entendre. Was she saying she only wanted to canoe with me and no one else? Or was she saying she believed I was qualified above all others to man her canoe? Or was it something else? The possibilities left me breathless, speechless, and rooted in place. She was even more beautiful all dirty and rumpled, her hair in a messy ponytail, her eyes sparkling, her face glowing. She smiled, turned, and sauntered down the road, the swish of her skirt doing things to my insides that were definitely non-platonic. I turned and hurried into the camper, glad that Mom and Dad and Boyd and Imogene were still talking and laughing and carrying on, too busy to notice the blush on my face. I was really starting to enjoy camping.

* * *

Thank God I didn't have a closet full of clothes here. My desire to change out of my already dirty skirt had me standing there staring at my backpack wishing I'd brought more than just one change of clothes, knowing that if I had more clothes, it would take me forever to decide what to wear. Why did I always fall on my butt in the dirt when I was around her? Mom walked into the room, snapping me out of my dilemma, and asked me if I wanted a sandwich for lunch.

"Yes, please. Um… I'm going canoeing."

"You're going canoeing?"

"Yes, I've been invited."

"At the lake?"

"Yeah. It's not far from here…" I began, then remembered that Mom knew more about the area than I did. She'd been camping here as a kid herself and loved telling the story of how she'd met her future husband in a very competitive volleyball game just down the road.

"Okay, but eat first, and I'll pack you a small snack for later."

"Thanks, Mom."

I slipped out of my sandals and pulled on my socks and sneakers. There was no way to get a good look at myself except through the tiny mirror hanging over the sink in the tiny bathroom, but I managed to dust myself off, wash my face, brush my teeth, apply just a little bit of mascara and some lip gloss, and change my earrings from the silver ones to the aqua green ones that really brought out the color of my eyes. Staring at myself in the mirror, I braided my hair and threw on Dad's baseball cap.

By the time I finished sprucing up, I had limited time to shove the sandwich Mom made me into my mouth and get out the door. I flew down the steps and out to the road, only to be called back to retrieve my packed snack. Mom stood on the steps, holding the bag out to me, pulling it back when I reached out to grab it. She smiled, kissed me on the forehead, and then handed it to me. "Thanks, Mom." I ran all the way to the meeting place, afraid that if I arrived too late, Jordan would leave without me.

The road dead-ended into an open area, where gobs of people milled about in groups, making it impossible to immediately spot Jordan. I did see four canoes lying in the grass, though, and when I scanned the group of young people loitering next to them, I saw her. She was standing right in the middle, talking and laughing, and I realized that this was not what I thought it was. It would not be just me and Jordan. What was I thinking? Of course not! There were only three types of social outings in the church, alone, in a group, or with your date, and Jordan and I were not dating. Suddenly, I was wearing way too much makeup and the wrong earrings. I looked ridiculous. I was dressed for a date. And to make matters worse, Jordan was hanging out with a bunch of cool kids—I mean, as cool as Christian kids could be—and I was technically not a kid anymore, and I was definitely not cool.

I would have turned and run, but Jordan saw me and loudly called out my name. Crap! There was no escaping this cool-kid situation, one that I usually avoided like the plague. But I could hardly worry about that now with Jordan running toward me. She looked very good when she was running; all the lovely parts of her moving together made me warm and happy and a little bit faint. I was a mess. I plastered on a smile, but it faltered, and I knew I wasn't going to make it.

Jordan came to a stop in a rush of excitement and breathlessness, reaching out her hand and touching my shoulder as if she knew I was about to make a run for it. "Are you okay?"

"Yes," I squeaked. What was wrong with me!

She laughed, and I started laughing too, and whatever was happening inside of me was suddenly completely okay. It didn't go away, but it was okay.

Jordan looked behind her and then back at me. "Come on. Our canoe is the last one on the left."

We grabbed our canoe and followed the other six canoers onto a narrow path with tall trees and low brush on either side. The sounds of birds chirping, kids laughing, and the smell of pine and warm dirt filled my senses. I was the last in line, with Jordan in front of me, both of us holding the canoe above our heads. It wasn't a date, but it kinda was. I was Jordan's canoe mate, and no matter what happened during the rest of the outing, this was the best part. I couldn't imagine anything better. I was able to covertly check Jordan out, mesmerized by the way she moved, thrilled each time she graced me with a view of the side of her beautiful face as she glanced back at me to make sure I was still there. Where else would I be? I was in heaven and hoped we never reached the lake! Her hips moved back and forth, her muscular calves flexing, her toned arms raised, her broad hands holding the sides of the canoe. A bead of sweat rolled down the nape of her neck, and an audible gasp escaped my lips as I followed its path, letting out a slow breath as it disappeared down the neck of her T-shirt.

Suddenly, I was surrounded by knee-high bushes, Jordan was not in front of me anymore, and the canoe I was holding was going in the wrong direction, bumping my head as it pulled from my shoulders. The momentum swung me around, causing me to lose my grip and then my footing, sending me tumbling into a sprawl of bushes. I struggled to my feet, startled when Jordan suddenly appeared next to me.

"Are you okay? That was quite a tumble you took."

"I'm okay. Really. No serious damage."

"Do you want to be in front? It's probably hard to see anything from back there with my big butt in the way."

"No, your butt is fine... I mean, I can see past your butt fine... Except when I can't..." Why can't I stop speaking! "I mean... I'm sorry, I didn't see the turn." I was looking at your fine butt!

Jordan laughed as she guided me around the bushes and back to the path. She had a hold of my arm, and I could feel the effect all the way down to my toes.

"Take the front. I'm sure the view is better."

"No, it's not... I mean, I don't mind being in the back, and besides, you know better where we're going."

She looked right into my eyes, and everything slowed down, our breath mingling in the air between us, her eyebrows furrowing in concern. "Are you sure you're okay? Tell me if you need me to slow down. I get carried away sometimes and get to walking too fast."

"I'm fine. Really. I can be a bit of a klutz sometimes."

"Well, there is nothing wrong with that. It's actually kind of sweet. I hope the canoe isn't too heavy for you."

Sweet? Oooh, I liked the sound of that.

She smiled, gave me one last look-over, and let go of my arm. I instantly missed her touch. She walked around the canoe and lifted her end, hesitating as she looked up at me. Oh, yeah! The canoe!

I snapped out of my daze, hoping she'd not realized that my preoccupation with checking her out was the real reason for my path deviation. Thank God it was bushes and not a cliff, or I would be lying at the bottom of a canyon right now. I'd always been a bit clumsy, but this was ridiculous. When she was near, I couldn't keep myself on my feet.

Thankfully, we made it to the lake without further incident. The other three canoes were already in the water, and I was glad. They were far enough away so that it was just me and Jordan, but I also didn't want anyone to see me operate a canoe. I had no idea what I was doing. I shielded my eyes from the sun with my hand and gauged their distance from us. I didn't want them too far away either, just in case I capsized us and we needed saving. We put on our life jackets, climbed into the canoe, and started paddling. I was in front this time, so I couldn't see Jordan unless I looked back at her, and I wasn't about to do that. But there was something tantalizing about knowing she was looking at me. And I knew she was looking. I could feel it, and it took every bit of concentration I possessed not to squirm under her watchful eye.

It was a warm, cloudless day, and the lake was calm, the only sound coming from the faraway voices of the other canoers and the water splash from our oars rowing, steady and synchronized. Jordan started talking about her grandfather—whose name was also Jordan, the mystery of the origin of her unique name revealed—and how he had taken her fishing during the summer when she was a kid. She described her grandfather's boat in detail and joked about the first time she hooked a worm and how proud she'd been the first time she caught a fish. Lulled by the sound of her voice and the rhythm of our movement through the water, I fell into a deeply relaxed state. There was nothing in my experience that compared to this moment. It was just the two of us and the whole wide world. I wished we could stay like this forever.

As we approached the island shore, a growing burning sensation on my legs made itself known, but I was quickly distracted from it when we jumped from the canoe into the water. After we pulled the canoe onto the beach, as Jordan tied it to a tree, the intense burning sensation on my legs roared back to life. I looked down and, to my horror, found them covered in an angry red rash. Please, God, help me! I was as concerned by the way they looked as by the fact that they were on fire. I stood there helpless, my legs slightly spread, my hands hovering at my sides. How could this be happening to me!

"It's okay. Relax." Jordan's hand touched my arm as she lowered herself down on her knees in front of me. I looked down at her head as she inspected my legs, so completely freaked out that I could not even protest as she lifted my skirt over my knees.

"Looks like a bad case of poison ivy." She looked up and gave me a pained smile. "From the bushes, I'm guessing."

I closed my eyes and groaned. I had just recovered from the previous catalog of excruciating faux pas and mishaps, and now had this indignity to add to the list. If it were possible to die of embarrassment, I was flat-lining!

"I've got some calamine lotion in my backpack."

Jordan led me away from the beach and into the shade, sitting me down on a tree trunk before heading back to the canoe to retrieve our backpacks. Being in the shade seemed to irritate my rash even more, tempting me to just reach down and give it a good scratch. Jordan returned a second later—preventing me from succumbing to my need to scratch—dropping to her knees in front of me. Oh, dear Lord! Seeing her on her knees like that was driving me crazy!

Jordan shook the little bottle of calamine, opened it, and dabbed the lotion on her fingers. She hesitated, looking up at me. "I don't have anything to smear this with."

"It's okay, Jordan," I said, pressing my lips together, stifling an anticipatory moan.

With the first touch of her fingers, my nipples hardened and a gentle pulse erupted between my thighs. When she reached my knees, I moaned. I tried not to, but there was nothing I could do to stop it. Hopefully, she'd think I was in pain. It took every ounce of will to control my breathing as she smeared the pinkish lotion on my legs, torn between wishing she would never stop and wishing… well, wishing she would never stop. I clapped my hand over my mouth to stifle another moan as she raised my skirt a bit higher and carefully rubbed her fingers on my inner thigh just above the knee. My whole body clenched as I willed my legs not to move, feeling panicked as they seemed determined to part. Then she was finished, and I didn't know whether to thank God or curse him.

"Okay. That should feel better soon. Sit for a while. Let it dry." She fixed her eyes on me. "Are you okay?" The look on her face robbed me of my breath. She was so beautiful, and she looked so worried, and I didn't want to spoil her day with my complete inability to act like a normal person.

"It feels better already. Thank you." This made her smile, and I added, "You're so prepared. What else do you have in your backpack?"

"I have this first aid kit, some water, and a couple of sandwiches."

"Oh. You didn't eat lunch yet?"

"I did, but I brought us a snack just in case we got hungry."

"Oh, God," I breathed, my heart pounding hard in my chest.

"Are you okay?"

"Yeah. It's just that you're so thoughtful. Thank you."

"You're welcome. Are you hungry?"

I could not say no to her sandwich. "Yeah. It's very kind of you to think of me."

Our eyes locked for several seconds, and a small humming noise welled up in my throat as I quickly licked my lips, Jordan's eyes tracking the movement with stealth-like precision. I was a heartbeat away from jumping into her arms. The only thing holding me back was the calamine lotion all over my legs, though, in reality, I would never do such a thing whether I had calamine lotion on my legs or not.

She broke eye contact, and a smile ghosted her lips as she turned and pulled two bagged sandwiches from her backpack. She handed me one, and when our fingers briefly touched, all the touching she'd done to my legs pulsed back to life.

"Thank you," I managed, breathless.

"How about some water?" She pulled a water bottle out of her backpack, opened it, and handed it to me, and when I hesitated, she said, "Oh. Um... I don't have any cups. You can drink from the bottle. I don't mind." And so, I did, and when she took the next drink, I could only stare as her beautiful lips touched the same place mine had just been.

I offered her a brownie and an apple from my snack bag, and we ended up having a very lovely picnic, Jordan providing the entertainment with hilarious stories of her encounters with poison ivy. She had the ability to make me feel like a regular person, whether I was assaulting her with an empty fried chicken container, rolling around in the dirt on a baseball field, head bumping her in the parking lot of a campground, or taking a dive into a poison ivy bush. She made me feel like everything I did was relevant, none of it embarrassing, all of it human.

After we finished eating, Jordan wanted to take me back to my campsite, but I insisted we at least walk to the other side of the island first. We found the others there, and Jordan explained what had happened and told them we were heading back. They were very sympathetic and offered to go back with us, but Jordan assured them they didn't need to, and so they stayed. And I was glad for that, and Jordan seemed glad for that as well.

The canoe ride and the hike back to the campsite left me tired, sweaty, and itchy but did not dampen the new sensations my body was experiencing. Nothing could stop what was happening to me, not even a massive rash caused by a forest of poison ivy.

* * *

"How on earth did this happen?" Mom asked as she spread another coat of calamine on my legs.

"I fell into a poison ivy bush."

"You fell? How did you fall into a poison ivy bush?" She laughed.

"Mom, please. It's embarrassing enough. Don't make a big deal out of it. It feels a lot better."

"Well, at least someone had the presence of mind to bring a first aid kit." She stood up and gave me an amused look before planting a kiss on my forehead. "We're eating at the Massengale's barbecue. You want to come?"

"Yes." I knew she was waiting for me to smile, so I did and added a quick eye roll to let her know I was really all right.

"Good." She gave my arm a squeeze, then led me out of the camper and down the road to the Massengale's campsite.

The Massengale barbecue was already in full swing, everyone halfway through their first helping, some already lined up for seconds. Grabbing a paper plate, I got in line, my mouth watering at all the wonderful smells. I was hungry and took what the cook gave me from what was left on the grill— a chicken breast and a spare rib. I added some noodle salad and some baked beans from the buffet, then found a seat at the end of one of the tables. I took a bite of my spare rib—a rather large bite, unintended, the meat would not let go of the bone—and struggled a moment before the meat finally pulled free with a snap, leaving a large chunk of spare rib hanging out of my mouth.

"Hi! Is this seat taken?"

I looked up, distressed to find Jordan standing there with her plate in hand, catching me in another ridiculous state of klutzy dweebiness. My hand instantly jumped up and covered my barbecue-sauce-smeared mouth as I attempted to fit the rest of the meat inside. I grabbed my napkin and added it to the mix while nodding and incoherently mumbling at Jordan to please take a seat.

She sat across from me, looking amused, watching the

spectacle as I chewed, swallowed, and wiped. God, help me! She started laughing, and I started laughing too. There seemed nothing I could do to repel her—nothing she found objectionable, too uncool, or unacceptable. Of course, if she knew how her sparkling eyes, her sun-kissed skin, and her blazing smile affected me, it might change her kind behavior toward me. Needless to say, I wasn't going to tell her.

"I bit off more than I could chew," I said, feeling the heat of my blush.

"Yeah, ribs are tricky, but they are so good."

She took a large bite of her rib, ripping a big chunk of meat from the bone, and my heart fluttered. I almost started crying. She corralled the bite into her mouth, chomping, licking, and giggling, her beautiful lips smeared with barbecue sauce. I stared. I couldn't help it. Especially the licking part. I tore my eyes from her mouth and took another bite of my rib, not worried anymore about making a mess.

"How's the poison ivy?" She asked.

"It itches."

"Yeah, but don't scratch it. Believe me, I know."

We laughed as thoughts of scratching her poison ivy flashed through my mind, interrupted as she lifted a large forkful of my coleslaw and carefully fit it into her mouth.

"Mmmm," she moaned, and I moaned with her, but my moan wasn't about my coleslaw. It was about the utterly delicious sound of her moan. "It's good, isn't it?" she agreed, referring to our shared moans. She looked down at my plate, her brows pulling together in confusion when she didn't see any coleslaw on it. "Did you get some of this? It's incredible." She looked over her shoulder at the buffet table, then back at me. "I don't think there's any more left, but you can have some of mine if you want."

"No, thank you. I've had some," I said, glad she'd not realized the reason for my moan. She slid another forkful of my coleslaw into her mouth, moaning and rolling her eyes at how good it was. I smiled, careful not to moan with her this time, pleased that she liked it so much.

We finished eating and then enjoyed a bowl of homemade ice cream, Jordan talking and me listening as the rest of the world slipped far, far away. She was so beautiful and so kind. Being in her company was like being wrapped in warm light. I was abruptly pulled back to reality when a guy walked up beside Jordan and put his hand on her shoulder. I blinked and looked up at him as he asked Jordan if she'd already saved her place at the clearing.

"It's already pretty full," he said, glancing at me.

"Yeah, my stuff's already there," Jordan answered, glancing at me before looking back up at him. His name was Bill. I'd dated him briefly years ago. He was my first kiss, and I gagged a little at the memory, praying to God he didn't have his sights set on Jordan. "I'll be over in a few minutes," Jordan said, and finally he released her shoulder. I suppressed a shudder.

He looked at me, cocked his head, and smiled. "Hi, Shannon."

"Hi, Bill." I suppressed an eye roll and smiled back.

Bill strutted away, and I wanted to ask Jordan about her place at the clearing, but thankfully, I didn't have to. "Some of us are meeting up at the clearing tonight. You know, where we met this afternoon. We're sleeping under the stars. You wanna come?" she asked me.

"I don't have a sleeping bag."

Jordan let out a surprised snort, biting down on her bottom lip as she tilted her head sideways, looking at me as if she couldn't quite figure me out. "I can find you one."

"Okay," I breathed. Her adorable lip-biting rendered me unable to say much more than that.

"I'll pick you up at your campsite in fifteen minutes."

"Okay," I said as we gathered up our plastic bowls and tossed them into the trash.

"Don't forget to bring a flashlight," she reminded me.

"Okay," I said.

And then she smiled at me.

I loved camping.

* * *

I walked out of the camper all bundled up in my button-down sweater, a red ski cap, and black wool knee socks. If it looked like my mother dressed me, it was because she had. She refused to allow me out of the camper without the ski cap and knee socks, afraid that I would catch a cold. I relented because I saw no other way out, planning to remove them as soon as I was down the road and out of sight.

Jordan was already waiting for me out front, a rolled-up sleeping bag tucked under her arm. When she saw me, she got the same look on her face she'd had when I told her I didn't have a sleeping bag. Amazed? Bemused? Curious? Maybe a little of each.

"Hi. You look warm," she said.

"I am warm." I rolled my eyes and added, "My mother."

"Ah. Yes. Mothers."

And then something I'd wanted to say all day slipped out of my mouth. "Thank you for not laughing at me."

"Because of you, I have laughed a lot today," she said, teasing.

"Yeah, but it never felt like you were laughing *at* me."

"I would never laugh *at* you, Shannon." She smiled, still teasing but not.

"Thank you," I smiled back.

The clearing was crowded with young people sitting on their sleeping bags, some of them already tucked up comfortably inside, boys on one side, girls on the other, of course, circling a large campfire, where four grown-ups lounged on lawn chairs. Chaperones, of course.

Jordan found her sleeping bag and laid mine out next to it. We sat down on top of them, and Jordan was instantly included in the conversation surrounding us. I knew everybody there, I'd grown up with them, but Jordan was new to this area, and she knew most of them better than I did. That's how she was—open and fun, giggling and joking with the girls around her, enjoying this special kind of fellowship.

Every word that came out of her mouth captivated me, every playful gesture and every expression filled my body with warmth and my thoughts with ideas about sleeping next to her and how that made me feel.

The campfire burned low, one of the chaperones led us in evening prayer, and we all crawled into our sleeping bags, looking up at the stars, feeling blessed, special, and full of light. Me more than the others; I was sure of that.

* * *

The sound of birds woke me. Lots of them. The noise level was deafening. How was everyone else still asleep? I turned onto my side and came face-to-face with a peacefully slumbering Jordan. My breath caught at her beauty; her face was angelic; serene. I stared and dared not move for fear of waking her. I may not get another chance to look at her so close up. I studied her face while remembering all the different expressions I'd seen there, not one of them negative or mean. She was good, she was innocent, and she didn't know what was in my heart. I didn't deserve to be near her. I didn't deserve to be looking at her, especially with her so unaware.

Her eyes opened, and I quickly slammed mine shut, hoping she hadn't caught me staring at her, waiting a moment before slowly opening them again. Jordan grinned at me and snuggled deeper into her sleeping bag, her beautiful long lashes fluttering as her eyes locked with mine. She sighed softly. She didn't speak, and neither did I. We just lay there looking at each other as if the rest of the world didn't exist.

I don't know how long we lay there like that before the first campers began waking, but Jordan's expression of disappointment made my lips curl slightly upward in agreement. Her eyes darted up and around as she raised her head and looked out over the clearing, her expression turning thoughtful as her head returned to her pillow. Her brows pulled slightly together as her gaze became more intense, pushing something toward me, some meaning I was sure was just for me. I was desperate to grasp it and returned her gaze just as intensely, wanting to tell her everything.

The girl next to Jordan sat up in her sleeping bag and stretched, yawning loudly, her arms up over her head and then down, the left one landing on Jordan's hip. "Wake up, sleepy head," she said, and the connection between me and Jordan was broken.

Jordan turned and looked at the girl. "Good morning," she said, while the girl's hand lingered on Jordan's hip.

Swallowing hard, I looked away, suddenly very warm and desperate to get out of my sleeping bag, pulling at it as I sat up straight, wiggling my arms out of it and pushing it down to my waist. I took a deep breath and ran my hands through my hair, knocking my ski cap off in the process. I yanked at the neck of my sweater, blew out a quick breath, and turned to find Jordan staring at me. "I'm wearing too many clothes."

"You look hot." Her eyes went wide. "I mean, your cheeks are flushed."

"I meant to take off my socks and ski cap, but I forgot."

"Yeah...well."

"The socks, at least, were helpful. They kept the calamine from getting on the sleeping bag."

"Yes...right."

Jordan's speechlessness was new to me, and I didn't know what else to say to keep the conversation going, so I gave her a quick smile, unzipped my sleeping bag, and crawled out of it. She helped me roll it up and offered to walk me back to my campsite so I could get ready for church services. I gladly took her up on her offer, and we made our way through the mass of waking campers and out onto the road.

Jordan was quiet all the way to my campsite, almost bashful, not speaking until she dropped me off. "See you at church."

"See you at church," I replied as she walked away from me, a sleeping bag under each of her arms. I was still affected by the thrill of waking up next to her and curious about her uncharacteristic shyness, wondering what it meant and whether something I did caused it. I cautioned myself to be more careful, then went into the camper to get ready for church.

* * *

Services were held in the same clearing three hours later—parishioners brought their own chairs to sit on; some sat on the grass. Dad's sermon was especially suited for our surroundings. He spoke about God's many gifts, how we were all stewards of this earth, and how we were bound by duty to take care of it. It was pretty good, I had to admit, and all the birds chirping, the breeze whispering in the trees, and the sound of rushing water in the distance certainly added to the power of his message.

I hadn't seen Jordan during services, and afterward, I searched amongst the crowd for her as I said my goodbyes. But people were already dispersing, eager to get on with their camping trip, and I guessed she had better things to do—camping stuff, adventures, hanging out with way cooler kids than me. I had monopolized most of her time while I'd been there and didn't begrudge her getting back to her fun.

I loaded the car while Mom and Dad said goodbye to Boyd and Imogene. I was on my second trip when I saw a vision of loveliness waiting for me, leaning up against the passenger-side door.

"Hi. I missed you this morning," she said in greeting.

I hesitated, the words, *I missed you too*, on the tip of my tongue, greeting her with a simple hello instead as I rounded the back of the car and dumped everything into the trunk. I turned as she joined me, standing so close that I had to resist the urge to take a step back. Something about her bold stance made me feel lightheaded. Her hands were behind her back, her front on full display, and I scanned her breasts, stomach, and hips before I could stop myself. I looked up at her face, hoping she hadn't noticed my blatant scrutiny. She smiled and removed her hands from behind her back, the right one holding some kind of cactus plant, perfectly potted.

"Something to remember your weekend by."

"What is it?"

"It's an aloe vera plant. Winston grows them. Elena, Vicky, and I are staying with Winston and Shelly for the week. They are seriously into plants. We're going on a botany hike this afternoon."

"A botany hike?"

"Yeah, searching for plants. He has a list. Anyway, he said aloe vera has anti-inflammatory properties. It's very helpful against poison ivy."

"Anti-inflammatory?"

"Yeah. It helps soothe the rash. It cools it down. Keeps it from itching so much."

I didn't know what to say. This was the sweetest thing I could imagine, and it was squeezing my heart. "Thank you, Jordan," I croaked, slowly shaking my head, hating that I had to leave her and feeling like I might cry.

"You're welcome. And don't scratch it. It just spreads the poison all over the place."

"I won't scratch it. I promise." I took the plant and stared at it, racking my brain for something to say, hoping to keep us talking. "Thanks for spending so much time with me," I blurted. "I had fun."

"I had fun, too. Are you going to the Young People's Meeting in Stockton next month?"

"Yeah, I think so. Are you?"

"Yeah, I'll be there."

"I'll see you there then."

I really wanted to hug her, but I didn't because I knew what I was, and she didn't, and that wasn't fair. It wasn't right, so I gave her a friendly smile instead. She smiled in return, her eyes holding mine.

"Okay, great. I'll see you there."

CHAPTER FOUR

Young people from all over Northern California attended the Young People's Meeting in Stockton because it was centrally located and easy to get to, making time for it was not an issue because it only lasted the weekend, and they always had fun activities planned for after services. Not going this year was not an option. Jordan had practically invited me, and there was no way I was going to stand her up.

I arrived at the church building a few minutes before the start of services and found a potential seat in the last pew—relying on the good manners of a gentleman in training, his parents giving up his seat and making him stand in the back. He found a spot on the back wall with all the other gentlemen in training while more and more people continued to walk in. Soon there would be no standing room left.

As the first hymn began, I peered over my hymnal and scanned the huge room. This building was much bigger than the building where I went to church, making it perfect for such popular meetings but a challenge when trying to locate a particular person without knowing where they were sitting. I didn't locate Jordan until halfway through the second hymn.

I actually gasped when I saw her, then glanced around to be sure no one heard. No one heard because hundreds of people were singing about how much God loved them at the top of their lungs, Jordan included—her mouth moving, her lips touching, her neck straining with each high note. I followed along, mumbling the words, wondering what she sounded like when she sang and what it would be like to touch her lips. That was pretty much how I spent the rest of the service, working myself into a frenzy over how it would feel to be squished into that pew right up next to her. I missed the entire sermon and was mildly irritated at the interruption when the last hymn was sung, the last prayer prayed, and we were released for an evening of fellowship.

I pushed through the crowd, saying quick hellos, keeping

my eye on Jordan as we both made our way to the foyer. She hadn't noticed me yet, but I got the distinct feeling she was looking. I tried to make myself noticeable but ended up getting the wrong person's attention. It wasn't unusual at these types of meetings for some random guy to introduce himself and ask me to accompany him to whatever activity the church had planned for the evening. Tonight, the church had the local ice-skating rink reserved for two hours, and no less than three guys asked me out before I reached the front door. These young people's meetings were regular pickup joints, making it nearly impossible to attend without being asked out, and I usually gave in just to get it over with. But not tonight.

I power-walked through the crowd, politely declining the three invitations and avoiding two others, sucking in a lungful of air as I burst through the double doors leading out to the front lawn. I made my way through the crowd, planting myself at the slightly elevated back part of the lawn near the parking lot, out of the glare of the outdoor lights. The bright lights inside put everyone exiting the building on display, including Jordan. She was surrounded by guys and gals alike, all of them vying for her attention, all of them looking at her with the same wonder I felt every time I saw her.

She walked out onto the grass, the glow of the outdoor lights behind her, leaving her face in shadow. The slightest turn of her head, first one way, then the other, made my heart beat faster. It looked like she was scanning the crowd. I wanted her to be scanning it for me. When her head suddenly stopped, I smiled. Even though I couldn't see the details of her face, I knew she was smiling too. She excused herself from her group of friends and made her way toward me, and suddenly I could not breathe. I began nervously primping, stopping myself mid-primp when I realized she could see me way better than I could see her. Lightly holding on to the fabric of my skirt to keep my hands from moving, forestalling my affinity to act downright silly whenever she was near, I begged myself to at least appear cool and collected.

"Hi," she said as she walked up to me.

"Hi," I said, eyeing her light cotton blouse, quickly licking my lips at the thought of it touching her skin.

"Are you going skating tonight?" she asked.

"Yeah. Are you?" I inhaled her scent into my lungs, carefully exhaling so she wouldn't notice.

"Yeah, I am. Are you going with someone?"

"No. Are you?"

"No. I'm hanging out with Vicky and Elena tonight."

"Okay." I wanted to ask her if she'd like to ride with me, but I just didn't have the courage. "Well, I guess I'll see you there then."

"Okay, I'll see you there. Bye."

"Bye."

She gave me a smile that I would have done anything to see again and again, and then she turned and walked away, her skirt swishing back and forth with each step, revealing the back of her knees. I literally had to rip my gaze from her backside. I raised my hand and began fanning my face, then thought better of it, casually tucking some hair behind my ear instead as I slowly took in my surroundings, relieved to see everyone deep in conversation and not at all interested in me and the show I was putting on. They seemed oblivious to the fact that I had feelings for someone I wasn't supposed to have feelings for.

I took a deep breath and tried to calm myself. I was high from just that little bit of contact with her, intensely aware of my body to the point of distraction, my desires hidden in plain sight as I tried to hold my awkwardness and fluster at bay. The control she had over me was exhilarating in a way that made me feel like my body could defy gravity and take flight. A nearby snicker had me scanning the crowd again, completely paranoid that everyone knew what was happening to me. How could they not? I was practically levitating.

Groups of kids began migrating toward the parking lot, signaling that it was time to depart. There was no use driving out to the skating rink until the appointed time; we would just end up hanging out in the skating rink's parking lot waiting until the open-skate session ended, and that experience was always a little uncomfortable. It happened without fail. When the worldly kids left the skating rink, fanning out across the parking lot to their cars, the looks they gave us were almost as bad as the things they said to us. I wanted to avoid this at all costs.

I jumped in my truck and drove out of the church parking lot, feeling dread for this small part of the evening. I'd gotten bullied a lot in school for the way I looked, and the only consolation was that no one from church witnessed it. Walking into a skating rink past a group of worldly kids was high on my hard-to-do list. If someone said anything ugly to me in front of my Christian peers, especially if that Christian peer was Jordan, I feared my whole evening could implode.

Parking as close as I could to the skating rink, I timed my dash through the parking lot to coincide with a small group of young Christians approaching the entrance. I scurried up alongside them, using them as a buffer between me and a group of worldly boys loudly exiting the skating rink. I looked down at my shoes, avoiding eye contact, hoping that no one in our group lingered or tried to engage them.

"Ooh, the redhead's hot!" someone shouted, and I pushed past, knocking shoulders with a couple of my fellow Christians as I squeezed through the door, panic threatening to overtake me as I hurried to the skate rental window. I tried to catch my breath as I stood in line. I couldn't let this scare me away. Jordan was here, and I wanted to spend a couple of hours with her, even if those couple of hours came at the cost of public insults from worldly boys and the humiliation that came with it. And it wasn't like I'd have her to myself or anything, but still, I could openly watch her doing something unassociated with church, something different, something exciting, something potentially vulnerable and human.

I found a spot on one of the large round changing tables and changed into my skates, slipping my flats into a shoe cubbyhole on the wall. I wobbled toward the ice rink, wanting to get out there and get warmed up before it got too crowded. I was a horrible ice skater, but a little less horrible if I warmed up first. I concentrated on my balance, the key to mobility, and let go of the wall, the fear of falling on my butt keeping me on my feet. I glanced around as the rink became more and more crowded, the boys whizzing by at breakneck speed, the girls, like me, being more careful. It was embarrassing enough to fall on your butt in public; it was a whole other level of humiliating doing it in a skirt.

"Hi!"

I took my eyes off my feet for a moment as Jordan flew past me, her skates dancing as she took the turn like Dorothy Hamill. Wow! She was an excellent softball player and an even better ice skater! Was there nothing she didn't excel at? Determined to skate like I knew what I was doing, I accelerated around the bend, chopping my skates at the ice, waving my arms, struggling to keep my balance as I made it around to the straight part of the rink.

Risking a glance across the ice, I spotted Jordan surrounded by a bunch of girls, talking and laughing as if they were taking a stroll in the park. I stood up straighter, trying to display a bit of elegance, jerking back down into position when my balance began to wane. The turn was approaching, and staying on my feet was imperative. I could practice elegance when I survived the turn and was safely on the straight part of the rink again. I chopped my way around the bend without falling and was rewarded with light contact on the small of my back.

"How are you doing?" Jordan's voice was like honey. I blinked and grinned, my body jerking in response. My grin faltered, but when I remained upright, I risked another.

"Good. I'm doing good. And you?" I asked, trying to make conversation, hoping she would stay awhile.

Before she could answer, a voice thundered over the loudspeaker. "Couples only! Okay, gentlemen, ask your favorite lady for a dance around the rink! Don't be shy, guys!"

Three things happened in quick succession. The first notes of a Chicago song I couldn't remember the name of blasted over the loudspeaker. The lights went out, throwing the rink into complete darkness for what seemed like an eternity. And some very annoying strobe lights came on, sending the room spinning around me, delivering the final death blow to any form of equilibrium my body possessed, literally knocking my feet out from underneath me. I landed on my butt, legs up and spread, skirt riding high, rotating in a circle as I slid down the ice, moving faster than I had all evening on my feet. I crashed into the wall at the far end of the rink and sat there in shock as Jordan came to a screeching halt right in front of me, the blades of her skates digging into the ice, sending a sheen of frost into my lap.

"Are you okay?" she asked as she kneeled down, balancing on the tips of her blades.

I glanced at her exposed thigh, then looked up at her concerned face. "Yes! Yes. I'm fine," I answered.

She shook her head and offered me her hand, a smile spreading across her face. "You went down so fast. One minute you were there, and the next you weren't." She started laughing.

"I'm glad my lack of coordination amuses you," I said, grabbing her hand as she stood and yanked me decisively to my feet. I gasped. It was the surest two seconds I had ever spent on ice, and for a moment, I knew exactly what it would feel like to be able to skate.

"It's not so hard. Relax your body. Just go with it. Feel the natural movement. Don't fight it."

I listened to her voice as she pulled me across the ice, explaining to me how to ice skate. It didn't occur to me until we were gliding around the opposite bend that we were still holding hands. She changed subjects from skating technique to family life with her brother, to her job search, to the latest movie, the latest song, and before I knew it, the lights had turned back on, we were still holding hands, and I was skating like my body wasn't mine. It was like Jordan had control over it. She had cured me of bad ice skating. It was a miracle and high time we stopped holding hands.

She gave me a regretful smile and let go of my hand. I looked down at my empty hand, still feeling the strength of her fingers and the warmth of her skin, sad that we would probably never get to do *that* again but hopeful as she continued to talk to me, sharing with me her love for the rock band *Journey*. It was potentially scandalous that a Christian might enjoy such music, and I was both shocked and delighted that she was sharing this secret with me. It made me feel special, and I was sure that was why she entrusted it to me. It was a gift, a consolation, something to hold on to as she let go of my hand.

We talked and skated together the rest of the evening, and when the last skate, couples only, was announced, we left the ice, foregoing the main event, opting out of another pairing ritual. We sat alone in the dark, changing out of our skates, giggling as we got used to walking on solid ground again. We returned our skates to the rental window, then walked together through the parking lot to my truck.

"That was fun," I said, chuckling as I unlocked my door.

"Why are you laughing? What's so funny?"

"I never thought I'd use the word fun to describe ice skating."

"Ice skating is fun with the right person," she said.

I stared at her, and she stared at me, and I didn't know how to respond, unsure if she had said something important or had said nothing at all. But I couldn't unhear it, ignore it, or pretend it didn't mean something to me. Because it did, and that was all that I had.

"Goodnight, Jordan! Goodnight, Shannon!" a chorus of gleeful voices sounded.

Startled, we turned to find a group of church girls crossing the parking lot, headed for their cars. Other church people were exiting the building as well, and I wondered how long we'd been standing out there together, briefly worried that someone may have seen us. But we were standing a good two feet apart and weren't doing anything questionable, like holding hands or anything like that, and I doubted anyone heard anything. We hadn't said anything worth hearing, at least nothing that could be interpreted as something. I took a deep breath and tried to calm myself. I was more than a little paranoid.

"I better go. Elena and Vicky will be looking for me. I'll see you later," Jordan said, giving me one of her lovely smiles.

"Okay. I'll see you later."

I watched Jordan walk away, ready to bet my life that something was happening between us, unable to believe that what I hoped was happening was even possible, hoping that if something was happening, no one else could see it.

* * *

The days that followed were a blur. I worked, went to church, and thought of Jordan. A couple of weeks had passed since I last saw her, and missing her became my constant, which was everything in a world where I couldn't have her. But still, if I could just see her for a moment, I would be so thankful. I was leaving for a meeting in Oklahoma in a couple of weeks and desperately wanted to see her smile before I left. On Wednesday, I thought about going to her church for midweek services instead of mine but was afraid someone would somehow know that I had come to see her. It seemed too risky, and when the possibility popped into my head that Jordan might also think it strange, I abandoned my plan altogether, glad that I had when she walked into my church that evening.

I stared as Elena and Jordan made their way up the aisle, looking for a seat. Jordan turned and met my gaze, and my breath caught. My heart jumped in my chest when she grabbed Elena's arm, pulled her to a stop, and pointed in my direction, and when they came over and sat in my pew next to me, I nearly fell out of my seat.

"Hi," Jordan said, smiling, looking me directly in the eyes.

"Hi," I said, blinking way too much, trying to control my breathing.

By the time the sermon began, my heart was beating so loud, I couldn't hear anything the preacher was saying. Jordan seemed to listen to the sermon intently, and a couple of times leaned toward me and whispered a comment into my ear—her breath on my face, her arm and thigh touching mine, sending electrical shocks racing through my body, making it impossible for me to understand anything she was saying. My physical reaction to her was overwhelming, leaving me in a complete fever and a state of surprise when services were suddenly over and everyone stood up.

I jumped up out of my seat and headed for the exit, not wanting Jordan or anyone else to see me in this condition. I needed the cover of darkness and the cool of the evening to help me recover. I could have gone home, but I needed to see her one more time, hear her beautiful voice, bask in the warmth of her smile, and say something meaningful to her. She walked out of the building a few minutes later, slowly scanning the crowd, smiling when she found me. I approached her, struggling with the desire to tell her how she made me feel. It was irresistible, and I knew I had to be careful. I couldn't tell her I had an enormous crush on her or anything remotely related to *that*. I didn't want to scare her away, but I had to somehow let her know how important she was to me.

"Uh… So… Skating. I really, really enjoyed that. Thanks for your help. It was…fun," I sputtered, blushing, mentally head-slapping myself. What was wrong with me? I was a complete dufus and now she knew!

She glanced down at her shoes, her olive skin faintly flushed, her body language bashful and adorable, turning my words into perfection. This was how I felt about Jordan, and now she knew. She smiled, her eyes locking with mine.

"Yeah, it was fun. Next time I'll show you how to crossover on the turns." She held my gaze, and it was as if we had been the only ones there at the ice-skating rink that night and had shared something exclusive, something meaningful.

"I'd like that."

"Then, it's a date."

My mouth dropped open at her use of the word *date*, but I quickly shut it when she smiled at me teasingly. It was just a figure of speech, the words themselves the closest I would ever come to a real date with her. But still...

"Walk me to my car?"

"Sure."

I walked Jordan and Elena to their car, where we said quick goodbyes. After they drove away, I jumped in my truck, replaying the entire wonderful exchange over and over again in my mind as I drove home.

I walked into the house, said goodnight to Mom and Dad, then went directly to my bedroom and did something that I did not often do. I touched myself, and for the first time, I did it with Jordan in my head. I did not have the visuals all sorted out, but that didn't matter. It worked, putting all my previous attempts at masturbation to shame.

I began masturbating very regularly to Jordan, so much so that I began to worry that Mom and Dad would notice the sudden change in my bedtime or my propensity to shower more often and longer. But they didn't notice anything. Nobody did. Nobody was watching, nobody was suspicious, nobody could tell that I was falling head over heels for Jordan.

CHAPTER FIVE

The Oklahoma meeting was the biggest meeting I had ever attended, the venue so large and all-encompassing, it was as if the world had turned into a Christian. I had heard about this phenomenon, where a meeting had so literally taken over an area that everything in and around it became completely Christianized and made you feel like you were already in heaven. It certainly looked and felt like the heaven I had always imagined.

I'd started planning my trip to this meeting last year, having heard how intense the meetings in the South could be. I had hoped to benefit from coming into contact with a new group of young Christians, hoping to find the man I could fall in love with. Of course, I hadn't planned on meeting Jordan in the meantime, a consideration that slowly faded as the power of the church flooded all of my senses, the atmosphere potent with that old-time religion, oozing with goodness, friendly and warm, where everyone was welcome and nobody judged, where happiness was a permanent state of mind and worries about life were mundane at best.

It was as if my entire spiritual future depended on this very moment, like a final test or a conspiratorial group interview to see if I was truly ready for my next step as a Christian woman. With a stage so perfectly set, surely it was impossible for me to mess up this rite of passage. The attention I received was overwhelming, filled with encouragement and goodwill, praise and compliments, not to mention best wishes for my mom and dad.

Services were held outdoors in a huge tent that sat at least a thousand people inside and another five hundred or so in the overflow area. I was never in want of a place to sit, a group to hang out with, or a person to talk to. The sermons were rousing and inspiring, and the fellowship with other Christians my age, thoroughly enjoyable. Four different guys asked me out, all of them impressive and attractive, the last one so over-the-top handsome, I was at first speechless when he asked to sit with me during services. Cinderella herself could not have been more impressed. I exchanged addresses with all four of them and promised to write as soon as I returned to California. The whole experience was awe-inspiring, challenging me to recommit to the church, convincing me that what was happening inside me was a misguided, passing fancy and that I still had a chance at the life I had been raised to want and value.

After the meeting ended, I shared a ride back to California with an older married couple. The plan was to drive to LA, then up to Sacramento, where they would drop me off before they continued north to Oregon. In LA, we stayed with a family I knew pretty well. I had last seen them a few years earlier at a summer meeting in the Sacramento area. They regularly attended meetings all over California and were best known for their many sons. They had five of them, one of them my age, and at dinner that evening, I was surprised to see him walk in a bit late from work and sit across from me at the dinner table. His name was Dennis, and he was obviously surprised to see me too.

"Hi, you're Shannon, right? I remember you from that meeting in Sacramento a couple of years ago."

I smiled, flattered that he remembered my name. The last time I'd seen him, we were shy, awkward teens. Not anymore. He was tall, handsome, and intelligent, and we talked together the rest of the evening until late that night about the church and religion, and even about current events and politics. He was funny, and he made me laugh. He was respectful of my opinions and had a progressive side to him that I had never experienced with another man before. I genuinely liked him, and when he asked me out to dinner the following evening, I said yes, and I had to admit, he was just as impressive out in the world. I felt all grown up sitting across from him in candlelight with soft music playing in the background, surrounded by other couples and polite waiters who didn't seem to notice how long my hair was or how strange my dress looked. I was like another person, like the person I always wished I could be.

The next day, around lunchtime, as we prepared to leave for Sacramento, I found Dennis waiting for me next to the car. We talked for a few minutes, and he told me he was thinking about attending the late-summer church meeting at my congregation next month and asked whether I would like to see him there. I said yes, and we exchanged phone numbers and addresses. He gave me a very chaste goodbye kiss, his message clear. He wanted to date me. The obvious question was, did I want to date him? The answer even more obvious: why wouldn't I?

During the drive home, I reflected on all that had happened on my trip, feeling stronger and more confident about my faith than ever before, ready to try one more time to get my life in order. I was hopeful that I could make a new start, get myself going in the right direction, and stop acting like a child. At the same time, after several days on a spiritual high, pretending that my gayness had been miraculously cured, thoughts of Jordan slowly crept back into my mind. My condition was slowly making itself known again, reminding me that it was still with me. I was desperate to be rid of it, it would ruin my life, and I prayed to this all-powerful God to do for me what I obviously could not do for myself. This should be easy for him—an effortless gesture, the correcting of a mistake, a simple flipping of my switch to put an end to the way I felt about Jordan. I hadn't asked for this affliction. I didn't want it. It was completely against everything I needed to believe. As we drove through the night, I begged him to help me. He had eight hours to do so, but he chose not to, again. It wasn't the first time I'd asked him, and his answer was just as clear. If I was going to conquer this, I was going to have to do it alone.

* * *

The details of my trip preceded my arrival home, and when I walked into the church building for Wednesday evening services, all the ladies were abuzz with excitement and gossip. I confirmed that I was dating Dennis, to the delight of all, while I avoided eye contact with Jordan, who I was surprised to see there. She kept her distance, and I kept mine. She was reserved, watching me from afar, perhaps as curious as the others about my new self-confidence. I had lost a bit of my shyness and awkwardness during the trip. I was suddenly growing up.

After services, as I headed through the parking lot to my truck, I glanced at Jordan as she and Elena headed to their car, ignoring the pang of desire and the pull on my heart as our eyes met. I shook my head, jumped in my truck, and drove home.

I didn't see Jordan in the weeks leading up to our late-summer church meeting. Out of sight wasn't out of mind, though, and I constantly had to renew my efforts to keep her out of my thoughts, determined to make the most of my new commitment. I believed if I stayed the course, I could move beyond my struggles and get my life back on the right path.

Dennis was making plans to fly up for the first weekend of the meeting, and the church even gave him the Sunday morning speaking slot. He had to fly back to LA on Sunday afternoon. I spent the week before the meeting preparing myself, taking care of a hundred little things—planning my wardrobe, cleaning the house, and keeping a tight rein on my thoughts. On Friday evening, I was ready. Dennis met me in the foyer when I arrived for services, giving me a quick kiss before escorting me to our seats. During the sermon, I noticed that I was not as enamored with him as I remembered being in LA. His charm, composure, and good looks were not having the same effect on me as they'd had during my brief stay.

I tried not to panic when, after services, I could not feel awestruck and thrilled that he was here because of me as we stood and were surrounded by people who wanted to shake his hand and say hi to him. As the evening wore on and I struggled to reclaim the connection I had with him in LA, the desperate hope that feelings of love and desire would somehow emerge from someplace inside me dwindled as well. But I could not give up. I powered on, insisting that I could right my ship, invoking all the power I'd experienced in Oklahoma. If this was beatable, I could beat it!

Saturday was full of fun activities, starting with a pancake-breakfast potluck, followed by softball for the guys and volleyball for the girls, and ending with a big barbecue. After Saturday evening services, everyone gathered at the local ice cream parlor for ice cream and fellowship. Afterward, I drove Dennis to the house he was staying at. We parked across the street and talked a few minutes inside the cab of my truck before he leaned in and gave me a much more passionate kiss than we had yet shared, further degrading any hope that romantic feelings for him would somehow materialize. He broke our kiss sooner than I expected, explaining that it was already late and he still had to prepare for the sermon he would give the following morning. I said goodnight and drove home, trying to ignore that familiar feeling of relief at being rid of my date. I knew what this feeling was and what it meant, but I was determined not to give up.

On Sunday morning, I got up early and spent a good hour preparing for the sleepover I was hosting that evening. A group of visiting single females had been assigned to my care, and I had every empty room in the house converted into a small dorm, fitting at least two comfortably, up to four if necessary. When I had everything ready, I bolted my breakfast, got dressed, and drove to church. Dennis was waiting for me outside. He smiled as I approached, not looking at all nervous about being the Sunday morning guest speaker.

He gave me a quick kiss, then led me inside, where we sat in a pew near the front. As we greeted other members sitting around us, a strange sense of guilt overtook me. It took two hymns for the feeling to fully evolve, finally slapping me right in the face when Dennis stood up and walked to the pulpit to deliver his sermon. I felt like a fake and a liar. Over the last couple of weeks, I'd let myself entertain thoughts about what it would be like being married to Dennis, and now, all I could think about was how unfair it was to let him think about me as a potential partner. I felt guilty for allowing him to get so close to me. He was blissfully unaware of my secret side, believing he was dating a normal woman.

If he ever found out what I was, our relationship would end and he would never want anything to do with me again. He could get any woman he wanted just by snapping his fingers. Why would he stay with me? It was like a super-hard puzzle that was impossible to figure out. If I told him, I would lose him, but if there was any hope of a future for us, I had to tell him. Not telling him, if not a sin in and of itself, was certainly morally reprehensible and something I just couldn't do. So, the question became, *when* should I tell him? After he fell in love with me? That would be akin to entrapment, like a trick, a lie of omission. It was hopeless.

And then there was Jordan. What was I going to do about Jordan? I had feelings for her—strong feelings, feelings unlike I had ever had for anyone. Simply ignoring her hadn't worked. I couldn't get her out of my mind even though I hadn't set eyes on her since just after my return from Oklahoma.

The thought of her warmed my body, and I pulled at my collar, trying to rid myself of the blush that covered my face. I took a deep breath and straightened in my seat, fighting the feelings of desire and guilt swirling around in my mind and body, that familiar sense of panic rising up in me as well.

I shut all of these thoughts down and tried to listen to Dennis' sermon, desperate for any respite. His words began to make their way into my brain as he explained the impossible dilemma *riding the fence* created, ironically describing the exact situation I found myself in—stuck between two opposing realities, unable to fully commit to either one of them. Hope surged as I listened to his solution, followed by disappointment when he offered nothing but the basics—a firm recommitment to God. I knew this already; I had recommitted myself a million times. If this was the only solution, I was in deep trouble.

After services, Dennis and I said quick goodbyes in the parking lot. His host was driving him to the airport, and he promised to call when he was home safe. I waved as they drove away, then went back into the building to join the others. After potluck, I went home and took a short nap. Hosting a house full of young women was no easy task, but it was a mindless, routine task, one I had done a hundred times before. And this time, I didn't worry about what it could evoke in me. I was already taken in that regard.

* * *

I sat with my parents at Sunday evening services, and afterward, we all drove out to the local miniature golf course for a round of fellowship and putt-putt golf. On hole number seven, familiar laughter hit me like a Mack truck, and I swung around to find Jordan four holes back, celebrating a hole-in-one with a group of girls. It took me five attempts to get my ball in the hole. The next hole was a bit better, though, as relief and the tiniest bit of satisfaction crept into my heart. At least she wasn't with some guy on a date. Just the thought of her with a guy made me jealous, another emotion I had no right to have when it came to her.

The battle was never-ending, and my heart ached as I turned my golf club in at the front desk and walked through the parking lot to my truck, struggling to keep Jordan out of my thoughts while missing her badly. Maybe if I put more distance between us. Maybe if I moved to another city or state. Maybe knowing she wasn't nearby would keep me from thinking about her. But the thought of never seeing her again was worse. I wanted her in my life, even if it broke my heart. I needed to get a rein on myself, or I would lose her altogether.

My guests started arriving fifteen minutes after I got home, and the twelve female visitors I'd planned for turned into seventeen. I spread them throughout the house, in vacant beds, on sofa pullout beds, and for those who thought to bring a sleeping bag, there was plenty of room on the floor. I was making one of the sofa beds in the family room when the doorbell rang. "One more," Mom called out. If female visitor number eighteen didn't bring a sleeping bag, I wasn't sure where I was going to put her. I then realized I didn't have enough pillows and walked into the kitchen to ask Mom where all the extra pillows were. I came to an abrupt stop in the doorway. It was Jordan, sitting on a kitchen barstool next to three other young women, charming every one of them, including my mom, with some story about turtles being able to breathe from both ends. I watched for a minute, trying not to stare, fighting my growing amusement at seeing her so animated. Her eyes were as big as saucers, her smile wide, her laugh adorable, and her voice, music to my ears.

"Hi. I hope you have room for one more body," Jordan said as she suddenly turned to me.

Everyone turned and looked at me, waiting for my reply, but totally hung up on Jordan's word choice, I started blushing profusely instead.

"Are you blushing?" Mom asked. "You are so silly and very pretty." She planted a kiss on my forehead, then turned to go. "Come on, ladies, I'll show you where your beds are." As the three young women followed Mom out of the kitchen, I turned to Jordan, wondering why she was still standing there. Before I could ask, Mom popped her head back into the kitchen and said, "I put Jordan in the living room with you. Good night, you two." Mom disappeared from the kitchen doorway, and I brushed by Jordan, refusing to look directly at her as I led her into the living room.

"Are you enjoying the meeting?" I asked.

"Yeah, I am. And you?" Jordan replied.

"Yes... I'm enjoying it," I mumbled as I came to a stop in the middle of the room, Jordan right behind me.

I found myself confronted with several blankets and some throw pillows piled up on the couch. I stared at them, feeling very unprepared to deal with the simple making of our beds, hers and mine, her presence behind me making it impossible for me to concentrate. I decided to delay the bed-making for the time being and change into my nightgown first. I needed to regroup and figure out what was happening here.

"I need to go to the bathroom," I announced as I turned on my heel, coming face-to-face with her. "You can change here," I added. She nodded her head.

I stepped to the side, meaning to walk around her, while she took a step in the same direction, effectively blocking my way.

"Sorry," she mumbled, taking a step in the other direction at the same time I did, causing me to bump right into her.

We did this one more time, clumsily bumping, our hands briefly touching. I had to put a stop to it!

"Okay! Stop!" I flustered. I brushed up against her as I stepped around her, hightailing it the heck out of there.

As I brushed my teeth, I stared at myself in the bathroom mirror, questioning Jordan's presence while reminding myself that Jordan went to a different congregation and was technically a female visitor in need of a place to stay. But still…

I leaned over and spat toothpaste into the sink, hovering a moment before slowly looking back up into the mirror. Oh my God! She was here! And we were about to spend the night together! I flipped into panic mode, madly swishing water around in my mouth as I prepared to fight the demons inside me, staring at myself in the mirror like a deer caught in headlights. I spat the water out, hesitated, then frantically splashed water on my face, trying to cool myself down and calm my galloping heart. I grabbed the edges of the counter with both hands, willing myself to relax, suddenly aware that the constant noise in my head had gone silent.

She was here, and we were about to spend the night together. A feeling of liberation hit me as every single moment I'd spent trying not to think about her since I returned from Oklahoma burst apart inside my heart, freeing me from the impossible task of pretending I didn't love her. My breathing calmed as I let go, allowing the only thing that mattered to take over my thoughts. I would have her all to myself for the night. This excited me in a way I had never experienced before, and I knew with complete clarity that I wanted her. My body was vibrating, and the area between my thighs was unapologetically warm and wet. I slipped into my nightgown without a thought to Dennis, the church, or what a night alone with Jordan might mean for my future. All I could think about was being close to her.

I threw on my robe and walked out of the bathroom, making my way down the hallway, past the dining room, and through the kitchen, clicking off the light as I stopped in the living room doorway. A small lamp was still on, illuminating the room in soft, dim light. Jordan was lying on her back on the floor under the covers on her side of our makeshift bed. I was relieved and excited at the same time, glad that Jordan had taken it upon herself to make the bed—a task that seemed daunting to me just a few minutes ago—and excited by her choice of sleeping arrangements. A vague feeling of crossing a line overtook me. I could turn back now and find another place to sleep, but I did not want to do that. Every piece of me wanted to lie down next to her. I stepped into the room. Jordan didn't say a word or move a muscle; she just looked at me and waited.

I took another step and then another, making my way across the room toward the lamp. I swallowed hard, reached out, and took the lamp's chain in my fingers, pulling it and throwing the room into darkness. I waited for my eyes to adjust—the only light coming from a full moon pouring in through the front windows—then removed my robe and draped it over the arm of the couch. I blew out a quick breath and carefully stepped around to my side of our makeshift bed, hesitating a moment before kneeling down and crawling under the covers next to her.

Jordan's head turned, and her shadowed eyes looked straight at me as my heart pounded hard against my ribs, my body tingling with anticipation—of what, I could only imagine. Since the camping trip, when we slept together under the stars, I'd often thought about being with her in this particular position, lying down next to her alone in the dark. But still, I was not quite sure what might happen next.

Movement from under the cover caught my eye, and my breath caught as I realized what it was. I lay stock-still as her hand approached my hip, then gasped when her fingers touched the fabric of my nightgown. A surge of heat shot through my body, and my head pushed back into my pillow as pure want erupted between my thighs, my hips slightly lifting and rolling, completely consumed by lust.

Desperate to get to her, I followed my body's lead, scooching and sliding, nudging and fumbling, feeling my way to her without any real plan of what I was going to do when I got there. I ended up with my face scrunched up against her upper arm, my hand clambering up onto her stomach, and my leg easing itself onto her thigh—her hand wedged between us, still over my nightgown, snuggly nestled up against the source of my want. We were both breathing like cross-country runners. I stifled a whimper and held on to her tighter, the covers on her stomach balled up in my fist as my hips pushed forward.

The next thing I knew, it was morning. I was lying in the exact same position, and Jordan was gone. Panic hit me, and at first, I couldn't move as the incredible events of the night before flashed through my mind. I looked around for any sign that someone may have seen us, but there was no evidence that anyone was even up yet. It was completely quiet except for the very first birdsong as early morning dawned.

I got up, put on my robe, and walked into the kitchen. There was no sign that anyone had been in the kitchen; not even the coffee was made. I stepped through the opposite doorway into the dining room and peered down the hallway. The sound of one of the showers running gave me hope, and I hurried back through the kitchen and looked into the living room, searching for any clue that Jordan was still here. I spotted her purse lying on the floor next to the sofa, and a sigh of pure relief left my lips. She was still here! I put on some coffee and waited.

A few minutes later, Jordan walked down the hallway and entered the kitchen. I practically gasped when I saw her. Her hair was wet, pulled back in a messy bun, and her robe was damp around the shoulders. Her face was glowing; she looked incredible. Every inch of me ached to take her into my arms. Someone opened a door and started down the hallway, snapping me back to reality. Mom! My eyes widened in panic, and Jordan immediately left the kitchen, hurrying into the living room. I poured myself and Jordan a cup of coffee and followed Jordan into the living room just as Mom entered the kitchen from the dining room.

"Good morning, sweetheart."

"Good morning, Mom."

I set our coffees on the coffee table, then reached over and grabbed the opposite corners of the blanket Jordan was attempting to fold. I stepped forward, took her corners into my hands, and when she didn't let go of the blanket, our fingers touched and held, the intimate contact turning my body warm and wet in a matter of seconds. How could I want her so openly and so badly while standing here in my parent's house surrounded by Christians? I wanted to tell her what was happening to me, but I didn't know what to say. And how could I ever explain my behavior last night? I practically jumped her in my own living room. I had striven my whole life to keep this part of me in check, but now it was loose, and I couldn't make it stop, and I didn't want to, which scared me to death but made me feel more alive than I had ever felt before.

Girls' laughter sounded from somewhere in the house, startling Jordan, and she let go of the blanket, picked up her coffee, and walked back into the kitchen. I stood there gaping after her for a moment, then finished folding the blanket, grabbed our pillows off the floor, and stacked everything on the end of the couch. I considered going after Jordan and talking to her, but what could I say and where could I say it? The house was full of Christians. I had no idea what to do next, so I hit the showers while the bathrooms were still free.

After I got dressed, I went to the kitchen to help Mom with breakfast. She was making a smorgasbord of scrambled eggs, bacon, and pancakes, refilling the platters that were sitting on the kitchen bar. I grabbed one of the platters, took it into the dining room, and placed it on the table, where five of our guests, including Jordan, were already eating breakfast. I picked up the empty platters and turned toward the kitchen.

"Good morning," Jordan said, stopping me in my tracks.

At least she was speaking to me, which gave me hope that I hadn't completely mucked everything up. Maybe she wasn't too freaked out by what happened.

"Good morning," I said as I turned back to the table.

We held each other's gaze for a few seconds before she graced me with a small smile, and it was like a lifeline. I returned her smile, buoyed tenfold, then hurried out of the room, suddenly filled with energy, that smile still plastered on my face as I busied myself around the house, making beds, rolling up sleeping bags, and generally straightening everything up. I gathered all the used towels from the bathrooms and threw them into the washing machine, then grabbed the trash and took it out back to the trash cans. I opened the lid, dumped the trash inside, then froze when someone cleared their throat behind me. I turned to find Jordan standing there with two bags of trash I had missed.

"Oh, I didn't see those. Thank you," I said, my heart suddenly racing.

"No problem," she said with a slight smile, looking as nervous as I was.

She walked to the trash can, threw her bags inside, then turned to face me, hesitating before reaching out and touching my arm. I looked down at her fingers touching my skin, my mouth and chin quivering as I attempted to swallow. We were both breathing so hard, it would have been comical had the moment not been so serious. She took a step back, looked left from where she had come, then looked back at me. I would have given my life to know what she was thinking.

We walked back inside the house together and were not alone again for the rest of the meeting. I scarcely saw her in the weeks after it ended, but what happened between us that night before I passed out consumed my thoughts, forever changing me. I would no longer fight the feelings I had for Jordan. Dennis wrote me several letters, as did the men I'd met in Oklahoma. I never replied to any of them.

CHAPTER SIX

Several weeks had passed since I'd last seen Jordan, and I was nearly out of my mind with missing her, especially at night, lying in bed, lost in a world of what it would be like...if. And that was the problem. I had no idea how Jordan felt about all of this, leaving my thoughts woefully incomplete. I needed all the pieces of this puzzle to get a full understanding of whether the *what if* might actually be something. I lay there frustrated, unable to sleep, the need to know filling my body with desire and my heart with hope.

When dawn broke the following morning, I drove to her house. It was risky, and I almost lost my nerve, nearly turning back twice, but I had to see her. I had to talk to her about what happened, find out what she thought, and somehow tell her how I felt about her. She was either going to fall into my arms and help me figure this out, or she was going to scream in horror and swear ignorance about the whole thing. My plan was simple. Deliver my message, stare into her beautiful brown eyes, take in her gorgeous smile, give her the chance to tell me how she felt about what was going on between us, and then drive back home before Mom and Dad noticed I was gone.

I knocked on her front door, relieved when she opened it and not Shawn. She wore pajama bottoms, a T-shirt, and a three-quarter-length, light blue cotton robe. Her hair was perfectly tousled, and she looked adorably sleepy like she had just gotten out of bed. My mouth opened, and nothing came out.

"Shannon, hi. Um... Come in."

She was surprised to see me standing on her front porch, of course, but I could definitely tell she was happy to see me, which gave me a little courage. I sat at the kitchen table staring at her as she poured us some coffee, racking my brain for something clever, interesting, or complimentary to say, something to let her know how extraordinary she was. She brought me my coffee and sat down next to me, smiling shyly. Even if something clever, interesting, or complimentary had popped into my brain, it would have been inadequate. She was beautiful, and she smelled like wildflowers, and even though her pajamas were nothing special, they looked really special on her. She was not wearing a bra, and her T-shirt clearly displayed the outline of her breasts. It was all I could do not to stare at them. She was breathtaking, rendering me speechless, which was stupid because I had come here to talk to her. I hadn't said a word since I arrived. I had to say something or risk looking like an idiot.

"How are you..." I began.

"Good morning, Shannon. You're up early for a Saturday," Shawn chipperly greeted as he walked into the kitchen, totally interrupting our moment.

"Good morning, Shawn. Jordan and I are going jogging this morning. You wanna come?"

"No thanks." He laughed, shaking his head as he walked back down the hallway, taking his coffee with him.

"Can we take a walk?" I asked Jordan in a whisper.

She nodded, stood up, and went to get dressed. I waited for her out on the front lawn, relieved that my ability to speak had returned but nervous about how she would react to the words I hoped I had the courage to say. The door swung open and she stepped out onto the porch, and when she started down the steps, I took the opportunity to check her out. I had never seen her in sweatpants before and had to rip my eyes away from the new details they revealed about her beautiful backside. She walked to the sidewalk and turned to me, tilting her head as if to say, "*You coming?*"

We walked in silence, just enjoying the act of walking next to each other—one more thing I could spend hours doing with her. But not today. I had to start. There was no way I was leaving here without a better understanding of what was going on between us.

My heart fluttered wildly in my chest as I thought of a

way to begin. I took a deep breath, blew it out, gathered all my courage, and finally forced what I wanted to say out of my mouth. "I don't know if you think about me, but I think about you, a lot. I...ah...like you." I winced at how immature, stupid, and unromantic I sounded. She spoke, and my words didn't sound so stupid anymore.

"I like you, too."

I nearly fell off the sidewalk. Her hand reached out to steady me, releasing me almost immediately, but the place where she touched me tingled with warmth. I wondered what it would take to get her to touch me again as her words repeated themselves in my head. *I like you.* Daring threatened to overtake me, but caution stepped in, grabbing me by the collar and pulling me back.

What did her words mean? Did they mean what mine meant? Should I ask? My feelings for her had been near bursting for weeks, and now I had no idea what to say. The problem was that I was afraid that if I said the wrong thing, I'd scare the crap out of her and she'd never want to see me again. I kicked myself for not having formed a better plan before I came here and was ready to give up when she suddenly spoke.

"Where could we be alone together?"

I was again surprised at how direct and to the point her words were but managed not to trip over my feet. I was seriously out of my depth. I mean, her question was already ten questions ahead of mine, and although her question was encouraging and very informative, I still could not be sure how she meant it. I didn't know how to respond. I was stuck and running out of time. I'd been so confident lying in my bed earlier this morning, the words I wanted to say to her rushing through my mind like a wild, untamed river, a feeling of invincibility so strong, there seemed no other option but to get to her as soon as possible and pour my heart out to her. And now, I couldn't get two words out of my mouth if my life depended on it.

"I don't know," I answered, while my brain screamed at

me, *Say something to her!*

We returned to the house and stood on the front lawn, looking at each other for a moment. Jordan gave me a small smile, then turned toward the porch. I completely panicked, fearing that if I let her disappear into the house, I would never see her again. Before I could overthink it, I let my heart speak for me.

"Can I take you to breakfast?" I blurted.

"Yeah, okay," she blurted back, swinging around to face me, her expression changing from disappointment to relief in one second flat.

I nodded and smiled, and she walked inside to ask Shawn if she could go to breakfast with me. I waited for her on the lawn and was at first disappointed when she walked back out still wearing sweatpants, sure it meant that Shawn had said no. But he hadn't, and Jordan smiled at me as she walked past me on the way to my truck.

As we drove out to the main road, it surprised me how little traffic there was, reminding me how early it still was. I asked Jordan if she knew of a breakfast place nearby, and instead of answering, she leaned forward in her seat and peered out the windshield.

"Pull in there," she said, pointing along a line of parked cars.

As I pulled in between two large Chevy trucks and turned off the engine, Jordan unfastened her seat belt and turned in her seat, facing me, placing her right hand on the dashboard and her left hand on the back of the seat. She waited as I unbuckled my seatbelt and then moved toward me, hesitating when her knee touched mine. I practically gulped when she nervously moistened her lips and all but swooned when she slowly leaned in. All I could hear was how heavy we were both breathing, the urgency of it amplified in my head. She put her hand on my thigh, and I knew she was going to kiss me.

She glanced at my mouth, then looked into my eyes, seeming to ask my permission. The smallest of noises escaped my lips, and a heartbeat later, her mouth was on mine. Both of us inhaled sharply through our noses and then moaned in unison when our tongues touched, our bodies melting into each other for a moment before our kiss turned hungry and hot. She grabbed my hip and squeezed, and I grabbed onto her shoulder and pushed myself up against her as my body erupted into liquid heat. Our breathing became urgent, our groans and whimpers filling the cab of the truck as we frantically touched arms, thighs, hips, and waists for the very first time. It was like nothing I had ever experienced before. And I wanted more.

Without losing contact with her beautiful lips, I climbed up on top of her and straddled her in her seat. She didn't seem surprised, and if she was, she didn't let on, kissing me even deeper, with more urgency. It was intoxicating; I wanted to climb into her mouth! Up until now, I thought I hated kissing. I didn't hate it. I loved it! And it was her I loved kissing, and boy could she kiss, and thank God she was just as into it as I was! How would I survive if her lips never touched mine again? They were so soft and seemed to know exactly what to do. They wrapped themselves around mine and moved as if they only existed to make mine happy.

The obsession boys had with kissing was suddenly clear—but boys had nothing on us. This was in another realm entirely, the purest form of expression as I let her know that my mouth, lips, and tongue belonged to her. Forget climbing into her mouth; I wanted to swallow her up!

"Please," I whimpered, breathlessly sucking on her mouth as I fisted the hem of my skirt. I desperately wanted her hands on me and had a pretty good idea where I wanted them but had no idea how to verbalize it. Without meaning to, I bit her. Freudian? We both gasped as I quickly pulled away from her, mortified that I may have hurt her, worried that she would never want to kiss me again. "Are you okay? Did I hurt you?" I asked.

"No, you didn't hurt me," she said, chuckling as she swiped the tips of her fingers over her bottom lip. "I love kissing you." And then she kissed me a whole different way. It was soft and slow, and so good, I couldn't decide which of her kisses I liked best. She broke our kiss slowly, hesitantly touching my hair, reverently smoothing it back away from my face. "You wanted to talk."

"Yeah, I did," I said, taking a quick breath as I tried to organize my thoughts. "I came over to talk, you know, about what happened at my house during the sleepover." Jordan was silent, seemingly very interested in my face and neck as she slowly ran the tips of her fingers from my cheek to my jaw, down my neck to my collarbone. She was driving me crazy. "I feel like I should...tell you what's happening with me...what happens to me when I'm near you. Everything turns on, Jordan. I don't know how to explain it."

"Shannon. I think you've been very clear about what's happening to you."

"You've noticed? I mean, I hope you don't think..."

"Think what, Shannon? Listen. You have nothing to explain. I feel the same way. Can't you see that?"

"Yes. I see. I want to see."

"Then see that I want you too."

Unable to speak, I nodded my head. Her words were incomprehensible.

I slid off her lap, and we sat there holding hands, looking into each other's eyes, and eventually kissing again, which had me breathing hard and squirming in my seat in no time. When we came up for air, she said, "You are beautiful, and I love your red hair." I had to laugh a little at the 'I love your red hair' part, and blush a little at the 'You are beautiful' part. She was so sweet and very sexy. I looked down at our fingers intertwined, amazed.

"We should air out the truck," she said.

Air out the truck? I looked up to find her craning her neck to the side, looking through the slightly fogged-up truck windows, trying to get a better look at the area around us.

She opened her door, so I opened mine, and we both stepped outside. It was mid-morning, and traffic had increased, something I hadn't noticed sitting with her inside the cab. I had no sense of time when we were together. As she paced back and forth alongside the truck, I was suddenly aware of how stressed she looked, worried that she'd freak out as the reality of what we had done came into focus. She looked at me over the hood of the truck and smiled.

"Thank you for today."

"Thank you, Jordan." Relieved that she was okay, I shook my head at her and smiled back, astonished at what we were thanking each other for.

We climbed back into the truck, and I immediately understood why she wanted to air it out. The thick, heady atmosphere we'd created was gone. I missed it, and apparently, so did she. She pulled me into another kiss, and I never wanted her to stop as thoughts of what else I wanted her to do to me spun around in my head. She ended the kiss slowly, reluctantly, and I let her go, equally reluctant. There was no more time. I had to take her back.

I put on my seatbelt, turned on the ignition, pulled out onto the road, and drove her home. Her house looked exactly the way we'd left it, showing no sign of whether Shawn was home or not. His car was either inside the garage or he was gone. I couldn't remember seeing his car parked in the driveway when I first came over.

"Don't be nervous. Everything is okay," Jordan said, blowing out a quick breath, her house key at the ready. "How do I look? How do I smell? I mean…"

"I know what you mean. You look beautiful, and you smell incredible." She was obviously as paranoid as I was about getting caught, somehow making me feel even more connected to her.

"Okay. Wish me luck." She jumped out of the truck, gave me a small wave, and took off running across the lawn and up the steps to the front door. She let herself in with a quick glance back at me and disappeared into the house. I held my breath, waiting for something to happen—like Shawn chasing Jordan out of the house, screaming at the top of his lungs. God forbid! But I couldn't stay any longer; it could look suspicious. I put the truck in gear and drove down the street before making a U-turn and slowly driving back past her house. Everything looked okay.

* * *

On the way home, I began to worry about whether I could make it into my own house undetected. I had not intended on returning so late. Wishing I had paid more attention to the details of Mom and Dad's schedule, I tried to remember what they had planned for the day. I was sure they would be busy with meetings until the evening, but I couldn't remember exactly when they were supposed to leave. Surely, they were already gone. The possibility of being caught had me nervously nauseous. My hands were trembling, and my mouth had gone dry. Was this the cost of what we were doing—besides the whole going-to-hell thing we would definitely be doing later? With this thought in mind, I full-out panicked. My heartbeat accelerated and my breathing turned shallow and fast. I was on the verge of hyperventilating. I pulled over to the side of the road and tried to catch my breath, realizing how indiscreet and irresponsible it had been to drive over to Jordan's house, not to mention making out with her in my truck in broad daylight.

It took a few minutes for me to calm down enough to drive, and then, when I turned onto my street, I totally freaked out again, horrified to find my parents' car still parked in the driveway. I drove past the house and parked around the corner, frantically trying to figure out what to do. I could go in and head straight for the bathroom, or I could sit here and wait until they left. But how long would that take, and what if they were sitting in the house waiting for me?

I drove back to the house, parked next to their car, grabbed my purse, and hurried to the front door. As I reached for the doorknob, the door swung open, surprising me. I jerked my hand back and deftly stepped to the side as Mom and Dad walked out, deep in conversation about photo albums and how they should be sorted—chronologically or subjectively. Mom turned and closed the door, noticing me for the first time.

"Hey honey, we're late. There's lasagna in the fridge. Don't wait up," she laughed over her shoulder as she headed for the car.

Dad was already unlocking doors and loading stuff in the trunk. He waved.

"Thanks, Mom," I croaked, struggling to speak as I returned Dad's wave.

After they drove away, I walked into the house, closed the door, and started crying, which was probably understandable after such a remarkable, emotional, monumental morning. I eventually regained enough composure to get myself to the bathroom, where I undressed, jumped in the shower, and cried some more—but only a little bit and more out of relief than anything else.

I took my skirt, blouse, and underclothes and threw them into the washing machine, thoughts of what Jordan might be doing floating through my mind as I added way too much detergent. The washing machine tumbled to life, and I stared at the growing body of suds as I thought about her hands on me and her soft moans. I closed the lid, and the memory of her lips, and especially her tongue, shot through my head. My knees gave, and I gripped the washing machine, holding on to it for support, amazed at how just the thought of her affected me. She had complete control of my body. When I was not blushing and speechless, I was wet and throbbing. My heart beat like a base drum whenever she was near me, and I got weak knees just thinking about her. I'd given up all potential suitors and was obviously ready to risk heaven itself for the possibility of a few moments alone with her.

All the times I'd wondered what being in love was like, I never imagined this. It was both wonderful and terrifying. It was extraordinary—too extraordinary to let go of—and I knew I would risk everything to hold onto it for as long as I could.

CHAPTER SEVEN

Over the next few weeks, I took refuge in my routine—church, sleep, work—a routine that perfectly embraced my state of mind, allowing me to completely lose myself in thoughts of Jordan at the expense of all else. I became distant and quietly detached from the people around me, some of them sitting right next to me, talking directly to me. Amazingly, nobody noticed. When I was at home and my parents were not, I was glad for the solitude, perfectly content to sit for hours and think of her. I was often far away in a daydream about what we would do together the next time I could get her alone. I didn't have much to fall back on for these daydreams—I had no experience sexually—and tried to hang on to what happened during the sleepover and in my truck. It all happened so fast; too fast. If I were given another chance, I would kiss her more perfectly, and I would take my time. I longed to know what the rest of her looked like, what the rest of her tasted like. Her neck, her ears, her shoulders, her…hmm…yeah…

Then it was suddenly November, the beginning of winter, my favorite time of the year. It had been several weeks since I'd seen Jordan, and I missed her terribly, but I didn't know how to get to her without drawing attention to us. Elena and Shawn were busy planning their wedding and hadn't visited my congregation in months—which was how I usually got to see Jordan—so now, even those short visits were gone. I was constantly trying to think of opportunities where we could be together, but each possibility seemed as improbable as the next, the mortifying thought that we could be discovered driving me to inaction.

December passed, and in the second week of January, my wedding invitation arrived. May tenth. There was no way I could wait another four months to see Jordan. I was so desperate that I seriously considered showing up at her house again. But then she surprised me with a visit of her own.

It was Sunday morning, and she was there. I couldn't believe it. She was with Shawn and Elena, and they had just taken their seats when I walked into the church building. They sat in a pew four rows from the front, and I found a seat on the opposite side of the building, four rows from the back. Services hadn't started yet, and as the buzz of whispered greetings died down and members found their seats, I prayed for a sign that Jordan hadn't forgotten me. Suddenly, her beautiful face came into view for the first time as she looked over her shoulder, her eyes locking with mine. She gave me a brief smile, then turned to the front again.

I was instantly aflame and suddenly aware of everyone singing as the sound blasted into my ears. I grabbed my hymnal, snapped it open, and began singing too, hardly able to contain the smile spreading across my face. She hadn't forgotten.

After services, I beelined it to the foyer and planted myself near the front door, busying myself greeting members and shaking their hands, catching glimpses of Jordan as she made her way toward the foyer. Our eyes met as she appeared in the doorway. She smiled. I smiled back. It took a minute or two for her to move through the crowd, greeting everyone, and then she was standing next to me.

"Hi," I said as I reached out to shake her offered hand. "How are you?"

"Good, how are you?"

"I'm good, thank you," I said, still holding her hand, reluctant to let go.

"Let's go outside." She signaled with a nod toward the front lawn.

I let go of her hand and followed her, stopping on the edge of the grass near the parking lot, where not so many people were standing.

"You look beautiful," we both whispered at the same time.

"I've missed you."

"I've missed you, too." I looked down at my shoes, then

back up at her, completely thrilled to be near her again.

"Listen, Elena and Shawn are spending the day with Tod and Rebecca. Would you like to come?"

Her unexpected invitation took me by surprise, and I stared at her for a moment, the word *yes* balancing on the tip of my tongue. And then a better idea popped into my head. "Please come to my house today. My parents are in Oakland and won't be home until this evening. I can fix us something to eat. Please, I miss you, the house is empty, we would have it to ourselves..." I rambled, whispering loudly, begging, my desperation on full display.

"I don't know, Shannon. This visit is wedding-related, and I think I'm expected to be there."

"Please!" I pleaded, surprised when my eyes filled with tears.

"No! Don't cry." Jordan's eyes widened with panic as she looked around to see if anyone was watching us, reminding me that we were not alone.

"I'm sorry." I wiped at my eyes, vigilantly scanning the crowd, knowing I had to leave before I made a spectacle of myself, knowing darn well why I wanted her alone in my house. "I have to go." Feeling rejected and a little embarrassed, I left her standing there, helplessly looking after me.

Jordan was nowhere to be seen as I exited the parking lot and drove by the front of the building. She had already gone back inside. She had better things to do than worry about me falling apart. I pulled into my driveway ten minutes later and sat for a moment before pulling a tissue from my purse. I blew my nose, then took a deep breath, letting out a cynical grunt. I got out of the truck and slammed the door, shaking my head in irritation. She was so close—a spontaneous opportunity to have her alone taken away from me!

Inside the house, I removed my coat and shoes and went straight to my bedroom, dejectedly flopping face-first onto my bed. It wasn't long before regret wrapped itself around me, and I sat up and slapped my palm against my forehead.

How could I reject her invitation like that? How could I walk away from an opportunity like that? My overwhelming desire to be alone with her had caused me to forfeit a whole day with her. What the heck was wrong with me? It was like nothing else mattered to me but getting her alone. I had taken Jordan's offer to spend time together and unceremoniously thrown it in the garbage, treating her like crap and leaving me sad, sorry, and totally empty-handed. I was a complete idiot!

I got up and went into the kitchen to make coffee. Taking a cup from the cupboard, I put it on the counter in front of me and just stared at it, wishing I had handled things better. I took a deep, contemplative breath and turned, crossing my arms in front of me as I leaned back against the counter, facing the kitchen window leading to the front yard.

My eyes widened in disbelief and my mouth fell open in shock as Jordan's face suddenly appeared in the window. For a moment, I questioned whether she was really there, half convinced I'd conjured her up. As if sensing my doubt, she smiled and gave me a little wave, snapping me out of my shocked state. I ran to the front door and opened it.

"Hi. I didn't want to ring. I was afraid your parents might be home. I wasn't sure…"

I grabbed her by her coat lapel, pulled her inside, and closed the door, tears filling my eyes as I pushed her up against it. "You came! You're here!"

Before she could speak, I kissed her, desperate to taste her, while my fingers quickly unbuttoned her coat. I released her lips as I pushed her coat from her shoulders and down her arms, letting it fall to the floor, my hands practically frisking her as they moved over her sweater, around her waist, and up along the sides of her breasts. I gasped, astonished at how big and full they were. She whimpered, and it was music to my ears. Grabbing the hem of her sweater, I lifted it, pulling it up over her head and dropping it on the floor next to her coat. Transfixed by the brightness of her white cotton, button-down blouse against the brown of her skin, I swallowed hard as I fumbled with the top button. Jordan watched as I unbuttoned the rest, both of us gasping when I pulled her blouse open with a decisive snap. The sight of her before me left me breathless. I slowly raised my hand and touched her skin along the upper hem of her bra, staring in wide-eyed wonder at her heaving breasts.

She moistened her lips, drawing my attention to her beautiful tongue, and I leaned forward and kissed her while my fingers slipped under her bra and pulled it up. She moaned, thrusting her breasts forward, and I immediately broke our kiss, leaned down, and took her right nipple into my mouth.

Jordan's head fell back against the door with a *thunk*. "Oh, my God!" she gasped.

I didn't know how she was still standing. I moved to her other breast and gave it the same attention while my hands squeezed and stroked, making Jordan whimper and moan. I had never seen anything so beautiful in all my life—the feel of them in my hands, the taste of them on my tongue, so much more than I had imagined. And Jordan? Wow! Her condition in my presence, under my touch, was shockingly erotic. She was breathing so hard, her mouth was hanging open, and the lovely whimpering noises she made, begging me to touch her, drove me crazy. I had complete control over her body, and her body had complete control over me. I would do anything to keep her whimpering, moaning, and saying God's name.

My right hand made its way over her hip and down the front of her thigh, where my fingers found the hem of her skirt. I hesitated a moment as our eyes locked, then lifted her skirt and slipped my hand into her panties. Jordan's legs gave way, and she slid halfway down the door, her hands grabbing onto my shoulders as she whimpered, "Oh God!" We were panting like animals. I slid my fingers between her thighs and gasped at what I found there. She was slick-wet, drenching my fingers in an instant, her vagina warm, soft, and swollen, begging me to touch her more boldly. And I did, and she collapsed to the floor, dragging me with her. I landed on my knees and covered her open mouth with mine, kissing her wet and sloppy as I hung onto her with one arm, my fingers sliding back and forth over her wet flesh as I pumped madly with the other.

She came, moaning into my mouth, slumping further down and sideways until she was lying on her back, her left leg bent up against the door. Lying half on top of her, I broke our kiss, my hand still in her panties, my fingers wanting more. Her breathing calmed as we lay there, and after a moment, I reluctantly removed my hand from between her thighs. I was a little nervous as I turned and looked at her, my pounding heart skipping a beat when I met soulful eyes filled with adoration.

I sat up and let my eyes roam the length of her, taking in the havoc I'd wreaked. Her blouse was still unbuttoned, her bra still pulled up over her breasts. Her skirt was wrapped around her hips, and one of her knee socks had slipped down to her ankle, but her shoes were still on. She looked very sexy. Jordan slowly raised up on her elbows, then abruptly sat up and quickly adjusted herself as she pulled down her bra, covering her breasts, and pushed her skirt down over her panties. She started buttoning her blouse, and I placed my hand on hers, stopping her.

"Come to my bed."

After my crazy, chaotic ambush, I wasn't sure how she'd respond. She hesitated a moment, then moved to get up. I took this as her answer and grabbed her hand, pulling her to her feet. I led her through the kitchen, through the dining room, and down the hallway, and a second later, she was miraculously standing in my room and I was helping her out of her clothes and into my bed. She looked at me expectantly as she slid under the covers.

"Aren't you taking off your clothes?"

"Yes, of course," I said as I fingered the buttons of my blouse, feeling super shy about exposing myself to someone for the first time. There was nothing I wanted more than to be naked with Jordan, and I would not let my weird shyness trip me up now. I quickly removed my clothes, and when I slid under the covers next to her, my shyness disappeared. I pushed the covers away; I had to see her. And then my hands took over; I had to touch her. I climbed on top of her and awkwardly attempted to touch every inch of her with every inch of me. Although my moves were novice and unpracticed, her body seemed to understand mine, our movements becoming beautifully fluid, achingly sweet, and incredibly effective. When her hand slipped between my thighs, I was more than ready.

A noise I'd never heard myself make before shot out of my mouth as heat erupted from my core, searing into my brain the incomprehensible first-time quality of being so intimately touched by fingers other than my own. And her touch was exquisite, her fingers breathtakingly precise as they slid through my wet, swollen folds with reckless abandon. It was perfection, and I did not want them to ever stop. But my body was already taking over, my hips already rocking as her arm pumped and her fingers touched, my lust overwhelming as I rode her hand unashamedly toward my coming orgasm.

I collapsed on top of her as aftershocks rippled through my body, my hips still moving, my vagina still rubbing itself on her, wanting more. I couldn't help it; it felt so good. I could not believe that something this amazing could come out of my body and that Jordan was the key to it. I raised my head and looked at her. Her face was flushed, her breathing labored, and she looked about as blown away as I was. We were both kind of speechless. I mean, what do you say after something like that? And then she smiled, words unnecessary.

We snuggled our bodies closer, the sheer intimacy of it stealing my breath, Jordan looking down the length of me, clearly checking me out as her hand followed the curve of my hip. "Your body is beautiful. You are beautiful. You really shouldn't be so shy."

"You're beautiful, Jordan! I've never seen anything so

beautiful in my life!" I returned, blushing a little at my earnestness. She let out a soft chuckle and smiled, and I smiled, too. We couldn't stop smiling at each other. "Why did you change your mind today?"

"About coming here, you mean? I didn't. I wanted to come as soon as you asked, I just didn't know how to bring it up with Shawn. After you left, I went in to talk to him, but it was never the right moment, and before I knew it, we were in the car. I had pretty much given up on seeing you, but then we were driving by your street, just over there," she indicated toward the traffic light on the corner. "The light turned red, the car stopped, and I just did it. I told them to let me out, I was going to spend the afternoon with you. They even wished me a good time."

"Wow, you're wonderful."

"Yeah, it did take a little bit of courage. They said they would meet me back at church this evening." Jordan smiled, and as she squeezed me tighter, her stomach let out a loud growl.

"Are you hungry?" I asked, but she didn't answer. I was about to ask her again when the question I really wanted to ask stumbled out of my mouth instead. "I wanted to ask you... Do you...you know...have you thought about..."

"What? What's wrong?"

"I thought I would die if I didn't see you soon," I said. "I know this is a complicated situation, Jordan, but I need to ask you... Do you think about me, too? About seeing me? I mean, do you think about how we could see each other more?"

"Every day. I can't stop thinking about you. I had this day all planned out for weeks, for us to spend the day together after church at Tod and Rebecca's house. What a stupid plan. Your plan was way better." She smiled as tears sprang into her eyes. "Nothing is more important to me than seeing you, Shannon."

"Jordan, don't cry. You are so sweet."

"Don't ever think I don't want to see you or that I'm not

trying to get to you. It's all I think about." We shared a bittersweet kiss, and then she turned and glanced at the clock. "It's already three o'clock."

"Let me make you a sandwich. I'm starving. Aren't you?" I asked.

"I can eat later. I don't want to waste our time together."

But I insisted and got up and made us a quick ham and cheese sandwich, which we ate in bed, practically laying on top of each other. There were crumbs everywhere.

Afterward, I spent at least half an hour kissing her as thoroughly as I could while she reciprocated with equal attentiveness.

We showered together, touching and exploring, lathering each other up and rinsing each other off, much too quickly, leaving me wanting her badly as we toweled each other dry between kisses. I was shamelessly wet and throbbing as we dressed and hurried out to the truck with only ten minutes to spare.

Inside the church building, we sat down next to Shawn and Elena just in time for the first hymn. I couldn't hear the sermon, just Jordan's voice in my head, her breathless moaning, and her other sweet noises. I glanced at her, then looked away, my breathing accelerating, remembering the longing in her eyes, unable to stop the thoughts of her beautiful body spread out before me. How would I make it through until next time? I grunted silently, and Jordan turned and looked at me, giving me a small smile before looking away. I had already been given much more than I could have ever hoped for. I would simply have to make do with what was possible and continue to dream that there would be a next time.

CHAPTER EIGHT

I didn't see Jordan again until early March. It was completely unexpected, just a coincidence that we'd both received the same invitation to a member's house for Sunday lunch.

I rang the doorbell, and Amanda, the host, opened the door and invited me in. She took the chili and cornbread I brought for potluck, showed me where to hang my coat, then pointed me through the foyer toward the living room before disappearing into the kitchen. I entered the living room, where fifteen or so other guests already sat waiting for lunch, and almost dropped my purse when I saw Jordan. She smiled and gave me her little wave. I immediately turned around and walked back into the foyer, hoping to hide the deep blush that had broken out all over my face. If someone saw me have a physical reaction to Jordan, it would cause undue attention, and that was the last thing I needed. I caught a glimpse of Amanda in the kitchen headed for the foyer, and I turned and quickly walked back into the living room, where I was met with silence, curious stares, and Jordan, her eyebrows raised in amusement. Crap! Now I had undue attention!

"Is everything okay, Shannon?" Amanda asked as she walked up behind me.

"Yes. Um… I thought… I forgot something… In my truck."

"You need to get something out of your truck?"

"No. I forgot it at home."

"Okay…" Amanda smiled, looking a little confused, then, with more pressing things to do, she walked back into the kitchen.

I sat down on the couch and pretended interest in a conversation between two women. They were talking about dresses. I looked down at mine, wishing I had worn something else. I hated this dress and hardly wore it unless I had nothing else. Today, of all days, I had nothing else. My hips were too narrow for it, and it never hung quite right. The bodice was too snug for my taste, and the buttons in front were too many. Glancing at Jordan, I caught her staring at me. I held her stare for as long as I dared, then looked away as Amanda walked in and announced lunch.

I remained seated while the first group filed into the adjacent dining room to fill their plates at the buffet, jumping when a voice from behind me said my name. I swung around to find Jordan standing next to the couch, smiling down at me.

"Sorry. I didn't mean to sneak up on you. Did I startle you?"

"No, it's okay." I stood up and faced her. "How are you?"

"I'm doing okay," she said, looking me up and down. "You look nice."

I let out a gasp before I could stop myself, abruptly clapping my hand over my mouth when I realized how loud I was. I glanced around the room and let out a quick breath, glad that no one heard me, irritated by everyone's presence, and frustrated that I couldn't see Jordan more often.

Jordan suppressed a smile, obviously finding my behavior amusing. "Hey, I want to show you something." She turned and walked into the foyer, opened the basement door, and disappeared inside.

I furtively looked around at the other guests making their way toward the buffet table, then followed Jordan, finding her waiting for me on the basement staircase, a few steps down. "Close the door," she whispered.

I took the first step down and pulled the door closed behind me as Jordan descended into the basement and disappeared around the corner to the left. I slowly followed her, and as I reached the bottom and stepped around the corner wall, a huge room opened up in front of me. It was a rec room and Jordan was standing at the other end of it, leaning against the back of a couch. There were two couches and two recliner chairs in front of a big-screen television. Between us stood a small billiard table, and on the wall to my left was a door, and next to it, a small corner kitchen with a sink, a refrigerator, and a microwave oven. There were little windows along the upper outer walls. It was surprisingly nice and fresh.

"Wow, this is really something," I said, trying to sound casual and cool—I was anything but—suddenly aware that we were completely alone.

"Do you believe in love at first sight?"

Surprised by her question, my mouth dropped open. Not sure how to answer, I quickly snapped it shut. I was already certain I was in love with her but had never even considered telling her. I decided to just answer the question and see where it led. "I do believe in love at first sight. Do you?"

"Yes, I do."

There was a moment of silence, the enormity of our declaration hanging between us. They weren't the exact words, but it was a lot. I hadn't realized how much I needed to hear the rest until the words spilled out of her mouth.

"I love you, Shannon."

Hearing those words spoken to me by the woman I dreamed of hearing them from nearly stopped my heart. I licked my lips and swallowed hard. This was happening. "I love you, Jordan."

"Come here."

My whole body wanted to run to her, and it took every ounce of control I possessed to keep my feet firmly planted in place. "Jordan, someone might come down here," I cautioned.

"No one will come, they're eating. Harry doesn't want them down here. Come here." Her voice was soft but insistent.

I turned and looked at the stairs, realizing that anyone who walked in wouldn't be able to see us until they were all the way down. I looked back at Jordan and blew out a quick breath. God, this was a bad idea! "But only a quick kiss, okay?"

The tilt of her head, her intense stare, and the very sexy

smirk on her face told me she had other ideas in mind. But what could I do? She had just declared her love for me. For me!

I quickly walked across the room, hesitating when I got to her, reaching out and touching her arm with my hand. "I love you," I said, and then I repeated it. I loved saying it, and I wanted to hear her say it again.

"I love you, Shannon."

I took a moment to revel in her words, then threw my arms around her neck and kissed her. She had her tongue in my mouth a half second later, and her hands were all over me—my waist, my hips, my backside. I managed to push myself out of her arms and take two steps back, catching my breath as I wiped my mouth with the back of my hand. She stood there looking at me, her desire written all over her face. "I don't want us to get caught," I whispered.

"We won't get caught."

That was all the reassurance I needed, and I was back in her arms, her hands back on my behind, then on my hips, then up my sides, cupping my breasts and squeezing, sending a bolt of electricity to my core. I released her mouth in a gasp, hugging her close, panting in her ear as she fondled me, my throb so intense, it was unreal. I was wet and ready, desperate for her to touch me, and in a remarkable set of moves, she did just that, leaving me feeling deliciously handled—my left knee suddenly propped up on the back of the couch next to her, my dress pulled up over my hips, her hand in my panties, her fingers inside of me, "Oh! God! Jesus!" My head fell back as I gasped, whimpered, and moaned, hanging onto her as I pumped my hips, the feeling of her long, elegant fingers sliding in and out of me making me wetter and hotter with each thrust. My orgasm was fast approaching, and I humped for all I was worth, desperate to have it as it rolled in big and slow, holding on to me for several seconds before releasing me in an explosion. I let out a loud cry—Jordan's voice softly shushing me—then feebly attempted to moan quietly as my eyes rolled back in my head. I collapsed against her as my contractions faded, my arms wrapping themselves around her neck as I covered her mouth in a deep, wet kiss. God help me! I could not stop kissing her!

"How did you do that?" I breathed, still able to feel her inside me as I pulled my leg off the back of the couch.

"I love you, and you love me," she said, her answer insightfully simple. She smiled, lifting her eyebrows as she looked down at my dress still hiked up around my hips. I stepped back and quickly pulled it down, noticing Jordan's right hand at her side. Her fingers were bloodied.

"Oh no, what happened?" I asked, reaching for her hand.

"It's you, it's your blood," she said, holding it out to me.

"No, I don't have my period..." And then I realized what it was. "You deflowered me!"

"Yeah, I popped your cherry. You are not a virgin anymore."

"I love you, Jordan!" Tears sprang into my eyes as I threw my arms around her neck. I gave her another kiss, this one sweet and slow, then led her to the sink to wash her hands, both of us silent as my blood disappeared down the drain.

"There's a bathroom through that door," she said as she reached over and grabbed two paper towels. "Do you have a pad?" She doused the paper towels with water, wrung them out, and handed them to me.

"Yeah, I do. I always carry one with me."

"Good. You'll need something to protect yourself if you hope to sit down without messing up your dress."

"Wow, you really thought this through."

"Actually, I did. Right after I arrived, Amanda mentioned you were coming, and all I could think about was how to get you into the basement."

"You thought about getting me down here and seducing me?" I asked, teasing but curious to know how she thought about me in this regard.

"Seduce?"

"Well, no. I am hardly in need of persuading when it comes to you. You know what I mean. Your only thought was how to get me alone?"

"Absolutely. It took me less than a minute to lay out a plan."

She had no idea what she had just given me. The mildly disconcerted feeling I'd been harboring about always wanting to get her alone, as if I were some kind of sex fiend, vanished. "How did you know I would follow you?"

"I knew. I can feel how much you want me. Am I wrong?"

The cocky smile on her face told me she knew she wasn't wrong. "No. You're not wrong."

"Shannon, I don't know how long we have. I will take every opportunity to have you."

My heart ached and soared at the same time, her words bittersweet but full of promise. "I feel the same way, Jordan," I said, wanting to convey complete consent for what had just happened, not wanting her to feel one ounce of apprehension about it, either now or in the future.

She took my hand and pressed it to her mouth, leaving a soft kiss on my knuckles—which I found totally romantic—and then she led me to the bathroom. "Hurry."

I came out a few minutes later and washed my hands in the sink. Jordan was sitting on the couch, and the television was on. "Come, sit," she said, pointing at the other end of the couch.

"Shouldn't we go back up?" I asked as I sat down.

"No. I want Harry to come looking for me. It might look strange if we walk back up together after being down here for the last fifteen minutes. I want him to find us down here watching TV."

"We've been down here for fifteen minutes?"

Jordan looked down at her watch and nodded her head. "Yeah. Harry knows I like watching his television, and when he can't find me, he'll come looking for me. I expect him any minute."

I was enthralled by her whole planning thing. "This is the nicest thing anyone has ever done for me. Thank you." I wanted to kiss her and wondered if I had time before Harry came.

"Thank *you*," she said, chuckling. "By the way, I love your dress."

I looked down at my dress and touched the hem of the neck, tracing the line of buttons with my fingers down to my lap. "It's my new favorite dress," I replied. I would never look at this dress the same way again.

"Well, it looks very sexy on you, especially when it's hiked up around your beautiful hips."

I was instantly warm, wishing we had more time. Jordan smiled as she looked me up and down. The basement door opened, and I jumped.

"*Relax*," Jordan mouthed, holding eye contact.

"Jordan, you down there?" Harry called out.

"Yeah, we're watching TV."

"You and that television." He sounded annoyed but somehow pleased.

Harry started down the stairs, and panic rose in me. I glanced at the stairs, then back at Jordan. She nodded her head and mouthed, "*It's okay*." I took a deep breath and tried to relax, and as Harry came around the corner, we both turned and smiled.

"This television is wonderful! I've never seen anything like it!" I said, way too enthusiastically.

"Ah... Thank you, Shannon. The picture quality is not bad." Harry's voice changed when he addressed Jordan. "You need to turn that off, Jordan, or everyone up there will be down here watching it, and Amanda will kill me."

"Okay, okay." Jordan stood up and turned off the television.

We followed Harry upstairs, and as we circled the buffet table and filled our plates, Harry told Jordan about the newest television on the market with an even bigger screen and better picture quality. He had purchased his two years ago and was annoyed that there was already a new one out there better than his. He and Jordan were kindred spirits when it came to television, rambling back and forth about screen size and

VCR compatibility, some of the others joining the conversation as well with their opinions on HiFi stereo hookups for improved sound quality—no one the wiser about where we had been or that we had even been gone.

I found an empty seat near the sliding glass doors, and Jordan sat on the other side of the room next to Harry. I didn't mind that she didn't sit next to me; it would have made me nervous. It was actually nice observing her from afar as she talked and laughed. She was open and very friendly, and she looked incredibly sexy. Our eyes met often throughout the afternoon, her stare so intense once, I blushed and had to look away.

At four o'clock, everyone began preparing to go, saying quick goodbyes before heading out to their cars and evening services. I grabbed my chili container and my coat, thanked Harry and Amanda for having me, and headed out to my truck.

"Shannon!" Even though we were about to say goodbye, the sound of my name on her lips made me smile.

We walked down the sidewalk to my truck, silent, unable to keep our eyes off each other.

"I miss you," she said as I got into my truck.

She gave me a brave smile and took a step back, and I turned on the engine and drove away. I didn't see her again until the wedding.

CHAPTER NINE

Church weddings were grand affairs, and any woman who had ever attended one was sure to have been out shopping at least once to find the perfect dress. I hated shopping, always feeling frustrated and nervous as I navigated the malls hunting for my unique style of clothing, hardly ever finding what I was looking for, which was probably why it took me three shopping excursions to find my perfect dress and another trip to find the right shoes. But it was worth it because I loved weddings, especially May ones, and this May wedding in particular. Not only was it an opportunity to see Jordan, but it was our anniversary. It was one year ago that I first laid eyes on her, and I smiled when I thought about it, marveling at how much had changed in the last year and how much I had changed. I was in love.

The day of the wedding finally arrived, and I could hardly contain my excitement at the thought of seeing Jordan in just a few short hours. I didn't expect to spend much time with her—she was one of the bridesmaids—but I would get to see her, and that would be enough. I showered, then sat at the breakfast bar drinking coffee and thinking of Jordan in ways that would shock my parents if they could read my mind.

"Good morning, sweetheart."

I jumped in my seat. "Good morning, Mom." As Mom poured herself and Dad a cup of coffee, I tried to conceal the blush on my face.

Mom threw me a smile as she left the kitchen and walked back down the hallway to the bedroom. She had other things on her mind—like saving every soul on the planet—with barely the time to consider my awkward behavior in the kitchen.

I did my hair and makeup with great care, thinking of Jordan as I put on my dress, hoping she would know that I picked it out especially for her, hoping that seeing me in it would conjure up thoughts of how to get it off me. I'd certainly had all kinds of naughty thoughts about her when I first tried it on. I wished I could give her more than a silly dress, but in our situation, it wasn't nothing.

Mom and Dad complimented me on how nice I looked, bolstering my confidence, and I hurried out of the house feeling pretty. I jumped in my truck and raced over to the church, hoping to get there a little early so that I could get a good parking spot.

I ended up parking half a mile down the road, as the parking lot was already full, and walking back to the church in my really nice dress and pumps in California's late spring heat, the sun already high and blaring down on my long red hair. I lifted my mane to let air waft over my neck as I caught up with Phillis and Tim and their two kids, also headed for the church.

"Good morning, Phillis," I said, giving her an uncomfortable smile. I was starting to sweat.

"Good morning, Shannon. Pretty dress."

"Thank you. You look very pretty in yours."

We all walked into the church foyer together and waited in line to be seated. I was ushered to the bride's side, and a few minutes after I took my seat, the music changed, signaling the beginning of the ceremony. A loud hush filled the room, and all eyes turned as the flower girl and the ring bearer entered and slowly walked up the center aisle, joining Shawn and his best man at the altar.

The bridesmaids were next. I was nervous for Jordan. She was probably not nervous at all given her outgoing nature, but I would have been. Thank God no one had ever asked me to be a bridesmaid. Walking down the aisle in a fancy dress in front of all these people was unimaginable to me. This was the only advantage to not having any close female friends. I'd always hoped for a best friend, but it was never to be. Instead, I settled for the casual company of women, friendly but distant, never daring to get closer, afraid they would discover what I was.

The maid of honor walked up the aisle and stood across

from the groom and his best man, and then the first bridesmaid and groomsman walked through. The dresses actually looked very pretty. Sometimes they were awful, but these you could probably wear again.

My excitement grew. Jordan was next. She walked in on the arm of the second groomsman, and my mouth dropped open as the whole room let out a gasp. I sat there in awe as she walked past me, hushed whispers and craned necks following her up the aisle. She was stunning. I had never seen her in a dress like this before. She usually wore loose, casual dresses and skirts and hardly any makeup. This dress showed how magnificent her body was. You could see her femininity. Her makeup was perfect, her hair pinned up with soft ringlets around her neck. Her posture was regal, her gait measured, showing off her lovely curves and beautiful long legs. She was gorgeous. She looked like another person. I mean, Jordan was beautiful, but *this* Jordan was exquisite. She separated from her groomsman and stood next to the other bridesmaid, her stunning appearance and aura making her stand out by comparison.

Suddenly, a hefty feeling of inadequacy, mixed with a bit of guilt and a smidgen of shame, hit me right in the solar plexus. I looked at Jordan, then quickly looked away. How was I even worthy of such a beautiful person? Could I really let her risk her future and good reputation for me? Tears sprang into my eyes, and the lady next to me gave me a Kleenex. "I cry at weddings too," she whispered.

"Thank you," I whispered back.

The bridal song started, signaling the bride's entrance escorted by her dad, and everyone in the building stood up at once. The *oohs* and *ahhs* they offered as Elena entered, however heartfelt, were practiced and predictable and so noticeably different from the ones Jordan received, I kinda felt sorry for Elena.

There was a short sermon, the vows were taken, and Shawn and Elena were pronounced man and wife. They kissed, and the wedding party slowly proceeded back down the aisle, starting with Shawn and Elena and ending with Jordan and her groomsman. As Jordan approached, that feeling of inadequacy returned, and an overpowering need to hide took hold of me. I backed myself more snuggly into my pew, slumping a bit as I raised my hand to my forehead, my heart pounding as I stole a glimpse of her from between my fingers. She was scanning the crowd, her beautiful face hopeful and expectant, and I realized she was scanning for me. I lowered my hand and sat up a little. This caught her attention, and a brilliant smile broke out across her face, her eyes literally twinkling as they locked with mine. I let out an astonished laugh, close to tears, my heart near bursting. The lady next to me handed me another Kleenex. She was crying too.

As Jordan and her groomsman disappeared into the foyer, everyone stood up and poured into the aisle. There was a call from up front, "We're ready!" signaling that the wedding party was set to receive the wedding guests, and the mass began shuffling forward toward the foyer. This might be my only interaction with Jordan today, and I didn't want to mess it up by breaking down in tears in the receiving line. I rose to my tip-toes, trying to get a better view of how the receiving line was set up. Jordan was sixth in line, standing next to her brother. Guests were moving forward quickly, and I realized there really wasn't enough time for much more than a handshake and a quick hello for each of them. I needed to make this count and that meant not losing it. I had five people to practice on.

"Hi, Rebecca," I said, offering my hand to the first bridesmaid. "Great dress."

"I know, right?" She grabbed my hand and beamed a big smile at me. It was contagious; I beamed back.

"Hi, Vicky," I said, offering my hand to the maid of honor, Elena's sister.

"Shannon, hi. Wasn't it a wonderful ceremony?" Ignoring my hand, she pulled me in for a very excited, extremely tight hug. She was so emotional and over-the-top happy, I couldn't help but hug her back just as tight.

I didn't know the best man, so the handshake and hello went a lot smoother.

Elena gave me a hug and a kiss on the cheek. "Thank you for coming, Shannon." She looked beautiful.

Shawn shook my hand and thanked me for coming, his voice a little shaky, his eyes a little teary. I immediately started blinking, determined not to tear up, taking a quick breath and giving my nose a good sniff as I prepared to step in front of Jordan.

The first thing I did was look up into her beautiful brown eyes, and sure enough, my eyes teared up. She was so beautiful. She looked like a goddess. I was unable to speak, so there was no hello, and I completely forgot to offer her my hand. She smiled, and my heart squeezed, and when she pulled me in for a hug, I melted into her embrace. God, she smelled good.

"You are beautiful," she whispered in my ear.

My knees threatened to buckle, but she squeezed me tighter for a moment, keeping me on my feet. When she finally released me, I let out a huge, trembling sigh as tears rolled down my cheeks. So much for not losing it. She held my gaze until I stood in front of the groomsman next to her, and then she turned and addressed the person next in line. Okay, not exactly how I wanted to present myself, but not bad considering she looked like a supermodel. I looked like a mess in comparison.

I barely acknowledged the groomsmen as I stumbled past them, making my way out of the church building, crying and blowing my nose with gusto, relieved to find half the guests gathered on the lawn in the same condition as I was. I strolled amongst them, basking in the mutual euphoria of utter happiness and hope—because of the wedding, of course, but also because I was in love.

I walked out to the street and headed for my truck, sniffing and wiping my nose, reflecting on her words. Beautiful? How could she say that? There was no way I even deserved to breathe the same air as her, much less have her sweet attention, her lovely words in my ear.

I unlocked my truck and got inside, seriously considering not attending the reception. I would probably not get to interact with Jordan anyway and locking myself in my bedroom for the rest of the afternoon with the knowledge that she was only a short drive away was preferable to being in the same room with her and not being able to touch her. It would be torture either way, but at least I wouldn't make more of a fool of myself than I already had. Better to cut my losses. She was probably already asking herself why she had even started anything with me.

Looking at myself in the rearview mirror, wiping at the mascara smears under my eyes, I jumped and grabbed my chest when someone knocked on my side window. I swung around to find Stephanie peering in at me. I rolled down the window.

"Sorry, did I startle you?" she asked.

"No, it's okay. What can I do for you, Stephanie?"

"Oh, I'm so glad you asked, Shannon." She began a complicated explanation as to why she desperately needed my services. "Long story short, you have a truck, and we need the ice at the reception hall, now. Can you take me?"

"Yes, of course. Hop in."

"Oh, thank you, Shannon." She excitedly hurried around the front of my truck, opened the passenger-side door, and jumped in, talking non-stop about the wedding ceremony all the way to the ice warehouse.

Three men filled the back of my truck with fifty bags of ice while Stephanie paid at the front desk, and then we hightailed it to the reception hall.

We parked in back, Stephanie thanking me three times before disappearing inside while six young men unloaded my truck. When they were through, I drove to the front of the building and looked for parking—thoughts of barricading myself in my bedroom forgotten—deciding a quick peek wouldn't hurt. I was here; why not? Besides, it was obvious that fate and my raging hormones wouldn't allow me to leave without seeing Jordan one more time.

I was unable to find a parking spot, and instead of taking this as a sign that I should probably leave well enough alone, I returned to the back of the building and parked my truck in one of the last remaining reserved parking spots, next to a service van.

I walked back around to the front of the building and followed some of the last guests into the foyer, where we were held up at the book signing table. While I waited my turn, I stood on my tiptoes, looking over people's shoulders, trying to get a glimpse inside the reception hall to see if Jordan was already there. There was no way to tell; I could only see part of the room. I would have to go in. I quickly scribbled my name in the book, then went inside, astonished at how crowded it was. There was music playing in the background, the noise of people talking all but drowning it out. I moved through the room, looking for an inconspicuous place to stand. A place on the back wall beckoned.

The tapping of a mic got everyone's attention, and a booming voice shot through the loudspeakers, announcing that the bride and groom had arrived and would enter shortly. As people found seats and sat down, I could see more clearly how everything was set up. On the right side of the room stood a long table covered with a fancy white tablecloth and several bouquets of flowers, where I assumed the wedding party would sit. On the left side stood several tables set up near the kitchen entrance, covered with every conceivable potluck dish known to man. And scattered throughout the room were chairs set up in an assortment of arrangements—the typical setup for a church buffet.

There was another mic tap, and the same booming voice introduced the bride and groom. Everyone stood up, and a great wave of applause followed as the newlywed couple entered and crossed the large room, taking their seats at the center of the wedding party table. The music started back up as the rest of the wedding party shuffled in, and I stretched my neck to get a glimpse of Jordan as she made her way to the table and sat next to her brother. A groomsman sat down on her other side and immediately engaged her, and before long, they were talking jovially, shoulders touching, heads close together—probably so they could hear each other over the volume of noise in the room. Suddenly, Jordan's head rose back in a hearty laugh, sending a bolt of jealousy and a surge of lust through my body. Her beautiful white teeth, her gorgeous lips, her luscious pink tongue! It was sexy and hot and totally indecent, and I didn't want anyone else to see it! Who was this guy!

I took a deep breath and looked away, trying not to think about all the wonderful things her mouth could do. My thoughts were interrupted a moment later when the booming voice announced that the buffet was open.

People began moving toward the tables of food, and a space cleared out in front of me, leaving me exposed as glances and nods of greeting were thrown my way. I couldn't just stand there and spy on Jordan in peace. I either had to leave or grab a plate. I looked over at Jordan to find two men standing at her end of the table talking to her. Who were these guys! I had half a mind to march right over there and… And do what? Aargh! Instead, I headed for the buffet and grabbed a plate, glancing at Jordan as I got in line. Her group of admirers was growing—now five men in total. I rolled my eyes and looked away. She'd be engaged before the day was over.

As I stood in line, I reflexively began the necessary calculation required for such a long buffet table: the approximate length of the table in feet, divided by the approximate number of food items on the table, times four. One did not want to have so much food on one's plate at the near end that one could not fit a preferred item on one's plate at the very, very end. One also did not want to be so choosy that one rejected items that one truly wanted at the beginning only to find that one wanted none of the items at the end, thus leaving the buffet line with a near-empty plate. It was a dilemma. Thank God there was a formula to help one wisely navigate such a long buffet table.

Unable to concentrate on anything but Jordan, I filled my plate without regard to the formula and ended up with exactly what I deserved: two different kinds of spaghetti, a fried chicken wing, and an indiscernible chunk of casserole. I got back in line and added a spoonful of chicken salad, a deviled egg, and a sourdough bun. I grabbed some Pepsi and wondered how it could be that there was no ice in my glass given that Stephanie and I had just picked up fifty bags of it.

I found a seat—this time on the other side of the room—and sat down, picking at my spaghetti and cautiously glancing at Jordan as people began filling the seats around me. Soon, I was sitting in the middle of a sizable group of young people about my age. Pleased at having created the perfect gawking location, feeling very incognito in my group of young people, I openly stared at Jordan until a young man asked me if the seat next to me was taken, totally interrupting my undercover stakeout.

"No, please sit," I replied, peeved by his interruption and general existence.

He introduced himself just as I stuck a fork full of chicken salad into my mouth. I finished chewing, swallowed, and reluctantly told him my name, glancing over at Jordan to find only three men now gathered at her table. They had pulled chairs over and were eating with her like bees to a honeypot. Of all the pompous, arrogant... Who were these guys, and did they really think they could just sit down and eat with the woman I loved!

That was it. I couldn't take it anymore. I stood up, threw my food in the trash, and marched toward the exit. The guy who sat next to me, whose name I couldn't remember, was probably offended. Who cared! I didn't!

As I stepped outside, I remembered that my truck was parked out back by the kitchen entrance and stomped off in that direction. As I came around the corner of the building, I stopped in my tracks when I didn't immediately see my truck.

What the heck! My eyes began to tear in frustration as I combed the lot. It was not there.

"Shannon?"

My breath caught at the sound of her voice behind me. I turned.

"Jordan... Hi." My god, she was beautiful.

"You're not leaving without saying goodbye, are you?"

"Apparently not. I can't find my truck."

She laughed and pointed. "It's there between those two vans. I can see the bumper."

I walked over to the front of the van and looked around it, immediately spotting my truck. I could see what had happened. A second van, identical to the one I had parked next to, parked next to me, sandwiching me in between. I let out a loud sigh, feeling a little bit silly. "Thank you. I was about to call the police."

She laughed again and began walking toward me. My hand jumped out in front of me, palm out, and I took a step back. I was frustrated and irritated, feeling totally inadequate, while my body vibrated with jealousy and need. I seriously feared I would swoon and faint if she came any closer. Jordan stopped a few feet in front of me, looking mildly amused and not at all deterred.

"I wanted to give you something before you go," she said, stretching out her hand to me, showing me a small box.

"What is it?"

"Open it." She was obviously excited, quickly glancing at the kitchen entrance before taking a step closer. "Please, open it."

I took the box from her and removed the tie and paper. She smiled, encouraging me. I removed the lid and found a lovely gold pendant necklace inside. I pulled it out and looked at it closely. It was a tree with six red points of light on it. When I held it up to the sun, the red points grew brighter.

"It's beautiful. Thank you."

"Happy anniversary. It's a cherry tree."

I opened my mouth but could not speak. She glanced at the kitchen entrance, then took me by the arm and led me around the service van to my truck. Leaning me up against the door, she took a quick look around before stepping closer. I was already breathing heavily and practically gasped when she leaned in and whispered in my ear. "Cherry tree. Your cherry. It's mine forever."

Jordan leaned back and looked me in the eyes, daring me to look away, our faces so close, our noses briefly touched. She took another quick look around, and when she turned back, I kissed her right there in front of God and everybody, although technically no one was there except God. She moaned, letting out the most amazing sigh as she slipped her tongue into my mouth, and from under the façade of makeup, hair, and dress, *my* Jordan emerged. She had never left. She deepened the kiss, pressing herself into me, her hands slipping around my waist, well on their way to my backside.

Startled by a metallic, clattering sound from the kitchen, we instantly disengaged, Jordan quickly stepping away as she scanned the area for anyone who may have seen us. Seeing no one, she sighed in relief and flashed me a quick smile.

"I need to ask you something," she said, a bit breathless.

I nodded, a bit breathless myself.

"Tomorrow, after morning services, Shawn and Elena are leaving on their honeymoon. They will be gone for one week, returning on Monday. I want you to come and stay with me at the house for the week."

I blinked at her, taking in the meaning of what she was saying. A whole week alone with her!

"Take the week off from work. Tell your parents I'm alone at the house and you're keeping me company. I'm sure they'll understand. I can't imagine them saying no. Please, Shannon," she pleaded.

I hesitated, amazed that she had even thought of this, then nodded.

"Whew! For a minute there, I thought you were going to say no." She stepped closer, quickly looking around before leaning in, her full front pressing lightly into me. Her lips parted slightly as she looked into my eyes, everything about her demeanor promising me. "I want you."

I responded with a gasp, pushing my hips into her, unable to stop myself.

She smiled, pleased with my reaction, then stepped back, reached down, and took the necklace out of my hand. "Let me help you."

I lifted my hair, and she fastened the thin gold chain around my neck, her fingers lingering on my skin as she looked over my shoulder at the pendant resting on my chest.

When I turned to face her, she reached out and touched the pendant with the tips of her fingers. "I know what I'm asking is a lot. If you can't stay, I'll understand…"

"Jordan, I'll be there, even if they say no…"

"No. If they won't let you stay the week, we'll find another way. I don't want you to get into trouble, and I don't want to bring attention to us."

"They won't say no…"

"They might, and if they do, we'll figure something out."

I nodded, and she reached up and touched my cheek.

"I'll see you tomorrow."

"Okay… And Jordan, thank you for the necklace. Happy anniversary."

"Happy anniversary."

As Jordan disappeared around the front of the service van, I tried to fathom this turn of events. I looked down at my necklace and clutched it briefly, then jumped in my truck and drove home, the beginnings of a plan on how I was going to do this already forming in my head.

The first thing I did was change my clothes. It was tradition to wear your wedding-guest dress the next day at church, so I checked mine was clean and hung it outside to air. I then packed an overnight bag, quickly throwing in clothes and toiletries, and safely tucked it in the back of my closet. As I straightened up the house, I decided on the best way to break this to my parents.

Respecting your elders—parents in particular—was a core value within the church, and that included seeking advice and approval for important choices and decisions, or more accurately, asking permission for almost anything you wanted to do. But I was an adult; I needed to act like one. Tomorrow morning, I would tell them that I was staying with Jordan for the week as a matter of fact, but casual, like, *Oh, by the way... Just letting you know*, removing any possibility that they could decide not to let me go. I finished the dishes, folded the laundry, took a shower, and climbed into bed, repeating to myself that I could do this. I would not let what promised to be the most romantic week of my life simply pass because I was nervous about confronting my parents.

* * *

When I woke the next morning, Jordan was instantly in my thoughts, the conversation I was about to have with my mother taking center stage. I needed to time my casual announcement just right, so I went into the kitchen, put on some coffee, set out a bowl of cereal, sat down at the breakfast bar, and waited. Fifteen minutes later, Mom started down the hallway. I got up, poured myself a cup of coffee, added milk to my cereal, and sat back down just as Mom entered the kitchen.

"Good morning, sweetheart."

"Good morning, Mom."

Mom poured herself a cup of coffee, but before she could pour one for Dad, I mumbled at her with a mouth full of cereal, hoping to distract her before I hit her with my casual news. Mom turned and looked at me.

"Shannon, I can't understand you if you speak with your mouth full of cereal."

She watched me carefully as I finished chewing, tilting her head curiously, waiting patiently. I swallowed, then said, "Sorry, Mom." I took a sip of my coffee, filled my spoon with more cereal, and held it at the ready.

"I'm spending the week at Jordan's while Shawn and

Elena are on their honeymoon." I shoved my spoon into my mouth and started chewing.

Mom looked at me as she sipped her coffee. "Jordan? The girl who was in the wedding? Now that is a pretty girl. How long would you be staying?"

Yesss! That was definitely not a *no*. "A week," I said after I swallowed. "You know her, Mom. She stayed with us during the meeting last summer." I shoveled another spoonful of cereal into my mouth, hoping the word *meeting* would further distract her. This was her all-time favorite subject, but would she bite?

"Yeah, I remember. She looked a lot different at the wedding, though." Mom took another sip of her coffee, pondering, while I waited for any sign that my plan was working. "Your Dad and I wanted to canvas in Lodi next week. Thought you might want to help?"

Yesss! "Next week?"

"Yeah, next Monday or Tuesday. They're having that meeting in a couple of weeks, and we wanted to see if there's any interest in the neighborhood. Maybe Jordan would like to come too? We need all the help we can get."

"Yeah, I'll ask her."

Between my uncharacteristic bad manners—which was sure to have Mom scratching her head for months—and volunteering to help her canvas in Lodi next week—I rarely volunteered, and she was always short on canvas workers—my news about staying the week with Jordan would seem non-eventful in comparison and certainly nothing to be concerned about. And with the extra points for offering to help canvas, well, I practically had this in the bag. But just in case, I shoveled another spoonful of cereal into my mouth, knowing that one wrong word could trigger a reversal. I watched Mom closely, chewing my cereal, ready to counter if she so much as suggested I couldn't go.

She filled Dad's cup with coffee and gave me a smile as she left the kitchen, softly humming as she walked down the hallway toward the bedroom. I let out a huge sigh of relief, jumped up, and threw my cereal into the sink. I retrieved my bag from its hiding place, tossed it in the cab of my truck, then headed back inside to get ready for church.

* * *

As I entered the church building, I could see Jordan sitting way up front with Shawn and Elena. I took a deep breath and made my way toward them, taking a seat right next to Jordan. As I greeted those sitting around me, I could feel her eyes on me, and when I finally turned to her, it was like she'd been waiting forever and could hardly contain herself. I smiled and gave her a quick nod, letting her know that our week together was really going to happen. She smiled back, obviously thrilled.

"Hi, good morning," I said, nervously clearing my throat.

Before Jordan could reply, Elena leaned forward and addressed me from her seat on the other side of Jordan. "Thanks for staying over with Jordan while we're gone. She's afraid of the dark, scared to be home alone." Elena let out a teasing "Ha, ha," and leaned into Jordan affectionately.

"No problem, it'll be fun." I looked at Jordan and smiled.

The look she gave me in return made me blush, and I seriously feared that if she didn't stop looking at me that way, everyone would be able to see that we were sleeping together. I wasn't doing much better. I looked her up and down before I could stop myself. She was wearing her dress from the wedding, and I couldn't wait to get my hands on it. Her hair was down, and except for a touch of pink gloss on her beautiful lips, she wasn't wearing any makeup. She didn't need to. Her eyelashes were long and dark, her skin flawless. My blush deepened, and Jordan raised her eyebrows, smiling, giving me a very cute blink-wink before turning toward the front as the first hymn began.

After services, we all gathered on the front lawn to bid Shawn and Elena farewell, as well as Shawn and Jordan's parents, who had flown up for the wedding. Shawn and Elena would drive them back to LA and then spend their honeymoon in a hotel there, dividing their time between seeing the sights and visiting with Shawn's family. Basically, a honeymoon-slash-family reunion, which was pretty standard in the church. We waved as they drove away, then hung out a while longer, talking about the wedding and the reception and how nice it was. Then topics changed and I was suddenly ready to go. I found Jordan standing in a group near the door, looking right at me, waiting for me to catch her eye. She was ready too. I said goodbye to the group I was standing in and headed out to my truck.

The adage, *The first day of the rest of your life*, suddenly resonated. There was nothing that rivaled the importance of this week with Jordan, something I wanted more than anything else in this world—quiet, unhurried, uninterrupted moments with the woman I loved and the once-in-a-lifetime chance to share the most exquisite fantasies with her, fantasies that had tormented me for the better part of the past year. Up until now, I had fought and struggled for every moment with her, every word, every chance meeting, every look, every smile, and now, she was giving me unfettered access, a gift so precious, I wasn't sure she realized what it meant to me. Yesterday, the idea of us seemed impossible. Today, it was the only thing that existed.

CHAPTER TEN

The silence inside the cab of the truck was deafening, the chemistry between us palpable. I could taste it, smell it, and the way it hung in the air left no question as to what we both wanted.

I looked down at our hands holding, our fingers intertwined, aware of the intense throbbing between my thighs and how it synced with the beat of my heart. Jordan gazed thoughtfully out the window as she rubbed her thumb over my knuckles, and when she swallowed hard, I was thankful she was nervous too.

I parked in the driveway, and Jordan got out of the truck as I grabbed my bag from behind the seat. She walked up the porch steps to the front door, glancing back at me before letting herself in, leaving the door wide open. I tentatively followed.

It was dark inside, and I couldn't see Jordan at first, but as I passed the threshold and stepped inside, she came into view, standing in the middle of the living room waiting for me. I set my bag down, then turned to close the door, and when I turned back, she was suddenly standing right in front of me, taking my hands in hers and pulling me further into the room. She smiled as her hands slowly made their way up my arms and around my shoulders.

"I can't believe you're really here," she said, her voice barely a whisper.

"Me either," I breathlessly replied.

The fabric of her beautiful dress was smooth and silky, the tips of my fingers tingling as I ran them slowly down her waist to her hips—something I'd been dying to do since I first saw her in it at the wedding. I couldn't take my eyes off her breasts; they looked perfectly packaged, and I couldn't wait to unwrap them.

We stood there a minute, arms wrapped around each other, looking into each other's eyes, and then she kissed me, at first soft and slow, then deeper, urgent, both of us breathing heavily, our mouths going at it as if it might be the last time we ever kissed. Reaching around with my right hand, I unzipped her dress down the length of her back. She slowly released my lips, her eyes dark with anticipation. I pulled her dress from her shoulders, down over her breasts, then over her hips, helping her step out of it before draping it over the arm of a chair. Reaching around again, I unclasped her bra, then slid my fingers inside the front of it and slowly pulled it away, letting it fall to the floor.

I hesitated a moment at the sight of her beautiful breasts, then leaned down, meaning to take one of them into my mouth, only to be intercepted by Jordan's fingers on my chin as she lifted my face back up and covered my mouth in another wonderful kiss. She licked and nipped and sucked, refamiliarizing herself with my lips, my tongue, and the entire inside of my mouth, taking ownership of it. All of it was hers, and as far as I was concerned, she could do whatever she wanted with it.

The moment she broke our kiss, unable to wait any longer, I hooked my fingers into her panties and quickly pulled them down to her ankles. She put her hand on my shoulder and elegantly stepped out of them, making my breath catch. I looked up at her beautiful naked body as I shifted to my knees, in awe, prepared to worship her.

Her breath quickened as my hands moved up her legs to the back of her thighs, her mouth slightly open in anticipation as she looked down at me. "Please, Shannon," she said, almost desperate.

I lowered my gaze to the apex of her thighs and what lay between them. She was wet and ready, and I was eager. I had to taste her; I'd thought of little else over the past year. I leaned forward and slid my tongue over her vagina.

"Oh God!" she called out, then lowered her voice in a whimpering chant, "Oh God, Oh God, Oh God," her hips swaying forward and back in sync with my tongue lapping her up. Her right hand moved to my head, and she spread her legs a little wider, bending her knees slightly, giving me more access. I licked her until her knees buckled, then took her hand and guided her gently to the floor, coaxing her backward and parting her legs as I got into position. I took her into my mouth without delay, licking and sucking every inch of her, thoroughly relishing her desire.

Her hands found my head, and she began making the most beautifully urgent noises. She was coming, and it was a wonder to behold as her hips bucked and her back arched, crying out my name as her legs suddenly wrapped themselves around my head, locking me into place, the roll of her hips and the litany of *ahh's* that followed, nearly bringing me to orgasm with her.

I kept sucking until she released my head and then moved to her smooth, silky inner thighs and lavished them with kisses. Jordan lay motionless on her back, breathing heavily as I climbed up her body, my head coming to rest on her chest, the pounding of her heart reverberating through my soul.

My dress was wrapped around my hips, and a feeling of being exposed overcame me, followed by panic. My eyes snapped open, and my heart galloped a few seconds before I remembered that we were safe. No one could hear us, no one could see us, we didn't have to hurry. No one would walk in on us and discover what we were. I had Jordan all to myself for one week.

She raised her head for a moment, then lowered it back down to the floor, sighing deeply. "How on earth do you know how to do that?"

"I think about it all the time. Sometimes I think it's all I've thought about, in one form or another, since I first saw you."

"What do you mean, in one form or another?"

"Well, for example, when I would see you licking an ice cream cone or eating a taco or a corn on the cob or even a barbecued sparerib, it conjured up oral fantasies." I smiled at the memory of our messy rib dinner during the church camping trip last summer, and Jordan smiled with me, remembering too.

"So, basically, finger foods," she said.

I let out a chuckle and could feel myself blush. "Okay, yeah. I see the pattern now."

Jordan smiled, raising her eyebrows at me.

"And it evolved from there. After a while, it was all I could think about, and the more time we spent together, the more explicit my thoughts became, making me very curious."

"I think you are much more than just curious."

"You're right. I'm obsessed with your vagina. I love doing that to you. I mean, it was so much more than I ever imagined."

I crawled off of her and stood up, suddenly feeling very overdressed, and without the slightest feeling of shyness, slowly removed my dress. I unclasped my bra, pulled it from my shoulders, then slipped off my panties, tossing them both in the direction I'd tossed my dress.

"God, Shannon," she whispered, her eyes gobbling up every inch of me.

I kneeled down and slowly crawled back on top of her, taking her breast into my mouth, fondling and squeezing the other, lost in their beauty. Jordan lay there entranced, her eyes half-closed but laser-focused on everything I was doing. Her breasts were perfect. Big and firm, her skin light olive silky, her nipples chocolate brown, hard and erect. I sucked her nipple more energetically, sighing in pure joy and contentment, then switched over to the other one and gave it the same attention. I couldn't imagine anything as good as this.

Jordan's hand made its way to my lower back, attempting to reach my behind, the tips of her fingers touching the sensitive spot between the upper part of my butt cheeks, eliciting from me a gasp. I shifted higher, suspending myself above her by holding myself up on my arms, straddling her waist and spreading myself wider as I lifted my backside, desperate for her to touch me. I turned and watched as her fingers disappeared between my cheeks, moaning when they slid under, drenching themselves in my heat.

Little sparks of energy shot through my core with each stroke of her fingers, my hips rocking as I loudly moaned, our eyes locking the moment I orgasmed, my head jerking back as I called out her name. I collapsed on top of her and into her arms, completely undone and out of breath, her fingers never faltering as she stroked me through to the finish.

"I love you," I finally managed.

"I love you," she replied, holding me tight as I tried to catch my breath. We stayed like that for several minutes before she spoke again. "Are you hungry?"

I crawled off of her and sat up, leaning back on my arms, the sight of her spread out naked before me making my mouth water. I was hungry, but not for food, and I considered telling her this but thought it might sound silly.

"You are beautiful, Shannon," she said, changing the subject.

"You are beautiful, Jordan. You took my breath away yesterday when I saw you walk down the aisle. I think the whole church took a breath when they saw you. Could you hear that when you walked in?"

"Yeah, but I thought they did that for everyone." She looked surprised.

"No, just you. I've never seen anything so beautiful in my life. I was so proud of you. Everything about you looked incredible. I know it's irrational, but I was overcome with fear that you would never want to speak to me again."

Jordan sat up and drew her knees to her chest, hugging them.

"And then I started crying over the loss that is sure to come. Thank God so many people cry at weddings; no one suspected anything. The lady next to me was crying."

The rest stuck in my throat when Jordan reached out and touched my arm, sending a shiver through my body. She ran her hand down my arm, picked up my hand, and held it to her breast. I didn't mention the shame and guilt I'd felt.

"And then you hugged me and told me that I was beautiful, which I found absurd but very sweet, so I went to the reception because I couldn't bear not seeing you again, only to watch men line up at your table, make cow-eyes at you, and eat lunch with you. I felt a little jealous, I think. You are beautiful, charming, funny, and sexy." Jordan's left eyebrow arched seductively at this. "And it was just so much all at once." I took a deep breath and smiled at her. "And then you were standing behind me, saying my name. You remembered our anniversary, and you gave me this." I looked down at my pendant and touched it. "Making it clear that taking my cherry means just as much to you as it does to me."

"Popping your cherry, not taking your cherry," Jordan teasingly corrected as she kissed my hand.

"And now this." I gestured to the room. "I can't believe we're alone together... How did you get out of going to LA with your family?"

"I told them I had a couple of job interviews this week."

"Do you?"

"No, I don't. The only reason I'm not in LA with my family this week is because I want to be here with you."

"How long have you been planning this?"

"A while, but this last part was the trickiest. I couldn't drop the news that I wouldn't be going to LA until the very last minute."

"Right, of course. Something last minute that you can't get out of."

"Exactly. And I couldn't tell you until I knew how they'd react. I mean, I was pretty sure they wouldn't say no, but they could have."

"It doesn't bother me that you didn't tell me sooner, Jordan. I'm just amazed that you planned this. Thank you."

"Thank you for saying yes. I love you, Shannon. I'm so happy you're here." She smiled, then moved up next to me and straddled me, wrapping her body around me, holding me.

She kissed my neck and squeezed me tighter for a moment. "Let me make you something to eat."

* * *

Showering took longer than usual because we showered together—not that I was complaining. Afterward, I unpacked while Jordan went into the kitchen to make us something to eat. Dressed in sweatpants and one of her T-shirts, I sat at the kitchen table and watched her put two chicken salad sandwiches together. She explained that she really couldn't cook very well but could make a pretty mean sandwich and heat things up in the microwave. She opened the freezer and showed me an array of frozen dinners, frozen pizzas, and frozen hot pocket snacks.

"I know my way around a kitchen a little bit. We can go grocery shopping if you want?" I offered.

"You know how to cook?"

"Yeah, I can cook."

"Do you by any chance know how to cook chili?"

"Yeah, I can cook chili."

Jordan walked to the table and sat down next to me. "Is that potluck chili yours?"

"There's a lot of chili at potluck, Jordan."

"Yeah, but there's this one chili that everyone wants. Sometimes it's already gone before I can get some."

My face broke out in a blush, and I looked down at my hands for a moment before looking back up at her. "Yeah, that's mine."

"I love you, Shannon." Jordan's voice was gorgeously sultry. "Could you make some of your chili for me?"

She could've been asking me to do some unimaginably erotic thing to her, and I would have willingly complied. "I'll do whatever you want," I said, suppressing a whimper as I stared deep into her eyes, glancing at her lips when she suddenly licked them. I let out a slow breath, trying to control the wild beating of my heart. "I would love to taste your...chicken salad sandwich, though."

Jordan smiled and stood up. "I would love for you to taste my...chicken salad sandwich."

I let out a small laugh at the intentional innuendo and shook my head, nervously pulling at my ear. I wanted her so bad. If she hadn't gone to so much trouble cooking for me, I would have taken advantage of a repeat performance right there on the kitchen table. God help me!

We ate our sandwiches in the living room on the couch in front of the television, and then she took my hand and led me to the bedroom. We undressed and climbed into bed, and she immediately came to me, moving on me, touching me, fondling me, kissing my neck, my ear, and then my mouth, driving me right up to the edge of what I could endure. She slipped her hand between my thighs, and I moaned, gazing into her eyes, so in love with her as her fingers strummed me like the sweetest melody. I came much too soon, my toe-curling orgasm the most powerful yet, the string of aftershocks that followed leaving me whimpering like a baby. She held me as I slowly came down, pulling me closer as we fell asleep in each other's arms.

* * *

I woke the next morning facing the window, momentarily forgetting where I was. I rolled onto my back and looked to my right, finding Jordan in bed next to me facing the other direction, a blanket covering her hip. Oh, yeah... Jordan. I smiled. Her back was exposed, her legs folded together, tucked up. My eyes focused in on her hip, tracing its curve to the dip in her waist, then up to her shoulder, her silhouette resembling a roller coaster.

I wanted to go to her, but I didn't want to wake her. She looked so beautiful, her breathing soft and sweet, her shoulder slightly rising and falling. I waited, enjoying the view, admiring her pale olive skin—flawless—her hair tossed about her head.

She stirred. "Come here," she groggily murmured.

I immediately spooned her from behind, ready to take us

back to the passion of the night before, when a loud buzzer noise rang through the house. The doorbell! Someone found us! Someone knows! I bolted out of bed, yanking on sweatpants and a T-shirt, ready to jump out the window if need be.

"Relax," Jordan reassured. "It's probably just a package. Shawn said some of the wedding gifts would arrive by mail."

I couldn't believe how calm she was. "Okay. Do you want me to answer the door?"

"No. I'll do it," she said as she climbed out of bed. "Stay here... No! Come with me, just in case. If it's someone from the church, it's better if they don't find you hiding in my bedroom."

"Someone from the church! Why would someone from the church be here!"

"It's not someone from the church. I'm sure of it, but just in case."

The doorbell rang again.

Jordan slipped into sweatpants and a T-shirt, beckoning me to follow her as she left the bedroom.

I walked into the kitchen and tried to casually arrange myself against the corner wall in the entryway. I tried the same thing against the refrigerator, then against the counter, and then the table, finally sitting in one of the chairs, trying out different innocent, unassuming positions before crossing my legs and folding my arms in front of me, hoping I didn't look too guilty. My heart was beating so hard, my ears were pulsing. I tried to loosen up a bit but couldn't and feared I would never be able to convince anyone who walked into the kitchen that I was not having sex with Jordan.

Jordan returned to the kitchen carrying a large package. "It's one of those mini-ovens with a built-in toaster."

I let out a loud, relieved sigh and even started laughing a little as my body slowly unclenched.

"Scared you, huh?" Jordan said as she set the package on the counter. The smirk on her face, as cute as it was, could not hide that she had been a little nervous too. Her trembling hands betrayed her, her anxiety exposed. "Help me open it. This will be perfect for our frozen dinners."

I stood up and took her into my arms, holding her until she stopped shaking. I could feel how relieved she was that the church had not shown up on our doorstep. She pulled away from me, wiping at her nose with the back of her hand before grabbing hold of a drawer and yanking it open. She pulled out a box cutter and looked at it intently as she blinked tears from her eyes.

We unpacked the oven, and as she cleaned it, I fawned over it, trying to move us past our close call. But she remained thoughtfully quiet. After a few minutes of this, I touched her shoulder and softly squeezed it, running my hand down her back, trying to soothe her, trying to make sure she was all right. Suddenly, she turned to me, her eyes bright, her intentions clear, and kissed me, her arms wrapping themselves around my shoulders, our breasts pressing together. That was the clincher; I wanted her right now!

My hand quickly made its way up under her T-shirt, cupping her breast, making her moan. My tongue slipped into her mouth, and she latched onto it, stroking it, making us both moan. I could have spent the rest of the morning kissing her, but I really wanted her naked and that meant getting her T-shirt off. I broke our kiss, quickly pulled her T-shirt up over her head, and removed her sweatpants, making her beautifully naked in five seconds flat as I backed her up against the table.

She laid back and spread her legs, her toes clutching the table's edge as I got into position in front of her, my hands on her knees, her hips already moving. She was beautiful, and she wanted me. I spread her wider, and she softly pleaded, "God, Shannon, please." Music to my ears. I bent down and took her into my mouth, sliding my tongue up and down the length of her, somehow trying to taste every inch of her all at once. She deliriously moaned in chant, taking in a sharp breath every time I passed over the top part where her cute little knot was. I licked her there a moment longer, then ran my tongue right down the middle of her.

"No! Go back!" she demanded, breathless.

I eagerly returned, licking energetically, showing her how irresistible she was. She moaned loudly, grabbing my head and pulling me closer, showing me where she needed me. It wasn't long before she came, crying out, holding me tighter for several seconds before releasing me. I continued licking and sucking until she touched my head again, and then I slowly straightened, looking down at her spread out before me. She was magnificent.

"God, I love you," she said as she held her hands out to me. I took her hands and pulled her up, and her arms immediately went around my waist, her head resting on my chest. "I can hear your heart beating." She looked up at me and smiled. "I love how good you are at that."

I blushed, she chuckled sweetly, and then she said, "Let's go to *Denny's* I'm starving."

"What about the new oven?"

"We have the whole week to use the oven, Shannon. I want to go on a breakfast date with you."

I liked how that sounded. "I want to go on a breakfast date with you too."

She kissed me quick on the mouth, then moved to get up.

I took a couple of steps back and could immediately feel my wetness, and without thinking, grabbed my crotch, pulling my sweatpants away from me.

Jordan stood naked before me, watching my display with amusement.

"I need to shower," I said, feeling a little embarrassed as I removed my hand from my crotch.

"Yes, you do." She reached up and ran her thumb over my mouth and chin—my crotch was not the only place that was wet—then leaned in and gave me an all-encompassing kiss, effectively removing any evidence of what I'd done to her, leaving me even wetter than before. I definitely needed a shower now.

* * *

As we walked out of the house for the first time since I'd arrived, I automatically scanned the neighborhood, looking for any sign that we had been discovered. It was irrational, but it was quickly becoming a cemented part of my behavior, especially after our special delivery wedding package. It really wasn't too much of an inconvenient exercise considering the alternative. Getting caught would not just be inconvenient, it would be devastating and tragic as well, particularly if it were due to a stupid moment of carelessness.

We jumped in the truck, and my excitement grew at the thought of sharing this very normal activity with Jordan. We had shared a picnic together on an island, just the two of us, and I would never forget that moment as long as I lived. And that rib-ripping, mouth-stuffed-full, face-smeared-with-barbecue-sauce meal we shared later that evening was equally memorable. But both of those meals were before we'd declared our love for each other. I loved cooking, and I loved seeing people who loved each other gathered around a table enjoying a meal. It was the ultimate rush for me, and I wanted to share it with Jordan.

A sudden nervous panic hit me when we entered the restaurant and waited to be seated. It was as if everyone knew what we had done and what we were. People stared at us and continued to do so as we were led to our table, and I realized they were looking at Jordan, not me. She was beautiful even dressed in her jean skirt and blouse, and these people weren't shy about looking. I had never been out with her in public before, in the outside world. I'd never seen the world react to her.

We were seated, asked if we wanted coffee, and then our waitress basically ignored me, looking at me only to take my order. She couldn't take her eyes off Jordan, who was speaking to her, smiling at her, and listening to her. They talked about the weather in LA; the waitress also came from there. She attended Cal State University in Sacramento and worked at *Denny's* part-time. It was extraordinary how much she revealed to Jordan, and it occurred to me that she might be flirting. Jordan smiled at me, and I blushed a little as I smiled back. It wasn't Jordan's beauty alone that affected our doting waitress. Jordan had the ability to make every contact seem personal—it was one of the first things I noticed about her—without making me doubt that I was the only one who mattered.

Jordan ordered pancakes, and I ordered eggs easy over, sausage, and hash browns. We talked and laughed, played footsie under the table, and gazed flirtatiously into each other's eyes. It was the most erotic breakfast I had ever had, and afterward, we took an intimate stroll along a nearby outdoor mall made up of restaurants and boutiques, a laundromat, and a drugstore.

"Wait here, I'll be right back," Jordan said and hurried off, disappearing into the drugstore.

I walked around the little mall, careful to keep the drugstore entrance in sight. Jordan walked out ten minutes later, smiling sweetly when she saw me, our eyes locking as we walked up to each other, our hands briefly touching. We quickly snatched them back, both of us scanning the area to see if anyone saw.

"What did you buy?"

She looked down at the little plastic bag in her hand, then looked up at me and smiled. "It's a surprise."

"I love surprises."

She gave me the sweetest look as she bit down on her bottom lip. "That's good to know."

"Is it?"

"Yeah, it is." We were totally flirting with each other right in the middle of the parking lot! "Let's go see a matinee. Do you like movies?" she asked.

"I do. I love movies." She was adorable, and I couldn't wait to go to the movies with her.

We walked back to *Denny's*, jumped in the truck, and drove to the movie theater. The theater parking lot was practically empty, reminding me that it was Monday afternoon, making it feel like Jordan and I were the only ones left on the planet. We parked in the shade in the back corner of the lot, then hurried toward the ticket windows. There was no one else in line, as if the theater had opened just for us.

We decided on the movie, *Terms of Endearment*, with Debra Winger and Shirley MacLaine. Jordan bought a bucket of popcorn and a large Pepsi at the kiosk, and then we walked together down a wide hallway to our theater, passing only one other couple on the way.

I usually preferred sitting in the middle of the theater, but Jordan insisted we sit way in back on the entrance side, and as I followed her up to our seats and sat down, it became immediately clear to me why she'd chosen these seats. I had just gotten settled when she leaned over and very nimbly slipped her hand up my skirt, brushing the fabric of my panties with her fingers, extracting from me a very loud gasp. This only encouraged her, and she giggled, whispering, "Shhhh."

I looked at her with eyes wide, my mouth hanging open in shock as she moved her fingertips softly over my crotch, brushing my knot. My legs jerked open, and I stifled a gasp, making her smile as she ran her hand down my inner thigh to my knee. She raised an eyebrow at me, then turned, picked up the popcorn, and settled back in her chair, looking very pleased with herself. I closed my legs and yanked my skirt down, scouring the theater for possible witnesses. I turned and looked at her very sternly. She was looking at the screen, still smiling, refusing to look at me. I cleared my throat, trying to get her attention, and finally she turned and looked at me, biting down on her bottom lip like a very bad girl.

"Can I have some popcorn too?" I asked, my attempt at indignation melting away, still a bit shocked but very turned on.

"Sure," she said, letting out a small chuckle.

The lights dimmed, the movie started, and about thirty minutes in, Jordan slipped her arm over the armrest and placed her hand in my lap, the empty bucket of popcorn sitting on top. I covered her hand with mine, slipping my fingers between hers. Our boldness was breathtaking.

* * *

It was late afternoon when we left the theater, and when we got back to the house, Jordan popped two frozen dinners into our new mini oven. We changed into sweatpants and T-shirts and ate our dinner on the couch, watching an episode of *Cheers* on TV, laughing together as the two main characters, Sam and Diane, sexually bantered each other back and forth.

"Whatever happened to your boyfriend, Dennis?" I was surprised by her question and did not have a ready answer. "He was good-looking, and I loved his sermon referencing milk-toast to describe uninspired Christians. You two were the talk of the town last year. Everyone thought, 'That's it, you're finally getting married.' What happened?"

"Finally? What do you mean finally? Do people talk about me? What do they say?"

"Everybody loves you, Shannon. No one would ever say anything negative about you, but it does come up that you date a lot—you know, a lot of different men. When will you get married? Who will you marry? Who will you date next?" She gave me a small shrug and smiled. "Why do you date so many different men?"

"I don't know. I mean, ever since I can remember, the plan has always been to fall in love, get married, and have kids. The falling in love part has always been a challenge for me, so I just kept looking, kept trying, and over the last eight years, since I started dating, there have been a lot of boyfriends."

"You've never been in love before?"

"No, never, not until now." I looked down at our hands, fingers entwined. "And you? Did you date much in LA? I haven't seen you with anyone here."

"No, not much. I can't seem to get past the friend part and move to the boyfriend part."

"So, you've never been in love either?"

"No, this is my first time," she said, squeezing my hand.

She leaned in to kiss me, but before she could, I crawled up on top of her, straddling her in her seat, and kissed her instead, slowly working her lips, passionately stroking her tongue. I kissed her beautiful face, every part of it, and then her ears and her neck. I moved back to her mouth and kissed her like there was no tomorrow, a kiss that came from deep inside me, a kiss to show her how very much I loved her.

We had been making out for the better part of an hour when Jordan finally led me to the bedroom. Who knew there were so many ways to kiss?

We undressed, climbed into bed, and began where we left off, kissing, while her hands touched me everywhere at once, driving me out of my mind. Our legs intertwined, and I could feel her wetness as she rubbed herself on me, her hand running along my hip, sliding over my stomach, and down, over my mound and between my thighs. We kissed long and deep, panting and moaning, rocking and rolling, so enthusiastically thrusting and grinding, we very nearly fell off the bed, our mutual orgasms saving us at the last moment. We lay utterly spent, draped in each other's arms, the weight of her body caressing mine as we slowly relaxed, our arms and legs pretzeled together, blissfully entwined as we fell off to sleep.

CHAPTER ELEVEN

The next morning, I woke to the sound of clattering and clanking in the kitchen. I jumped out of bed, pulled on a pair of sweatpants and a T-shirt, and went to the bathroom to pee. I brushed my teeth, washed my face, and looked closely at myself in the mirror. My face was nothing like Jordan's. Her skin was golden-brown and flawless. I was Irish, with typical pale skin and freckles. I applied face moisturizer, comforted by the fact that Jordan seemed to like what she saw. I took one last look at myself in the mirror, then walked down the hallway to the kitchen.

"Good morning," I said as I sat at the kitchen table.

"Good morning. Did I wake you?" Jordan smiled and poured me a cup of coffee.

"If you did, thank you."

She brought me my coffee and sat on the corner chair next to me with her cup, looking at me with a sweet smile on her face, making me squirm in my chair. She let out a chuckle, obviously pleased with my reaction, and took a sip of her coffee.

I took a sip of my coffee, and when I put my cup down, Jordan reached over and covered my hand with hers, softly rubbing her thumb over my knuckles. I could barely control the quivering of my chin when she lifted my hand and kissed every one of my fingers.

"I have a project planned for us today," she said, releasing my hand and jumping up from her chair.

The sudden change in her focus surprised me. Her thoughts were obviously headed in a different direction than I had hoped. She was excited about something, though, evidenced by the way she enthusiastically moved about the kitchen—bending, stretching, reaching, and kneeling—looking very domestic and extremely sexy as she put away plates, cups, pots, and pans.

She wiped down the countertop and arranged the kitchen

towels on hooks along the side, then leaned back against the counter, crossed her arms, and bit down on her bottom lip.

Those lips. I was already warm, and watching her bite her lip, kiss my fingers, or do kitchen work made me even warmer. It really didn't matter what she did, she was beautiful, we were alone in the same room together, and she had a project planned for us today. I couldn't wait to find out what it was and could tell by the look on her face that she couldn't wait to tell me.

I waited.

"Are you hungry?" she asked.

I blinked—not the question I was expecting—and before I could answer, she was putting bread in our new mini-oven toaster.

She took the butter and marmalade out of the refrigerator, a knife out of a drawer, and a plate out of the cupboard. When the toast popped up, she gave me a cute eyebrow waggle before plucking them from the toaster. She buttered them, spread marmalade on them, then brought them to the table, quickly licking her lips as she sat down next to me. She picked up one of the pieces of toast and took a bite, chewing slowly as she looked into my eyes, smiling sweetly, excitedly jiggling her crossed leg under the table.

I took the remaining piece of toast, and she immediately picked up the plate and put it in the dishwasher. She wiped down the counter, leaned back against it, and smiled.

Whatever she was planning, she seemed to be totally enjoying herself, stretching out the wait to tease the living daylights out of me.

"Please, tell me," I begged, unable to deal with the suspense any longer. "I'm dying of curiosity."

She laughed, grabbed my hand, pulled me out of my chair, and dragged me into the living room. She sat us on the couch, facing each other, and cleared her throat.

"There is something I want to do, but I need to check if you are okay with it."

"What have you got in mind?" I asked, curiously excited.

"Okay." She took a breath. "I love what you do to me."

I was unclear about which part of our intimacy she was referring to, but whatever it was, I was all in. I smiled. "Go on…"

"Have you ever thought about trimming or shaving your hair?"

My head tilted slightly and my brows pulled together as my hand reached up and touched my hair. "My hair?"

"Yeah," she grinned. "And I don't mean the hair on your head."

The detail of what she was suggesting didn't quite compute, and I could tell she found the clueless expression on my face amusing.

"This…" She clutched herself lightly between her legs, instantly making me pulsate in the same place. "I want to do to you what you do to me." She took my hand for reassurance. "But I would like to…explore you with no hair."

I had no idea such a thing was even an option and wasn't sure how it would work. It made me realize what a sheltered life I lived. I had learned so much about myself of late, yet I was still so naive. I pondered her suggestion, a little embarrassed by my lack of sophistication, hoping she wasn't put off by it.

"I just thought, it would make my first time, you know, more successful," Jordan explained, looking shy and awkward—an expression I'd not seen before. She hesitated, then added, "It's fine if you don't want to…" obviously misreading the look of uncertainty on my face.

"No, it's not that I don't want to. It's just that I never considered it before."

"I just wanted to experiment…" Jordan's expression turned thoughtful for a moment, and then she announced in a rush of excitement, "I know! You do me! Shave me first!"

Suddenly, the notion of her suggestion was incredibly sexy, awakening another side of me that I didn't know was there. I was still unsure how this would work, but the idea of getting her even more naked than she had already been, made me wet.

"Really? Are you sure?"

She leaned forward and kissed me. "If you like it, maybe you'll let me do you?"

"Okay, that's fair." I grinned.

She excitedly sprung from her seat and disappeared down the hallway, reappearing with the little plastic bag full of the things she bought at the drugstore the day before. She sat next to me and emptied the bag's contents onto the coffee table in front of us.

I picked up some of the items and looked at them. A bottle of soap, three razors, disinfectant, cotton pads, small scissors, and a package of bubblegum. I picked up the bubblegum and smiled.

"Do you have a plan?"

"Of course."

She began describing her plan, and as she spoke, a picture slowly formed in my mind: towels, pillows, and a bowl of warm soapy water, surrounded by the romantic ambiance of the bedroom.

"What do you think?" she asked.

"Yeah, but I don't think we should do it on the bed. The angle is all wrong, and I wouldn't want to get your bed wet." The image of sloshing water was one thing, but sharp objects anywhere near her vagina on a wobbly bed made me nervous. Not wanting that image in her head, I decided not to say that part out loud. "I need you elevated so I can get to you at any angle. I need you comfortable so I don't feel rushed." I looked around the room for something fitting that description. "The kitchen table!"

We walked into the kitchen to inspect the suitability of the table.

"Oh, this is perfect," she said. "And we already know it will hold me." She grinned and leaned into me, teasing. "You could have me at any angle you want."

I chuckled at her innuendo. She was so cute. "Yeah, it's elevated and big enough. We can make it comfortable.

You're the expert. What do you think?"

She threw her arms around my neck and kissed me. "Let's do this!"

* * *

We spent the next half-hour setting everything up, during which I explained to Jordan how I would like to proceed and why. I did this more for myself than for her. I had no idea what I was doing, and talking it through helped me better visualize and make adjustments where necessary.

Jordan went into the bedroom to remove her clothes and then walked back into the kitchen wrapped in a towel. This show of modesty made me smile. She unwrapped herself with a showy flourish, handed me her towel with a cute suggestive wink, and climbed up onto the table, staging her backside perfectly in the air in front of me. I hesitated for a moment at the sight of her, realizing that the towel had nothing to do with modesty. I wanted to comment on how beautiful she looked from behind, but I did not want her further distracted. I needed her to be very still. I collected myself, trying to adopt a more clinical approach to the view of her before me.

"You're so serious," she teased.

"This is serious. It's not the easiest of surfaces to shave, and I want it to look nice," I said, using my most serious voice.

She laughed.

Shaving the woman you're in love with, the woman you've non-stop fantasized about every waking moment of the past year, was an honor and a privilege, but no easy task. It required concentration and nerves of steel and left me wet and throbbing and completely distracted. I was just finishing up the most difficult part of the shave when Jordan had a reaction of her own. Her hips moved.

"You okay?"

"Yes," she squeaked. She didn't sound sure.

"You sure? Do you need a break?"

"No. Sorry."

"Try not to move, Jordan. I would be so upset if anything happened to your vagina."

This made her smile, and I wanted to crawl up on top of her and kiss her. Instead, I returned her smile—basking in the pure intimacy of the moment—and concentrated on the task at hand, methodically working my way up to her mound and finishing her off by framing her bush into a neat triangle. I stood back, taking a moment to appreciate her *new look*. She let out the sweetest sigh of contentment, and I looked up at her, absolutely crazy in love with her and completely satisfied with the job I had done. I cleared my throat, announced that I was finished, and pulled Jordan up by the hand as I handed her a mirror.

"Wow, that didn't take nearly as long as I thought it would." She positioned the mirror between her legs and took a long look at her reflection before letting out a vague, "Huh." She looked up at me. "It looks great, Shannon."

I wanted more feedback but didn't want to press her on it. "It really wasn't as difficult as I thought it would be. I think I was just nervous. I didn't want to hurt you."

"Come here." I leaned in, and she met me with a soft kiss. "Thank you, it's perfect."

"You're welcome. Thank you for letting me do it." I blushed.

She went to the bathroom to shower while I rearranged our bush-trimming implements, readying them for my turn. I then made us both a peanut butter and jelly sandwich, grabbed us a Pepsi and a bag of chips, and made myself comfortable on the couch, eagerly awaiting her return, curious to know what she thought of her new bush. She appeared in the doorway wearing a T-shirt, sweatpants, and a big smile. I sat up and looked at her expectantly.

"It looks really nice, Shannon. Thank you," she said as she sat down next to me. "And everything is intact. No razor injuries."

I smiled, super pleased with myself. "Sandwich?"

While we ate, she asked me questions about the art of shaving a woman—as she put it—specifically questioning me about which part I thought was the most difficult and whether I had any tips for her.

"I think if you go slow and do it in the same order I did, you'll be fine."

"Have you ever looked at your pussy?" she asked.

I choked a little on my sandwich at her use of the word *pussy*. "No. Have you ever looked at yours?" I gestured at her nether region with my finger, "Before today?"

"Yeah. Actually, I have." And then she hesitated, looking intently at the side of her sandwich before scooping up an errant jelly glob with her tongue. "Erm…you have much more hair than I do." She glanced at me, then back at her sandwich, obviously trying to avoid eye contact with me, obviously trying *not* to tell me something. "Do you want to see yourself before I shave it off?"

"Yeah, why not? A before-and-after look. But first, I have to clean myself. I'm a bit…affected."

"You're wet?"

"Yeah, a little."

"A little?" She smiled, teasing me.

"Yeah, a little, and I would rather have my first look without all of *that*. And, of course, I don't want you to have to deal with it either, you know, while working."

"You do realize that it will most likely return during the course of my *work*?"

"Yeah…probably," I admitted, blushing a little.

"Shannon, I like that part, a lot. Dealing with it, as you put it, will not be an issue."

"Yeah, okay…"

"But I want you to feel completely comfortable. I want you to enjoy this, so take a shower if you want to."

I got up and went to the bathroom, and as I showered, I wondered why I had never taken the time to look at my undercarriage. I spread my legs, grabbed my knees, and took a look, but the angle was not optimal, so I squatted, almost slipping as I leaned further down. I grabbed the faucet to steady myself. I couldn't really see very well, but Jordan was right, I did seem to have quite a bit of hair. When I returned to the kitchen, Jordan was standing next to the table, ready with the mirror. "Okay. Sit on the edge here and put your feet on the chairs."

She handed me the mirror. Wow! *Quite a bit of hair* was an understatement. I could not even see my vagina. "Maybe we should get a professional for this," I joked, slightly sheepish.

Jordan took the mirror and gestured for me to get onto the table. "Now you'll see how hard it is to be still."

Jordan's approach to shaving me was much more playful and flirtatious than mine had been, exciting me whenever possible by touching me unnecessarily and teasing me by blowing on my sensitive, freshly shaved parts. It was delectable torture. The added challenge of shaving me while I squirmed and pleaded pleased her enormously.

"Just relax," she cooed, giggling.

She gave me a moment to gather myself, then added the last *touches* to my already perfectly manicured bush.

When she finished, she straightened, wiping the back of her hand across her forehead, emphasizing her hard work and effort. "I think that's it."

"Really, that's it?" I was a little disappointed she was finished.

"Yeah, that's it."

I gave her my hand, she pulled me up into a sitting position, and I let out a small gasp of surprise. There was red hair everywhere.

"Yeah, I know. You have a lot of hair." She gave me the mirror, and I took a good look at myself, a bit shocked at seeing my vagina for the first time. It looked totally different than hers. For one, hers was bigger.

"Do you like it?" I asked.

"Do *you* like it?" she asked back.

"Yeah, I like it."

"Good. Now, go shower," she said, never really telling me whether she liked it or not.

I jumped off the table and hurried down the hall to the bathroom. In the shower, I couldn't stop touching myself. Having no hair down there made me extra aware of my vagina, and even more so when I put on my sweatpants. The cushion I was used to between my vagina and my clothing was gone, the feeling of my clothing on my bare skin exhilarating.

I finished dressing and returned to the kitchen to find everything tidied up and in its proper place.

"And? What do you think?" Jordan asked.

"I love it. Thank you."

Before I could ask her what *she* thought, she glanced at the wall clock and said, "It's twelve-thirty. Let's go for a walk. Just an hour. Thirty minutes down the street and back." She took my hand and led me into the bedroom. "Jean skirts, no underwear."

"Really?"

"Trust me," she grinned.

As we walked out the front door, I immediately scanned the area, looking for anyone out and about. But there was no one—just the two of us—and I relaxed.

We walked across the lawn to the sidewalk, followed it left, then turned right at the corner. Wow… Okay… A slight breeze… One that I never would have noticed before my shave. The air moved under my skirt, touched my skin, and healed it. I felt naked, and the sensation was delicious.

We walked in silence, and I wondered what Jordan was thinking, hoping she was enjoying this as much as I was.

"Thank you for this," I said.

"You're welcome." She gave me a cute blink-wink.

We walked longer than an hour and didn't get back to the house until almost two-thirty. As we stepped up onto the porch, my heart took off in a gallop. I was nervous. Jordan unlocked the front door and entered in front of me, and I closed and locked the door behind us, turning to find her standing in the kitchen, waiting.

"Come to bed with me," she said, reaching her hand out to me.

She led me into the bedroom, where she quickly undressed and jumped into bed. She propped herself up against the headboard, crossed her legs at the ankles, and folded her hands in her lap, giving me the most amused look as she quickly licked her lips. "Please, undress," she said, biting down on her bottom lip. She was thoroughly enjoying my nervousness.

I gave her a weak smile, she let out a chuckle, and I responded with an eye roll. I was stalling. I was nervous as heck. I hoped she liked doing this to me; I didn't want her to be disappointed. I gave my head a shake, let out a quick breath, and got undressed, trying really hard to act cool and not nervous as I stood before her naked, my hands clasped together in front of my newly trimmed bush.

She sat up and patted the mattress with her hand. "Come here."

I unclasped my hands and let them fall to my sides. Her eyes moved down to my bush, and her head tilted to the side as if seeing me for the first time. She let out a small hum. I looked down at myself, then back up at her, nervously shifting from one foot to the other.

She moved to her knees and sat back on her heels, slightly spreading her legs, exposing herself. Wow! She stretched her hand out to me, her fingers begging. "Come here."

I crawled to her from the foot of the bed and sat back on my heels facing her. She reached out and touched my hair, tucking strands of it behind my ear as she scooched closer, placing her knee between mine.

"Don't be nervous. Your pussy is beautiful. I love you, Shannon," she whispered.

The back of her fingers brushed up against the bottom curve of my breasts, lingering a moment before moving around to the sides. She released a soft moan as she took them into her hands, completely focused as she fondled them, stroking them just right, making me wet again and throbbing so intensely, my hips were vibrating.

She moved closer, her left hand sliding around to my back, holding me, while her right hand continued to gently stroke my breast, pleased when I let out a whimper. She leaned down, took my nipple into her mouth, and I moaned, arching my back, encouraging her to take more of me into her mouth. And she did, her efforts taking on an almost hypnotic rhythm. My arms at my sides, the tips of my fingers touching the bed, holding me steady, I watched, enthralled as she worked my breast, her beautiful lips releasing me much too soon, my nipple emerging wet and erect as it left her mouth.

"You are beautiful," she whispered as she looked into my eyes, her expression so full of love. She looked down at my lips, then leaned forward and kissed them, at first soft and then more demanding, making us both moan. I wrapped my arms around her and pulled her closer, and she deepened our kiss even more, taking on the same rhythm she had with my breast. She kissed me and kissed me, and it was like I had been lifted off my feet and was hanging from her mouth, floating. She slowly released my lips and moved to my neck, her mouth wide, her tongue wet, her lips sucking.

She gently pushed me back onto the bed and began where she left off, kissing, working her way down my body, ending with a soft kiss in the bend between my thigh and mound. She spread my legs wider, and a whimper escaped my mouth when her breath brushed my newly shaved parts, accentuating my wetness. Then she licked me, and my head snapped back into my pillow, my mind undone by the sensation of having her lips on me, her tongue on me. She licked me again, and I cried out, fighting to catch my breath. She hesitated, but just for a moment, then took me into her mouth, and I swear, I almost fainted right there on the spot, the intense pleasure making me gasp for air. Before long, she had me withering and bucking, calling out her name. "God! Jordan! Please!"

LEAP OF FAITH

She answered my call by entering me with her tongue, introducing a new level of pleasure, taking on the same rhythm as before, her nose nudging up against my knot, over and over again, turning me into a gibbering, panting mess. I grabbed onto the sheets and held on tight as my back arched, the feeling that I might launch into space overwhelming as the pressure between my thighs intensified. My core erupted a few seconds later, my body turning liquid as I collapsed to the bed, warm waves washing over me as Jordan stroked me through the last of my aftershocks. And then she was on me, wrapping me into her arms, holding me tight, whispering words of love.

CHAPTER TWELVE

It was dark when I woke, the mattress moving slightly as Jordan crawled off me and left the bed, her shadowed form disappearing through the bedroom door. She made her way down the hallway to the bathroom, the toilet flushed, and a moment later, the shower turned on.

I stretched, rolled over onto my stomach, and laid my head on my crossed arms, closing my eyes as I listened, picturing her standing under the shower, arms up, washing her hair, her breasts lifting, her beautiful thighs and lovely behind covered in lathery soap. I was instantly warm.

The shower ran a minute or two more, then slowly stopped—the squeak of the shower faucet turning. I listened. My eyes popped open at the sound of her humming, and I smiled, feeling her happiness.

A few minutes later, the bathroom door opened, and Jordan walked down the hallway past the bedroom into the kitchen. She turned on the light and began to make coffee.

I got up and took a shower, then dressed in the bedroom before walking down the hallway, the sight of her making my heart beat faster as I stopped in the kitchen entryway. She was leaning back against the counter with her arms crossed, lost in thought. I crossed my arms and leaned up against the wall, mimicking her pose. She looked up at me and smiled.

"Want some?" she asked.

"Yes, please."

She turned, poured me a cup of coffee, then hesitated. Leaving my cup on the counter, she picked hers up and slowly turned as she raised it to her lips. "I love you," she said before taking a sip.

"I know." My voice broke, and tears instantly filled my eyes, but she didn't move to come to me. She just stood there, smiling softly. I sniffed and cleared my throat. "What time is it?"

She turned and squinted at the microwave's digital clock.

"Midnight."

My mouth dropped open, and I took a couple of steps forward to look for myself. "Wow. I can't believe we slept that long."

"Yeah, eight hours." Her cup still in hand, she picked mine up and brought it to me, both of us taking a sip as she slipped her hand under my T-shirt and softly rubbed my lower back.

I looked into her eyes. She smiled and looked away. "What?" I asked.

She walked back to the counter and turned, her face flushed, her expression earnest. "This thing we have, it's something special. I know it is. This doesn't happen to everyone." She hesitated a moment. "Nothing has ever felt so right to me. Since I first saw you, every thought, every decision, every move I've made has been to get to you, to be near you. I know what we're doing is technically wrong, but it doesn't feel wrong to me. I'm happy. I feel sane for the first time in my life. Everything makes sense to me now. When I'm with you, I don't feel ashamed anymore. It's just you and me, and it's wonderful."

I blinked several times and tried to swallow. My heart was beating so hard, I was sure it would burst. She looked down at her feet, then back up at me, and said, "Please tell me you feel the same way...that you understand what I'm saying."

"I feel the same way. I understand what you're saying." My voice cracked, and I took a shaky breath, letting it out slowly.

"Come here."

I went to her, my eyes full of tears, and took her into my arms. "I love you," I whispered in her ear.

"I know you do."

* * *

The next day, we didn't even bother leaving the bed except to grab something to eat or go to the bathroom. We talked about everything, anything, and nothing at all. We ate microwave dinners and mini-oven pizzas, laughed a lot, kissed a lot, and made love. She would turn twenty-two in August, and I would turn twenty-four in December. She played softball in high school, and I loved to cook. Her favorite bands were *ACDC* and *Journey*. I listened to John Denver and Barry Manilow. She laughed easily and loved to tease. I didn't tell her that I was ticklish, but she found out anyway.

I told her that when she looked at me, my heart beat faster, and when she smiled at me, I felt like the most important person on earth. When she kissed me, it was like floating, and when she made love to me, I left my body for a moment and only returned because I knew she was here waiting for me. She told me over and over how beautiful I was, and by late Wednesday night as she made love to me, I actually believed that I was. We fell asleep in each other's arms.

CHAPTER THIRTEEN

Thursday morning, when I woke, Jordan was not in bed with me. I jumped up, pulled on sweatpants and a T-shirt, walked into the kitchen, and poured myself a cup of coffee, wondering where the heck she was. I walked through the house, cup in hand, looking for her, a breeze touching my skin as I walked back through the kitchen to the living room. The windows were open, and I could hear birds chirping and smell wet grass. I went outside, first checking the backyard, then the front. That's when I noticed my truck was gone. Back inside, I checked the time on the microwave clock. Nine forty-five.

I poured myself another cup of coffee, took it out to the front porch, and sat on the steps, letting out a blustering breath, a little overwhelmed by a sense of loss and abandonment. Where was she? She just left without telling me where she was going, without waking me up. Why would she do such a thing? Why didn't she take me with her? I couldn't figure it out. It was so unexpected that it left me a little shaken. I would never have done such a thing.

This was the first time we'd been apart this week, and I hated it. We only had a couple of days left, and I wanted to spend every minute of them with her. She must know how precious our time together was—how costly. There was probably a good reason for her little outing, although I couldn't think of one that required my absence. My self-doubt was off the charts at what this implied. She didn't want me with her.

I sipped on my coffee and tried to shake off the chronic insecurity that plagued me, an insecurity resulting from years of bullying I'd endured in school, an insecurity that left me questioning myself, doubting myself, even after a day like yesterday when I had never felt more loved and desired in my life, a day so special, so lovely, and so uniquely exclusive, another would not soon equal it. We spent the whole day practically sitting on top of each other, wrapped in each other's arms. I had never felt so close to anyone. Jordan's love was so good, I felt incredibly vulnerable at the thought of losing it.

Maybe she just needed some time alone. I was on her nonstop. I didn't give her a moment's peace.

I wracked my memory for any indication that she was bothered by me, finding none. But I couldn't be sure.

If she needed a break, why didn't she say something! I would have understood! I'm not a complete dufus!

Maybe she didn't feel like she could. Maybe I didn't let her.

So, then what? She just up and takes off without a word instead!

I tried to control the back-and-forth in my head, hoping her sudden disappearance wasn't because of an emergency but rather a last-minute interview or a forgotten appointment, something that would confirm that her leaving had nothing to do with me.

A good explanation would really be helpful right now! She should have woken me!

Tears sprang into my eyes when the truck appeared at the other end of the street and made its way toward the house. I stood up as she pulled into the driveway, thrilled that she was back, more insecure and unsure than I'd been when I originally found her gone, and unmistakably angry and hurt that she left me here. She got out of the truck, grabbed several plastic bags out of the back, confidently swaggered to the foot of the porch steps, and theatrically held up the bags in both hands.

"Ta-dah," she sang, grinning ear-to-ear.

Shopping! She left me here to go shopping! This screamed of trying to get away from me! I turned and stormed into the house, slamming the door behind me, already pacing by the time she walked in.

"Is everything okay?" She pushed the door closed with her foot and walked past me, dropping all the bags on the kitchen table. She turned and looked at me, raising her hands before dropping them despairingly. "What's going on?"

"Where were you?" I demanded, hands on my hips.

"I was shopping." She turned to the table, lifted one of the bags, then another, finally picking them all up and putting them on the kitchen counter as she scanned the room looking for something. "I left you a note."

"Why didn't you wake me?" I was livid that her excursion was so minor—not an emergency, not a forgotten appointment—She could have taken me with her!

"I just thought it would be nice to let you sleep, I didn't…"

"You didn't want me to come with you? Did you need to be alone?"

"No, of course not. Shannon, what's wrong?"

"Nothing is wrong with me; I'm not the one who left!"

Jordan hesitated, then threw up her hands in bafflement. She turned to the bags on the kitchen counter and began putting the contents away. "I thought you would enjoy sleeping in. I thought I was being nice. I thought I could quickly do some shopping and save us some time so that we could spend more time together here. Whatever," she mumbled to herself, loud enough for me to hear.

"Really! That's what you thought? You would leave me here and save us some time? I don't believe you. I think you wanted to go shopping alone without me!"

"Are you crazy?" Jordan swung around and placed her hands on her hips. "I hate shopping!"

"Well, for someone who hates shopping, you certainly spent enough time this morning out alone doing it!" My voice dripped with sarcasm as I put air quotes around the word *alone*. I immediately realized air quotes didn't make any sense unless she wasn't alone, and that possibility irritated me even more.

"You cannot be serious! You think I left you here to get away from you? Are you out of your mind?"

"I am not crazy! I know when someone is avoiding me!

You could have woken me up! I could have come with you! You left me here! You were gone for more than an hour! *Walmart* is just on the corner! Did you meet with someone?" I was overreacting, but I could not stop myself. I was angry and hurt and scared, and she was the reason.

"I didn't go to *Walmart*; I went to *Albertsons*! And no, I did not go out alone just so I could meet up with someone!"

"Ha! So, you did meet someone!"

"Yes. Okay? I bumped into Poppy, and we talked for five minutes. But I did not plan it, and that's not why I went out alone!"

"And who is Poppy!"

"She's a woman I met in the mailroom at my last job!"

I was instantly jealous. "A woman from your last job! And? Are you sleeping with her?" I was completely losing it, but still, I could not stop myself. If I was going to lose her, then by God, I was going to deserve it!

"You *are* crazy!" Jordan huffed as she turned and began yanking items out of the shopping bags.

I took in a sharp breath, a gasp of outrage at what her non-answer suggested. "Oh my God! You're sleeping with her!" I waited two seconds for a reply, then announced in a low, angry voice, "I'm leaving!"

I stormed through the kitchen and down the hallway, and Jordan was on me before I got to the bedroom door. She grabbed me by the arm and swung me around. "You aren't going anywhere," she said, her voice trembling.

I pushed her away, then turned, but before I could take another step, she was on me again, grabbing me, attempting to pull me back. I tried to pull my arm from her grip, but she held me too tight.

"Get off me!" I yelled.

We struggled together, grunting with effort, and as I strained against her, attempting to twist my arm from her grasp, I turned, pulled, lifted, and jerked, landing a hefty punch to her face with my right elbow.

I immediately snapped back into reasonable thought,

gasping as Jordan let go of me and took two steps back, her mouth open in shock as her hand covered the side of her face.

"Jordan... Oh, God... I'm sorry..." I stammered, not only sorry for hitting her but for my irrational behavior, leading to this stupid, ugly scuffle in the hallway. "I'm impossible, I don't know what to say, I messed up." I swallowed hard, unable to look her in the eye, waiting for what I knew must come next. It was over, she would leave me, and I would die.

"It doesn't matter. It's over..."

Jordan's words vibrated in my head as I squeezed my eyes shut, clutching my chest, sure I was about to be sick, barely registering the next few words that came out of her mouth.

"I'm here with you now. I won't ever go shopping unless you are with me. I won't ever leave you alone in bed sleeping. I'll wake you before I go, and I won't ever sleep with anyone but you. I promise. Please, don't go. I love you."

My eyes blinked open, and I raised my head, shaking it in disbelief. Her face was twisted in anguish, bright red and streaked with tears, but she wasn't angry with me. She was pleading with me to stay, not breaking up with me.

I burst into tears, and a moment later, her arms were around me. She held me until I finished crying, then led me into the bathroom, where she sat me down on the toilet seat. She started running a bath, then went into the kitchen, returning with a small bag. She removed three candles, some matches, body oil, bubble bath, and a package of bath salts and arranged them on the counter. She opened the package of bath salts, poured it into the bath, then added a cap full of bubble bath.

She removed her clothes, threw them into the hamper, then began undressing me, pulling my shirt off over my head and removing my sweatpants. She helped me into the bathtub, turned off the water, then placed three candles around the faucet end of the bathtub before lighting them. After turning off the bathroom lights, leaving the door open, she slid into the bath behind me and carefully put her arms around me.

"I'm sorry," I began, and then all my pathetic insecurities tumbled out of my mouth. "I let myself think all kinds of horrible things about you. I worried you'd grown tired of me. And then I accused you of sleeping with someone else. I actually felt jealous. I don't know what came over me. It was like I was trying to sabotage us. I think I lost my mind for a moment."

Jordan kissed the back of my head, then leaned in next to my ear as she held me tighter. "Everyone loses their mind sometimes. It happens. I do it all the time. We're getting to know each other, and that can be a challenge under the best of circumstances. It takes time, Shannon. Sometimes I don't think, and I make mistakes. Please be patient with me."

"Jordan, you did nothing wrong. I did. I totally overreacted, and I'm so sorry." I swallowed hard, fighting back tears. "I swear, Jordan, I did not mean to hit you. It was an accident."

"I know, Shannon. It's okay. It's over now." She slowly moved her hands along my shoulders and down my arms to my hands, slipping her fingers between mine. I leaned into her, pulling her arms around me, her soft breasts pressing into my back. "Mmm," she moaned, her hips moving forward for a moment before relaxing.

I laid my head back on her shoulder, enjoying the sensation of our skin touching underwater, and then her toes broke the surface of the water in front of me, and a small smile touched my lips, the first one that day. I turned my head toward her, and she leaned over and covered my mouth with hers, kissing me deep and long, her left hand on my neck, her thumb stroking the length of it, resting in the hollow at its base. She released my mouth and slowly moved her hands down my body as I leaned back against her and took a deep breath, slowly letting go of the last remnants of fear, enjoying her touch, grateful that she was still mine.

"This feels wonderful, Jordan."

"Yes, it does."

Her hands made their way up along my arms to my

shoulders, and I closed my eyes and let out a long sigh as she rubbed them. No one had ever rubbed my shoulders before, and I was overwhelmed by the effect it had on me. It was exquisite. I could feel all the hard parts of me breaking apart and melting away.

"Did you buy all these things at the store today?" I asked, my voice soft and languid.

"Yeah. I thought about doing this yesterday, but I didn't have any bubble bath or candles."

"You are very romantic."

"Yeah, I am a little bit," she chuckled. "I always have been, I guess. I've just never had anyone I wanted to be romantic with."

"Please don't be romantic with anyone but me."

"I won't. I promise."

My heart squeezed at the thought of losing her and leapt at what her words meant, her promises soothing me, knowing she wouldn't be able to keep them, not wanting to think about that now.

We held each other another ten minutes or so, and then my stomach growled loudly. "Are you hungry?" she asked.

"I'm starving."

"I am going to put the rest of the groceries away and make us something to eat, okay?"

"Okay."

Jordan climbed out of the bathtub, dried off, kissed the top of my head, and disappeared down the hallway. I laid back in the tub and submerged to my chin, still feeling her hands on me but also hearing her in the kitchen. Suddenly, I didn't want to be in the bathtub anymore. For two seconds, I considered staying in the tub, not wanting to encroach on her alone-time, but I let those thoughts pass. She had been clear about her feelings for me and how much she wanted to be with me. I needed to stop letting my insecurities determine my actions. I wanted to be near her, and there was nothing wrong with that.

I blew out the candles, opened the drain, and jumped out

of the tub. After drying off, I got dressed, went into the kitchen, and sat at the table, watching Jordan as she chopped up some onions and tomatoes. She threw them, along with two cans of tuna, into a bowl, then came over and knelt down on her knees in front of me. She took my hands in hers, looked into my eyes, and very seriously asked me how I felt about tuna-melts for lunch. She was adorable.

"Tuna-melts sound perfect."

She kissed my hand, then laid a small piece of paper on the table in front of me. "I found this on the floor. The breeze from the open windows must have blown it off the table." She then stood up and turned back to the kitchen, pulling a skillet out of the cabinet and placing it on the stove. She grabbed some sliced cheese, mayo, and butter out of the fridge, set them on the counter next to a loaf of sourdough bread, and got to work.

I fingered the thin strip of paper before holding it up and reading it. "*Good morning. I didn't want to wake you. I'm out picking up a few supplies. I took your truck. I'll be back soon, Jordan.*" I shook my head at myself and let out a sigh, looking over at Jordan as she finished assembling our tuna-melts.

She laid them in a simmering skillet, flipped them once, turned off the burner, then came over and pulled me up off my chair and into her arms. "Is there anything else I can do for you?"

"If you could just keep loving me even when I do really stupid stuff, that would be great."

"I can do that," she said, holding me tighter.

We sat on the couch and ate our tuna-melts while we watched TV. I still felt bad about our fight earlier, but I was slowly letting it go. Jordan was right; no one was perfect, everyone had a bad day, and our situation was not the easiest. It was a miracle we were coping as well as we were, juggling guilt, worry, and self-doubt while hiding what we were from our families, the church, and the world. What we were attempting was enormously difficult and risky.

We were trying to be like a couple, whatever that meant in this situation, and even though no one was allowed to know and it would never be official, I needed to start thinking about us like a couple. If we were going to be together, for however long that was possible, then I was going to have to be more patient and understanding. This was going to be hard enough without me freaking out about nothing. There were sure to be plenty of real issues to freak out about later.

We spent the afternoon on the couch, Jordan lounging back against me as she watched TV, my arm draped over her shoulder holding her as I listened to her talk about her job search and her plans to buy a car. She talked about high school and softball, how she had felt a bit lost after graduation, and how hard it had been to make the decision to move to Sacramento, knowing she'd miss her mom and dad but hoping to make a new start.

We sat like that for a couple of hours before Jordan announced that she had to pee. While she was gone, I gathered our plates and glasses and took them into the kitchen. After putting everything into the dishwasher and cleaning up a bit, I returned to the couch just as Jordan walked back into the living room.

I gasped when I saw her, covering my mouth with my hand in shock at how bruised and swollen her cheek was. Standing up, I timidly approached her, reaching out and carefully touching her arms as I looked at her face from all angles.

"My God, Jordan."

"Don't freak out. I already saw it in the mirror."

I put my hand on her cheek, and her head jerked back slightly. "Sssss...ouch!" she hissed, her face twisting in pain.

"Did I do this?"

"We did this, and I bruise very easily."

I pulled her face to mine and kissed her, then took her into my arms and held her. "Jordan, I'm so sorry."

"It was an accident. Stop blaming yourself. It's partly my fault." She chuckled, giving me a squeeze.

"I hate that this happened. If I had not freaked out..."

"You feel bad, don't you?"

"I do..."

"You want to make it up to me, don't you? It's the only way you'll feel better."

I looked at her, a bit confused, and was met with a very cute grin and eyes filled with mischief. She was teasing, trying to make me feel better. I gave her a playful shove, then inspected her face more carefully, relieved that I hadn't broken her nose or busted her lip. But her cheek was swollen, and a big bruise was beginning to form.

"I already have an explanation for it," she said.

I squinted at her, not quite sure what she meant by that.

"People will notice; they'll ask."

"Oh...right, okay."

"We were playing catch in the backyard. You threw the ball, I missed it, and it hit me in the face."

I was already shaking my head as she finished. "No one will believe that, Jordan. Everyone knows you play softball, and they know I don't. No one will believe that I threw a ball that you could not catch."

"No one will think that much about it, believe me. Don't worry, and don't forget the story. Someone might ask you about it."

"Okay." I nodded. There was no way I could come up with a better story. I mean, I was living proof that it was possible to miss an easy ball and get smacked in the face, or in my case, smacked in the stomach.

Jordan put her hands on my hips and pulled me closer, tilting her head back and looking upward as though she were thinking hard about something. "Now, how can you make this up to me?"

I laughed, and she looked back down at me and smiled. I was instantly warm. How did she do that? "Amazing."

She murmured her agreement as she tucked her head in next to mine, running her lips along the curve of my ear, nibbling on my earlobe before running her mouth down my neck. Her left hand slid into the back of my sweatpants, and her wonderful fingers slipped between my cheeks.

"I want you," I panted, turned on like a switch.

My legs were already spreading, letting her leg in between mine, my hips already moving as she very decisively grabbed my butt and pulled me snugly up onto her thigh. I grabbed her shoulders, holding on as I rolled my hips, grinding myself on her as I gazed into her eyes, feeling amazed at how much I wanted her.

"Take me to bed," she said, her expression full of desire, her voice husky with want.

We hurried through the kitchen, pulling our T-shirts off as we went. My sweatpants were already down to my knees when I got to the bedroom door.

Jordan passed me on the left, already naked, and jumped onto the bed. She flipped over onto her back and propped her head up on her pillow, spreading her legs, looking cocksure and very sexy.

I finished removing my sweatpants and crawled to her from the foot of the bed, bending my arms and lowering my body as I predatorily approached, ready to take her directly into my mouth.

"Say it, Shannon!"

Hesitating, I looked up at her. "Say it?"

Her eyes locked with mine as she quickly licked her lips. "Tell me what you want. I want to hear the words."

"I want you...in my mouth?" I said, unsure of exactly what she wanted me to say.

The smirk on Jordan's face told me I wasn't far off. "Say it."

"Pussy?"

"Oh, God, Shannon," Jordan gasped as her hips let out an inviting thrust.

Wow! I did not expect that reaction. Apparently, I had hit a nerve. "Pussy," I repeated.

Jordan let out a moan, her eyes glossing over with lust as she squirmed in front of me.

"I want your pussy in my mouth," I said, inflecting as much raw lust as possible into my voice.

Several gaspy moans fell out of Jordan's mouth as if she'd lost all ability to speak but desperately wanted to communicate something to me. She was begging. I gave her a sly smile and slowly ducked my head between her thighs, taking her into my mouth and making her call out my name. Quite by accident, in my enthusiasm to get as much of her freshly shaven pussy into my mouth as possible, I sucked her luscious, engorged knot between my wet, puckered lips.

"God, Shannon! Yes!" she practically screamed.

With those words of encouragement, I sucked her lovely knot until she came. She cried out long and loud, her back arching, her thighs shaking, collapsing to bed in a moaning, gasping heap.

"Come here," she called to me, breathless.

I crawled up her body and snuggled into her, laying my head in the crook of her neck, scanning her body from her breasts to her toes, thinking for the first time, this is mine.

"Wow, that was good," she said as she kissed the top of my head. "That was very good. It was more than good. It was great!"

"You liked it?"

"Yeah, I liked it," she said, still a bit breathless as she let out a small laugh.

"What? Tell me." I sat up and looked at her.

"You sucked directly on my clitoris. I mean, it was in your mouth the entire time. It was very effective. It was perfect. I liked it…a lot." She sighed and added, "It was awesome."

"The clitoris?"

"Yeah, the clitoris."

I let out an exasperated breath. "If you know something, Jordan, please tell me."

"I don't know that much about it. I had a sex-ed class in high school, and they explained the parts of the vagina, and that's how I know about the clitoris. It's very sensitive. It's what makes the orgasm happen."

"The little knot at the top?"

"Yeah... I mean, little is relative."

"I didn't mean it that way. I meant it like, compared to what the guys get."

"Oh...right. But still, the clitoris is twice as sensitive as the entire penis."

"Really?" I said, surprised and impressed, wishing I had known about the clitoris earlier. "This is important information. There must be an easy-to-hide, how-to book about this that I can get my hands on." I ran my fingers through my hair, frustrated. Jordan smiled, amused, making me blush at my obvious lack of knowledge on the subject. "Don't make fun of me, Jordan. It was only a few years ago I found out how men and women have sex."

Jordan laughed at this, shaking her head. "A few years? When did you find out?"

"I was seventeen."

"Seventeen!"

"And the revelation about the erection was even more recent. Actually, very helpful in clearing up a lot of the confusion I was having about positions and how the sperm travels from the man to the woman."

"How can it be that you know so little about sex? I mean, not even the basics?"

I thought for a moment, then shrugged my shoulders. "My mom never told me. My parents pulled me out of high school sex-ed, so I missed out on that. The stuff I do know, I managed to piece together from conversations I overheard at school and then later at work. I just... I don't know. Sex has always been presented as this thing everyone just knows about without needing to be told, so I never asked. I didn't want to look like an idiot, and also, *that* version of sex has never been very appealing to me, so I never went out of my way to find out about it. The only organic sexual thoughts I've ever had were fantasies about women, but even those were not very clear. I had no sense of the mechanics of it, you know? No examples, no visuals." I laid my hand on her chest,

"Just you," adding, "I know, I'm a bit of a freak."

"How did you know what to do, you know, with me? I mean, you explained your oral fascination, but what you do to me is much more than that. It's like you know what you're doing."

"I know a lot more than I did a couple of months ago, but not near as much as I want to know. I want to know everything about you, Jordan."

Jordan looked at me like she couldn't quite figure me out, a look I'd seen on her face more than a couple of times. "I'll tell you anything you want to know if you keep doing what you do to me."

"Really?"

"Yeah."

"Okay. Deal."

She smiled at me, and I smiled back. I knew she was teasing, joking around with me, but I was completely serious. I loved touching her, and I loved the way she touched me. There was nothing like it. It was perfect. If I could make her feel the way she made me feel, I would be the happiest woman on the planet.

CHAPTER FOURTEEN

The next morning, as I rubbed the sleep from my eyes, a beautiful view of Jordan's back came into focus. Without thinking, without hesitating, I leaned in and kissed the place between her shoulder blades. I was rewarded with a luxurious moan, causing my whole body to glow.

I placed my hand on the curve of her waist, fascinated by the contour of her hip, following the slant of her thigh as far as my reach would allow. I returned the same way, continuing up her side, shifting closer to spoon her from behind.

She let out a fervent whimper as her lovely backside pushed into my lap, and what started as an innocent morning cuddle turned into a feat of balance, coordination, strength, and rhythm as I embarked on a mission to satisfy her at all costs.

I jumped to my knees and grabbed onto her hips, pulling her into me as I thrust up against her, wanting to give her what she so shamelessly begged for. Her begging was my kryptonite, and it was all I could do to keep my wits about me as I took her from behind—her beautiful heart-shaped butt in the air, her legs spread wide, displaying her gorgeous sex in all its glory.

It was the first time I'd ever been inside Jordan, and I wanted to get it right. It was amazing—her moans and whimpers, her grunts and cries of encouragement, telling my fingers exactly what to do. I was astounded, but only for a moment. I had to concentrate or this could go sideways fast. It was imperative that I keep my head as I balanced on one knee, the other one up and bent, my foot strategically placed alongside her for leverage, fighting the urge to thrust my hips into her because that would totally mess everything up.

She was coming! I redoubled my efforts, huffing and puffing, pumping my arm for all it was worth, knowing that one wrong move could make it all for naught. Driven by a sense of mutual understanding, we held our positions a moment longer, and then she practically burst apart in front of me as her orgasm ripped through her body, its force vibrating from the tips of my fingers all the way up my arm. I could not have been prouder as she collapsed on the mattress while I caught my breath and cradled my arm. I had given her my all, and the expression on her face as she turned and looked up at me, so full of love, so very satisfied, made all my awkward, fumbling attempts over the last ten minutes well worth it. She smiled at me, and I was in awe.

"Come here," she said, still a little out of breath. She leaned forward and grabbed my hand, pulling me down on top of her as she fell back onto her pillow with a satisfied huff.

I snuggled against her, my head on her chest, feeling like Wonder Woman.

"Did you like it?" I asked, hoping for a little constructive critique.

"Yes, I liked it. I've thought about this with you, and it was exactly how I imagined it." Our eyes met, and she asked, "What?"

"You've imagined this with me?"

"Yes, Shannon. I have. Who else would I imagine it with?" She sighed and let out a chuckle, squeezing me tighter.

I pressed my lips together for a moment, pleased by her admission and the light blush on her cheeks. "I've thought about this too, but it was much more than I imagined." Jordan raised her eyebrows at me, inviting me to elaborate. "At first, I could hardly think straight. When we do it, I hardly think at all. I just move. But this time, my position, holding my rhythm, my coordination, my balance. In the end, that's all I was doing—thinking. And my arm…" I raised my right arm and let it drop. "It's useless now."

We both laughed.

A comfortable lull surrounded us, the silence suddenly broken as we both agreed in unison, "We have to do that again."

"I know, right?" I sat up and turned to face her, sitting cross-legged as I prepared to discuss sex with the woman I loved. "I mean, I have no upper-body strength. I need to start doing push-ups."

Jordan smiled, shaking her head.

"What? I can do it better. I want to do it better. I just need practice."

"I think you did it pretty good."

"You weren't so bad yourself," I said, giving her a lustful smirk.

"I really didn't do anything at all," Jordan laughed, blushing again."

"Oh, but you did. I was very inspired. You should see yourself, how you look. And the noises you make. They make me crazy. I mean, my God, Jordan, your body is beautiful, and you up on your knees like that. Your pussy is so big and full, I don't know how to describe it."

And then I went on to describe it, babbling along at a hundred words a minute, surprised when Jordan suddenly lunged at me. She grabbed my legs and pulled, totally freaking me out as I realized she was about to tickle me. I fought her all the way, backpedaling as I slapped and kicked her in a full-blown, ticklish-person panic.

"I just want to give you a massage," she huffed, straining against me as she pulled me closer.

"No! Jordan! No! No foot massages! I can't! You know I'm ticklish!" I screamed like a banshee.

Grunting and laughing, she pulled me up on top of her—my head landing between her knees, my butt landing on her stomach, my legs spread eagle, my crotch right in her face. I thrashed and squirmed, determined to escape, going stock still when her finger touched my pussy, gasping when her other fingers joined in, moaning uncontrollably as she proceeded to give me the best massage I had ever received and an orgasm so earth-shattering, any doubt to whom my body belonged shattered along with it.

She wiggled out from underneath me and gathered me in her arms, whispering "I love you" in my ear. I was perfectly happy to remain cuddled in her arms the rest of the morning, but she had other plans—she was hungry and needed to pee. She jumped out of bed and disappeared down the hallway toward the bathroom, leaving me lying there, basking in the afterglow of our rigorous and very enjoyable morning activities. She reentered the bedroom and, as she dressed, asked me what I wanted for breakfast. My answer came in the form of a languorous, satisfied hum. She chuckled sweetly, then dragged me out of bed and sent me to the bathroom to shower.

After I showered and dressed, I walked into the kitchen and sat at the table just as Jordan was pouring my coffee. She set my cup down in front of me and gave me a soft kiss on my mouth before turning to the toaster and then the stove, maneuvering around the kitchen like a master chef as she tended to a skillet full of scrambled eggs and a plate of toast in need of buttering. As I sipped my coffee, watching her lay the table, I couldn't help but wish we could have exactly this every day for the rest of our lives.

We ate in silence, gazing at each other, head over heels and completely in love. It was overwhelming, and my eyes teared up as a burst of emotion surged through me. I looked down at my plate, blinking my tears away, filling my fork with the scrambled eggs Jordan made for me.

While Jordan showered, I cleaned up the kitchen, and afterward, waited for her on the couch. She entered the kitchen and smiled, acknowledging that I had cleaned it as she rubbed a hand towel through her wet hair. She walked into the living room and came to a stop right in front of me, still smiling as she put her foot on my knee and gave it a push.

"Let's do something; go somewhere."

"Okay."

A field trip with Jordan sounded wonderfully exciting. I jumped up and hurried to the bedroom to get dressed.

* * *

We jumped in the truck, and Jordan directed me to drive toward the city with no particular plan in mind, she said.

We found a parking space right on the street, then headed off on foot through the city toward the capitol building, and as we walked, I was hit with the desire to touch Jordan—to hold her hand or take her arm. But I couldn't, not out here. I was afraid someone would see. I wondered if she was thinking the same.

We strolled along, taking seemingly random lefts and rights, and after a while, I had no idea where we were. I followed her blindly, not really caring where she took me so long as she took me with her.

Soon, our surroundings began to change; we were no longer in the city center. There were more houses, apartments, little grocery stores, and small shops. We turned left onto a side street and walked another minute or so before Jordan stopped and leaned into me, pointing toward a large building across the street on the corner.

"What is it?" I asked, not sure what she was pointing at.

"It's a gay club."

My eyes widened, and I took in a breath, holding it, half expecting an alarm to start blaring, alerting the occupants that we were there. Thank God, that didn't happen. I quickly scanned the neighboring area, then looked at Jordan.

"We can't go in there, Jordan. We should go. Someone will see us," I whispered.

"It's Friday afternoon. Everyone is at work," Jordan whispered back, scanning the neighborhood just to make sure. "No one will see us. Besides, it's not even open yet. See? Look." She pointed, but I couldn't see what told her that the club was not open. "Let's just walk by. I want to see what it looks like." We started walking, always on the lookout for people who might see us, trying to act nonchalant just in case someone did. "See, it's closed."

We stared at the huge building as we passed it, the words *Club Imagine* painted in big, bold letters over the door, then turned left at the corner and made our way back to the main road. We found a diner on the next corner block, went in, and were promptly seated. Our coffees were poured, our orders taken, and then we were left alone.

I put my elbows on the table and leaned forward. "How do you know about this place?" I whispered.

"I saw it advertised in a small newspaper—a gay newspaper," Jordan whispered back as she leaned over the table toward me.

"Where... How did you get this newspaper?"

Jordan explained that late last year when Shawn's washing machine broke down, she had to do laundry in a laundromat. While waiting for her clothes to dry, she found a newspaper left on a chair and began reading it.

"In public?" I whispered loudly.

"No one saw me. It looks like a regular newspaper. It also advertised an office here in the city for gay people."

"An office?"

"Yeah, to help gay people get situated. To give them information about gay activities in the area. To get them involved in the gay community."

"Gay community?"

"Yeah, but I can't remember where the office is. I didn't take the newspaper with me. I was afraid Shawn would find it."

The waitress brought us our food, and after she left, Jordan asked me if I had ever read anything about gay clubs. I shook my head, then told her about the Christian bookstore in Colorado and about the pamphlet I had bought and then thrown away. "Other than that, I haven't read anything about being gay or where they go to hang out."

"I believe inside this club, we could sit together and hold hands and kiss, you know, in public."

The very idea of this made my heart beat faster. "Yeah, you're probably right."

I looked at Jordan's hand on the table and tried to imagine reaching over and covering it with my own, and for a moment, I thought I might do it. But then I couldn't. I just didn't have the courage. I looked around the diner, then looked at Jordan. She gave me a thin smile and nodded as if she were thinking the same thing.

We finished eating, then drove back to the house in thoughtful silence, my hand absent-mindedly caressing Jordan's thigh. From time to time, she would pick up my hand, press it to her lips, then lay it back down on her thigh as if it belonged there. We went straight to bed and made love. I lay in her arms after, listening to her heartbeat, thinking about the obvious. Tomorrow was Saturday.

* * *

The next morning, I woke to kitchen noise. I raised up on my elbows, listening, and just as I decided to get up, Jordan appeared in the doorway holding a breakfast tray.

"Good morning," she said, perky and bright.

As she walked around to my side of the bed, I adjusted my pillow and leaned back against the headboard. "Good morning."

Jordan placed the breakfast tray on my lap, then kissed me so deeply my eyes rolled back in my head. She released my mouth, leaving me breathless, and walked around the foot of the bed, removing her T-shirt and sweatpants as she went. She crawled up on the bed and edged up next to me, arranging her pillow and sitting sideways against the headboard, facing me. She grabbed her coffee from the breakfast tray and took a sip, looking at me intently over the rim of her cup. She put her cup down, picked up a slice of apple, and slowly moved it toward my mouth. I bit off half. She put the other half in her mouth and began chewing, her gaze so penetrating, I literally felt myself heat up. She moved closer, and her breast pushed up against my arm, making my breath catch. She shared the rest of the apple slices with me and then began feeding me grapes.

She put a grape in my mouth and let her finger linger on my bottom lip. I stared at her, my mouth hanging open as she picked up another grape, put it in her mouth, and began chewing. She looked down at my breasts and smiled. My nipples hardened in response. She leaned in and kissed my ear, and my eyes fluttered shut, and when her tongue probed inside, the words "Oh God" left my mouth. She pulled away, and I took a quick breath, steadying myself. She smiled and continued feeding me grapes until they were gone.

Next were the strawberries. She picked one up and steered it toward my mouth. I opened wide to receive it, and when I bit into it, juice ran down my chin. Jordan immediately leaned in and took my chin into her mouth, slurping and licking as if I were the most delicious thing she had ever tasted and she didn't want to waste a drop. She made her way to my mouth, reached in with her tongue, found my strawberry, and removed it, sucking on my bottom lip before releasing it with a smack. By then, I was practically panting. She smiled as she chewed my strawberry, then picked up another and held it up to my lips. I bit off half, forgot to chew, and swallowed it whole.

Jordan chuckled.

When we finished the strawberries, Jordan leaned over and kissed me, big and wet and sexy, making me wet and ready and breathlessly surprised when she broke our kiss and hopped off the bed, leaving me in a very aroused and frustrated state. She walked around to my side of the bed, picked up the tray, and turned, showing me her beautiful naked backside as she walked out the door and disappeared down the hallway toward the kitchen.

I swung my legs off the side of the bed, ready to go after her, when she suddenly reappeared in the doorway, hands on either side of the door frame, naked and beautiful, sexy and wild. I couldn't take my eyes off of her, and she gave me plenty of time to take in every inch of her before she suddenly moved toward me, practically pouncing as she pushed away from the door frame and jumped onto the bed. I started backpedaling, landing up against the headboard as she wantonly crawled over me, straddling me as she leaned forward and grabbed the headboard behind me.

Her hips began moving, and I grabbed ahold of them, her gorgeous breasts bobbing up and down in front of me. Wow! I had never seen her move so erotically. I eagerly leaned forward, my lips puckered and ready to savor her nipples, when she suddenly released the headboard and sat upright, taking my target out of range and leaving me in a gasping state of surprise. I swallowed hard and gave her my most earnest, *What are you doing to me?* look.

But she was not finished teasing me yet.

I wasn't sure how much more of her taunting I could take. She was driving me crazy, the throbbing between my thighs growing so intense, I was desperate to spread my legs to give it room.

I released her hips and slowly raised my hands, intending to touch her breasts, speculating that maybe she preferred them over my mouth. But she grabbed my hands and held them down, clearing up any misunderstanding. This wasn't teasing; this was torture!

I quickly licked my lips as she released my hands and slowly raised hers to her breasts, cupping them. "Oh, my God," I panted, gawping at her breasts in awed disbelief as she slowly massaged them, bucking my hips and sucking air through my teeth when she squeezed her nipple between her forefinger and thumb.

I looked up at her when she licked her lips and caught her suppressing a smile. She was enjoying this just as much as I was! I licked my lips back at her, gobsmacked at how good she was at this. I looked back down at her breasts and watched as she fondled them, groaning at the unbearably torturous effect she was causing between my thighs. I attempted a confident huff and whimpered instead. "Jordan, please…"

She grabbed me by the back of my neck and pulled me forward, burying my face between her breasts. My hands were around her waist in a heartbeat, pulling her closer, my mouth desperately sucking and licking from one breast to the other. She slowly leaned backward, and I followed, laying her on the bed, her big beautiful breasts the center of my universe.

I ravaged them until I had my fill, then made my way down her body, kissing her stomach, her hips, and her mound, working my way to the prize. I took her pussy into my mouth, and she moaned softly, spreading her legs wider, her hips already moving in sync with my mouth, greedily sucking.

I sucked every inch of her, avoiding her clitoris for as long as I could, wanting to torture her like she had me, wanting her to beg. But, of course, she never did. Because she didn't have to! She had me wrapped around her finger, and she knew it! She let out a satisfied sigh when I finally sucked her clitoris between my lips, followed by a sweet chuckle as if she knew I wouldn't be able to wait.

In retaliation, I entered her with my fingers. She gasped. Ha! I bet she didn't see that coming! I tortured her for all of thirty seconds before she grabbed my head and pulled me closer, and then I couldn't go slow anymore. Her hips rocking, her grip on my head tightening, she rode my face as I held onto her clitoris for dear life, eagerly thrusting my fingers into her, wanting her to feel every inch of me. In no time at all, her opening clenched around my fingers, announcing her coming orgasm. She came louder than I had ever heard her come before, thrashing and bucking, crying and moaning until the last contraction echoed through her body.

Her grip on my head loosened, and her hands fell away, landing on the bed. I slowly slid my fingers out of her, crawled up next to her, and took her into my arms.

"That was..." I began, unable to find the words to describe what she'd just done to me.

"Yeah..." She let out a contented sigh. "Not exactly what I had planned, but I am not complaining."

"I'm not complaining either. That was..."

"Yeah..."

We luxuriated in each other's arms for a good half-hour before my bladder began to protest.

"I have to pee."

She nodded, then released me, and I stood up and hurried to the bathroom to pee, quickly taking a shower before returning to the bedroom. Jordan was gone. I put on sweatpants and a T-shirt, then walked down the hallway, through the kitchen, and into the living room, where I found her sitting on the couch watching TV. I snuggled up next to her, thrilled to be near her again, trying not to think about the fact that tomorrow was Sunday. Our time here was almost finished, and I could feel the coming loss strongly. Admiring her profile as she laughed at something funny on TV, I pushed the thought away. I didn't want anything negative to touch our last day together.

She made grilled ham and cheese sandwiches for lunch, and we ate them with chips and drank cold Pepsi out of the bottle. I inspected the bruise on her face. It was fading and the swelling was completely gone. I rubbed her feet, which she loved, and she tried to rub mine, but my feet were just too ticklish. She gave me a back rub instead, which turned out to be a very effective aphrodisiac. We made love, then spent the rest of the evening on the couch watching TV, me sitting between her legs, reclined against her, her holding me, making me feel loved and cared for, her words in my ear, soothing me and giving me hope.

"I will always love you. I will never leave you. You mean everything to me."

* * *

On Sunday morning, we woke up, made love, and then rushed around the house getting ready for church. I packed my bag, and Jordan carried it to the truck for me, both of us nervous as we climbed inside. On the drive to church, Jordan tried to reassure me.

"It's just church, try to relax. No one knows but us."

"No one knows but us," I repeated.

We walked into the church building and sat next to each other without even thinking about it. As services started, I nearly had a panic attack when I realized what we had done, absolutely certain that someone would be able to see what we were just because we were sitting together. I quickly glanced around the room, knowing I was just being paranoid, fighting the overwhelming urge to run away and hide. I tried to relax.

After services, we split up, greeting other members, making small talk about the weather, the latest news in the congregation, and still about the wedding and how lovely Jordan looked in her dress. I looked over at Jordan from time to time and even caught her looking at me a couple of times. She would smile encouragingly, and I slowly relaxed. Everything was okay.

I moved through the foyer and out to the front lawn, reluctant to go, not wanting to leave Jordan until I had to, but also wanting it over with. The thought of leaving her was crushing me. She walked out of the building, and when I caught her eye, she nodded toward the parking lot. I began walking in that direction, dreading the moment we would have to say goodbye.

She didn't come immediately, and I stood in front of the truck, waiting for her. I tried to smile when she finally walked toward me, but it was a struggle. I took a couple of steps back as she approached. Keeping my distance was paramount. Every inch of me wanted to grab her and hold her, and I just didn't trust myself to not do something inappropriate. She had a pained look in her eyes, her face sad and tense, so different from the face I had kissed that morning.

"I'll miss you."

I looked over her shoulder, scanning—no one was near us—then looked as deeply into her eyes as I possibly could, metaphorically holding her. "I'll miss you, too."

I had to make myself turn and get into my truck. I backed out of the parking spot and drove slowly toward the exit, looking at her to my left as she walked alongside the building, looking at me. And then it hit me. I slammed on the brakes, the truck screeched to a stop, and I rolled down my window and called out to her just as naturally as any good friend would do.

"Jordan, do you have a ride home?"

She hesitated for a split second. "No. Do you mind?"

Everyone in the parking lot walking to their cars could hear us, and an odd sensation of giddy excitement hit me as if for a moment we were doing something *normal*, audaciously being ourselves in plain sight. I could hardly contain the broadening smile on my face as she hurried around the truck, opened the passenger-side door, and jumped in. I drove out of the parking lot and down the road, waiting until the church building was well out of sight before looking at her.

"I can only stay the afternoon. I have to work tomorrow."

"Okay," she said, nodding her head eagerly.

We spent the afternoon in bed, making love, over the moon happy at this gift—this extra time together. We were lounging in each other's arms when I suddenly remembered the chili.

"I never made chili for you."

"Sweet Shannon, you have your whole life to make chili for me."

Her words perfectly encapsulated the meaning of this beautiful week. It was much more than how it started—my fantasy week with the woman of my dreams. This was the beginning, a promise of all that was to come, and I was hopeful and happy. I could not be worried, afraid, or unsure anymore. No matter what the future held for us, I loved Jordan, and Jordan loved me.

CHAPTER FIFTEEN

My life quickly returned to its routine—church, work, and missing Jordan. Jordan occasionally attended services at my church, but another opportunity to meet intimately never materialized, and by August, I was missing her very badly. Her birthday was two weeks away, and I wondered if she had any plans with her family to celebrate. I decided to find out. Her birthday fell on a Thursday, and if she was free on that Saturday, I would ask her out on a date disguised as a friendly birthday dinner. With all the risky contact I'd avoided over the last couple of months, a friendly birthday dinner would not look too suspicious. After all, this type of occasion was exactly what I had been saving for; it made months of being so careful worth it. We deserved this.

Planning to call her after Sunday morning services, I was glad when I didn't have to, thrilled when I pulled into the parking lot at church and saw Shawn, Elena, and Jordan climbing out of their car. I parked in the next row over, jumped out of my truck, and hurried after them.

"Good morning," I greeted as I caught up to them outside the front entrance.

Jordan turned and looked at me, but she barely gave me a smile. "Good morning." She didn't look very happy to see me.

"Good morning," Shawn and Elena chimed in.

We all walked in together, and I followed them to their seats, sitting next to Jordan, smiling adoringly at her when she looked at me, her expression pained and a little sad. God, I hoped everything was okay.

After services, I made a beeline for the foyer as a group of parishioners made a beeline for Jordan. She was like that. People had to say hi to her. A few minutes later, she approached the foyer, her eyes darting around the main room before peering through the foyer doors, locking with mine. I smiled, then ducked outside and made my way to my truck, quickly glancing around at other parishioners as they made their way to their vehicles.

My heartbeat accelerated when Jordan appeared around the corner of the building and made her way toward me, looking so fabulous that several heads turned and followed her progress—too many heads. Taking a step back, not wanting to draw any attention, I arranged my expression into something that didn't announce how thrilled I was to see her. I attempted a casual smile, scanning the parking lot behind her as she walked up.

"I miss you, Shannon." She was speaking way too loudly, and I again scanned the area behind her, hoping nobody heard.

"I miss you, too, Jordan," I said, almost whispering, trying to counter her loudness. She seemed irritated with me, and I needed her to smile to reassure me everything was okay. Hopefully, my invitation would do the trick. "Do you have plans for your birthday next week?"

"No... I mean, yes. Elena is making dinner for me on Thursday, but no, nothing official, no party."

"Would you have dinner with me on Saturday night?"

"Yes! I would!"

Finally, she was smiling.

Increasingly more people were walking out into the parking lot, and I sighed in frustration, wishing we could talk a bit longer, wishing I could touch her. It was impossible to have a moment alone with her. "Great. I'll pick you up at six." I stood there, not wanting to move, not wanting to leave her orbit, not wanting to miss her anymore.

"Okay. Six o'clock. I'll wait for you outside."

I nodded at her and smiled, then turned and jumped in my truck, looking out the window at her as I turned on the ignition, the thrill of being near her still racing through my body, already feeling desperate to see her again. She smiled back, and I put the truck in gear and drove away.

* * *

On Saturday morning, I drove out to the mall and bought Jordan a birthday gift, returning home just in time to help Mom stuff envelopes. Stuffing envelopes was a very normal task on a Saturday at our house, filled with talk about any number of meetings, including the one coming up in the Bay Area, scheduled for September. Mom wanted to canvass the neighborhood near the church there, which meant she'd need several boxes of canvassing flyers. She asked if I wanted to help, and I agreed—just like always, nothing new, nothing suspicious, very routine. When we finished at three o'clock, Mom asked me if I wanted to join her and Dad for dinner. They had plans with another couple, and she wanted to know if I wanted to tag along. I often did and hoped declining to do so this time wouldn't set off any alarm bells.

"No thanks, Mom, but thanks anyway. You guys have a nice evening." I wasn't lying when I neglected to tell Mom about my birthday date with Jordan. It was a question unasked, and I left it at that, deciding it was better that my parents didn't know. The way I saw it, the less they knew about the number of times Jordan and I met, the more they'd think we didn't meet that often, so when we did openly meet, it wouldn't seem like it was that much. It seemed important in the whole scheme of things to manage people's perceptions of us. Out of sight, out of mind was the main tenet if this was going to work.

Mom and Dad were out the door by four-thirty. I showered, got dressed, and was out the door and on my way to Jordan's by five-thirty. When I drove up, she was standing on the front porch waiting for me as promised. She hurried down the porch steps and across the lawn, smiling as she opened the truck door and jumped inside.

"Hi," she said, her voice cracking, bringing a smile to my lips.

"Hi. Happy Birthday." I reached over and gave her hand a quick squeeze.

"Thank you." She blushed adorably, and I wanted to kiss her.

"You look beautiful, Jordan."

"Thank you, Shannon. You look beautiful, too."

Our eyes held a moment, and then she looked away, shy or uncertain, I wasn't sure. I put the truck in gear, made a U-turn, and headed out toward the *Sizzler* restaurant by the mall, and as I drove, Jordan filled me in on how much her home life had changed since Elena moved in. I only half listened. Being in the cab alone with her, able to smell her and hear her breathe, had me tempted to skip dinner and find a place for us to park. But it was too early; it was still light out, and I didn't want to reduce our visit to sex. It was her birthday, and I wanted to celebrate it with her, and that meant dinner first. I could ravish her in the cab of my truck later. The restaurant was busy, but we were lucky and got a booth next to a window. The waitress took our drink order, then left us to peruse our menus.

"So, it sounds like everything's good at home," I began, picking up from where she'd left off in the truck, trying to sound like an adult out on a date and not like a horny teenager. "Other than that, how are you doing?"

"Except for missing you, I'm okay. Good actually. I found a job."

"That's wonderful, Jordan. Congratulations. Where?"

She explained that she would be working in the receiving department for *UPS* in the city. "It's not much, but it's a start, and it's a good company. I start on Monday. I have six months' probation, and then, if nothing goes wrong, I'm permanent."

"Wow, Jordan, that's great. I'm so happy for you."

"I may be able to afford a car by next summer." She gave me a quick smile, then looked down at her hands. "And you... How have you been?"

The waitress walked up with our drinks and asked us if we were ready to order. We hadn't looked at the menu yet but did not want her to return, so we ordered the special.

"I'm doing okay. Work is good." I hesitated, then whispered, "I miss you, too."

I slid my foot forward and touched her ankle with my toe, causing her to gasp. She blinked, then practically glared at me. Not the reaction I was going for.

"Shannon, when I say I miss you, I mean it. I miss you. Deeply. It's brutal." Her easy-going manner from earlier was gone, replaced with a vulnerability I'd never seen before, her voice raw and desperate. "Why can't I see you more often? Why can't we do this more often? I don't understand, Shannon. I thought after what happened in May, we would see each other more."

"It's hard for me, too, Jordan, but I don't see another way to do this."

"There has to be another way!"

"Jordan, if we were found out…"

"There is such a thing as being too cautious, Shannon!"

"Jordan, try to understand…"

"I do understand!" Jordan's voice had gotten louder and louder, and a couple of diners glanced in our direction. She took a deep breath, leaned forward, and lowered her voice. "You are afraid that someone will become suspicious, that someone will find out about us. I get that, and you're right. If someone finds out about us, it would be catastrophic. But I have to see you. We need to figure out a way to be together." She leaned back in her seat and crossed her arms in front of her. She didn't even try to soften her message with a smile.

Jordan's directness and forcefulness surprised me, but she was right. I had been willing to keep her at a distance, willing to make do with a few visits here and there and maybe a nice birthday-dinner or a once-in-a-lifetime week together if we were very, very lucky. It was not enough for her. It was not enough for me either, but given our situation, it was all I could risk. Certainly, she could understand this.

"Then tell me! How do you suggest we do this!" I stomped my foot in frustration, and Jordan finally released a very small smile. Tears sprang into my eyes, and I blew out a trembling breath, relieved that she was smiling but scared to death I'd lose her if I couldn't figure this out. I squeezed my eyes shut, desperate for the answer, flinging them open when Jordan's hand took hold of mine. I stared at our hands, clasped together on top of the table in public for all to see, then looked up at her, surprised to find her expression sympathetic and contrite.

"Relax. I apologize for my outburst. I do understand, and I know you're trying. We'll figure this out. I love you."

"We'll figure this out, Jordan. I love you, too."

Our waitress approached with our plates, and Jordan quickly removed her hand from mine as we straightened in our seats. As soon as the waitress placed our plates in front of us, Jordan proceeded to overwhelm her with attention, thanking her for bringing two kinds of steak sauce and an extra portion of Tatar sauce, distracting her from any hand-holding she may have seen between us.

The waitress blushed as she explained that these were the preferred condiments, offering to bring Jordan anything to make her meal more enjoyable. They laughed together, and the waitress invited Jordan to please ask her personally if she needed anything else at all.

"Thank you," Jordan said, smiling charmingly.

The waitress turned and walked away with a noticeable spring in her step. Jordan directed her beautiful smile at me, and I had to smile back as I quirked my eyebrow at her, blushing a little myself. She started laughing.

"Is there anything you can't make blush?" I asked, glad for the sudden levity. "Really, Jordan, you could make a dog blush."

We teased and flirted as we dug into our *Sizzler* specials—steak and shrimp—slowly relaxing as we got reacquainted with one another. It was nice, and after the waitress cleared our table, I gave Jordan her birthday present.

"Wow, a present. I love presents." She took the little box and shook it next to her ear, jokingly looking up as if trying to guess what was in it. She looked at me and smiled. "Thank you. May I open it?"

"Yes, please, open it."

I watched with excitement as she removed the little bow and wrapping paper and opened the lid, her silent gasp confirming that I had chosen well. She stared at a beautiful pair of diamond earrings for several seconds before looking up at me, her eyes moist and full of emotion. "Oh, Shannon, you shouldn't have."

"I wanted to. I wanted to give you something nice for your birthday."

"Thank you, Shannon. These are beautiful."

I got up, stepped around to her side of the booth, and sat down next to her. I took the box from her and took one of the earrings out. "Here, let me help you put them in."

Jordan pulled her hair back away from her ear, displaying her very lovely neck, and my breath caught. I gathered myself and tried to concentrate on putting her earrings in without stabbing her. As I fastened the backs, I ran the tip of my finger along each lobe, letting her know how just the act of putting her earrings in affected me.

"Let me look." She turned to me, and I smiled. "Perfect."

"I would kiss you right now, but I can't," she murmured.

"Later," I whispered. Our eyes locked, and all I could think about was getting us out of there.

I tried to get the waitress's attention, which turned out to be impossible. I could never quite catch her eye even when she seemed to be looking in our direction. It was as if she couldn't see me. Jordan waved at her once, and she came skipping over.

"We'd like to pay, please," I said, and the waitress turned to me, almost surprised to find me sitting there.

I looked over at Jordan, my lips pressed together in a smirk. She started laughing.

* * *

We left the restaurant, exchanging suggestive glances as we walked through the parking lot and climbed into the truck, making it clear we couldn't wait to get our hands on each other. I had been on enough dates with guys to know that the optimal time for kissing and petting in the cab of a truck was after the sun went down. The obvious exception, as Jordan and I proved, was early morning before a universe of possible witnesses were awake and out and about. We were about to share another first kiss, and I couldn't wait.

We drove around a good ten minutes before I spotted a series of little shops already closed for the day. It was the perfect place to park. I hit the brakes, made a tire-squealing right turn into the parking lot, and drove around to the back, where a dark, deserted delivery area awaited. I turned off the ignition, and Jordan was on me before I let go of the keys, her hands all over me as she backed me up against the door, her lips smashing into mine in a desperate kiss, her breathing completely out of control. She pulled my right leg out from under the steering wheel and pinned it up against the back of the seat, then reached under my skirt and slid her hand up my thigh. Her fingers had just found their way under my panty crotch when the sound of an approaching vehicle froze her in place. We both turned and looked out the windshield as a car swung around the corner of the building and pulled up right in front of the truck, the glare of its headlights hitting us square in the face. Rotating lights on top of the car turned on, and a siren-bleep sounded and then went silent. It was the police.

"Oh, God," we both sputtered in disbelief.

Jordan grabbed my leg and pulled it back around, trying to help me get it back underneath the steering wheel. I quickly adjusted myself in my seat, pulling my skirt down and straightening my blouse. Jordan was frantically doing the same.

Through slightly fogged windows, I could see a police officer holding a flashlight approaching the truck. He shined his flashlight into the cab and made the roll-your-window-down motion with his hand. I smoothed my hair back, took a deep breath, and rolled down the window.

"Good evening, Ma'am. License and registration, please."

I reached into my glove box, pulled out my registration,

and grabbed my wallet out of my purse. I gave the officer my registration and pulled my license out of my wallet.

He examined both with his flashlight, handed them back to me, and then shined his flashlight at Jordan.

Her eyes darted guiltily back and forth between me and the police officer.

"Ma'am, have you been drinking this evening?" he asked, shining his flashlight at me.

I turned and looked at him. "Ah... No, sir."

"This is private property. I could cite you for trespassing and loitering."

He drew an impatient breath when I didn't respond.

"You can't be here doing whatever it is the two of you are doing."

When I still did not respond—because, let's face it, what was I going to say—he straightened and clicked his flashlight off. He looked over at his vehicle for a moment, then back at me as he leaned down and put his hands on his knees. "I'm going to let you off with a warning this time, but you need to find another place to do this. Don't come back here anymore, and be careful where you choose to park in the future." He touched the brim of his hat. "Have a nice evening, Ma'am."

He walked to his police car, got in, and drove away.

I started my engine and drove out the opposite way, barely holding it together as we sped toward Jordan's house, careening into the parking lot of the *Walmart* on the corner at the last second and coming to a screeching halt in the nearest parking spot.

I turned off the engine and sat there, gripping the steering wheel as I stared out the window, the police officer's voice bouncing around in my head. He knew what we were. He knew what we were doing. He let us go. This was what shocked me the most, and I let out a bark of laughter as I slapped my palm against my forehead. I took a couple of deep breaths and looked at Jordan.

"Are you okay?" I asked her.

She reached over and pulled me into a hug, her shoulders

tense, revealing how stressful the situation had been for her. "I am now, but that really scared me."

"Yeah, me too." I leaned back and looked at her. "We need to find a place to be together."

She smiled and nodded her head, and after a quick scan of the parking lot to make sure no one was near, she leaned in and kissed me.

As I drove her home, we came up with a couple of ideas on how we could see each other more often, all of them iffy and woefully inadequate, but better than nothing. Jordan looked hopeful, though, and that was enough. Then, as I pulled up in front of her house, I had to tell her that she couldn't wear her earrings in public, which I hated doing.

"People will think it strange that I gave you such a gift."

She deflated a bit, but quickly recovered, smiling even as she removed her earrings and put them back in the box.

I reached over and squeezed her hand. "Please be careful, Jordan. I love you."

"I love you. Thank you for dinner."

She jumped out of the truck and ran to the front door, giving me a wave before disappearing inside.

Over the next few weeks, I thought often about the incident with the police officer, my reaction running from fear and horror to relief that we hadn't been ticketed, or worse, charged with trespassing. And it wasn't just luck that saved us, it was bumping into a tolerant cop. I knew full well that the officer recognized what we were doing and could have charged us with indecent exposure. The thought of my parents having to bail me out of jail, not to mention them finding out the reason for my incarceration, had me rethinking my low-risk, minimal-contact approach to having a relationship with Jordan. While less public contact kept us out of the spotlight and reduced the risk of detection, it also led to pure, unadulterated desperation when we finally did have a chance to be together, which led to risky behavior and would eventually lead to discovery. I could not let that happen.

* * *

In early October, I attended a young woman's gathering in Placerville with Mom. She was running one of the workshops, and I was there to help her set up and generally give her support. It was a popular gathering, and I had heard a lot about it but had always avoided it, partly because I was just too busy but also because I secretly associated it with gatherings for old maids. But now that it looked like I might be headed in that direction, when Mom asked if I could help her out, I agreed, thinking it would be a good idea to check it out and see what all the hoopla was about. The seminars were surprisingly informative and fun.

During one of the breaks, after helping Mom set up for her next group, I browsed the room mingling and discovered a small group of women trading recipes. I joined them, hoping to add something new to my cooking binder, and overheard a very intriguing conversation coming from behind me.

"Did you get your car fixed yet?" one woman asked.

"No, not yet. Pat has been driving me to work," a second woman answered.

"Which means I have to get up at six o'clock, an hour earlier than I'm used to," a third woman complained, presumably Pat.

"Oh stop. I pay for the gas, and you get to park your car in the garage," the second woman said, obviously teasing.

My head was buzzing. I could not fit the tone of the conversation with its content and connect it to the years of hearing such conversations and knowing where they belonged and who took part in them. I slowly turned and saw two women in a group of other women talking about their homelife together. I watched them the rest of the day. They seemed normal enough; they didn't sit together, they didn't work any of the exercises together, but they lived together, or so it seemed.

I asked Mary, the host, who they were, and she told me

that their names were Marion and Pat, that they were older, in their early thirties, and that they lived together and went to church in the area. She explained how Marion had tirelessly cared for her ailing parents over the last ten years and how they had suddenly passed away last year within a month of each other. Mary gushed over Pat, explaining how nice it was that she had moved in with Marion to help her with the house.

"It's so big and way out there on the edge of town. I don't know how Marion would have managed without Pat," Mary explained.

I was electrified. This opened up a whole new way of thinking about me and Jordan's problem. There were women in the church who lived together. Jordan and I could live together—get an apartment together. Okay, I wasn't as old as Marion and Pat, but I was old enough. My brother, a year older than me, and my sister, a year younger, were both married with children, living their own lives. I wanted to live mine and began for the first time to question why it was considered so wrong for adult singles to live out on their own. Didn't unmarried people deserve a life? Would it really be so dramatic and unusual if I moved out of my parent's house at my age?

It was all I thought about for the next two weeks, and slowly a plan began to take form. I looked in the rental section of the newspaper every Sunday and noted the apartment complexes in my area, apartment availability, and cost. All of them wanted a security deposit and first and last month's rent upfront. Rent ran from two-fifty a month to five-fifty, depending on how many bedrooms and bathrooms and in which area of town the apartment complex was located. At one point, I realized that we would need two bedrooms. It would be impossible to explain a one-bedroom apartment.

I began driving by apartment complexes, checking out the area, occasionally stopping by the manager's office to pick up a brochure. My main concern was the distance to Jordan's work. She didn't have a car yet, and Shawn was taking her to work every morning and picking her up in the afternoon after her shift. I was prepared to do the same, but without knowing how she felt about moving out, there was really not much more I could do. My next step was to talk to her about it.

I'd been able to see her more often since her birthday. Shawn and Elena were coming to my church more regularly, and whenever Jordan or I knew we had plans to be at some gathering or occasion, we would tell the other one ahead of time so that we could both be there together if possible. We already had plans to meet the following Sunday at the church in Modesto for morning services, so I decided to condense all the research I'd done on the subject of apartments into a one-page report and present it to her after services at potluck.

* * *

I rose early Sunday morning, hyper-excited and full of energy, eager to see Jordan. I barely noticed the hour-and-a-half drive to Modesto, my mind preoccupied with the details of my plan and how I could most persuasively present them. I arrived twenty minutes early and was tempted to sit in my truck and wait for her, but I knew it was better to wait until potluck. The loud buzz of hundreds of people visiting and conversing together while stuffing their faces was the perfect cover for having a conversation about our future. Okay, it wasn't the ideal venue, but where else could we have such a conversation without anyone noticing? Certainly not in the cab of my truck. And who knew when we would get to see each other again?

I went inside to find a seat, and as a visitor, was greeted warmly by members, many asking if I would like to sit with them for services. I declined, thanking them, and sat in a pew near the back on the outside aisle, careful to leave a little room on either side of me, but not too much so that it looked like I was saving a place for somebody, but enough so that I could casually scoot over when Jordan casually asked to sit next to me.

The building filled quickly, and soon there were hardly

any empty seats left and still no sign of Jordan. The empty space next to me was looking bigger and more available by the minute, and sure enough, someone looking for a seat tapped me on the shoulder. I looked up and saw a tall young man looking down at me. Poop!

"Good morning," he said. "May I sit with you?"

I didn't know what to say, but I definitely couldn't say, *No, I'm saving this seat for my girlfriend,* and the seats were filling up fast, so I moved over, and he sat down. The church doors opened again, and I looked back to see if it was Jordan.

"...Samuel, and yours?" the guy sitting next to me asked.

I turned and looked at him. "Shannon. Nice to meet you."

"From which congregation are you?" Samuel asked.

We began a conversation of short questions and answers, and then services started. During the first hymn, Jordan walked in and sat on the opposite side of the building in a pew in the back where there were still a few seats left to squish into. I made eye contact with her. She wasn't smiling.

As the singing part of the services ended and the sermon part was about to begin, Samuel stood and went up to the pulpit. He was the preacher this morning, and I was instantly irritated with him and the empty seat he left behind—the seat Jordan should be sitting in.

I was way too preoccupied with Jordan to listen to the sermon and was surprised when it was over and Samuel sat back down next to me. Communion took longer than usual because of the large attendance, giving me half an hour longer to worry about the fact that Jordan wasn't smiling. She was upset about something.

After services, I had to fight my way out of the pew as a crowd gathered around Samuel. I headed toward the entrance, trying to reach Jordan, but she kept moving away from me, and she would not make eye contact. One person I did make eye contact with was Samuel, who seemed to have escaped his group of admirers and was following me. And that was how I spent the next ten minutes, chasing Jordan while Samuel chased me.

I lost Jordan in the crowd as I bottlenecked in the foyer, greeting and shaking hands with everybody, not wanting to be rude. By the time I got to the front lawn, Jordan was nowhere to be found, and when lunch was announced, I went back inside to hang out by the buffet tables, thinking that she would sooner or later show up there for a bite to eat. As the buffet crowd thinned out, I got in line, filled my plate with noodle salad, and found an empty seat up front on the pulpit steps, giving me a good view of the entire room.

"Hi," a voice came from my left, and I looked up to find Samuel standing there. "May I?" he asked.

"Oh, sure." I hesitated, then scooched over to make room for him, glancing at the buffet table for any sign of Jordan.

Samuel talked about his sermon, and I kept my mouth shut and listened. I'd heard none of his sermon and wouldn't even know how to start to have a conversation with him about it. I barely ate, and when his plate was empty, I excused myself, walking down the center aisle, scanning the room for any sign of Jordan in case she'd walked in during Samuel's accosted moment with me. The room was packed with people talking, laughing, and eating, and young kids running all over the place, making a racket. But no sign of Jordan, and I hoped she hadn't already left. I threw my plate in the trash and headed outside.

Even though the front lawn was crammed full of young people, I spotted Jordan almost immediately. She was staked out in the far righthand corner near the parking lot, seemingly hiding. There was no other way to describe it. She was ensconced with three cackling young women, peeking at me from between their animated conversation. When I started toward her, she bolted through the parking lot away from me. Panic hit me—she was definitely running away from me—and I hurried after her, grabbing her by the arm in the last row of cars.

"Hey! Jordan!"

She turned, and the look she gave me, startled me.

"What's wrong? Why are you avoiding me?"

"Is that your new boyfriend?" She asked, pointedly removing her arm from my hand.

"What?"

"The guy you were sitting with. Is he your boyfriend?"

"No! Of course not!"

"Shannon, do you know who that is?"

"I just met him. His name is Samuel."

"He's a very well-known preacher from Alabama."

"So what... I don't care who he is. Why are you acting this way?"

"He's one of those ultra-conservative guys. Why are you sitting with him?"

"I am not sitting with him. He keeps sitting with me."

Jordan dropped her head to her chest, took a deep breath, then looked back up at me. "You don't know him? You didn't plan to meet him here?"

"No! Jordan, please. I do not know the man. *He* sat with *me*. There were hardly any seats left." My hand trembled as I reached out and touched her arm. "Please, Jordan. I'm here to meet you. I swear, I gave him no reason to sit with me."

"Shannon, the reason he sat with you is because you are beautiful, everyone knows your dad, and you're the ultimate good girl. Men are going to sit with you."

"You know how I feel about you, Jordan. I don't want them, I want you." I was on the verge of tears, desperate to make her understand that there was no one but her.

Jordan quickly glanced behind me, then took a deep breath. "Okay, okay. Don't cry. I'm sorry. I was jealous. I felt sick seeing you sitting with him."

"Jordan, you have nothing to be jealous about. I love you."

"I know, and I love you. I'm sorry."

She gave me a small smile, and my heart did a summersault in my chest. I wanted to hold her and erase any doubt she had about the way I felt about her. I closed my eyes for a moment, wishing we could hold each other whenever we wanted to, letting out a small gasp when I suddenly remembered my plan. If I could convince Jordan to move in with me, we could hold each other every day.

"I have something for you," I said, pulling my purse forward to retrieve my report.

"Another present? For me? You shouldn't have," she said, wincing a little at her attempt to lighten things up.

"A present for us… I hope." I gave her my report, and as she read it, I explained my plan. "The only thing I really worry about is getting you to work and back. But other than that, I mean, it's possible, right? We could do this?"

Jordan looked up at me, then pointed at the row of cars to her left. "I have a car."

My eyes followed to where she was pointing as my mind tried to process what she'd just said. I just assumed she'd ridden over with someone. She led me along the row of cars, stopped in front of a green Chevy sedan with a faded black top, and nodded at it.

"It's used and hideous, but it's mine. It's the reason I was late this morning. Shawn had to help me get it started. It still needs a few minor repairs."

I stared at Jordan's car for a moment—the final hurdle to my plan suddenly eliminated—then recounted what happened at the young woman's gathering. "Other women live together, and no one thinks anything of it. It's really not that unusual. We could be together by the end of the year. We can do this, Jordan."

She stood there in silent contemplation through my entire pitch and continued to do so even after I'd finished. I waited, racking my brain for anything I could say that would convince her to do this with me, ready to repeat my entire presentation if need be.

"Yeah. Okay," she finally said, slowly nodding her head.

"Okay?" I could hardly believe it! "Okay! Good!"

I would have jumped for joy, but we were surrounded by Christians. I hadn't really thought about what I would've done had she said no, and now I was a little surprised she'd said yes. It had taken me weeks to wrap my head around the idea of moving out, and she was ready to move out after a ten-minute conversation about it.

As we made our way through the crowd, headed for the buffet tables—Jordan hadn't eaten lunch either—I spotted Samuel standing in a crowd of young people. Our eyes locked, and I immediately looked away, wondering if he saw us in the parking lot. The thought quickly faded, though, my mind too busy to think about anything but Jordan and our plan.

* * *

Thanksgiving that year was a small affair at our house—just family. After my brother and sister and their spouses and kids were packed in their cars and on their way home, I helped Mom in the kitchen, putting leftovers away and drying dishes, wondering how best to introduce the topic of moving out. I had to speak. I had to say something. I had to start the conversation.

"Mom?"

"Yeah, honey."

"I've decided to move out. Get my own place." I was obviously past the mincing of words.

Mom abruptly stopped washing dishes and turned to me, her left hand landing on her hip. "Really? And when were you thinking about doing this?"

"In the next month or so."

She turned and resumed washing dishes, slowly shaking her head. "I don't know, Shannon. I hate thinking about you out there in the world all alone."

"I'm thinking about getting an apartment with Jordan."

Mom stopped washing dishes and turned to me, her left hand back on her hip. "Really? Do you think Jordan could do that? Do you think she wants to?"

"I don't know. I can ask," I lied.

Mom turned back to the sink and resumed washing dishes. "Well, that would be better. And when would you ask her?"

"I'll talk to her about it this Sunday at church," I lied

again.

"Well, let me know what she says. I hate to think of you out there in the world all alone," she repeated.

After we finished the dishes, Mom headed down the hallway toward the bedroom with two cups of hot tea while I went to my bedroom and started freaking out. My conversation with Mom had gone surprisingly well—too well—and I feared there had been some misunderstanding. I sat on my bed expecting Mom to come storming out of her bedroom any minute when she realized what she'd agreed to. But she didn't, and I began to relax, allowing myself to feel pride for my courage and my small but important victory, the first step in my quest to be with Jordan.

* * *

By December, I was ready to go. I had enough money in my savings account to cover move-in costs on almost any non-luxury, two-bedroom apartment in the Sacramento area. I'd been nothing if not frugal the last few years and had amassed a modest fortune. Money was not the problem. It was Jordan. She'd promised to let me know as soon as she spoke to Shawn, but I hadn't heard from her and hadn't seen her since before Thanksgiving. And then she called me on my birthday.

"I've been meaning to call you…about Bible study next week. I'm a little behind on the reading part," she said after she wished me happy birthday. "I didn't realize I needed to…have everything completed so soon."

We didn't have a group Bible study together, her being from a different congregation than I was, and I knew immediately that she was not alone and speaking in code, telling me that she had not yet talked to Shawn about moving out.

"I was hoping by the end of the year at the latest," I said.

"I need a little more time. It's been difficult to find the right moment to…sit down and finish the assignments."

I didn't know what to say. I didn't want to pressure her.

She sounded almost uncomfortable, giving me the impression she was trying to end the conversation, so I said goodbye and let her go.

By Christmas, I had given up all hope that she would ever talk to Shawn. In fact, I began to suspect she had changed her mind. Gone was her self-assured confidence from a couple of months ago, replaced with tepid acknowledgment at best of what we had agreed on—living together by the end of the year—making me question whether we had ever agreed at all.

Maybe she was just nervous, and I could understand why. She was a long way from home, living with her brother and his new wife, and the only reason her parents allowed her to move up here was because her brother promised to look after her. It was hard to tell how Shawn would react to his little sister moving out. He took his brotherly responsibilities very seriously. But still, I had not anticipated that it would take this long for her to get her courage up. I just assumed our desire to be together would overcome any nervousness she felt about telling her brother. Apparently not. I began to think it would take an act of God to get her to move into an apartment with me, and at this point, I would take any help I could get, including His.

CHAPTER SIXTEEN

On a glorious Saturday morning in early January, as I bustled around town running errands—dropping Mom off at Karen's for Bible study and picking up Dad's dry cleaning—an apartment complex I'd never seen before caught my eye, and on a whim, I pulled up in front of the office and went inside.

I was flipping through a brochure when the manager walked in.

"Hi. How can I help you?"

"Hi. I'm out apartment shopping and saw your vacancy sign. These look nice."

"What exactly are you looking for?"

"A two-bedroom, one bath."

"I've got four available. Let me show you. There's an empty one just around the corner, and the others are basically the same."

He walked right back out the door he'd come in through and disappeared down the corridor. I had no choice but to follow, and a minute later, found myself standing in the living room of a very cute little apartment.

"Do you have any vacant two-bedroom apartments on the second floor?" I asked.

"Except for this one, they're all on the second floor. I'll show you," he said, already walking out the door.

I hurried alongside him as he hustled through the complex, pointing out one apartment and then another, circling back toward the office before pointing out the third one. I stopped and looked at it, knowing it was special, hoping I was right. It was a corner apartment, the front facing the parking lot, the side facing a courtyard.

"Can I see that one?"

We took the stairs to the second floor and walked the open hallway to the apartment door. He unlocked it and stepped aside, letting me enter first. I smiled when I saw two big windows in the living room, one on each of the corner walls, exactly as I had envisioned. The living room was full of light, much brighter than in the other apartment, which only had one living room window. The kitchen was to the left and had a refrigerator, stove, dishwasher, cabinets, and a small window facing the front of the apartment. A tiny dining room nook sat just off the kitchen, and in the back corner of the living room was the entrance to a hallway leading to the bedrooms and bath.

The hair stood up on the back of my neck—not easy, given the length of my hair. I had a very good feeling about this place. I walked down the hallway and checked the bedrooms. The smaller one was on the right, and the bigger one was at the end of the hall, both with a built-in closet and a window facing the courtyard. The bathroom was on the left and surprisingly big, with a combination bath and shower. There was a small hallway supply closet for towels and sheets and three hallway lights along the ceiling. I switched the lights on and off, then turned to the manager.

"I'll take it." My heart was beating like a jackhammer.

"Great!" he said. "Let's go down to the office and do the paperwork."

I signed a six-month rental agreement, wrote him a check for twelve hundred dollars, gave him Jordan's name, and told him she would be rooming with me beginning in February. He gave me a copy of the rental agreement, my apartment key and a spare, and pointed out my parking space as he walked me to my truck.

"You can start moving in today," he said. "Congratulations."

I drove out of the parking lot feeling like a person I hardly knew but really liked. A person who had just taken a monumental leap of faith without any safety net. I had no idea if Jordan was even interested in moving in with me anymore. I had no idea if I would ever get to be with her in any meaningful way for that matter. But I had to at least make it a possibility, and that meant showing her that the possibility was real. There was a place for us—a real place—if she wanted it. I couldn't wait for an act of God. I needed to know where she stood. Now. She was either going to move in with me or tell me to my face that she had changed her mind.

* * *

The next morning, when Jordan showed up at my church for Sunday morning services—her unexpected appearance more star-alignment than act-of-God, as it just so happened I had spent half the previous night devising a plan to confront her—I was encouraged. I waited for her in the foyer after services.

"Hi, how are you?" I greeted her, thrilled to see her again as she walked up and stood next to me.

"I'm fine. How are you?" Jordan smiled, but her eyes seemed incapable of making contact with mine. She looked uncomfortable, her expression vulnerable, as if pleading with me not to give up on her. I had no intention of doing that.

"Hi, Jordan."

I heard him before I saw him, his hand appearing on Jordan's arm as he stepped up next to her.

Jordan rolled her eyes, then turned to the young man, giving him a subdued smile.

"Hi, Rodger. How are you doing?" Jordan threw me a quick nod, letting me know to wait outside for her, then turned her attention back to Rodger.

I walked around to the side of the building, pulling my coat tighter around me as I looked out over the parking area. There was a light drizzle and it was windy, and I considered sitting inside my truck to wait for Jordan but decided against it. It would look conspicuous. I walked a little further down the walkway, putting a little more distance between me and the people pouring into the parking lot, but not too much distance so that it looked like I was standing out here all by myself, hiding something.

A couple of women came around the corner of the building, but not Jordan. What was taking her so long? My impatience had everything to do with the appearance of Rodger and his hand on Jordan's arm. I was more than a little jealous when it came to guys giving Jordan attention. They were my rivals, and I hated thinking that one of them would have her someday. I let out a slow breath and pushed the thought away. Far away.

Another young woman caught my eye as she came around the corner and hurried into the parking lot, shooting glances behind her as she power-walked to her car. She looked like she was running from something, and then I saw who she was running from. Samuel. I was relieved to see he had found someone else to chase, but then felt sorry for the girl he was chasing and hoped she could…get away? She did. She made it to her car, jumped in, revved the engine, and tore out of there, leaving him standing there looking…angry? Yes, he looked a little peeved as he watched her drive away, and I was somehow glad. I had avoided my share of unwanted attention, escaping boys I didn't like, my reasons for not liking them much different than for most girls, but still, it felt good to watch her win. And then Samuel turned and looked at me. Poop!

Jordan came around the corner at that very moment, a smile exploding across her face when she saw me. Her timing could not have been worse. I ducked my head and quickly shook it twice, and she hesitated, her smile slowly disappearing. I motioned her toward the end of the walkway with a tilt of my head as I casually walked away from her, stopping and turning when I heard her walk up behind me, my breath catching a little at how very beautiful she was. I took a moment to just look at her. It never ceased to amaze me how my feelings for her continued to grow, and I suddenly felt even more brave, more in love, and more convinced that we were doing the right thing. My gaze followed hers as she looked over her shoulder. Samuel was gone, thank God, and no one else seemed poised to interrupt us. My heart beat hard and fast as I considered what I was about to do.

"Sorry that took so long," she said, taking a deep breath.
"Don't worry about it."
"I miss you."
"I miss you, too," I returned, smiling at her as I took a quick breath. "I have something for you." I pulled a box with a ribbon on it out of my coat pocket and gave it to her.

"A present? For me? I love presents." She put the box up to her ear and shook it, and this time looked mildly surprised when she heard something move inside. "What is it?"

"Open it."

She glanced behind her, then quickly removed the ribbon, looking up at me for a moment and smiling before opening the box. Her smile wavered as she stared at the box's contents—her key to our apartment. Underneath the key was a slip of paper, which she pulled out and read, her expression serious. And that was exactly what I wanted. I knew she was nervous about this, but I needed her to get serious.

"This is your key to our apartment. That's the address. You are welcome to join me there whenever you wish. I will start moving in tomorrow." I looked over her shoulder to make sure no one was watching, then reached out and touched her hand. "I love you, Jordan."

I gave her a hopeful smile, letting my hand linger a moment longer, then turned and hurried to my truck, not wanting to pressure her further or hear that she had changed her mind.

* * *

I drove to my parents' house to tell them the news. Mom wanted to help me decorate. She had lots of extra dishes and pots and pans, and she insisted we clean the place from top to bottom before I moved one piece of furniture into it. I was happy she was so excited, but I didn't want her so involved that she felt comfortable stopping by unannounced.

"Thanks, Mom. I definitely want the pots and pans and dishes, but you have to let me do this alone. I will clean the apartment and decorate it, and if I need help moving or with anything else, I'll let you know."

She looked at me, blinking, her mouth opening and closing, obviously not knowing what to say.

I gave her an apologetic smile, hoping I wasn't being too rough on her.

Dad walked up and put his arm around her shoulders. "Honey, she'll be fine." He looked at me and winked. "You are always welcome back, sweetheart." Dad kissed me on the forehead, and then they both hugged me. There was an element of guilt attached to the moment—they were completely unaware of all that this move signified—but still, it meant a lot to me to have their approval and support.

I gave them my new address and told them I would give them my phone number as soon as I got the phone hooked up. Then I went straight to my bedroom and started packing.

* * *

The next morning, I made a couple of phone calls. First, I called into work and took the week off. Then I called the phone company and secured the next available appointment for a technician to come by and hook up my phone—Thursday afternoon between noon and four. I borrowed as many cleaning supplies from Mom as she could spare, including the vacuum cleaner, then drove over to the apartment and spent the rest of the day cleaning.

I slept at my parents' house one last time, and early the next morning, started loading my stuff into my truck. It took me two trips to get everything over to the apartment. That evening, my brother, Simon, and my brother-in-law, Doug, helped me dismantle and transport my bedroom furniture, including reassembling my bed in the big bedroom at the end of the hallway. That night, as I sat on my bed, I made two lists: one of everything I needed to buy immediately, and one of everything I wanted to buy with Jordan. We definitely needed a couch and TV; I would buy that with her. And we definitely needed a coffee machine; I would buy that tomorrow.

On Wednesday morning, I walked into the living room and smiled. The room was lit up with sunlight coming in through the windows. I sat down on the floor with my back against the wall and looked at the empty room. It was beautiful, and I could see us in here sitting on the couch, watching television together and eating pizza. This was our place, and it was perfect. I just had to get Jordan to move in with me. I let out a deep sigh, stood up, got dressed, and went out to buy a coffee machine. I ended up spending half the day shopping—we also needed our own vacuum cleaner and some basic groceries. I spent the rest of the day in the apartment arranging what little furniture we had and adding small touches to make it homely. We didn't have much, but what we did have, I wanted to look nice for Jordan.

On Thursday, my phone was turned on, and that evening, the first call I made was to my parents, reassuring them I'd settled in just fine. They told me they missed me and that they were proud of me. "We love you very much, Shannon," they said, and I almost started crying.

The next call I made was to Jordan. Shawn answered the phone. "I thought she was with you."

My heart flipped in my chest, and I let out a surprised "Oh!" followed by an awkward "Right..." ending with the clearing of my throat as I tried to act like I'd been expecting Jordan any minute and was only calling because she was late. "Ah... She's not here yet. When did she leave?"

"About thirty minutes ago. I hope she didn't break down. That car of hers...it's a disaster waiting to happen," Shawn groaned. "Have her call me when she gets there, and Shannon, you take care of her, okay? And be careful. And make sure she calls from time to time. She's horrible about calling. And don't let her stay up too late. She loves watching TV, and she needs her sleep."

"Shawn, don't worry," I jumped in. "She'll be fine."

He reminded me to have Jordan call him as soon as she arrived, and then we hung up.

I let out a squeal of delight. "Yes! She did it! She's

coming!" I could hardly believe it. I took a deep breath as I looked around the room. Everything looked perfect. A bit empty, but perfect. I did a quick walk-through, then nervously paced until a click at the door stopped me in place.

The door slowly swung open, and I was barely able to contain my excitement at the sight of Jordan standing in the doorway—suitcase in hand, overnight bag and purse hooked over her shoulder, and a small bouquet of flowers tucked under her arm.

"Hi."

My heart rate accelerated NASCAR-style. "Hi." I put my hand on my chest and just stared at her.

She stepped over the threshold and closed the door, dropping her suitcase, shoulder bag, and purse at her feet before bringing the flowers to me with arm outstretched.

I smiled and let out a nervous laugh as I took them from her. "Thank you, Jordan. They're beautiful."

"You're beautiful," she replied.

She stepped closer and leaned in, obviously intending to kiss me, and I almost let her. "Wait! You have to call Shawn and tell him you're here."

I turned to the phone, picked up the receiver, and handed it to her.

A look of wonder spread across her face. "We have a phone."

"We have a phone." My eyes instantly filled with tears, and Jordan's did too. Over a phone no less.

Jordan called her brother, then basically stood there the next couple of minutes, listening, punctuating his conversation with the occasional, "Yeah" or "Okay."

She eventually turned to me and rolled her eyes. I smiled, marveling at the fact that she was standing in *our* apartment using *our* phone. As their conversation neared its end, I began straightening my skirt and arranging my hair, catching myself before I went into full primping mode. I blew out a quick breath and willed myself to relax, impatient for her to hang up.

"Yeah, okay, I love you, too. Okay, bye." Jordan hung up the phone and turned to me, shaking her head. "Wow, that was interesting."

"What did he say?"

"What didn't he say? My goodness, he got so emotional."

"When did you tell them? How did that go?"

"I told them last night after work. Shawn didn't say anything, and Elena practically helped me pack. She was so excited for me. And then tonight, the same. Shawn was quiet, and Elena carried my bags to the car. It was like she wanted me to go."

"Jordan, it's not that she wanted you to go. She wanted to be alone with Shawn. They are a newlywed couple. You know how thin the walls are in that house. I could hear you from the bedroom no matter where you were in the house." Jordan looked at me, confused. "Think about it," I said. "You can be very loud. Anyone in the house would be able to hear you."

"I'm not sure I know what you're talking about."

"Sex, Jordan. And if you don't know what I'm talking about, that means they are not having a lot of sex, and when they do, they're either doing it when you're not there, or they are being extremely quiet about it."

"You think so?"

"I'm sure of it. Elena doesn't want to get rid of you; she just wants to...well, get rid of you so she can be with Shawn."

"Yeah, I think you're right."

"And I think Shawn is a bit torn. He wants to be with Elena, of course, but he also wants to take care of you."

"Well, that would explain the phone call. I thought he was going to cry." She then added, "I'm not loud. You're the one who's loud."

"Really? I'm loud?" I said, teasing.

"Yeah, you are," she said, smiling, stepping toward me.

I reached out and touched her arm, reassuring myself that she was really there standing in front of me in our new apartment. I took a deep breath, then took her by the hand.

"Let me show you around." I told her about my plan to furnish the living room. I showed her the kitchen, the small bedroom, and the bath.

The door to the larger bedroom was open, and she walked in ahead of me. She stood in the center of the room and slowly turned in a circle, looking at everything.

"It's nice, right?" I offered.

"Yeah, I like it."

We looked at each other for a moment, and then Jordan began undressing. I did the same. She climbed into bed from her side, I from mine, and we met in the middle, wonderfully naked, lying on our sides, propped up on our elbows, staring into each other's eyes.

My face was the first thing she touched, and then my hair. She ran her hand down my arm and over my hip, making her way along my thigh and then back up, her fingers gliding lightly over my stomach to my breasts. She leaned in to take my breast into her mouth, and I hooked my finger under her chin, lifting her face to meet mine. I kissed her soft and sweet, wanting to take my time. But our kiss turned hot in a matter of seconds. Our bodies merged, and nothing else existed except her touch on my skin, the beat of her heart, and her love for me. I wrapped my arms around her shoulders, and she held me closer, our breasts pushing together, our thighs intertwined, our hips rocking and grinding, trying to touch deeper as we moved together.

My orgasm slowly enveloped me, lingering on the precipice before barreling down on top of me, making me cry out. Jordan came a moment later, using all of me, her breasts pressing into mine, her arms pulling me closer, her rolling hips riding my thigh, her body shuddering.

"I love you," she breathed as she slowly caught her breath.

"I love you, Jordan," I returned, holding her tighter, never wanting to let her go.

* * *

The next morning, I woke with a start, the bed shaking with

Jordan literally jumping out of it. I caught a flash of her naked butt as she hurried out of the bedroom.

"I'm late," she called out as she ran down the hallway.

I sat up as she returned to the bedroom with her suitcase and overnight bag. She threw the suitcase on the bed and opened it. After looking through its contents, she snatched out a skirt and blouse, grabbed her overnight bag, and headed for the bathroom.

I got up, walked into the hallway, and leaned up against the wall, watching her dress, her toothbrush hanging out of her mouth as she buttoned up her blouse. She smiled at me, and I smiled back, shaking my head in disbelief, feeling like I was in a dream.

She hurried to the front door, shouldering her purse as she turned to me, grabbing me around the waist with one arm as she quickly looked down at my still-naked breasts. I let out a small gasp when she pulled me closer and gave a soft moan when she covered my mouth with hers. And then she said something I never believed I would ever hear her say.

"Is there anything I can pick up at the store after work on my way home?"

"No. Just you...just bring you."

"Okay. I love you. God, I can hardly wait to see you tonight."

* * *

When we weren't at work or in church, we were at home in bed making love. We could not get enough of each other, and every time was like the first time—the most special, somehow even more special than the time before. Every night when Jordan walked in the door, it was like a miracle, I just couldn't believe she was mine. I could barely get us through dinner before I would drag her to bed, pulling her clothes from her body, unable to keep my hands off her. I don't think we slept eight hours that first week.

We bought a television and a small TV cabinet in February to celebrate Jordan's new permanent status at work, and in March we bought a couch and a small coffee table. By April, we had made love in every room at least twice and on the living room floor more times than I could count. Jordan said she loved the way my skin glowed in the morning sun. We spent every free moment together in that apartment, just me and her, in our own little world, free to do whatever we wanted with no interruptions.

On a Thursday evening in late April, as Jordan and I cuddled together on the couch watching TV, Mom called and asked if she could stop by on Saturday afternoon. She hadn't seen the apartment yet and wanted to bring a care package over as a housewarming gift. I'd known this was coming but had done nothing to prepare for it and stood there trying to think of how to answer.

"Shannon, are you still there?"

"Yeah, Mom, I'm still here..." I let out a quick breath, realizing there was only one answer. "Yes, of course you can come. What time?"

"About four o'clock. I have to drop a box of leaflets off at Karen's, and I thought I could swing by after. Is that okay?"

"Perfect, Mom. See you on Saturday." I hung up the phone and turned to Jordan. "We have to go shopping! Now!"

I thanked God all the way to the furniture store that Mom had given us a courtesy call and hadn't just dropped by. We bought a twin bed and a small dresser, then stopped at a nearby *Walmart* and bought a pillow and sheets. We unloaded the truck and carried everything up to the apartment, and on Friday after work, we assembled the bed in Jordan's room and filled the dresser with Jordan's clothes. We made the bed, then threw in a couple of knickknacks, adding a picture of Jordan's mom and dad to give it that personal touch. Slowly, it began to resemble a real bedroom.

We then began looking for anything else in the apartment that could seem suspicious. Everything seemed suspicious to me, so I began separating all of Jordan's things from mine. I started in the bathroom, separating our shampoo, makeup, towels, and dirty laundry. In the living room, I separated books, papers, coats, and shoes. I checked my bedroom for any sign of Jordan. It took hours, and even after we'd gone to bed, I lay awake worried, uncertain we'd caught everything.

The next morning, after breakfast, we started cleaning. By three o'clock, we were ready. By four-thirty, Mom still had not yet arrived, and by five, I was getting worried. Just as I picked up the phone to call her, the doorbell rang. I opened the door, and there she stood with two bags of groceries in one hand and a casserole dish of lasagna in the other, right in the middle of a monologue.

"...then I would know how many boxes and which ones to bring. Oh! Hi, honey, I'm sorry I'm late. I brought the wrong leaflets to Karen and had to drive all the way back to the house to get the right ones. It took me another fifteen minutes to find them. Your dad has all my boxes stacked in the garage. I don't understand what he's thinking sometimes."

"Hi, Mom. Come in."

She walked into the small foyer and quickly scanned the living room before turning to the kitchen, where Jordan stood waiting. "Jordan, hi. Here, put this in the freezer, these in the refrigerator, and the rest in the pantry." She handed everything to Jordan, then grabbed me and gave me a great big hug. As she pulled away, still holding me by the arms, she smiled apologetically. "I love you. I have to go. I'm so late. We'll do this again. I promise." She headed for the door, giving me a quick wave as she scurried down the outside walkway to the stairs, calling out to me that she loved me and that she would call me later. I closed the door and turned to Jordan just as she closed the refrigerator.

"Okay... Good. I think our first visit went well."

Jordan smiled as she walked over to me. She slipped her hands around my waist and pulled me into her as she leaned in and ran her lips along my neck. The panic and stress of the last forty-eight hours instantly drained away.

LEAP OF FAITH

"Let's break in the new bed," she whispered in my ear, and then she took me by the hand and led me down the hallway to our newly furnished spare bedroom.

CHAPTER SEVENTEEN

Two weeks later, Jordan and I were sitting on the couch together, kissing, holding hands, and murmuring sweet things to each other. We were celebrating our two-year anniversary and were happily satisfied and full to the brim after eating an entire large delivery pizza. We were about to retire for the night when the doorbell rang.

We both scrambled to our feet and stared at the door. Jordan looked at me, I gave her a tentative nod, and she tiptoed to the door and looked through the peephole. She turned and grimaced, mouthing the names *"Shawn and Elena."* Exchanging hurried hand signals and hissed whispered instructions—*Pick up your skirt and blouse... put them in your bedroom... make your bed and check if I left anything in there*—we frantically dashed around the apartment, putting things in order until the doorbell rang again. While Jordan opened the front door, I slipped into the bathroom to gather myself, trying to calm my wildly beating heart. I took a deep breath and, as casually as I could, headed down the hallway to join Jordan as she welcomed our guests.

Elena held two bags of groceries while Shawn carried a square Tupperware container full of fried chicken.

"Hi. Sorry we didn't call first," Shawn said.

"Hey. No problem. Come in," Jordan invited.

"Hi, you two," I greeted as I entered the living room.

I took the container of chicken from Shawn and followed Elena into the kitchen, where she began unpacking the bags of groceries, holding up each item one by one and explaining what it was and how to cook it—as if I were an incapable culinary novice.

I didn't have the capacity to be insulted, too preoccupied listening for clues to what Shawn and Jordan were up to. To be honest, I was enormously grateful that Elena talked so much. If she stopped, I'd have no idea what to say. I was still a bit shocked that they were here. Just a few minutes ago, I was sitting on the couch with Jordan, thinking about her breasts, and now Elena was in my kitchen talking about how nicely creamed peas complimented fried fish.

The sound of Jordan's voice told me they were coming back down the hallway. Jordan must have given Shawn the apartment tour. They walked into the living room and stood in front of the windows with their heads together, talking quietly.

Elena sidled up next to me and put her hand on my arm. "Martin is in the hospital. It's serious," she whispered.

As Shawn delivered the same news, Jordan's demeanor slowly withered away. She looked at me for a second, her face turning horribly ashen, then turned back to Shawn and nodded.

I couldn't think, not quite able to take in what I'd just heard, suddenly desperate to console Jordan, while Elena sprang into action, filling four glasses with ice and Pepsi and taking them into the living room. I followed.

Shawn explained that their dad had had a stroke earlier in the day and was not expected to survive through the week. They were planning to drive down to LA early the next morning and thought it best that Jordan stay the night with them so they could get an early start. Jordan agreed and went into her bedroom to pack.

"I'm sorry, Shawn," I said.

"Thank you, Shannon. And thank you for looking after Jordan for me. You're a good friend."

Jordan walked in with her suitcase, and we all stood up, Shawn and Elena turning toward the door, Jordan and I staring at each other, knowing that we couldn't say goodbye the way we wanted to.

"I'm so sorry, Jordan." My words sounded painfully hollow. She looked so sad, my heart broke and my arms ached to hold her. I turned to Shawn and Elena. "Please, be careful driving and say hi to your mom for me and tell her I'm thinking about her."

"I will. Thank you, Shannon. And we'll be careful."

They filed out the door and down the walkway toward the stairs. I closed the door, took a few steps into the living room, and stopped. The emptiness without her there slammed into me, its impact robbing me of my sense of self for a moment, making me feel like I might be sick. A click at the front door spun me around. It opened.

"Jordan!"

She caught me as I threw myself into her arms, and gave me a deep, bittersweet kiss. I held onto her until she reluctantly released me, our faces wet from tears.

"I love you." Her voice trembled, then cracked. She turned and left without looking back.

* * *

Mom called on Friday evening and told me that Jordan's dad had passed and that the funeral would be held on Monday. I didn't expect to hear from Jordan—the others might find it strange if she called, and long-distance was expensive—so I had no idea when she would return. I hated that I could not go with her to LA and help her while she went through this. I hated that we could never be a couple in this way. That we had to hide what we meant to each other angered me. I stewed and waited, missing her terribly.

The following Wednesday evening, as I sat on the couch watching TV, I heard a click and was at the door before it opened. I pulled Jordan inside and into my arms, holding her as she dropped her bag and wrapped her arms around me tight. We stood like that for a long time.

"Can I get you something? Can I do something for you? Anything?"

"I need you."

She looked tired and so sad. I'd never seen her this way before and worried I wouldn't be enough to help her. I took her to our bedroom, undressed her, and put her to bed. I climbed in beside her, holding her as she told me everything that happened in LA. She cried, and I cried with her, wanting to take away her pain, comforting her the best I could.

* * *

Over the weeks that followed, Jordan's sadness slowly lifted, and by mid-June, she was all but her old self again. Her dad's passing did take its toll in one regard, though, and I couldn't help but worry a little. We hadn't made love since before she left for LA. I didn't want to put any pressure on her and decided to give her a little more time before talking to her about it. Certainly, I could go six or seven weeks without having sex with her. I'd done it before, just never while she was lying naked in bed beside me every night. It was not easy.

One early Saturday morning, as I stood in the kitchen drinking coffee and flipping through the newspaper, Jordan walked in, rubbing her eyes, looking very sweet and very sexy. "Could you come back to bed, please?" she said, not really asking.

She walked back down the hallway toward the bedroom, and I put down my cup and followed her. When I entered the bedroom, she was already in bed, propped up on her elbow, holding up my side of the cover, signaling for me to get into bed next to her. I began to do just that when she stopped me, looking me up and down, gesturing at me with her finger.

"Could you take that off, please?" Again, not really asking.

I pulled off my sweatpants and T-shirt and climbed in under the cover next to her. She waited only a moment or two before pulling the cover away, slowly exposing me inch by inch. Her eyes roamed my body from my breasts to my toes as her hand moved softly over my skin, making me tingle all over. What she was doing was totally working. I was wet and throbbing, practically panting, praying she would do to me what I very much needed her to.

"I missed you really bad when I was in LA."

"I missed you, too."

Her eyes followed her hand as it continued moving softly over my skin. "I felt sick about leaving you here, and I also felt sad about my dad. I didn't like having these two feelings at the same time. It made me angry. Do you know what I mean?"

"Yes."

Her hand abruptly stopped, and she looked up at me.

"You know what I mean... What do I mean?"

"I was angry, too. I couldn't go with you. I couldn't help you or comfort you in any way because no one can know what I am. I was sad for you and sad for your dad, but I missed you, and I wanted you, and I started feeling guilty about having both of these feelings at the same time. I became angry. Everyone else can be with the person they love during this time of sadness, except us, and I..."

Jordan leaned in and kissed me before I could finish my sentence. I needed her bad, and she did not make me wait.

She made love to me with such fervor and depth of emotion that all the hurt, uncertainty, and bitterness over our separation was instantly healed, making me feel complete again in a way that only she could accomplish.

"Come here." I pulled her up from between my legs, and she laid her head between my breasts. Her body relaxed into mine, and we held each other like that for several minutes before she suddenly spoke.

"What are we going to do?"

I had no idea how to answer her.

* * *

At the end of June, we decided to renew our rental agreement. We didn't officially decide. We didn't sit down and discuss it. I didn't actually ask Jordan about it at all. As we left for work one morning, I mentioned that I would be stopping by the manager's office after work to renew. I renewed our rental agreement for another year.

In July, we bought a sofa chair, a side table, and a lamp for the living room, and in August, I did something I'd always dreamed of doing. I enrolled in a culinary class for beginners, taught by a real chef on-site at a restaurant in the city. Jordan knew I was passionate about cooking, and I had mentioned the idea of attending a cooking school to her before, but always in the context of *maybe, someday*, in a wishful thinking kind of way, nothing serious—until now. I was excited to tell her my news.

That evening, I was surprised by her reaction. She was not very pleased about the news, to say the least.

"After work?"

"Well, yeah, I mean…"

"So, you won't be here when I get home."

I hadn't thought about it that way and tried to ease her concerns. "It will only be two nights a week, and I'll be home by nine-thirty at the latest." I took her hand in mine and explained to her how important this was to me. "My parents were against college or any type of additional education after I graduated from high school. You know the plan. Church, marriage, children. They would never have let me go to a cooking school. But I'm not living with them anymore. Jordan, I may never get another chance to do this."

"Why do you need to learn to cook? You already cook well enough for me?"

I found her comment hugely misogynistic and let out an incredulous huff. "Jordan, you don't really mean that, do you?"

"You know what I mean." She looked slightly abashed, but then quickly added, "You work in an office for the State as a supervisor. Wouldn't business classes be more appropriate?"

Now she was trying to pretend it wasn't me taking classes she had a problem with, but that they were hobby cooking classes and not serious business classes. It seemed pretty obvious that she didn't want me taking any classes at all.

"Jordan, can you hear yourself speaking? You sound like my dad. Listen, I love cooking, and I want to learn how to cook properly. Besides, who says I'll be working for the State the rest of my life? I actually dream of having a restaurant of my own someday."

"Are you kidding me? You never told me that."

"No, but you know how passionate I am about cooking, and dreaming about owning a restaurant is part of that." I sighed, feeling a little defeated. "Indulge me, Jordan. It's just a dream."

"I just hate that you won't be here when I get home," she said, repeating the crux of the matter.

"I'll make it up to you. Please be okay with this."

Jordan gave in grudgingly, but she definitely wasn't crazy about the idea. I sat next to her, watching her watch TV, wanting to soothe her and make her smile. I did not want her to stress out about this or think about it in a negative way. I grabbed hold of her foot and pulled it into my lap. She watched as I began rubbing it, giving me a brief smile before returning her attention to the television.

After rubbing her foot for more than ten minutes without a peep from her, not even a groan of delight, I leaned over, took her big toe into my mouth, and began sucking it softly. Jordan jumped and took in a sharp gasp of air. I had her full attention now. She stared at me in disbelief, eyes wide, mouth open, her right hand holding onto the back of the couch, her left hand holding onto her crotch. She swallowed hard as I continued bobbing my head, letting her big toe slide in and out of my mouth between my puckered lips, her face taking on that wonderful, sexy, sultry look that told me she wanted me.

I released her big toe, and Jordan watched as I stood up, grabbed her sweatpants by the legs, and slowly pulled them off her. I moved the coffee table to the side, and she swung her legs around as I got on my knees in front of her. She spread her legs while shifting to the edge of the couch, breathing the words, "Oh God," as I put my hands on her knees and spread her wider.

When I was finished with her, she was no longer feeling threatened by my culinary plans, and we were finally able to have a rational conversation about my ambitions.

"I just panicked. I'm sorry. I'm such an idiot. I want you

to go to school. I want you to do what makes you happy," she said as she held me in her arms.

"I was really nervous about enrolling, Jordan, but you make me feel strong like there's nothing I can't do. Well, I can't do this without knowing you're okay with it."

She kissed my forehead, then looked down into my eyes. "Do it. I'm okay with it."

* * *

We celebrated Jordan's birthday at home, eating a delivered pizza for dinner and a pint of Haagen-Dazs ice cream—chocolate-chocolate-chip—for dessert. We reminisced about her last birthday, recounting the incident with the police officer. We could laugh about it now, a little, but those feelings of fear and panic were not quite gone, reminding us of how badly that situation could have turned out, the stark contrast with our current surroundings reminding us how far we had come.

My cooking classes started in September, and after two weeks, I was ready to quit. Between church, work, and Jordan, it was difficult to find time to study, and secretly, I felt kind of dumb. I knew how to cook but knew almost nothing about the science of cooking. I was overwhelmed by all the new terminology and a bit frustrated that we weren't doing much cooking at all. I divided my free evenings into an hour of studying and the rest in the kitchen, where I felt more confident. Jordan tried to be helpful, always encouraging me to keep trying, careful not to take up too much of my time for the attention she was used to getting from me.

I kept going to classes, kept reading the material, and kept trying new techniques out in my kitchen, and by October, the material started to make sense and my uncertainty slowly faded. I became more organized about my time, which helped Jordan know when it was—or was not—a good time to talk to me about something non-cooking-related. She even tried helping me in the kitchen, sometimes as a taste-testing guinea pig, sometimes as a dishwasher, but mostly she was distracting, often growing bored with all the technical cooking stuff with nothing but a funny-tasting sauce or an experimental side dish to show for it. More than a few times, she actively seduced me, and we'd end up doing it on the kitchen counter, table, or floor, my lab homework conveniently forgotten.

The more I learned, the more time I spent studying. Most nights, I was either in the spare bedroom reading through my books and going over my notes, or I was in the kitchen practicing techniques and perfecting recipes, completely committed to creating the perfect finished product for class.

At first, Jordan was always there waiting for me when I came home from class, excited and asking questions about what I had learned and volunteering to help me with my lab homework. But after a while, she began to let me alone, knowing I was busy and sensing how important my work was to me. She felt she was in the way, and neither of us wanted that. I was relieved when she didn't interrupt me while I was working. I knew she needed my attention, but I thought I could give it to her later. But later rarely came.

On my non-class evenings, she would always look a little bit sad when I hunkered down to study after dinner, and then, after a while, she barely registered that I was studying at all, her disinterest becoming more distracting than her distractions were. She stopped asking questions about what I had learned, stopped volunteering to be my guinea pig, and then, one evening, she wasn't there waiting for me when I walked in the door. I sat on the couch waiting for her, and at ten-thirty, the front door opened.

"Where have you been? I was worried sick," I said, jumping up from the couch.

"I'm sorry I'm late," she said as she closed the door and locked it. "I had a thing with some friends from work, and suddenly it was ten o'clock. I raced home as fast as I could."

She plopped down on the couch, and I sat down next to her. "You smell like smoke. Have you been smoking?"

"No!" She grabbed the front of her blouse and pulled at it, sniffing. "Silvia smokes. It must be on my clothes."

Looking her over, noticing something but not sure what it was, I asked, "What was this *thing* at work?"

"It wasn't *at* work, it was after. Six of us went to a place for dinner. It was Linda's birthday."

"What kind of place?"

"It was a bar, but they serve food there."

"Was there drinking?"

"No… Yes! They drank alcohol, I drank Pepsi."

"Where is this bar? What's the name of it?"

"I don't remember, some bar in the city."

It was just a moment, but something crossed Jordan's face, and then it was gone. She looked away, stood up, went into the bathroom, and took a shower. I sat there, not knowing where to begin thinking about all of this. There had been a subtle change in Jordan the last few weeks, but I hadn't had much time to address it, not really sure if there was anything to address. But this was way out of the ordinary for her, going to bars, drinking with friends, coming home late, smelling like cigarettes…

"You coming to bed?" Jordan asked, startling me.

I stared at her as she stood there drying her hair with a towel. She cleared her throat, and I blinked, lightly shaking my head, knowing that something consequential was happening but unable to see the forest for the trees. "Ah, yeah, in a minute. I have to organize my notes from class."

Jordan went to bed, and I sat on the couch for another ten minutes or so, thinking. Something about what she said bothered me, but I could not put my finger on it. And then it hit me. 'I'm sorry I'm late.' Why did Jordan say that? Late for what? Late getting home, of course, but it somehow suggested that this was not the first time she'd been out with these friends—it was just the first time after a night out with them that she'd gotten home after I did. I got up, went into the bedroom, and climbed into bed. Jordan was already asleep.

* * *

Our situation worsened over the next month. Jordan was seldom at home when I got home from class, and more often than not, I was already in bed when she finally did get in, and she would always shower first before climbing into bed next to me.

On the evenings I didn't have class, she would come home later and later after work, once so late that instead of coming to our bed, she slept in the spare bedroom. The next morning, she explained that she hadn't wanted to wake me. I was flabbergasted that she thought to explain this and not explain why she had been out so late in the first place.

Jordan was changing. Her routine, her friends, and her interests were evolving. I could no longer ignore it, and although it bothered me, I couldn't really find any fault in it. She was an adult, and it seemed a bit hypocritical to forbid her activities and friends that she enjoyed when I had just convinced her to give me the same respect and allow me activities that I enjoyed. Still, the whole thing made me nervous. It was time to talk to her about it, but I didn't know how to start or what to say, and we were both busy and hardly saw each other long enough to schedule a quick sit-down, much less have a substantial, meaningful conversation about a problem I didn't even know how to define.

Even when we did have a little time, something about the topic kept us from talking about it, and we began to avoid it, trying to enjoy the moment instead of turning it into something uncomfortable. But after a while, whatever was happening between us seeped into those moments as well. Jordan took me to dinner for my birthday, and it was lovely, but the subject we'd been avoiding seemed to hover around us, turning our dinner conversation into something strained and shallow.

By January, I was not only worried about us, I was scared. I couldn't concentrate at work, and I couldn't concentrate in class. Finals were approaching, but I barely gave them a thought. It was impossible to study, and I started skipping classes. I just sat home on the couch and waited for Jordan.

And then one night, after I had already gone to bed, I heard her come in the front door and go straight to her room. I got out of bed and went to her. When I turned on her light, she lifted her hand to shield her eyes from its brightness. She was lying on her bed, still fully clothed, and she was wearing pants. I'd never seen her in pants before. I had no idea she even owned a pair. I sat down on the foot of the bed and looked at her. She lowered her hand and propped herself up on her elbows.

"Hey," I said softly.

"Hey," she replied. I could smell that she'd been drinking.

"We have to talk."

She sat up and leaned against the headboard, taking in a deep breath. "I know."

"What's going on, Jordan?"

She looked down at her hands, then back up at me.

"Something is happening to me, Shannon." Her voice was soft and low, resigned, not defensive. "I found something that has changed me, something that is important to me. I don't know how to explain it, but I think it's what's missing from my life. It makes me happy, like I belong somewhere."

"Don't I make you happy? Don't you belong here with me?" I asked.

"Yes, you do make me happy. I have never been happier in my life than I have been with you." She gathered her thoughts a moment before continuing. "It's not you, it's our lives, the way we live, and the way I feel because we have to live this way. There is another way to live. I met some people who are free to live the way they choose. They do not live two realities like we do, trying to balance both at the same time while dealing with opposing feelings and beliefs all at once. The two realities and competing beliefs inside me are ripping me apart. These people live one reality, completely, fully, without guilt or anxiety. They are happy. I've seen it. I believe I will go mad if I do not change my life." Jordan's face twisted in pain, her eyes red and full of tears. "Do you understand what I'm saying?"

"Yes."

"I know you do." Her voice broke, and tears rolled down her face, dripping from her chin.

I swallowed hard. I didn't know what to say. I didn't know what this meant or how to help Jordan. I reached out and touched her leg with my hand, and she immediately leaned forward and grabbed it, taking it in hers. She pulled me toward her, and I crawled up next to her, holding onto her. She cried silently, tears falling from her face; her shirt was wet from them. She turned and laid on her side, then reached back and pulled my arm around her, clutching my hand to her chest. I held her as she cried herself to sleep.

* * *

I moved through the next couple of weeks numb and disoriented, unable to think about anything except Jordan, trying to understand what was happening. I barely got anything done at work, and my cooking classes were a distant memory, not important anymore. I sat home and waited for her, feeling suffocatingly sad, knowing we weren't the same as before and having no idea what to do about it.

She was just as loving and caring as always, but very quiet and thoughtful now. I couldn't imagine what was going on in her head, and she never said, and I didn't ask, both of us acting as if it were all very obvious. And maybe it was and I was just too afraid to understand. And then she would smile and give me her wink-blink, or she would say something so sweet or do something so familiar, like cuddle with me on the couch during a movie, and I would let myself rest on the idea that maybe time would correct this. Maybe she just needed time to think and realize that what we had was important.

One evening, after dinner, while we cleared the table and did the dishes, I asked Jordan about her friends, generally probing, curious about who they were and how she met them—a seemingly innocent question, I thought. She told me that she met a couple of women at work, and they all began going out once a week to eat. She got to know them and discovered that they were gay. Jordan didn't tell them that she was, but they knew. On Linda's birthday, they all went to a restaurant for dinner, and afterward, to a gay club to celebrate.

"You remember the one. *Club Imagine*, in the city."

I remembered the first time Jordan came home late, the look on her face when I asked her what the name of the bar was that had kept her away from me that night. She lied, making it seem as though the bar was some sort of restaurant, the name of which she couldn't remember. She wasn't lying anymore, and I didn't know what that meant. Well, obviously it meant she was ready to share a little of how she'd been spending her time, and I *had* asked, although I wasn't sure anymore if I wanted to know.

Jordan went on to explain that after Linda's birthday celebration, they started inviting Jordan to go with them to the gay club more often, and after a while, they were all going regularly just to hang out. Jordan met other women, got to know them, and even made some friends.

"And I could feel myself changing, growing, something happening to me. It was amazing, Shannon. I was becoming myself. I wasn't afraid or nervous anymore."

Her answers brought up more questions than I knew how to deal with. I briefly wondered why she never invited me to go with her. But I knew why. She would never ask. Associating with people in the world was a big enough step, but going to a gay bar was an enormous step, one that took courage—courage that I did not have. It was a step too far; the possibility unimaginable to me. I wondered how Jordan was able to go to such a place without feeling misfitted or conflicted, but then again, she was much more open and outgoing than I was, and her ties to the church were not as consequential as mine. The whole idea scared me, and maybe Jordan knew this. She never asked or even suggested I go with her, and I knew it was out of respect. I would have to ask her, and I was not about to do that.

And then I thought about the possibility that Jordan may have slept with someone else, and suddenly, I thought better of asking so many questions about her new activities. I didn't want to know how she'd been spending her time if it included hearing about intimate time she'd spent with another woman, and I certainly didn't want to catch her lying about it.

CHAPTER EIGHTEEN

It was a Sunday morning just like any other; a quick shower, a cup of coffee, and out the door to church we went. I hurried down the stairs, Jordan right behind me, and just as I hit the parking lot pavement and turned toward my truck, Jordan casually announced that she'd be taking her own car to Sunday morning services, explaining that she needed to pick up some things at her brother's house afterward. I hesitated, worried for a moment, but then let it go, thinking it not that important given everything else that was happening.

I got to church and took a seat on the outside aisle near the back, and Jordan came in a couple of minutes later and sat next to me just before the first hymn began.

About halfway through the sermon, Jordan took a small piece of paper out of her purse and wrote something on it. She waited a few moments, then handed it to me before standing up and walking through the doors that led to the foyer. I unfolded the paper and read it. *"Don't follow me. I love you."*

I sat there and stared at her message, not sure what to make of it. I turned and looked at the foyer doors, somehow thinking she'd gone to the restroom and would return any moment. Another couple of minutes passed, and I knew something was wrong. I left the building and walked out to the parking lot. Jordan's car was not there. I ran to my truck and raced to the apartment.

Jordan's Chevy was parked in her parking space, and I pulled in next to it. I hurried up the stairs and down the walkway to our apartment and let myself in. Noise from her bedroom led me down the hallway, and I came to an abrupt stop in front of her doorway. What I saw inside made me gasp. She was throwing clothes from her closet into her suitcase.

The sight of her packing nearly stopped my heart, and my

throat seized up. "What..." My voice broke. I tried to swallow. "What are you doing?"

"I told you not to follow me." She was cold and abrupt.

"I don't understand. Talk to me!"

She was moving fast, grabbing socks, underwear, T-shirts, and sweaters out of her dresser and throwing them into her suitcase. She continued as if I wasn't even in the room, snapping her suitcase shut when it was full.

"Jordan! Stop! Where are you going?"

She yanked her suitcase off the bed and brushed by me, striding out of the bedroom. I grabbed her arm with one hand and tried to wrestle the handle out of her grip with the other. "Wait! Please!" I pleaded. "Don't go! Jordan!" I didn't recognize my own voice as it begged her to stay.

At the front door, she turned and faced me. I let go of her arm, holding my breath, surprised that she had stopped, actually thinking for the briefest moment that she had somehow changed her mind and had decided to stay.

She was crying, her face racked with pain, her voice breaking as she attempted to speak. "Shannon, you have to stay here. You have to stay in the church and get married and have children. Think of your mom and dad. I can't stay. I love you, but I have to go." She hesitated, staring at me with eyes wide as if she herself could not believe what she was about to do.

"Jordan...please...I love you..."

She turned, opened the door, and walked out, closing the door behind her.

I let out a choked sob, trying to breathe, swallowing hard as I pushed down the bile rising in my throat. I had to stop her; I could not let her go! "No!" The word shot from my mouth, and I grabbed the doorknob and yanked the door open. I ran down the walkway and flew down the stairs to the parking lot, hitting the concrete running, yelling, "No!" just as Jordan backed out of her parking space.

I approached her car from the front as she started to drive forward, and in an attempt to somehow stop her, I dove onto the hood, grabbing the rim near the windshield with my fingers, begging her not to go. "No!"

She slammed on the brakes, and her car jerked to a stop. She looked at me through the windshield, tears streaming down her face.

"Please, don't leave me, Jordan!" I cried, pleading with her.

She turned to her left and looked out her side window.

"Shannon Rae!" came a voice from my right, and I turned my head to find Mom standing just a few feet away next to her car, staring at us in disbelief. She must have followed me here. "Shannon Rae Callaghan! Get down from there!"

I turned back to Jordan, the tortured look on her face crushing me, and let go of the rim of her hood, slid off the hood of her car, took a couple of steps to the side, and watched her drive away.

Mom looked me up and down, her expression one of shock and concern. My face was wet and my makeup was smeared. My nose was running, my hair a complete mess, and the front of my yellow dress was covered with dirt from breast to hem.

"Mom, she's gone," I sobbed as I covered my face with my hands.

Mom took me into her arms and held me with a soothing, "Shhhh," and then walked me back up to the apartment. I washed my face and changed my clothes, and when I walked into the living room, Mom was sitting on the couch, waiting. She patted the place next to her, and I sat down.

"What happened?" she asked, her voice full of concern.

"Jordan left," my voice rasped, rough and unfamiliar.

"You mean, she moved out of the apartment?"

"Yeah, she moved out."

"Did you two have an argument?"

"Yeah, we had an argument."

Mom touched my hair, tucking some stray ones behind my ear. I was numb. I could hardly feel her fingers touching my skin.

"Do you think she'll come back?"

"No."

"Is she moving back home?"

"I don't know."

"I see." Mom took my hand and let out a deep sigh. "Shannon, this happens sometimes. You can't stop Jordan from doing what she's going to do. I know you feel responsible for her, but you're not. She's an adult. You can't save her, Shannon. Only God can."

We were talking about two different things. She was talking about Jordan leaving the church, and I was talking about Jordan leaving me. Did she really think I would jump on someone's car to keep them from leaving the church? Then I realized there was no other explanation for my behavior as far as my mom was concerned. Even after the display I put on in the parking lot, it was unfathomable to her, not even an option, that Jordan and I were more than just friends.

"Do you want to come over to the house? Some fellowship might help. The McElroy's are coming over for lunch."

"No. Go. I'll be fine. I'm just tired," I said, my tone monotonic.

"Okay. I'll call you next week. Try to get some rest." She hugged me and then stood up and walked to the door, hesitating a moment before opening it.

She turned and looked at me, and for a split second, I considered telling her everything, but then she turned and left, closing the door behind her, leaving me alone.

I sat there unable to move. The very idea of movement or what I should do next was irrelevant. I sat there, my mouth hanging open as thoughts entered my mind and were immediately canceled. I sat there in this condition the rest of the day and through the night, stunned, frozen in a position of disbelief, my mind in denial, trying to jump-start itself, reboot, desperate to put everything back together the way it was.

Far away, the sun began to rise, and more and more of the

room appeared before me. Sunshine spilled in through the windows and crept across the floor toward me. I stood up, called in sick at work, and climbed into my bed. I didn't cry. I just laid there; my body pressed to the mattress by some invisible weight. I laid there for a week, only getting up to pee and drink water from the bathroom faucet.

* * *

I lay there in the dark, my mind playing with a single, faraway thought, turning it over this way and that, unveiling it slowly, examining it briefly. Not much more was necessary for understanding to wash over me.

As unprepared as I had been for Jordan's departure, I knew she was leaving me weeks before she did. She had to leave. The door had been opened, and she could see the life that awaited her if only she had the courage to break away from me and the church. It must have been so difficult for her—heart-wrenching—no one without courage could have made such an agonizing decision. Jordan was gone, away on a journey. I wished her farewell and let go of her.

I dragged myself out of bed and took a shower. I dressed slowly, often stopping and staring at the space in front of me for long moments at a time. I didn't think about anything. My head was empty. I didn't look at anything in the apartment for more than a second; I couldn't. I concentrated on what was right in front of me, just trying to get myself down the hallway, past the living room and kitchen, to the front door. The doorknob. I grabbed hold of it, took a deep breath, and turned it, pulling the door open and stepping outside. I found myself sitting in the church parking lot twenty minutes later, not remembering anything about the drive over and not caring. I crawled out of the truck and dragged myself into the building, sitting in the last pew, waiting for Sunday morning services to start.

I carried on like that for several weeks, dragging myself to work, to church, and home again, barely hanging on until I could crawl back into my bed at night. No one really noticed at work, but it was impossible to hide from the church. News spread fast that Jordan had left the church, and instead of members asking me how I was doing, they shied away from me, greeting me at services but not stopping to talk. They knew how I was doing. I could imagine what I looked like—my withered bearing, the dull, strange look on my face—not able to come up with much more than a half-hearted hello myself, making it clear that I did not want to talk.

The story that circulated was simple: Jordan had left the church, and Shannon felt responsible. Some probably held me responsible, like Shawn. After all, Jordan was living with me. *See, that's what happens when young singles leave their parents' home.* Some saw me as strong because I was able to fight off her evil influence and didn't leave with her.

And that's how it was in the church—someone was always at fault—clean and simple, uncomplicated, good over evil, and I never corrected the record either way. I never defended myself or Jordan. I didn't talk about it to anyone. How could I?

Then, in late February, as I sat in church waiting for Sunday morning services to start, someone tapped me on the shoulder. I looked up to find Samuel standing there, smiling.

"Good morning, Shannon. May I sit with you?" he asked.

He sat down next to me, and after services, he asked me to lunch. I said yes, and he took me to *Sizzler*. We sat in a booth near the window and ordered iced tea and the Sunday special. I vaguely remembered being there with Jordan as I numbly listened to Samuel's non-stop commentary on his work, his hobbies, and his plans. He had a new position working with a nearby congregation and would be living here for the foreseeable future. He didn't have many hobbies, preferring to donate all of his extra time to the ministry of the church, making it clear that he would be more than happy to make an exception for me whenever I wished. He sat with me again at church that evening, and afterward, he walked me to my truck, waving as I drove away. We saw each other every day for the next few weeks, and slowly, I began to talk to him. Outside of work, I had barely spoken since Jordan left, and the light conversations I had with Samuel helped return a bit of normality to my brain.

Oddly, Samuel became someone I almost looked forward to seeing, and in March, on a particularly warm Sunday afternoon, I asked him over to my apartment and made him lunch, feeling untypically social, glad to be cooking for someone besides myself, although I still could not manage more than a simple noodle salad with sourdough bread and butter.

Jordan's departure left nothing in my life untouched, even my ability to cook. But Samuel seemed not to notice and complimented me on my salad, saying that it was delicious, maybe the best he had ever tasted. Afterward, we sat on the couch together and enjoyed a bowl of ice cream while he talked about his family in Alabama.

I couldn't understand why he hung out with me so much, but he seemed to enjoy my company and was pleasant enough, I guess, nice enough, and I was happy that we were comfortable enough with each other to share and liked each other enough to become friends. I could really use a friend right now and almost smiled at the possibility. Then Samuel said something that cleared up any confusion I had about friendship or how much he liked me.

"I love you, Shannon, and I would like to marry you," he announced.

It shocked me when he proposed. I had given him no encouragement; we hadn't even kissed. But then again, we were in the church, and he was a guy, and I was a gal, and I guess technically we were dating. Why else would he be hanging out with me? And sudden proposals were not so uncommon, often redefining a flailing relationship and steering it in the right direction. And then there were those couples who weren't flailing at all and had only dated a month or two before suddenly getting engaged. It did happen, a dating couple who had accidentally gotten pregnant. I understood this, even in a religion where sex was not allowed before marriage. A sudden proposal, a quick engagement, a quick wedding.

But I was convinced that there were also couples in the church who met and fell head over heels in love with each other—complete and utter love at first sight—the kind of love that just knocked you off your feet, changed your life forever, changed the way you looked at yourself and the world. You married that person as quickly as you could because you needed them, you wanted them, you couldn't live without them, you didn't want to live without them, and if you had to live without them, you would be miserable and wish you were dead.

I knew this condition intimately and would be personally affected by it the rest of my life. I would make no judgments about quick marriages but, at the same time, recognized that Samuel and I did not fit into these three categories. We were about to create a category of our own.

"Samuel, are you sure you love me?" I asked. "We haven't known each other that long."

"I'm sure," he said, giving me a confident smile.

I stood up, went into the kitchen, and put on some coffee, trying to wrap my head around Samuel's proposal and what it meant. A chance like this—a chance to stay in the church, a chance to put an end to Jordan and me forever—would not come again. There would be no better suitor than Samuel. There was no reason to hold out for love. I had dated so many men in the last few years, I had more than proven I couldn't fall in love with them. I took a deep breath and walked back into the living room.

"Samuel, I have to tell you something, and you might reconsider your proposal when I do. It's very personal, but I trust that what I tell you will stay between us."

"Everything you say to me, Shannon, stays between us," he promised.

I sat down on the couch and began my story. "I had an affair with a woman in the church. It's over now."

I told him that it was Jordan and generally what had

happened. He listened without interrupting, and when I finished, I sat back in my seat, my hands clutched in my lap, and waited. My body was vibrating. It was the first time I'd ever told anyone what I was. Samuel didn't speak right away, and I found that I could not sit there and wait for him to. I got up, went into the kitchen, and poured us some coffee. I put the cups on the coffee table and sat down. He looked at me and pressed his lips together for a moment before speaking.

"I've seen you with her... You seemed close. I'm glad that you stayed."

This was his entire reaction, and I wondered if he ever suspected. He didn't seem especially shocked, but then he was a minister, used to private confessions. He gave me his confident smile, then reached over and took my hand.

"Do you want to marry me? Do you want to live a Christian life?"

"Yes, Samuel, I do," I answered, accepting his proposal.

I didn't love Samuel, and I never would. I would never love anyone except Jordan. Samuel wasn't going to save me from my broken heart, but he would marry me and give me children, and then I could die and go to heaven, leaving this horrible, painful, confusing life behind. The simplicity of it was almost a comfort. I gave Samuel a very sad smile—a wholly inadequate smile given everything he was about to do for me. But I hoped, in time, I would be able to give him the smile he deserved, the life he deserved.

He leaned over and kissed me, and then we drove over to my parents' house and told them the news. After evening services, Dad announced it to the church.

And so, it was official. I would stay in the church, get married, and have children.

* * *

We talked briefly about when we would marry and, not surprisingly, agreed that the sooner we married, the better. We were both in our mid-twenties, and it wasn't like I was a virgin anymore, so why go through a long, unnecessary engagement when there was nothing to show and nothing to prove? Marriage was the only goal, the only part of this that mattered. My parents were surprised by our quick engagement but also a little relieved, I think, worried that after all the men I'd dated, I would never find the right one and settle down.

We talked about the number of children he wanted and his views on child-rearing, the atmosphere turning vaguely intimate when he brought up the subject of contraception methods. He listed some of them off, ending with the biblical one, using an unnecessary amount of detail, being much too forward, and I realized he was fishing. I quirked him an eyebrow, almost in warning. I knew what was expected of me in a marriage, and I knew that he knew what was expected of me too. Was he testing me? He hesitated, then suddenly announced, "We can wait to have sex, give you some time to adjust." Talk about whiplash; his words were more unsettling than calming. It was like he had suddenly noticed my discomfort and his open disregard for it, his gesture meant to placate me, as if he were worried I might back out of our *arrangement*. But his manner was also authoritative, his tone slightly condescending, no discussion required, the subject suddenly closed, leaving me oddly irritated that he could just up and decide something like that for me, reminding me that he would be doing most of the deciding from now on. And maybe that was his message, but still, his promise was more than implicit, and I tried to take some comfort in it.

The wedding took place on the last Saturday in April. It was a very small wedding with an even smaller reception, which was okay with me. There had been no time to plan a big one, and I really didn't want a big one anyway. Afterward, we went to my apartment to pick up a few of my things—two suitcases of clothing and two boxes of personal items I had already packed and stacked next to the door. I could decide what to do with the rest later. The rental agreement wasn't up until the end of July, so I had plenty of time. At Samuel's apartment, I unpacked my suitcases, found a place at the bottom of Samuel's closet to store my boxes, then busied myself with getting to know where everything was. We had decided to postpone the honeymoon until the summer and drive out to Alabama to spend time with Samuel's family, leaving a very anticlimactic mood hanging over our wedding night, which suited my mood just fine.

We ate a late dinner, then moved to the bedroom and changed into our bedclothes. In bed, we lay separate, not touching, talking about the day, how nice the wedding had been, and how surprised we were that so many people showed up on such short notice. Then there was silence, a silence heavy with the very thing we weren't doing. Sex. After a minute or so, Samuel let out a deep sigh, bade me goodnight, and turned over on his side. I let out a sigh of relief when he started snoring.

* * *

By the end of the first week, my new routine began to take shape: going to work, coming home, making dinner, listening to Samuel talk about his day, going to bed, sleeping next to him, waking up, and starting all over again. And just as I thought I was getting the hang of married life, just as all worry about sex had disappeared from my mind, Samuel suddenly decided my adjustment period was over, my understanding of what *we can wait to have sex* implied, obviously very different from his. But still, I was more disappointed than shocked when Samuel made his move.

The whole thing lasted less than five minutes and was awkward at best. He was more nervous than I was, I think. I had had sex before, and it was obvious that he had not. He fell off to sleep soon after, and I lay awake, relieved that it had gone as quickly as it had, hoping this would satisfy him for a while. No such luck. The next day, Samuel was back for more, and the day after that, and the day after that. I had created a monster, but thankfully, a very quick monster. Sex with him was a wholly mundane exercise for me, not painful or scary, an activity that definitely had more to do with him than it did with me, a nightly occurrence that I would learn to live with.

It didn't take long for Samuel to grow bored of our nightly romps and seek more variety—two weeks to be exact—and on a Sunday afternoon, as we drove home from church, he introduced afternoon sex. The bulge forming in his pants as he worked the peddles of my truck should have alerted me, but it truly never crossed my mind, and I remained clueless until we got to the apartment, where all forms of decorum and good manners fell out the window. As he grabbed my hand and pulled me down the hallway and into the bedroom, I experienced my first feelings of nervousness and panic, and when he was finished, feelings of irritation and anger as well.

Afterward, as I prepared lunch, I realized that something very crucial to our relationship had changed. Samuel was not being a gentleman with me anymore, his respectful manner having all but vanished. He was still generally polite, but it was more a reflection of his upbringing than with me personally, and the whole notion that we could wait to have sex was brazenly being ignored as if the words had never been spoken, and I realized the words had always been a lie.

As I stood in the kitchen thinking about this, cutting up tomatoes for the salad, Samuel walked in, grabbed one of my cut cherry tomatoes, and popped it into his mouth. I looked at him as he chewed, and he slowly smiled at me. Clearly, he had lost his mind. His face was animated with emotion, but there was no sign of love in it—just arrogance and that weird pride that all Christian men carried with them after they got married. He was finally, officially, a man, the king of his castle, the master of his universe, something he could never have accomplished without me, his servant. His hyper-agitated state told me he was aware of the irony of this and was going to make me pay for it the rest of my life. I turned away, unable to hide my disappointment.

That evening after services, as we drove home, I could feel his sexual energy vibrating through the cab of the truck. He was hyper-fidgety and breathing way too fast. After what happened earlier in the day, I thought I was prepared for what was to come, but he managed to shock me again when he rudely and very aggressively grabbed my rear end as we entered the apartment. I couldn't say exactly what came over me, but I was instantly angry and even a little scared. Out of pure reflex, I spun around and snatched up his hand, making him take a step back, a look of astonishment exploding across his face.

"Don't touch me that way."

I dropped his hand, turned, and marched down the hallway and into the bedroom, trying to show a strength I did not possess. My whole body was shaking. I was angry and scared. What was wrong with me—besides the obvious—I knew what was required. If it had been Jordan, would I have reacted the same? Surely not. I quickly put the brakes on those thoughts, changed into my nightgown, and climbed into bed, feeling more and more nervous about what I had done and how I had spoken to him.

I could deal with typical bedtime sex. I could even handle spontaneous daytime sex—now that I had been warned—but I could not handle being grabbed by him like a piece of meat. It not only made me feel cheap, it angered me. Samuel approached the bedroom door, and I rolled over on my side and pretended to be asleep as I tried to figure out a way to make myself be okay with what had happened.

The days that followed were tense, each day a repeat of the one before: him attempting to continue where we left off without any discussion as to what was bothering me, me insisting we talk about it before we move on, him brushing me off and then coming on to me, me rejecting him, him storming off defensive and irritated, me nervously lying next to him in bed, listening to his agitated breathing, warning me how angry he was becoming.

* * *

Thursday morning began well enough, all things considered. I got up, made coffee, and got dressed for work. As I stood in the bathroom, looking in the mirror and applying makeup, I caught a glimpse of Samuel as he walked past the open bathroom door still wearing his pajamas. I'd never seen him leave the bedroom in pajamas before, and my senses immediately sharpened as an alarm went off in my head. I stared at myself in the mirror as I listened to Samuel take a cup from the cupboard. The cupboard door slammed shut, and I jumped. I quickly began straightening up the bathroom, putting all my things in a drawer, my heart pounding hard in my chest. I took a couple of deep breaths, then braced myself as I walked down the hallway, watching and waiting, half expecting him to pounce. He was leaning against the kitchen counter drinking his coffee as I picked up my purse from the table near the door, preparing to leave for work.

"Good morning," I greeted him with a nervous smile.

He was upset, which was nothing new, but there was something else. He looked desperate and angry, and the combination scared me. Before I could open my mouth to say goodbye, he slammed his right hand down on the counter next to him. I jumped, dropping my purse, no doubt delivering the reaction he was looking for—he almost smiled. And then he began yelling at me about being a Christian, a proper woman, and a good wife, and how I was none of those things.

For a split second, I believed him—humiliation and guilt wrapping themselves around my neck as I blushed—and had it not been for the person inside me, the one I had tried so hard to hide from everybody, I probably would have buckled and done whatever was needed to make this work with Samuel. But she wouldn't let me. She was furious.

"That's not true. And your opinion does not matter to me. Not liking the way you touch me does not make me a bad Christian."

"Actually, it does. That, and what you and Jordan did makes you a very bad Christian. And I'm beginning to think the two are related." He had taken two steps toward me and was pointing his finger at me. I took two steps back away from him. "Jordan did this to you."

"Jordan did nothing. You don't know anything about her, and you know nothing about me," I began. "You don't know anything about being a Christian, you know nothing about being a husband, and..." I let out a sarcastic snort, "You know nothing about being a man!" Samuel's face turned red, his eyes wide, obviously surprised to hear me speak this way.

"Your opinion does not matter to me and is irrelevant in any case! This matter is closed! You will submit!"

"I will not! To have you touch me is the most degrading, disgusting thing I have ever let anyone do to me." He continued walking slowly toward me, his face turning crimson as his brows pulled together and downward. I had hit a nerve, and I continued. "You are a coward, a fake, and a liar! You, Samuel, are ridiculous and a complete ass, and if you never touch me again, it will be too soon!"

We'd made our way into the living room, standing face-to-face, me looking up at him, breathing hard, my chest heaving, feeling so brave as he grabbed me, lifted me, and body-slammed me onto the living room floor. The crush of his body pushed all the air from my lungs, and I could not breathe. My head bounced off the floor as he slammed into me, the side of my face rubbing along the rug as his upper body settled into mine. He straddled me as he turned me onto my back, holding me down, struggling with me before realizing I wasn't struggling back. I was struggling to breathe, my mouth wide open, desperately trying to find some air. After a couple of scary attempts, I finally sucked in a big gasp of it, releasing it in a horrifying scream.

This seemed to affect him, and he loosened his grip. I sucked in another lungful of air and let out a second scream, louder than the first, and he slowly crawled off me. He climbed to his feet, looking at me with hate in his eyes as he tried to catch his breath. His eyes shifted, and I followed his gaze to my skirt, which had wrapped itself around my hips, exposing my panties. I quickly pushed my skirt down, covering myself, and he turned and walked down the hallway. The bedroom door slammed.

I sat up slowly and pushed my hair back, but it kept falling forward. I reached up to find my hairclips not where they should be. They had been thrust forward and were no longer holding my hair in place. I pulled them out, strands of my hair still clipped in them, and brushed my hair back away from my face. I touched my shoulders, my chest, and my hips, checking myself for injury. I tried to listen for Samuel, but all I could hear was a loud ringing noise. I slowly stood up and looked around the room, surprised at how normal everything looked. There was not a lick of evidence of what had just happened. I grabbed my purse off the floor and hurried down the hallway to the bathroom, my eyes glued to the bedroom door for any sign of Samuel. I slipped inside, closed and locked the door behind me, and sat on the toilet seat, waiting. Listening. A noise. The bedroom door opened, and then the front door opened and closed.

I put my ear to the bathroom door. The apartment was eerily quiet. As I stepped away, I caught a glimpse of myself in the mirror and turned. My hair was a mess, and the right side of my face was scratched from cheek to chin. I turned on the faucet and carefully cupped water onto my cheek, padding it dry as I examined it in the mirror, oddly thinking that no amount of makeup would be adequate to cover the damage.

I quickly ran a brush through my hair, re-clipped it, and then started packing. First the bathroom. I grabbed shampoo, cleanser, lotions, make-up—anything I could fit in my arms—then hurried to the bedroom, where I threw everything into a small suitcase. I threw in a couple of blouses, a couple of skirts, and a couple of dresses on top, then added a handful of underwear and three pairs of shoes. I left the rest. I shouldered my purse, grabbed my suitcase, and hurried to the door.

I raced to my apartment, and once I was inside, an unmistakable sense of safety returned, something I'd not even realized had been absent the last couple of weeks. After

I called in sick at work, I took a long bath, feeling almost human when I finished—my face notwithstanding. I put on some coffee, then sat at the kitchen table as I waited for it to brew, oddly calm, not nervous or panicked. I was probably in shock. I didn't know what was going to happen next, but I couldn't imagine it being any worse than what happened with Samuel.

CHAPTER NINETEEN

The next morning, I barely managed to roll myself into a sitting position on the edge of my bed. I was one big sore muscle. I carefully made my way to the bathroom and into the shower, grunting and gasping, bemoaning my impossibly sore body. My arms were sore, my hips were sore, my neck and shoulders were sore, and when I looked in the mirror, tears welled in my eyes at the condition of my face. It was swollen, and there was an angry red rug burn running down the right side of it. It looked like I was wearing a Halloween mask.

In the kitchen, I put on some coffee, then walked into the living room and watched sunlight pour in through the windows. A smile touched my lips, and I immediately winced at the pain it caused my face. Gingerly touching my cheek with my fingers, I walked to the side corner window and looked out over the courtyard below before turning to the front window. I scanned the parking lot, and when I saw my truck, I gasped, causing my face to explode in a new wave of pain.

I ran to the front door, yanked it open, and ran down the walkway, looking out over the railing at my truck as I hurried to the stairs. Samuel had been busy last night. Sheets and covers, coats and scarves, and all my clothing, including my underwear, had been draped over the cab and hood of my truck. It looked like he'd thrown each item, strategically piece by piece, on top of it so that it would be completely covered. In the truck bed, I discovered shoes, pillows, pictures, books, and the contents of opened boxes strewn everywhere.

I carried everything up to the apartment and immediately sorted through it, separating clothing, arranging papers, and organizing things into correct boxes. This process helped calm me, negating the impact of Samuel's message that I was not worth the respectful return of my belongings. By the time

I finished, it was early afternoon. I ate a late lunch on the couch in front of the TV, realizing what Samuel's actions really signified. He didn't want me back either.

Too exhausted to fully contemplate the ramifications of *that*, I dozed, images of my fight with Samuel flashing through my mind, mixed with pieces of memories of Jordan leaving me. The doorbell rang, and I bolted upright in my seat, glancing at the clock—four-thirty. I stood up and slowly approached the front door, holding my breath as I very quietly looked through the peephole. It was my brother, Simon. How did he know I was here? I opened the door.

"Hey," Simon said, his tone curt, waltzing right in without waiting for me to invite him in.

I hesitated a moment before closing the door, irritation rumbling within me at the entitled way he burst into my apartment.

"You wanna tell me what's going on, Shannon?"

"What are you doing here, Simon?"

"Mom called me this morning. She said you and Samuel had a fight."

Samuel already called my parents. Wow. I hadn't seen that coming. I sat down on the couch, and Simon sat down next to me, his gaze landing on my scratched-up cheek, officially acknowledging that something was up with my face. I thought he might ask if I was okay, but he didn't, getting right to the point instead.

"Something's wrong. After I talked to Mom on the phone this morning, I went over there. Mom and Dad were in the front yard talking, whispering. They were pacing back and forth. It was bizarre. When I approached them, they stopped talking and told me to go into the house and wait for them. They looked pretty stressed out. Dad actually raised his voice at me. I waited in the house for over an hour. They never came back in. I can't imagine them behaving so oddly over a fight. I mean, what kind of fight did you guys have?" His gaze darted to my cheek again, then back to my eyes.

"A bad fight," I said, stating the obvious. "Simon, why are

you here?"

"Well, Mom called this morning saying that you and Samuel had had a fight, then I go over to Mom and Dad's this afternoon, and they're standing on the front lawn whispering. You weren't at work, you weren't at Samuel's, so I thought my next stop should be here. What's going on, Shannon?"

"Simon..." My heart jumped in my chest and a large dose of adrenaline shot through my body. I stood up and took a deep breath. "I'm gay."

Simon's head jerked backward as if I'd slapped him in the face. "No you're not," he said, his face scrunching up in confusion as he forcefully shook his head.

"I'm gay. I had an affair with Jordan. Samuel knows. I told him. We had a fight, and this happened." I pointed at my cheek. "I left his apartment and came here, and he dumped all my belongings onto my truck last night. I believe he told Mom and Dad about me and Jordan, about me being gay, and that's why they're acting so strange."

I went into the kitchen to pour myself a glass of water, trying to calm my racing heart and catch my breath. When I turned, Simon was standing in the kitchen doorway.

"I have to go! You are *not* gay! And if you are, then...stop it!" he said, practically yelling.

Simon opened the door and walked out. I closed the door behind him, and the next thought that went through my mind was Jordan. I had to call her and warn her. Shawn would freak out when he heard about this. I called Jordan at work.

"Hi, it's me, Shannon. Listen, I can't explain everything right now, but Jordan...my parents know about us."

"You told them!"

"No! I did not tell them. It's a long story, but I had to warn you. Shawn will know soon. Everyone will know soon."

"Wow... Okay... Thank you for warning me."

"I'm sorry, Jordan."

"It's okay, Shannon. Are you okay?"

"Yeah, I'm okay..."

Even over the background noise of the mailroom's sorting

machine, I could hear Jordan breathing. I strained to hear her every exhale, the slightest nuance, whatever I could pull from the telephone line, remembering when she breathed for me.

"I have to go," she said, jolting me back to the present.

"Of course, right. Goodbye." Before I could hang up, Jordan's voice sounded, and I quickly brought the receiver back to my ear. "What?"

"Shannon, it's gonna be okay." And then she hung up.

My stomach lurched violently, and I ran to the bathroom, barely getting the lid of the toilet up before my lunch hurled itself out of my mouth. Holding on to the rim of the toilet, I pushed myself to my feet, my legs shaking as I dragged myself to bed, my body shutting down out of pure self-preservation, passing out before I could even crawl under the covers.

* * *

The next morning, I woke early—it was still dark out. I tried to move, but I couldn't. My muscles were much sorer than they were yesterday. I could barely raise my arms, and my neck and back muscles painfully spasmed every time I attempted to get up. I was a mess. As I lay there trying to locate a place on my body that didn't hurt, everything that happened the last couple of days played through my mind.

Samuel was obviously not the man I thought he was. I realized this weeks ago, but what he was doing now was a whole other level of creepy, scary, weird. Why was he behaving this way? He called *my* parents immediately after our fight. He told them about our fight but not about how bad it was. He told them about Jordan. He promised he wouldn't. Throwing everything on my truck like that was almost as aggressive as body-slamming me, not to mention totally unchristian and somehow much scarier. It was like a grown man having a childish temper tantrum. For what? I couldn't understand it. He won. He was the man. He put me in my place. What was the point of the rest?

And then it slowly hit me. He had to behave this way. He

had no choice. He was a Christian man, and his wife left him after a month of matrimony.

I had marks on my face, and everyone at church would be able to see what he had done. He needed to intimidate me, make me cower, scare me into passivity. He had to talk to my parents and the church before I did. His story had to be out there and circulating before mine was. He could lose his job if someone were to find out what really happened. Worse, his reputation would be so damaged that he may never be offered another job by any other church. And probably most important to him, he would no longer be an acceptable suitor for a good Christian woman looking for a good Christian man.

He had to behave this way, and fast, and just as a precaution, he needed to dirty my name as much as possible in the process. My sin was much more egregious than his, much more salacious, more than enough to dampen the battery issue, enough to confuse it for comeuppance. And Samuel knew this.

Less than two days had passed, and he had complete control of the narrative. I was so naïve. Even if I had the mentality and stomach for such tactics, it was too late, there was nothing I could do. I had already lost the public relations battle and lost control over this situation. My life had already been ripped from my hands, and I would never be able to get it back. Church, marriage, and children were looking very unlikely.

I lay there for a few minutes, shocked by this revelation, turning it back and forth in my head. But there was no other outcome possible. There was no way to put everything back together. It was falling apart too fast.

Finally able to climb out of bed, I showered, got dressed, and made coffee, cowering on the couch the rest of the day, waiting for the next horrible thing to happen.

I didn't go to church on Sunday morning. I couldn't. I was horrified and embarrassed at the prospect that everyone already knew what I was. I wouldn't know how to act. What would I say? I had never thought about leaving the church, never even considered it, and in that moment, quitting was the furthest thing from my mind. I hadn't even realized yet—as I sat on my couch and did not go to church because I was so ashamed as my life fell apart—that I would never go back to church again.

On Monday, I called in at work and took the week off. I couldn't let them see my face. I hunkered down in my apartment and licked my wounds. The next horrible thing did not happen, and I finally stopped flinching at every unexplained noise and stopped peeking out the window every time I heard steps on the stairs or a car door slam. I thought about the church rumor mill and wondered how long it would take before everyone knew. I thought about my family and how they would be humiliated by this, and I thought about Dad and how he would lose his position in the church because of this.

I healed, my face started to look almost normal, and on the following Monday, I went back to work.

* * *

Over the next couple of weeks, I fell into a routine much different from all the ones I'd had before. With my family, the church, and Jordan gone—and Samuel too, good riddance—I had much more time on my hands to think about myself and who I really was. I'd spent most of my life pushing the gay part of me away, trying to ignore it, trying to hide it, and had never taken the time to just sit down and analyze it. As I did, a barrage of questions stormed my brain. One very loud, dominant question kept popping up above all the others, repeating itself—Why me? This very juvenile lament occupied my thoughts for days until I pushed it aside, unable to come up with an adequate answer to it.

Then I started thinking about sex, the root cause of my predicament. Even as a Christian who grew up in the church and knew every rule in the rulebook, I still could not wrap my head around the question of why it was so immensely important who I was having sex with. Why did it matter so much? And why was everyone so obsessed with sex in the first place? All the thought put into fear-based laws, rules, and commandments, secular and religious, regulating my sex, and the energy it took to enforce compliance, left me flabbergasted. I had grown up knowing almost nothing about sex because no one thought it important enough to educate me on it, and now that I wasn't quite doing it the way everyone wanted, it was suddenly so powerfully important that it was changing the trajectory of my whole life. All I had to do was want to have sex with a man, and my life would be perfect and awesome and normal and none of this would be happening to me. But I couldn't. For some reason, having sex with a man was unnatural to me.

I also thought about the power of sex in the sense of how it influenced my behavior and motivated me to do things I once thought impossible. I had risked everything to have sex—a safe, stable home, friends, family, and my reputation—and then lost it all.

I thought about how sex had changed Samuel. Or had it? I slowly realized why Samuel agreed to marry me—to marry a woman he knew was gay. I remembered the young woman hurrying through the parking lot, running away from him. It wasn't the first time I'd seen a young woman avoid him. I always assumed it had something to do with how pious he was as a militant conservative. But maybe those women sensed something a little off about Samuel that I conveniently overlooked because he wanted to marry me and because I needed to get married. It didn't matter how off he was; he was a Christian man and that was enough for me. And he didn't care how gay I was, because he was having difficulties finding a partner. What a perfect match. He could have sex, something that was guaranteed within the bounds of a Christian marriage, and I could go to heaven. And then I took his sex away, and he got very angry. Sex hadn't changed Samuel; he was already who he was before he had sex with me.

The most important question remained, and I found it completely perplexing. Why was I sexually attracted to women? Where did this come from and why did I have it? I had come full circle. Why me? I was stuck and angry, confused and scared, yelling out in frustration one minute, crying in desperation the next. How could something like this happen to someone without their permission, without them doing anything to warrant it? I searched my mind for a possible explanation—anything that could explain the source of my condition.

I found the answer inside me. I was the source. It was me. There'd been no outside influence. I'd been taught nothing about it. I didn't know any gay people. I didn't hang out in gay clubs or in any place where gay behavior was propagated, and as far as I knew, I'd had this condition for as long as I could remember. There was only one explanation. I was miraculously, organically gay, and I wondered if it was like this for everyone.

These thoughts swirled around in my head for days, and I slowly made a decision without really making any conscious decision at all. I just couldn't struggle with it anymore, and I certainly couldn't deny it anymore. It was true. It was real. I was gay. Not knowing exactly how to proceed, I began to move forward in the only way I knew how, the way that felt most natural to me, and as I did, I realized that I had been moving in this manner the whole time, through the entire process, every decision, every misstep, from hiding who I was inside, to my mass dating strategy, to falling in love with Jordan, and even marrying Samuel. To think that I could have behaved in any other way than how I had, was absurd, and I was finished beating myself up for it.

* * *

One of the most natural things for me had always been cooking, so the first thing I did was register for next semester's culinary class. I had a new life to reschedule—a wealth of free time waiting to be filled—and no time to lose.

The next thing I did was go shopping. I needed new clothes—something relaxed and casual. I wanted to look like I was a part of this world, not separated from it. I bought slacks, jeans, normal shoes, and even a couple of T-shirts. I loved wearing dresses, but the occasional pair of jeans, a simple T-shirt, and comfy sneakers sounded heavenly.

Then I decided I wanted to visit a gay club. I remembered the one Jordan showed me, *Club Imagine*, but wasn't sure where it was, so, one evening, I jumped in my truck, drove into the city, and went exploring. My first excursion proved fruitless. I ended up getting lost in the city and spent most of my time trying to find the freeway entrance to get back home. But it wasn't entirely worthless. I did get a sense of the city's layout. I had accomplished something.

I went to the city a couple of times a week, sticking to the main strip at first, then venturing out onto side streets as I got more confident. Before long, I was parking the truck and setting out on foot, and even tried to retrace our steps from the capitol building to see if I could find the diner where Jordan and I ate lunch. I couldn't find the diner or any clue at all that there was any lesbian activity anywhere in the city of Sacramento. It was like being the only lesbian on earth—the same feeling I'd had about myself before I met Jordan.

As I walked back to my truck one evening, ready to call it a night after another unsuccessful search of the city, I spotted a laundromat. I crossed the street and went inside, discovering what I was looking for on a table in the back next to the detergent automat. There were stacks of pamphlets, brochures, booklets, and small newspapers. I looked through the newspapers, and the one titled *Barbed Wire* jumped out at me. Underneath the title in small letters was printed, *Gay and Lesbian News Letter*. I flipped through it and on the back page discovered a list of restaurants, bars, and clubs with addresses and telephone numbers. I folded it up, stuffed it in my purse, and hurried out of the laundromat.

Inside the safety of my truck, I unfolded the newspaper and scanned the back page for the words, *Club Imagine*, letting out a gasp of excitement when my finger came to a stop right underneath it. I turned on the ignition and started driving around, looking for the street. I drove past the diner Jordan and I had eaten at, and my heart skipped a beat. I was close and took the next left turn. It took three drive-bys to get up enough nerve to pull into the parking lot.

I parked near the back, then sat there for an hour watching women walk in and out of the club, several of them actually looking at me as they walked past my truck. It surprised me how many there were and how open they were. I could tell that they didn't care if anyone saw them. Some were even holding hands, and I witnessed two women by the side of the building openly making out. I studied their outfits, their haircuts, their gestures, and their movements. It was fascinating.

At eleven o'clock, I drove home. Sleep was impossible, and I lay awake in bed thinking about how different I looked from the women I'd seen. My new clothes were adequate—a little conservative maybe—but my hair was so long, it was almost strange. For the first time in my life, I began to consider cutting my hair. The next day, I made a hair salon appointment.

* * *

The day of my appointment arrived, and as I left work and drove to the salon, I was suddenly hyper-aware of my hair.

My hair was a thing. It was an independent object that hung from my head. My body and my hair had a bond, an understanding. They worked together so that I was able to move through my daily life with a little dignity and grace, so that I didn't look like a victim being attacked by an alien life form when the wind blew hard or suddenly from the wrong direction, or when it suddenly rained and every single strand of hair on my head searched for a separate spot on my face, neck, shoulders, arms, and back to dry itself.

I'd had it stuck in front doors, car doors, zippers, buttons, necklaces, watches, and the fingers of adults, children, and especially babies.

There was a whole dance I went through all night long, one that I was hardly aware of, the reflexive flipping and arranging of my hair while I tossed and turned in bed at night. When I woke, my hair was always lying next to me in the most correct and advantageous place it could possibly be and never in the place I'd left it the night before.

It was long, past my butt, and untrimmed. It was thick; two women could have an average, long, full head of hair from my hair alone. It was auburn red with other shades of red mixed in and natural blond highlights from the California sun. It was beautiful, or so I'd been told. It was not uncommon to receive compliments on my hair. At church, men and women alike would take the time to come to me where I sat in a pew, my hair hanging over the back, and whisper to me before they took their seats, "Your hair is beautiful." While waiting my turn in the supermarket checkout line, a perfect stranger would say, "Excuse me, I just had to tell you, your hair is beautiful."

I remembered a particularly difficult day during my freshman year in high school, being teased and mocked more than usual for my strange appearance and my obscenely long red hair. I sat on a bench at the end of an empty side corridor off the main hallway across from my next class, eating my lunch and feeling very sorry for myself. A fellow student hurrying down the main hallway glanced at me and suddenly stopped. I held my breath, hoping it wasn't me she was looking at, then let out a sigh of resignation when she turned and headed down the corridor toward me. Poop! As she came to a stop in front of me, I braced myself for the insult I knew would come, looking up at her, determined to look my bully in the eye.

"I've seen you around school, and I've always wanted to tell you, your hair is really beautiful," she said.

Expecting one thing but getting just the opposite, I flinched, squinting at her before giving her a confused smile. She smiled back, and I bashfully mumbled, "Thank you," to which she returned, "You're welcome. Have a nice day." She turned and walked back to the main hallway, continuing on her way in the direction she was going. I could not recall ever seeing her again, but with everything I was going through at the time, her words—a simple compliment for anyone else—were immense.

The evolution of my attitude toward my hair was painful but extremely satisfying, from when I was young, being teased for its color and length, to benefiting from its beauty as I became an adult. My hair was by no means a fashion statement, though. It was a symbol, a veil between me and God, the ultimate proof of my submission. I was more than ready to be rid of it.

To say I was a little nervous as I walked from my truck through the parking lot to the salon was an understatement. I did not know what to expect. I had no frame of reference. I had never been to a salon before. I walked in and sat down in the small waiting area, and a woman who was cutting an older lady's hair turned and looked at me and smiled.

"Sherri! Customer!" she yelled.

Sherri appeared from a back room, noticeably hesitating when she spotted me, smiling as she walked up and stood in front of me.

"Hi, do you have an appointment?" she asked while looking my hair up and down.

"Yes, five o'clock."

Sherri stepped behind a tall receptionist's desk and glanced at the appointment book lying open on top of it. "Shannon?"

"Yes. Shannon," I confirmed, starting to relax a little.

"And what did you have in mind? A trim?"

"I want it cut off," I announced a little too loudly.

"Cut off?" She looked confused.

"Well, yeah, short, you know, in a hairstyle," I explained, moving my hands around my head to show her what I meant.

"Okaaay," she said, drawing out the word. "Sit in that chair over there," she pointed, "and I'll be right with you."

I got up, walked into the salon area, and hesitated. "That one?" I asked, pointing at one of the empty salon chairs. They were big, scary, high-tech, swivel chairs, bolted to the floor. I wasn't sure if they were all the same or if they served different purposes. I didn't want to make a mistake and sit in the wrong one.

"That's fine," she said.

Still unsure which one she wanted me to sit in but not wanting to ask again, I just picked one, hoping it was the right one. I approached it, looked it up and down, then glanced at myself in the huge mirror on the wall. I could see Sherri and the other hairdresser behind me making hand gestures to each other, *Look at her hair,* mouthing the words, "*Oh! My! God!*"

I sat down, and Sherri abruptly turned to me and smiled. She walked over and stood behind me, slowly touching the long, hanging part of my hair. She lifted it and looked underneath it. She laid it down carefully and continued her examination at the top of my head, removing my clips and running her fingers through my hair over my scalp. The way she touched my hair was intimate, and I closed my eyes for a moment, enjoying it, letting my head move as she turned it left and right, pushing it forward and to the side, looking at God knows what and I didn't care. It felt wonderful.

"You have very thick hair, and the color is beautiful. Are you sure you want it cut off? Maybe just a trim to start," she said, making a line with her finger just above the back of my chair, suggesting a possible hair length.

"No. I want it cut off," I said decisively.

Sherri turned and looked at the other hairdresser, who had just finished her customer and was walking toward the receptionist's desk. Sherri waited as the customer paid and left the salon.

"Marg, call Florence. I need help with this."

Marg grabbed the phone and dialed. "Flo? Hi, it's Marg. Can you come in…now? We have a thing here. Yeah, okay, no, great." Marg hung up the phone, looked at Sherri, and then at me, quickly plastering a smile on her face. "She's on her way."

Marg joined Sherri, and together they inspected my hair, again touching it, lifting it, and running their fingers through it. "It's really very pretty," Marg said.

The door opened, and in walked Flo. "What's going on? Where's the emergency?" We all turned and looked at her. "Oh…" She abruptly came to a stop, first looking at me and then at Sherri and Marg.

"She wants it cut off…short," Sherri complained, as if my request were unreasonable.

"Well, that's what we're here for," Flo said, giving me a reassuring smile.

Sherri and Marg backed away as Flo approached. She went through the same routine with my hair as Sherri and Marg had. It was incredible. My eyes closed, and I stifled a moan. They should really consider opening a salon just for running fingers through hair. I would definitely make an appointment.

"Are you sure?" Flo asked, as if for good measure.

My eyes snapped open, and I turned and looked at her. "I'm sure," I said, hoping this would be the last time someone asked me this. I could feel my resolve slipping.

She stepped back and took a good look at my hair, slowly tilting her head to the left, looking neither daunted nor panicked. A challenge? "Do you know what you want?"

"I want it short in the back and around the ears and gradually longer from the sides to the top," I explained, showing her with my hands.

"Okay. You want a short wedge." She took a deep breath and, without taking her eyes off me, called out to Marg and Sherri. "Get me a clean medium-sized plastic bag from the closet and bring me number fourteen."

Marg disappeared into the back room, and Sherri retrieved a book from a shelf behind the receptionist's desk. Flo flipped through the book for a moment, then, finding what she was looking for, placed the book on my lap, pointing at the different pictures of hairstyles on the page before me.

"... and this one here is a little bit longer in the back. See what I mean?" she explained.

I took the book in my hands and slowly scanned the pictures. And then I saw it. "This one," I said, pointing.

Flo took the book from me and studied the picture for several seconds before closing the book with a snap and handing it back to Sherri without even looking at her. Flo was looking at me, her hair-cutting brain already at work.

"Is this your first visit to a salon?"

"Yes, it is. This is my first haircut."

Flo's eyes widened for a split second, and then she cleared her throat and began to explain what would happen next. "First, I'll trim the bottom off; it's dead hair. Then I'll cut off the bulk of your hair in four parts. What's left, I'll cut into a hairstyle. It's simple really," she said, looking in the mirror at Sherri, who was still holding the book, and Marg, who was holding a blue plastic bag.

And so, Flo began. She draped a long plastic bib over the front of me, fastened it around my neck, then brushed out my hair. She trimmed my extensive split ends and then rubber-banded my hair into four parts, cutting each part off and putting it into the plastic bag Marg was holding. We all took a deep breath as I stared into the mirror at the angry red, unruly mass sticking out in all directions on top of my head, certain I'd made a huge mistake.

Before I could freak out, Flo had me move to a chair that was attached to a sink, where she washed what was left of my hair. She had me return to my original seat, quickly ran a towel through my hair, and then brushed it. My eyes slowly closed, and I let out a soft moan. There was tugging and pulling and combing and parting, meticulously organizing everything before scissors even came into play. She used an electric razor around my neck and ears, the razor humming as Flo gently pushed my head forward and to each side. Then she started cutting again, snipping with deftness and precision. She brushed it, blow-dried it, and formed it with her hands as she arranged it into place. It was so relaxing, I nearly fell asleep.

Suddenly finished, she gave me two swipes across the shoulders with a brush and said, "You can open your eyes now. I'm done."

The first thing I saw when I opened my eyes was the three of them standing behind me, looking a little apprehensive. Then I looked at myself. The sensation of looking at myself in a mirror and seeing someone who wasn't me made me dizzy. I turned my head left, then right, unable to focus on any one detail. Marg handed me a hand mirror, Sherri held a bigger mirror behind me, and between the three mirrors, I got a good look at what Flo had created. I stood up, and gobs of red hair slid from my lap to the floor. Sherri began brushing me, removing cut hair from my shoulders and back as Marg removed my bib.

Refusing to let my eyes tear up, I turned to Flow and cleared my throat. "It's perfect. Thank you."

Flo pressed her lips together in a faint smile and nodded her head once. She looked at Marg, then back at me. "Do you want your hair?"

My eyes narrowed in confusion. "My hair?" Marg held up the blue plastic bag holding my hair, and I blinked at it, astonished at how full it was. The weirdest feeling came over me, as though I were losing a part of myself or was leaving someone behind that I had known forever. I stared at the bag for several seconds, stuck on the thought that what was inside the bag used to be attached to my head, attached to my whole life, its meaning and importance still hanging on me like the hair itself once had. I shook my head and took a deep breath, looking at Flo as I swallowed the lump in my throat. "No. Thank you."

"Okay. So, I'm going to warn you," Flo began. "Your hair will not look like this tomorrow when you wake up. You will have to fix it."

As we walked to the receptionist's desk, Flo gave me a few pointers on how to fix my hair and suggested a product that would help. I paid, threw in a generous tip, and then they sent me off at the door, wishing me luck and waving as I headed for my truck.

The first thing I noticed was a lovely breeze hitting the back of my neck, a simple perk that should not be discounted. I shivered all over. The second thing I noticed were the practiced movements I made as I got into my truck—movements that were no longer necessary because the mass of hair I had learned over my lifetime to maneuver around no longer existed.

When I got home, I jumped in the shower and noticed that I only needed a tenth of the shampoo I normally used to wash my hair, if that. The shampoo bottle in the shower was half full, and I always kept three reserve bottles, just in case. At this rate, it would take years for me to use up all my shampoo. I quickly scanned the shampoo bottle for an expiration date, surprised when I found one. The long, arduous process of drying my hair was now accomplished in a matter of minutes as I dried off, got dressed, and made coffee.

I caught myself in the middle of the night shifting positions, tossing and turning in my bed as my hands gathered, flipped, and arranged my missing hair.

People at work were shocked by my appearance but also a bit curious about the change. Without exception, everyone I came in contact with felt the need to tell me what they thought of the new me. Their approval was unanimous.

The most astonishing thing that occurred—another reminder of how much my hair was a part of me—was when I watched television. I would sit on the couch and start to relax, watching a sitcom or a good movie, and would suddenly become aware that my chin was resting on my chest so that I was effectively watching TV through upward rolled eyes. It was the weirdest thing, and at first, I couldn't understand why it was happening. I worried that I had a brain tumor or cancer or some other disorder that was causing my neck to malfunction.

I was sitting at my desk at work a couple of days later, completely engrossed in the stack of paperwork before me when it suddenly occurred to me what the problem with my neck was. I took in a quick breath and laid my pen down on my desk, stunned at the obvious explanation, astounded that I had not realized it before, in awe of how my body had always accommodated my hair. My neck had tirelessly worked for so long to support my heavy hair that it still did so even though I had no more hair to support.

CHAPTER TWENTY

It took me a whole week to get my courage up, deciding in the end that I would never be more ready to visit a gay bar than I was right now. To keep putting it off would just make it more difficult. It was your standard rip-off-the-Band-Aid solution to doing something really hard. It wasn't that I didn't want to go; it was that I had never been social out in the world before, and the prospect scared the crap out of me.

On Saturday afternoon, after an early dinner, I began to prepare. After picking through my closet, putting together the perfect outfit, and arranging everything out on my bed, I changed my mind and started all over again. By the end of it, there were clothes strewn all over my bedroom. Never before had I had this much difficulty selecting an outfit. This was all new territory for me—new clothing, new place, new people. I was totally flying by the seat of my brand-new pants.

Finally settling on a pair of jeans and a nice blouse, I took a quick shower and did my makeup. My hair was a challenge. After two hours fiddling with it, I gave up, irritated that I could not get it to look like it did when it was first cut. I finally settled for the messy, I-couldn't-care-less look and got dressed.

At nine-thirty, I drove out to the city, pulling into the parking lot of *Club Imagine* around ten o'clock. I waited until no other women were walking toward the club, then gathered the last of my courage and got out of my truck. I could hear music growing louder as I neared the building, and as I turned toward the entrance, two women exited, thoroughly ogling me as they passed. It was my first contact of the evening and surprisingly enjoyable, and I wasn't even inside the front door yet. I walked through the entrance into a small foyer, where a huge man sat on a skinny stool behind a tall desk.

"There's a five-dollar cover, and I need to see some ID," he said in a gruff voice.

I pulled out my driver's license and a five-dollar bill and handed him both. He glanced at my driver's license, then looked at me, narrowing his eyes as if to suggest he found it highly unlikely that I was over the age of twenty-one. He seemed to reconsider and handed back my license with a conspiratorial grin. It was confusing, and I wasn't sure I'd been allowed admittance until he gave me a stamp on the back of my hand, leaving two letters in wet black ink. *CI*.

I gave myself a silent pep talk, then pushed through a set of swinging doors, hesitating as a whole new world opened up to me. It was like walking through a wormhole to some other dimension, a secret place where only women who loved women existed.

I stood there and scanned the large room, taking in its four separate parts. The bar was directly to my right, and to my left stood two pool tables. The dance floor was across the room along the back wall, and in between stood ten round tables, all of which were occupied. The music was loud, the lights dim, and the air was filled with smoke. I took a deep breath and let out a surprised cough, clearing my throat as I looked around for a place to sit.

The bar was the only place left with available seating, so I grabbed a stool about halfway down, hesitating when I caught my reflection in the huge mirror on the wall behind the bar. Hardly recognizing the woman I was looking at, I wondered how long this effect would last as I swiveled to my right and took in the sprawling room. It was crowded with women, talking and laughing, drinking and smoking, flirting and touching, giving absolutely no thought to being seen. Well, maybe a little thought; there was no doubt they were here to be seen, and it was like eye candy—literally mouthwatering to look at.

The pool table area was the most crowded with women, some playing pool, others just hanging out watching. There was kissing and touching, arms draped around hips, waists, shoulders, and necks, and fingers hooked into belt loops and back pockets. I turned toward the dance floor to find more women kissing, holding each other close, lost in a world of their own. My eyes moved from one contact to the next:

couples sitting together, holding hands, looking into each other's eyes, and kissing. I smiled as I observed women interact intimately as if it were the most natural thing in the world. What I was seeing was almost unreal to me. I was, of course, personally familiar with this type of contact in private, but to see other women touching and kissing excited me in a way I had not anticipated. It was hard to look away, and then I did just that, my attention drawn to the entrance as a hoard of new women poured into the club. Where were all these women coming from, and where had they been hiding the last couple of weeks while I searched the streets of Sacramento looking for them?

The unmistakable sound of someone clearing their throat behind me swung me back around to the bar, where a very attractive woman behind the bar was wiping down the surface of it in front of me. It took me a moment to realize what she wanted, and another moment to come up with the name of a drink.

"Beer, please," I blurted, then smiled, pleased with myself.

She raised her eyebrows, waiting. At first, it was unclear to me what further information I could give her, but then I remembered how many beer brands were advertised on television every night. I picked the first one I thought of.

"Oh! Budweiser, please."

She reached inside a refrigerated compartment, pulled out a bottle of Budweiser beer, opened it, and set it down in front of me. Then she looked at me and again raised her eyebrows.

"How much?"

She looked almost offended by my question and a little annoyed as she held up two fingers.

I gave her two dollars, and she turned and walked to the cash register. I could not take my eyes off her. I had never seen so much attitude displayed by one person in such a short period of time. She was absolutely the coolest woman I had ever seen. I quickly roamed her body, blushing at how completely forward and feral it felt. She was really beautiful—low-cut tank top, tight jeans, and pixie-cut blond hair—the epitome of cool and sexy. She looked like she didn't care about anything, like she was above it all, like working as a bartender in a gay club around these women every night was normal, routine, just a job.

And then another woman came in behind the bar who was even cooler, a little taller, a little older, with shoulder-length auburn hair tucked behind her ears. She smiled at the customers, and they smiled back. She knew their names, and they knew hers. Mason. She began taking orders and mixing drinks. The two bartenders worked well together, and they looked really good together. I could definitely see the advantage of sitting at the bar.

Not wanting to get caught over-ogling my bartenders, I swiveled to the right and scanned the crowd, enjoying the wonderful displays of love and affection as if I were a third-party observer. Suddenly, it occurred to me that these women could see me too. The first couple of glances I dismissed as my imagination, but it quickly became clear that these women, as they walked by me or stood around talking in groups, were looking at me—not staring at me but glancing at me. A lot.

I swiveled back to the bar and looked at my beer. I took a sip and then another. It wasn't horrible, my first sip of beer, but it wasn't what I expected either. Commercials on television made beer look like the most delicious drink ever created. As I sipped my beer, watching the women behind me through the mirror in front of me, someone bumped my right shoulder.

"Oh, excuse me," a voice said, and I turned to find a tall, very attractive man standing next to me trying to get the bartender's attention. He had the face of a supermodel, and his blond hair was even messier than mine, giving me hope that mine didn't look as bad as I thought it did. "Sorry about that. Didn't mean to bump you. It's crowded tonight," he said. He was wearing a Levi's button-down shirt, loose-fitting jeans, and light brown work boots, and he was extremely well-built.

"My name is Sam," he introduced himself.

"Shannon, nice to meet you," I replied, offering my hand.

Sam smiled and took my hand, and then a woman pushed up against me from my other side. I swiveled to my left and was met with a very attractive smile. "Hi. I'm Sandy."

"Hi. I'm Shannon," I replied, offering her my hand.

She was dressed similarly to Sam, but her shirt was plaid and unbuttoned, revealing a very white tank top and ample cleavage. Then I noticed two similarly dressed women standing so close behind me that when I attempted to swivel my barstool, they had to step back to avoid my knees.

"Hi there. My name is Becky," one of them said.

"I'm Laurie," said the other.

"I'm Shannon. Nice to meet you," I said as I offered my hand, hesitating as I realized that Sam was not a man.

There was a moment of uncertainty as we all glanced at each other, and then they all started speaking at once. I tried to keep up, but aside from their mutual desire to know whether I came here often, the only noteworthy information I could glean from them was that they all knew each other and worked together. They were firefighters.

Feeling a little surrounded, I tried to turn toward the bar, but this made Sam think I was turning toward her, which just encouraged her to lean in closer. I was almost certain she was asking me to dance, but when her lips lightly brushed the shell of my ear, I found that I was unable to formulate an answer. My body began to tingle and my eyes fluttered closed. I let out a slow breath, a little surprised by my body's reaction to her. Who was this woman?

When I opened my eyes again, I caught Mason watching me. She held my gaze for a moment, then looked away, attending to one of the other patrons sitting at the bar. I tried to swivel away from Sam, but it was impossible. I was stuck and had no idea how to remove myself from what was slowly feeling like a blockade.

Movement from just outside our little bulwark caught my

attention, and a hand emerged from between Becky and Laurie, hovering a moment before reaching forward and picking up my hand from where it lay fidgeting nervously on my lap. Becky and Laurie turned to see who the hand belonged to, and Sam and Sandy stopped talking and were looking too.

"Hey you," Jordan said as she squeezed between Becky and Laurie. She raised my hand to her lips and laid a soft kiss on my knuckle. "Dance?"

Before I could respond, she pulled me up off my barstool and led me through the crowd to the dance floor. I noticed three things about Jordan immediately. My earrings sparkling in her ears, how adorable she looked with short hair, and that I was still very much in love with her. She put her hands lightly on my waist, and I held onto her arms as we moved slowly back and forth, her hands feeling wonderfully familiar on me but somehow foreign in this place, on a dance floor, dancing. She looked so different than I had ever seen her look before, and more beautiful than I remembered. I wanted nothing more than to forgive her for leaving me and beg her to come back. I quickly licked my lips as my reaction to her spread through my body, the strength and speed of it making me light-headed. I looked down at my feet, took a deep breath, and tried to concentrate. I didn't want to look like a complete fool on my first dance.

"You know how to dance," I said, looking back up at her, noticing for the first time the change in her features. Her cheeks were not as full, her cheekbones more pronounced. She'd definitely lost some weight.

"A little, I'm learning."

"Do you come here often?" I asked, taking a line from the firefighters.

"I come sometimes."

"Well, I'm glad you were here tonight."

"Were you getting nervous with all that attention?"

"You were watching me?"

"Yeah, a little. Listen, those ladies are nice. They're really cool. They're firefighters. They're like superheroes. I don't want you to think that they're not okay just because they're different from what you're used to. There are different kinds of women here…it's hard to explain." She hesitated, seeming to gather her thoughts. "I know you dressed down to come here, but here you look very feminine. These women have never seen you before. You're new, you're alone. Those women at the bar think you might like them—that you might like a more masculine woman. They're called *butch*."

"I understand. I know I panicked a little bit. It was nice of you to ask me to dance. I appreciate it."

"After you called me to warn me that we had been outed, I called Shawn, and he told me that you got married in April." The subject change was so sudden, it took me a moment to realize she wasn't talking about butch women anymore. "You had just left your husband when you called me." I nodded, but before I could explain, she continued. "I was afraid you'd show up here. You don't belong here, Shannon. You shouldn't be here."

"You're here," I shot back, defensive, confused by her change in tone, realizing a second later that there had been no change in tone. She hadn't once smiled at me since she rescued me from my barstool, and except for the light kiss on my hand, had not shown the slightest bit of affection for me. This wasn't a happy reunion; this was an intervention.

"Yeah, but I'm not married, my dad is not an Elder, and I don't have the same standing in the church as you and your family do. I will not be missed."

"I miss you," I blurted and immediately regretted it.

"You're here because of me? So, now I will be held responsible for leading you out of the church?"

"I did not come here looking for you, and you did not lead me out of the church. I have been gay my whole life."

"But they won't see it that way, Shannon."

"I don't care how they see it. I am not here because of you. I left the church because it became impossible for me to stay."

"It's not impossible. You can still go back. You don't want to do this, really. You have no idea what you're getting yourself into here. You are way out of your depth."

"What do you care, Jordan? You left me! You cannot tell me what to do! I do not belong to you anymore!" My eyes teared up, and I stepped away from her. "I'm gonna go," I said, feeling confused and thoroughly dumped again.

"Good. I'll walk you out." Jordan's jaw was set as she took my arm and escorted me through the mass of women toward the exit, pulling me along, eager to get me out of there.

A call sounded from the bar, and I looked over to find Mason waving at us. Jordan's grip on my arm tightened as she abruptly turned toward the end of the bar, where Mason stood waiting, drying her hands on a towel.

"Hi." Mason nodded at me, smiling.

"Hi." I returned her smile.

Mason looked at Jordan, then back at me. "I'm Mason. This is my bar. Welcome."

I looked at Jordan, then back at Mason. "Thank you, Mason."

Mason leaned toward Jordan and said something I couldn't hear, then gave me another smile, making it clear to both of us that I was welcome in her bar. Jordan did not look happy as she led me through the foyer and out the door, her grip on my arm tightening when a woman standing just outside gave me an approving head-to-toe check-out. The woman's eyes locked with mine, and her mouth broke out in a warm smile that instantly made me smile in return.

"Hi," I said, blushing at my boldness.

"Hi," she returned in a flirtatious voice, taking a step forward and standing a bit taller. Jordan stepped toward her, giving her a warning look, and the woman took a step back, losing the smile and looking a little confused.

"Be careful, Shannon," Jordan said as she led me to my truck. "You have no idea what you're doing. These women will eat you alive."

"If you don't want me, Jordan, why do you care?" I asked, pulling my arm from her grasp.

"I care what happens to you, Shannon. These women will take advantage of you. Look at you." She gestured at me, then rolled her eyes. "They will actively try to bed you. This is not the church where men control themselves. You're not prepared for this."

"Christian men are not at all what they seem."

"What the hell does that mean?"

"Oh! Now you use cuss words?"

"Yes, Shannon, I do. I cuss and drink and dance and…sleep with women and…a whole bunch of other things. I mean, what did you expect?"

"You sleep with women? Are you sleeping with someone?"

"Well, that's what this is all about, isn't it? I'm gay. I left the church. Who else would I sleep with?"

"Well, I'm gay too, in case you haven't noticed, and I have left the church, whether you want to respect that or not. So, I am here, like you, because of my desire to have sex and my preference for women. You are not my moral authority, and it comes off a little hypocritical when you, of all people, tell me what to do."

Seething and frustrated, Jordan raised her voice for the first time. "You…don't…belong here! Go home and don't come back!"

Several women walked by us in both directions, and one of them, on her way to the club's entrance, stopped and turned, looking at us. "Is everything okay here?"

Jordan turned, facing the woman, who seemed legitimately concerned with my well-being, and the woman's mouth fell open as a look of surprise spread across her face. I knew this look. I had seen it many times before. A look of surprised wonder at being in the presence of someone who looked like Jordan. Jordan was uniquely beautiful, undoubtedly the most beautiful woman this woman had ever seen.

"Yes, everything is fine. Thank you," I said, glancing at Jordan, who shot the woman a warning glare. I let out a huff as I half-rolled my eyes, turning to the woman and throwing out my hand. "Sorry. Very rude of me. My name is Shannon."

The woman managed to peel her eyes off Jordan and look at me. She shook my hand, and when it became clear that Jordan was not going to introduce herself, I said, "And this is Jordan."

"Hi. I'm Erin."

"Thank you, Erin, for stopping and checking," I said, giving her an apologetic smile. "We were just having a little argument, but it means a lot to me that you asked."

The woman blushed, smiling awkwardly. She was very cute, even more so flustered and blushing. "You're welcome... Okay... Right... Um. Have a nice evening."

She turned and walked away, and I couldn't get over how touched I was that she had taken the time to check on me, a stranger, making sure I was okay. "I think you're wrong about the women here. I think they're very nice," I said to Jordan. "I hope to be meeting more of them soon."

I turned and unlocked my truck, hating to leave Jordan standing there, hating that our conversation had gone so poorly. But there was nothing else I could do. She needed to realize that I was serious about leaving the church and was not going back. I jumped in the truck without another word, turned on the ignition, and drove out of the parking lot, watching her in my rearview mirror as she stood there alone. I wiped a tear from my eye and sniffed as I took a deep breath.

My first visit to a gay bar was nothing short of amazing, monumental, I couldn't find an adequate word to describe it, and seeing Jordan again was more than I had hoped for. It irked me and amused me in equal measure that she thought she could talk to me that way. I shook my head and let out a huff. I would not let her tell me what to do. I lifted my chin and straightened my shoulders, took another deep breath, and drove home.

CHAPTER TWENTY-ONE

I started going to the club every Friday and Saturday night and slowly began to meet women. At first, I was a bit shy and in awe of everyone I met. Just the act of being near another lesbian, being looked at, smiled at, checked out, flirted with, brushed up against, or danced with, made me nervous and generated such excitement in me, I could barely put two meaningful words together when trying to make conversation with them. That slowly changed.

I made friends, and this was helpful and very satisfying. Hanging out with women who were like me not only boosted my confidence but helped me feel more comfortable in my own skin. I learned popular vernacular, found that I enjoyed using profanity, and took advantage of every opportunity to express myself. Soon, I could carry on a conversation with almost anybody, even with women I felt attracted to.

Jordan was often in the club. Actually, she was there every time I was, and although she never talked to me, she always managed to remind me that I didn't belong there and that I needed to return to the church, shooting me her scary warning glare every time she got the chance.

At first, it bothered me, but after a while, I found it ridiculously silly and would respond with a quick, sarcastic smile. I could tell by the daggers I got in return that this infuriated her. I began looking forward to our little exchanges, and it became clear to me that the main reason I frequented *Club Imagine* so much was because she was there. Meeting other lesbians was just a bonus.

All the new social stuff I was learning was invaluable, but still, I could not master the nuances necessary to move from friendly conversation to more intimate contact. Several women flirted with me, but I could never get to the next step. I wasn't even sure what the next step was, often missing cues, never quite responding appropriately, and when the slightest feeling of lust made itself known, Jordan would pop into my head and I'd spend critical minutes trying to get her out. Of course, the woman who happened to be flirting with me would conclude that I had no interest in her and would get up and walk away, leaving me sitting there wondering what the heck happened. And then I'd scan the room and find Jordan sitting at a nearby table, glaring her disapproval at me, letting me know I didn't belong, making me more determined than ever not to give up.

When I wasn't busy failing miserably at flirting or trying to ignore Jordan's latest dirty look, I'd hang out with my new friends, enjoying the feeling of being accepted for who I was. I was doing just that one evening when a familiar face entered the club—a woman I recognized from my very first visit to *Club Imagine*, the woman who had given me an approving head-to-toe check-out as Jordan escorted me out of the club, the woman I had so boldly said hi to.

As she walked by the table I was sitting at, our eyes met, and she gave me the same warm smile she had back then. I returned her smile, just as warmly. As she made her way through the club, I noticed she didn't seem to be with anyone. She didn't dance with anyone, wasn't holding anyone's hand, or kissing anyone. She roamed the club, visiting with friends, kind of like me, just hanging out. She was about my height, about my size, and wore the same type of clothing I wore. She had short blond hair, her body was exceptional, and she was very cute.

A playful argument between two of my friends—Maggi and Barbara; they were a couple—interrupted my thoughts. Barbara was describing the noises Maggi made when she had an orgasm, hooting and howling, her face a mask of perpetual ecstasy. It was hilarious. Everyone was laughing and teasing, and Maggie became a little embarrassed, a little offended, and she playfully pushed Barbara, who pretended to fall over with exaggerated arm movements, knocking her beer over on the table. It quickly spread to my side, and I jumped up out of my chair to avoid the spillage, bumping into someone behind me and knocking the beer she was holding all over the front of her shirt.

"Oh my God, I'm sorry…"

"Jesus Christ," the woman mumbled under her breath, holding her shirt away from her breasts as she slowly straightened and looked up at me. It was the cute blond woman! Crap!

"Let me get a towel." I ran to the bar, got a clean cloth from Mason, and hurried back to the cute blond woman, apologizing again as I handed it to her.

She snatched it out of my hand and began rubbing it on her shirt, complaining when it became obvious the cloth was not helping. "My shirt is ruined."

"I have another shirt!" I blurted out, remembering the bag of clean laundry in my truck.

"Really?" she asked, sounding skeptical.

"Yeah…really… I do… Clean laundry…" I stammered. "I have a couple of clean T-shirts in my truck."

"Can you show me these shirts?" she asked, her tone mildly sarcastic.

"Yes, of course. Please, follow me." I led her through the club toward the entrance and was almost out the door when a hand landed on my shoulder, backing me up a step before swinging me around.

"Where are you going?" Jordan asked me with a hilariously menacing voice.

"Excuse me?" I replied, trying to sound indignant, very aware of Jordan's hand still on my shoulder and hugely frustrated at how her touch made my body tingle.

"Don't go with her," Jordan said, giving me her scary warning glare. I barely controlled the urge to laugh. She was really very adorable.

"I'm just getting her a clean shirt…"

"Shannon, she's not good enough for you. Don't do this. You don't belong here."

It was infuriating enough that Jordan didn't want me but was trying to control who I might leave with, but her making assumptions about my reasons for leaving with this very cute blond woman instantly pissed me off.

"Stop telling me what to do. I don't belong to you anymore." I jerked my shoulder away from her and took a step back.

"Is there a problem?" the cute blond woman asked as she stepped up next to me and slipped her hand around my hip, giving Jordan a glare of her own.

My eyes widened as I pressed my lips together, hoping that this did not turn into a brawl, a fight between two beautiful women for my attention. That would have been super cool but also kind of embarrassing. The thrill of the moment quickly passed as I remembered that Jordan wasn't after my attention. She believed that she had influenced my decision to leave the church, and all she cared about was sending me back, trying to make this place uncomfortable for me by bullying me and harassing those I chose to interact with.

A massive wave of anger bubbled up inside me. "There is no problem," I said, glaring at Jordan before turning to my new friend to offer her my best smile. "Come. My truck is out this way." I then did something that surprised even me. I took my liberator by the hand as I led her toward the exit, throwing a quick glance over my shoulder at Jordan, who looked very frustrated and, if I wasn't mistaken, a little rejected, much the same way I looked when she walked out on me.

I opened the passenger-side door of my truck, dug through my laundry bag, pulled out four T-shirts, one stacked on top of the other, and presented them to the cute blond woman.

"Please, take one," I said, smiling.

"Wow, clean and folded, and I get to choose. I'm impressed." She quickly fingered through them and picked the yellow one. "Thank you," she said, giving me a warm smile.

I put the remaining T-shirts back in my laundry bag, and as I closed the truck door and locked it, I looked over toward the entrance of the club, disappointed when I didn't see

Jordan. She hadn't even bothered to follow me out here and make sure I wasn't being seduced by her supposed adversary.

I turned back to the cute blond woman just as she pulled her beer-stained shirt up over her head. I blinked and swallowed hard. She wore a white laced bra, and her breasts were incredible. I looked up from her breasts, met her eyes, and immediately averted mine. She pulled my T-shirt on over her head, tucked it into her jeans, and neatly cuffed the sleeves up twice—a gesture that amused me. I took it as a compliment, as if approving of my fashion choice by adding the finishing touches to make it look on point.

"I'm sorry for ruining your blouse...erm..." I hesitated, not knowing her name.

"Diana."

"Diana... I'm Shannon."

"Yeah, I know."

"You know my name?"

"Yes. I know your name."

"Oh. Okay, then...it's nice to meet you, Diana." I smiled at her and she smiled back.

"I have to say, this is the most creative come-on I've ever had the pleasure of."

"I swear, it was an accident..."

"I'm teasing."

She was totally flirting with me, and it felt good, my inability to respond with much more than a shy smile, not at all deterring her. Her eyes moved over my face, the edge of her lips curling upward in an approving smile. She slowly looked down the length of my body, and as her eyes moved back up, they stopped at my breasts. Touché. She gave them a quick once-over, then locked eyes with me and took two steps forward, her fingers brushing against my hands.

Without even thinking, led only by a sudden strong desire to know what she tasted like, I leaned forward and kissed her softly on the mouth. She responded instantly, her hands moving up my arms to my shoulders and around my neck, her body pressing into mine. She slipped her tongue into my mouth, and my body began to heat up. She ended the kiss slowly, then leaned her head in next to mine.

"Come home with me tonight," she whispered in my ear.

"Okay," I said, breathless.

She smiled sweetly, took my hand, and very cooly escorted me to her car, whereas I very nearly got cold feet, quickly going through a checklist in my head—mismatched but adequate underwear, shaved legs, trimmed pussy, Jordan.

As we drove through the city, my nervousness dissipated, replaced by a bit of defiance as I resolutely insisted that this was the first step in getting over Jordan once and for all. If her breaking up with me and leaving me alone in a place where I would be miserable forever didn't do it, having sex with a beautiful blond woman with incredible breasts certainly would.

Diana let herself into her apartment, flipped on the lights, then turned to me and said, "Come in."

I stepped inside, closed the door, and looked around. Her apartment was small but nice and very tidy—her kitchen to the right, next to a small dining area, and her living room to the left, where a hallway entrance led to her bedroom and bath.

"What would you like to drink?"

"I'll have what you're having."

She gestured toward the couch. "Sit."

I sat on the couch and waited, my nervousness returning as thoughts of Jordan's glaring hypocrisy and ridiculous behavior clouded my mind. She cannot control my sex! I gave myself a curt nod, pushing Jordan from my mind as Diana walked in from the kitchen. She handed me a beer as she sat down next to me, and I immediately took a long swallow, hoping it would calm me. When she did the same, I wondered if she was as nervous as I was.

We talked briefly about interests and jobs. She was a Captain in the Air Force, a pilot who loved to fly jets. Her favorite movie? *Top Gun*. That was the last piece of information I was able to take in. She was not just cute, she was gorgeous. She had beautiful blue eyes and a sensuous mouth. I followed the slant of her jaw down her lovely neck to her collarbone, my gaze bushing across her breasts before landing on her broad shoulders, which, I must say, filled out my T-shirt spectacularly. My open appraisal of her was interrupted by her sudden silence. God, I hoped hadn't missed a question I needed to answer or a comment I needed to respond to! I was about to apologize for my lapse in concentration when she put her beer down on the coffee table. I did the same, and she moved closer, smiling sweetly as she leaned in and kissed me. Wow... Smooth.

We slowly kissed deeper, both of us moaning when our tongues met, her hand on my thigh, my hand already under her T-shirt, moving along her waist. Without warning, she pulled her T-shirt up over her head, revealing her lace-clad breasts, the clasp in front calling to me as it strained to contain her. I looked into Diana's eyes, and when she quickly licked her lips, I reached out and unclasped her bra, releasing her beautiful breasts. "Oh God," I breathed, hesitating only a moment before reaching out and cupping them. They were incredible—soft and warm and so touchable. I took one of them into my mouth, and Diana moaned as she arched her back, offering them up to me. The throbbing between my thighs intensified as I sucked and kissed and squeezed, fondling them until I had Diana bent back over the arm of the couch, laid out like a platter holding the most delectable treats I had ever feasted on.

"Let's go to my room." Diana's breathless voice brought me back to my senses, and I immediately stopped and pulled back, quickly crawling off of her and letting her stand up.

She grabbed my hand, pulled me to my feet, and led me down the hallway to her bedroom. I could feel how wet I was as I walked behind her, my eyes gobbling up every inch of her bare shoulders and back, her trim waist, and her Levi-covered ass. She flipped on the bedroom light, released my hand, and walked toward the bed. I stood in the doorway as she removed her jeans and panties, slowly revealing her trimmed blond bush and beautifully toned ass. My breathing increased each time she moved, and as she slid onto the bed and settled back against the headboard, I gulped loudly. I could see her pussy, and I wanted it very badly!

"Please." She waved her hand invitingly.

I pulled my T-shirt up over my head and let it fall to the floor, then unbuckled my belt and unbuttoned my jeans, experiencing a brief moment of body shyness as I shimmied out of them. I quickly removed my mismatched underwear, then walked to the foot of her bed, feeling encouraged when she smiled and scooched down a bit in anticipation. Her arms reached out to me, beckoning me, and I went to her, burying my face between her gorgeous breasts.

What happened after that was a marathon of pure lust. Although I revisited her breasts several times during our night of sex, I did not let the rest of her go unattended. She let me suck her pussy, and after she came for me, she returned the favor in kind. And she didn't stop there, and boy did she know what she was doing. She discovered parts of me that I didn't even know were sexual. And I came, and I came, and I came. I had no idea I could have that many orgasms in one night. And boy, what orgasms they were! I had one that was so strong, I nearly passed out!

We did it prone, from behind, and standing up on our knees. At one point, we were both sucking each other's pussies at the same time. It was heaven! She used every part of herself to make me come, and she had no problem showing me how to make her come. She was my sex guru, and I was her willing pupil.

Several hours later, spent and sore, lying in each other's arms, she sighed a sigh of deep satisfaction, kissed the top of my head, and we fell asleep.

At some point during the night, I woke up, instantly feeling guilty and immediately chastising myself for it, reminding myself that Jordan didn't want me anymore and had no right to tell me who I could sleep with. I mean, what did I have to feel guilty about? I had thoroughly enjoyed my night of pleasure, and I knew that's all it was. Diana was a beautiful, kind, and passionate lover and a very lovely person, but we were not in a relationship, and we were never going to be in one. This was a typical one-night stand, and I couldn't help but feel a little proud of myself.

What I felt guilty about was cheating on Jordan, which was ridiculous because we were no longer together. If Jordan didn't want me, then fine. Until I could come to terms with my feelings for Jordan, there were women willing to spend time with me who were totally open to doing so without the chaos and confusion of a relationship. I fell asleep mid-thought, too exhausted to continue contemplating the maddening, never-ending, emotional rollercoaster in my mind.

The next morning, Diana woke me in a rush. "Shannon, wake up!" I opened my eyes to find her standing next to my side of the bed wearing an olive-green T-shirt perfectly tucked into a pair of green camouflage khakis. "I have to go to work. I need to take you back to your truck."

I jumped out of bed, got dressed, and went to the bathroom. I didn't have a toothbrush or hairbrush with me, so I splashed water on my face, swished water around in my mouth, and ran my fingers through my thick, unruly hair, trying to shape it into some sort of style.

"Shannon, are you ready?" I hurried down the hallway toward the front door, where Diana stood waiting for me, the bottom of her camouflage khakis perfectly tucked into black leather, lace-up boots. "Sorry I can't offer you coffee and feed you breakfast this morning. I've been called into work. We have to go."

"No problem, I understand." And I did, but I could not ignore the feeling that she was trying to get rid of me.

She smiled apologetically as I bent down to lace my shoes, handing me her briefcase and her perfectly folded green camouflage shirt and cap as I stood up. "Can you hold these for me, please?"

She opened the door and led me out into the hallway, and

after she closed the door and locked it, she turned to me, her eyes meeting mine for a moment. I smiled, and she blushed. She cleared her throat, took her briefcase from me, and turned, marching ahead of me toward her car. I would have never guessed Diana was shy, especially after last night. Was she embarrassed about what we did together? Did she regret it? I was by no means an expert, but I was pretty sure we shared a spectacular night together. I couldn't imagine we had anything to be embarrassed about.

As we drove through the city, Diana seemed preoccupied, and I didn't want to interrupt her somehow. She was either already mentally on the job, readying herself for her day, or she was giving me the cold shoulder. And then she looked at me and gave me a shy smile, canceling all the doubts I had about the night we spent together.

"You look nice in your uniform," I said, wanting to tell her what a great time I had without saying something like, *I really had a great time last night*. I hoped she knew what I was trying to say.

"Thank you," she said, blushing again. "The military is like that. You have to go when they call."

A feeling of respect and admiration welled up in me. I was proud of her—a gay woman, a Captain in the U.S. Air Force, an airplane pilot. I wondered about her story, her background, her life, but I would never know these things about her. Such was the nature of the one-night stand.

She dropped me off with a quick goodbye and a super sweet "Thank you," and I jumped in my truck and drove home, feeling pretty darn thankful myself.

* * *

I spent the rest of my Sunday cleaning the apartment, feeling more relaxed than I had in a long time.

I heard nothing from the church or my family. I understood this, of course. There could be no contact between the willful sinner and the saved one. I mourned them, but I had to let go of them. They had certainly let go of me, and after a few weeks, I stopped wondering if I would ever hear from them again.

I spent my evenings after work in class, sharpening my cooking skills, and on the weekends, I visited *Club Imagine*, hanging out, dancing, and drinking beer. I deepened my friendships at the club, and a sense of belonging grew in me. I was a part of these women. They were definitely a part of me. Jordan was always in the back of my mind, and she was often in the club when I was, keeping her eye on me. I got used to it and actually started to feel comforted by it. It meant that even though she didn't want me anymore, she still cared about me a little, and even if her actions were a bit extreme, I didn't care. I would take whatever attention she could give me.

In July, a couple of days before my rental agreement expired, I got home from work and went directly to the manager's office to renew it. It didn't take long; the manager seemed to be waiting for me with all the paperwork required ready for me to sign. We talked a bit, me telling him how great it was living there, him telling me what a good renter I was—the usual renter-rentee banter I suspected. It felt good somehow, and I left the manager's office smiling.

As I rounded the corner of the building, my smile fell right off my face. Samuel's car was parked next to my truck. I looked up at my apartment to find him standing at my door, knocking. I slowly retreated, then turned and ran in the opposite direction, hiding behind some bushes on the back side of the building. Breathing hard, my heart beating impossibly fast, I peered through the bushes, waiting for Samuel to appear. I couldn't imagine him trying anything out here in the open. He was a Christian. He was in the church. But I sensed danger, something felt wrong about him just showing up like this without at least calling first.

A minute or two passed before he walked into view. He put his left hand on his hip and slowly scanned the parking lot, a large brown envelope hanging from his right hand, tapping impatiently against his leg. He turned and looked at my apartment for a moment, then down at his watch. He walked to his car, got in, and drove away. I leaned back against the building, took in a deep breath, and slowly blew it out. I waited another moment or two until I was sure he was really gone, then wiggled my way through the bushes and out onto the parking lot. I checked the area where he had parked—not really sure what I was looking for—then checked my truck for any sign of damage or forced entry.

I spent the rest of the night peeking out the living room window, watching for any sign of his return, unable to sleep as every bump in the night sent adrenalin shots through my body. At seven o'clock, I put on some coffee, then stood at the front window waiting for it to brew. Nothing. No sign of Samuel, thank God, but still, I was shaken, unable to imagine what he could have wanted from me, shaken to the core because he thought he could knock on my door.

* * *

In August, while hanging out in the club with my friends—I would never grow tired of this gratifying activity—a handful of us discussed the possibility of driving out to San Francisco for the famous Gay Pride weekend. It was way too late to get a hotel room in San Francisco, and Barbara and Denise had to work on Sunday anyway, so we decided to drive out on Saturday and stay for the day. We would miss the famous Pride Parade on Sunday, but I really wanted to go and promised everyone that I would organize everything next time so we could stay the whole weekend and see the Parade. Everyone agreed, and we all met early Saturday morning in Michelle's apartment parking lot. Her place was closest to the freeway and there was plenty of free parking for the rest of us to park our cars for the day. We piled into Barbara and Maggi's car—it was the biggest and could fit the five of us comfortably—and then headed for San Francisco. The drive took almost three hours, and finding a parking garage with vacancies took half an hour more.

As we walked from the city-center part of San Francisco

toward the Gay Pride part of San Francisco, loud music filled the air as more and more people crowded the streets, the majority of them gay, holding hands, arms around waists, kissing and touching as if it were the most natural thing in the world.

We rounded the corner of a tall building, and the music came in full blast. There was a live band playing rock 'n' roll on a scaffolded stage lifted ten feet into the air in the middle of a main intersection, surrounded by hundreds of screaming, dancing gay people. I thought I was on another planet. And this was just one corner. There were three other corners set up just like this one with bands playing different kinds of music, surrounded by hundreds of more screaming, dancing gay people. And this was just for today, for our visit. Gay Pride lasted the whole weekend. It was amazing!

We walked into an area that was completely devoted to information and activism. The most prominent topics included HIV/AIDS and gay marriage. There were booths encouraging political affiliation and petition signing on any number of issues, from environmental to socioeconomic and everything in between.

We walked into an area devoted to the arts, where artists displayed their paintings and photographs, and authors promoted and sold their books. There were vendors selling T-shirts, jewelry, hats, purses, backpacks, fanny packs, and just about anything else you could imagine in gay theme. There were street performers dancing everything from interpretive dance to breakdance, people playing instruments I'd never seen before, and actors reciting poetry and performing small, street corner plays.

There were booths promoting health and fitness, mental health, and support services, and booths selling sex toys, vibrators, dildos, and devices that left me scratching my head and too embarrassed to inquire about. There were a couple of massage therapy booths, and right next to them, seeming to suggest they were somehow related, was a very interesting booth that touted the dominant, submissive lifestyle. Several very tall, long-legged, gorgeous women were manning the booth. They were dressed in beautiful feminine leather outfits, some of them wielding whips and others wielding long, thick, erotic feathers. It was fascinating, and I wanted to stay a little longer and talk to these lovely ladies about their organization, but Barbara insisted we push on. We only had one day.

We turned at the next corner, and the whole street was filled with booths just for food—vendors selling hotdogs and hamburgers, burritos and chili, French fries and chips, ice cream and brownies, and so much more. All the different aromas were driving me crazy, and I almost said, *let's eat!* But we were already around the next corner, where we entered an area crowded with mini bars, each playing their own dance music, selling mixed drinks, beer, wine coolers, and ice-cold Pepsi-Cola. It was hard to keep track of everything, and several times we got turned around, not sure where we had come from or in which direction to proceed.

Barbara wanted to attend an amateur women's bodybuilding contest, but we were not sure exactly where it was, so we started asking random people around us and found a very cool, native San Franciscan, veteran Gay Pride attendee, who knew everything about anything Gay Pride San Francisco. Her name was Kandis, and she was friendly and very helpful. She showed us the way, and as we approached the building where the competition would take place, Maggi invited Kandis to join us. Kandis accepted, and we were all officially introduced. As we got in line to purchase our tickets, Kanis made eye contact with me for the very first time.

The competition was held in a huge auditorium with a big, round, extended stage, creating a very exciting circular runway. We chose a group of seats off the middle center aisle and filed in one by one, Kandis holding back a bit and sitting next to me in the aisle seat. As we settled in, her arm brushed mine, and a shot of electricity surged through me. It surprised me, and I turned and looked at her to see if she felt it too.

Wide eyes and raised brows told me that she had. Her expression quickly changed into an adorable smile that was so irresistible, I was smiling back before I even realized it.

"So, Shannon, are you enjoying your Gay-Pride experience?"

"I am. I'm completely impressed."

"What impresses you the most?"

"I think it's the number of people here and how open they are. I got the strange sensation that I was not on planet Earth anymore. Like I was in an alternate universe. It doesn't seem real."

"Where are you from?"

"Sacramento."

"Sacramento has a very strong gay community. Do you not get out much?"

"Yeah… I do. I try to. Actually, I have not been out very long. This is my first Gay Pride."

"Oh, in that case, it's an honor to accompany you on your first Gay Pride."

When Kandis gave me another one of her adorable smiles, it occurred to me that she might be flirting, but before I could process *that* possibility, the sudden hush of the crowd caught my attention. I looked toward the front of the auditorium and could not believe my eyes. Kandis noticed my expression and followed my gaze, and even though she didn't know who I was looking at, I could tell by her expression that she was looking at the same woman I was. Jordan was just that beautiful, and as she walked up the aisle toward us, heads were turning, following her progress, ogling her as she stopped a few feet in front of us. She was stalking me. That was the only explanation for her presence here. That, and the fact that every gay person in Northern California was here. But still, what were the chances that we would bump into each other at one of the biggest Gay Pride festivals in the world? She was definitely stalking me.

Jordan gave Kandis her go-to scary warning look and then walked on. Kandis and I and every other woman in the auditorium turned and watched her walk up the aisle and take her seat in the back. She had three friends with her, and I wondered if one of them was Jordan's girlfriend. I also wondered if one of them was Poppy or Linda or Silvia or whoever it was that was responsible for Jordan breaking up with me.

"Who was that?" Kandis asked as she turned back to me.

"Um, that was my ex."

"Wow. That would be a hard act to follow."

"She's intent on making it impossible."

"Unresolved relationship issues?"

"It's complicated."

"Isn't it always?"

I gave Kandis a weak smile, and then the lights dimmed and the competition started. Kandis looked at me several times during the competition, and I stole a couple of looks at her as well. Then, near the end, we looked at each other at the same time, our eyes holding for a long moment. I blushed. She was cute and had the most beautiful brown eyes, not to mention that killer smile. I resolved to think less about Jordan and more about the woman sitting next to me.

When the competition was over and the new bodybuilding champion was crowned, the lights were turned back up, and as we stood preparing to go, I took note of Kandis' body, her height and form, and the way she moved. I gave her an approving smile as I stepped out into the center aisle. Kandis returned my smile and stepped back, motioning with a wave of her hand for me to walk in front of her. I could feel her checking me out as we approached the exit, and then Jordan came into view. Kandis was probably looking at her and not at me anymore. Jordan was definitely looking at Kandis, again delivering a very severe warning look. I rolled my eyes at her and made my way through the exit into the foyer.

As we bottlenecked in the street entrance doorway, Kandis' fingers touched the small of my back, leaving me mildly aroused and a little worried that Jordan's presence might have something to do with my body's response. We inched our way through the doors and out onto the street, the six of us gathering in a huddle to decide where to go next. Kandis stood next to me, listening to Barbara and Maggi discuss our options, while Jordan and her entourage slowly strode by. I tried to ignore them, refusing to make eye contact with Jordan, concentrating instead on how close Kandis was standing next to me.

It was midafternoon, so we decided to get something to eat and made our way back to the food vendors we'd passed that morning. Kandis and I followed a couple of steps behind, both of us playing it shy, but when I saw Jordan up ahead hanging out with her buddies, seemingly waiting for us, I abandoned my shyness and grabbed Kandis' hand, giving Jordan a quick, thin-lipped smile as we passed. I looked at Kandis, hoping I hadn't overstepped, and was met with a surprised but delighted expression, letting me know that it was more than okay that we were holding hands.

It took a second or two for the importance of the moment to sink in, and I smiled. I was holding hands in public, and I was not ashamed or afraid that someone would see. Everyone was holding hands; I wasn't alone. It was my first time, and it was perfect. Our fingers intertwined, and a feeling of pride spread through me. I was a lesbian, and I could not have been happier. Denise and Michelle noticed the handholding first and gave each other a look as if to say, *Okay, that was fast*. Maggi smiled at me and winked, and I don't know if Barbara ever noticed. She was always very busy organizing everything.

We bought lunch, each of us something different, found an empty space on a wide set of steps in front of a nondescript, brownstone building, and sat down to eat. I had a chicken burrito, and Kandis had a fish sandwich. As we ate, Kandis told us a bit about herself. She worked in a bookstore on the pier and lived not far from where we sat, in a small apartment three blocks down from the park. She was thirty-two and single; she hadn't been in a relationship in a while but dated, which I assumed in a place like San Francisco was probably like breathing. I enjoyed her smile as I listened to her lovely voice and her contagious laugh. She had small laugh lines at the corners of her eyes, and her skin was tanned and clear. She wore no makeup, and her beautiful straight brown hair, casually tucked behind her ears, reached just past her shoulders. She was trim and fit, her neck long and her shoulders wide. She was pretty and friendly, and I was excited and proud to be her date at my very first Gay Pride.

After we ate, we strolled through the streets, taking in the festivities around us, and as we approached one of the large corner concerts, Kandis pulled me away from the others into a huge crowd of dancing gay people. She slipped her hands around my waist and pulled me to her, waiting a moment as we swayed back and forth before leaning in and kissing me. My arms went around her neck, and we danced and kissed like that through the rest of the song. She was a pretty good kisser, I had to admit.

"Come on, let's go find the others," Kandis said, and she pulled me through the crowd back the way we had come.

It only took a minute before I saw Michelle. We walked toward her, and the others came into view.

"This place is packed," Barbara said. "You could get lost in here forever."

"That would be wonderful," I replied.

Next, we decided to visit some of San Francisco's famous clubs, and Kandis knew where all of them were. She suggested three close by, then led the way, me in hand.

* * *

The first club was fabulous; there was no other word suitable to describe it. It was located in an old Victorian-style building, separated by floors into three distinct areas, each area uniquely decked out. The first floor had several floor-to-ceiling windows so that everyone outside passing by could see what was going on inside. There was a large bar on the back wall, several booths lined up along the wall to the left, and about twenty tables scattered evenly throughout. k.d.

Lang's voice sang in the background, but the dominant sound in the room was that of laughter and the voices of a couple hundred women talking all at once, drinking, smoking, and flirting, the air thick with nicotine, pheromones, and alcohol vapor.

The second floor had no window at all and was full of couches, big sofa chairs, and coffee tables, set in soft dim light, filled with women in pairs sitting close together, speaking in intimate whispers, behaving as if they were the only ones in the room, most of them openly making out. I stole a glance at Kandis, and she winked at me, her smile telling me she had spent some time in this room.

The third floor had a dance floor and was full to the brim with the steady beat of loud dance music, energy and excitement, and women dancing and having fun, kissing, touching, and moving together in a wave of celebration.

We drank a beer at the bar on the first floor, then headed to the third floor for a dance before moving on to another gay club that Kandis knew of, a typical gay bar; a dive, but nicer.

The dive bar was crowded, and Kandis grabbed my hips as we entered, steering me from behind to the left side of the room toward a big, beautiful, moon-shaped bar with a dozen or so barstools. She waved at the bartender as we all gathered together at the far end, reaching out over the shoulders of sitting customers to shake the bartender's outstretched hand. They obviously knew each other.

They exchanged greetings, and then Kandis raised her arm and pointed at us, moving her finger in a circle, signaling that she had just ordered us a round of something to drink. The bartender nodded her head, looked at me and winked, then turned and grabbed six shot glasses and a half-empty bottle of tequila. She set everything at the end of the bar for us to serve ourselves. Kandis filled the glasses, passed them out to us, and we raised them and clinked them together, shouting loud and proud, "To Love!"

It was amazing how crowded it was, how loud it was, and how festive it was. It was fun just watching everybody move and mingle. Denise and Michelle took a stroll through the bar, Barbara and Maggi found an empty corner to make out in, and Kandis and I just hung out together, her casually holding me from behind, her arms around my waist, her fingers playing with my belt buckle, her hips slowly swaying back and forth, bumping me softly to the beat of the music. My breath caught when her lips brushed my ear. It was astounding how she could turn me on even though I had no intention of being turned on. I had never been so openly hit on before and began to wonder what her intentions were.

A gap in the crowd opened in front of me for a split second, and I let out a silent gasp. The gap closed, and I was suddenly unsure if I had seen what I thought I saw. When it opened again, I let out an irritated huff. Jordan and her buddies were sitting in a booth on the other side of the bar, and she was staring right at me. I shook my head at her, bound and determined not to let her ruin my first Gay Pride. What was she thinking, and had her friends really agreed to spend their day at Gay Pride following Jordan's ex through the streets of San Francisco? They had to be very good friends to agree to that.

There was just enough tequila left in the bottle for one more round, and then we decided to go. We made our way slowly toward the entrance, Kandis' hands firmly on my hips, her breasts lightly touching my back as we inched forward through the crowd. She seemed to want to hold on to me and show this place that I was hers, a place she obviously frequented. I couldn't help but feel a little flattered and turned and smiled at her over my shoulder, surprised when her right hand suddenly jerked away from my hip. Kandis bumped me, then stumbled away from me, and I spun around, stunned to find Jordan, flanked by her friends, holding tightly to Kandis' upper arm.

"Don't touch her!" Jordan yelled, her voice clearly hearable over the noise in the bar.

This was a step too far, and I was instantly pissed. I grabbed Jordan's wrist and pulled at it, making her release

Kandis. "Don't *you* touch *her*! What on earth do you think you're doing? And stop following me!"

"I'm not following you."

"What, you just happen to be everywhere I am?"

"We're here for the weekend. I did not expect to see you here. You shouldn't be here, and you should not be picking women up off the street. You hardly know her!"

"You cannot tell me what to do, Jordan. I can pick up anyone I like!" I grabbed Kandis' hand and dragged her toward the exit, and as I turned, meaning to give Jordan a warning look of my own, my eyes landed on one of Jordan's friends, who, if I was not mistaken, had a very regretful, apologetic look on her face.

We stepped out into the street, Barbara, Maggi, Denise, and Michelle next to us, and I apologized for Jordan's behavior. Everyone was cool about it, even Kandis, and when I asked if Jordan had hurt her, she just laughed and curled her arm, giving me her best bodybuilding pose, showing me her very sexy biceps. I never made it to the third club.

* * *

We walked along the street together, past busy restaurants, bars, and cafés, Kandis and I bringing up the rear, holding hands and talking. "How long are you staying?" she asked.

"We're leaving tonight."

Kandis stopped and looked at her watch. "You're driving home tonight?"

"Yeah. What time is it?"

The others noticed that we had stopped, and they turned and looked back at us. Kandis let out an exasperated huff, squeezed my hand, and asked me a question I did not expect.

"Come with me just for a couple of hours."

"Hey you guys, come on," Barbara called out, and they all started walking back toward us.

I hadn't really considered spending intimate time with this tall, dark, and very handsome woman, partly because this was a day trip and partly because Jordan was everywhere I turned, reminding me that I still loved her. But I was ready to say yes to Kandis. I wanted to—who wouldn't—and knew if I didn't do what I wanted to do, Jordan would win. I refused to be intimidated by her, sent back, broken and ashamed, to the church and my husband, to a life of torture and sadness. I could not let her break me! She had no right to forbid me anything! I was not hers anymore!

"Okay, yeah, I'd like that," I said, accepting her invitation, turning to Barbara as she and the others walked up. "Hey, Barb. Kandis and I are going…" I hesitated when I realized I wasn't sure where we were going and didn't want to assume.

"We're going to my apartment," Kandis finished.

Everyone's eyebrows shot up as they exchanged knowing glances.

"We will only be a couple of hours. The club is just ahead on the right. We'll meet you there at…" Kandis looked down at her watch. "Eleven-thirty." She looked at me, and I nodded.

"Okay, you two. Have fun," Barbara said.

They all turned and walked toward the bar, leaving us standing there staring after them, surprised that the conversation had gone so well.

"Let's go!" Kandis suddenly shouted, and we took off running across the street, laughing and holding hands.

It took us only a few minutes to reach her building, and I was a little out of breath by the time we did. Kandis looked no worse for wear, though. She seemed to be in excellent shape. I couldn't wait to find out. She pulled her keys out of her pocket and let us in.

We walked up three flights of stairs to her apartment, and she took out another key and unlocked the door. She led me inside, and without even hesitating, with no time to pretend we didn't know why we were there, we began removing our clothes. I watched her as she quickly stripped down, defined muscles and several tattoos grabbing my attention as she pulled off her shirt. We removed the last stitches of clothing and began expressing our mutual desire for each other right there in the entryway up against the wall.

After that, we moved to the living room, where a beautiful multi-colored, natural-leather couch sat waiting for us. It was firm but soft, felt divine on my skin, and was obviously created for exactly what we were doing on it. We did it over the back of a lovely, deep burgundy sofa chair next, accommodatingly upholstered and neither too tall nor too short, but just right. The antique wooden dining-room table had me worried for half a second but proved to be entirely stable for what we had in mind next, holding up admirably under the weight of two completely high-on-each-other, horny lesbians without so much as a squeak or a tremor. The woman had excellent taste in furniture. We hit the showers next, where we continued our debaucherous activities until we were officially late.

"It's almost midnight. We're late," Kandis said as she strapped her watch back onto her wrist.

"They won't leave without me, but yeah, we should hurry," I replied as I buckled my belt and headed for the door.

We kissed once more, then hurried out of the apartment, down the stairs, and out the front door. Taking a shortcut through the park, we hit the main strip and turned left, crossing the street where the others had left us two hours earlier, both of us laughing and still holding hands. Kandis kissed me for the last time, and then we made our way to the club, where Barbara, Maggi, Denise, and Michelle stood waiting for us out front on the sidewalk.

"It's after midnight," Barbara complained as we walked up to them. "You're late."

"Sorry," I said, even though I wasn't really that sorry.

"Actually, we thought you would be even later," Maggi said, teasing.

I turned to Kandis and smiled at her, taking both of her hands in mine. "I had an amazing day. Thank you."

"Yeah, me too. Thank you." Her voice broke, and I let out a small laugh, touched by the bittersweetness of having to say goodbye after such a magical day. What did a person say in a situation like this? Should I ask for her number? Should I ask if I could see her again? "Look me up next time you're in the city. Pier 39, Premium Books," she said, answering all of my questions.

"I will."

I backed away from her with a smile on my lips, released her hands, and ran to my friends, catching up to them as they reached the corner. I glanced over my shoulder to find Kandis still standing there. She waved, I waved back, and then I turned to Maggi and put my arm around her shoulder, smiling to myself as I gave her a squeeze.

"How was your first Gay Pride? Did you have fun?" she asked.

"I did, Maggi. Thank you."

"What for?"

"For being my friend and coming with me today."

"You're welcome, Shannon. It was a pleasure."

We walked to the parking garage, all of us in good spirits, arms slung around each other as we joked and laughed, bringing to a perfect end my first Gay Pride. As soon as we were on the freeway, Michelle and Denise hit me with a barrage of obscene teasing, but it was late, traffic was light, and I only had to put up with it for two hours.

I was back in Sacramento before two-thirty, in my bed before three, and asleep shortly thereafter.

CHAPTER TWENTY-TWO

I couldn't recall exactly when I noticed the change in Jordan, but something was definitely different, and for the life of me, I could not figure out what it meant. She had completely stopped giving me scary warning looks, and I missed them, afraid of losing the last bit of contact I had with her. She also looked defeated and a little sad, which worried me but at the same time irked the heck out of me. What did she have to be sad about? Okay, she had not gotten what she wanted, which was for me to leave the club scene, stop being a lesbian, and return to the church and my husband. But that couldn't be it. There had been no sudden change in my behavior to make her less determined to send me back. It was like she didn't care anymore. She seemed to have given up. But why feel so defeated about it? Why didn't she just go on about her business, be happy, and live her life? I was living mine, if not exactly how she wanted me to, the best I could after she walked away from me! She was the one who didn't want me! She broke up with me! I was the one who should feel sad and down, not her! I was the one who respected her decision and was left to rebuild my life without her in it! Aargh!

I was barely able to look at Jordan's sad face anymore and left the club earlier than usual, saying goodbye to my friends and making my way to the bar to pay my tab. While Mason and I engaged in small talk, I noticed her glance over my shoulder, and I turned to see who she was looking at—a pitifully glum Jordan slouched in her chair staring at us. I looked back at Mason and let out a tsk.

"Don't be so hard on her," Mason said.

"Excuse me?" My eyebrows shot up at her.

"Jordan. You know, your ex. Don't be so hard on her. I don't know what's going on between you two, but lately, she looks like she's been dragged through the mud. I've never seen someone so love-sick."

"Well, it's not because of me."

"I don't see her staring at anyone else every night."

"I don't know what Jordan told you, Mason, but she broke up with me, and the only reason she stares at me all the time is to intimidate me into leaving the club and never coming back."

"Are you sure about that?"

"Yeah, I am. She's said as much, and as complicated as it is, I'm beginning to think it's really quite simple. She doesn't want me anymore but doesn't want anyone else to have me either."

"That sounds like pure jealousy to me. Are you sure you're reading her right? I mean, have you talked to her?"

"After everything she put me through, I should talk to her? If we ever talk again, she will have to come to me."

"Give her a break, Shannon. Talk to her."

"Give her a break? Mason, she doesn't deserve a break. And like I said, if she wants to talk, she knows where to find me."

"So, you're open to it?"

"Mason, what's going on?"

"Nothing. I'm a bartender. Bartenders love asking personal, probing questions. Sorry."

I shot Mason a skeptical look, said goodbye, and headed for the exit. As I unlocked my truck, I glanced over at the club, surprised to find Jordan standing under the light of the entranceway, looking right at me. A flood of warmth spread through me as I held my breath, waiting for what she might do. I walked around the truck and stopped a few feet away from it, feeling drawn to her, wishing she would come and talk to me, fighting the urge to run to her and take her into my arms. She turned and walked back into the club. I blinked, shocked at our sudden separation. Anger rose up in me, and I swung around and huffed back to the truck, jerking the door open and pushing myself inside. The woman was infuriating.

* * *

A couple of weeks later, as I sat in the club on a Friday night, enjoying myself at a table with some of my friends, someone I'd seen before and knew a little bit about but had never met, walked in. She was a beautiful, mildly flamboyant, feminine woman who frequented the club, her usual entourage in tow—a mix of gay men and butch women. She practically floated through the room, waving her hand in greeting as if every single person there was her fan. She considered herself an actress. I always enjoyed her dramatic entrances and her general presence. It made everything more interesting.

As she passed my table in a flourish, a scarf draped through the handles of her purse worked itself free and landed on the floor next to my chair. I picked it up, meaning to return it to her.

"Excuse me, your scarf…"

She turned and smiled, first looking at me and then at the scarf. I held it out to her, and she walked to me to retrieve it.

"Thank you," she said. "Please, let me buy you a drink." I walked with her to her table, and as we sat, she asked, "What are you drinking?"

"Miller Lite, please… Thank you."

She sent one of the women from her entourage to the bar to get our drinks, then turned her attention back to me. She told me her name was Maria, that she was an actress, and about some of the plays she'd performed in. She asked if I had ever seen a play at the community center and whether I had ever seen her in a play. I told her that I had not.

"Oh, you must. I invite you. Tomorrow night. You'll be my guest," she very dramatically insisted.

Maria smelled wonderful. She was beautiful and very feminine, and I was surprised at how strongly being near her affected me. I also had the feeling she was probably too much for me—a bit out of my league. I noticed feminine women in the club but had never shared more than a few words with two or three of them, and they never seemed that interested in me. In fact, they seemed irritated by my presence, unable to approach me because they couldn't quite figure out what I was. I had short hair, didn't wear a lot of makeup, and had never worn a dress at the club, but everything else about me was very feminine. Butch women were not at all confused by me. I never worried about it. I wasn't interested in role-playing and really only had my eye on one particular woman anyway, so the whole range of lesbian types never really became important to me.

I ended up sitting at Maria's table for well over an hour before she announced that she had to go. She stood up, and I stood up with her, taken off guard when she leaned forward as if intending to kiss me. I didn't know what the protocol was for this particular situation, and I didn't want to insult her or embarrass her, although I was pretty sure I didn't want to share a kiss with her this early in our acquaintance, especially in front of everybody.

I braced myself and was relieved when she leaned to my left as if aiming for my cheek. A cheek kiss would be perfectly acceptable, and I puckered up, ready to reciprocate, murmuring a surprised "Oh!" when she suddenly altered her direction and leaned to my right. She brushed my cheek with hers before quickly moving away, leaving me chasing her, unable to keep up with her, and, in the end, kissing nothing but air. She didn't seem to notice my awkward little dance and smiled sweetly, handing me a card with the address of the community center and her phone number on it.

She suggested I come a bit early, around seven o'clock, to experience the excitement of pre-show preparations and meet some of the cast. She invited me to visit her in her dressing room. I agreed, and then she left with even more fanfare than when she'd arrived.

I walked back to my table, looking at her card, excited to have been invited to a gay social event. I glanced over at Jordan, who was sitting at a table in the far corner with some of her friends. She looked a little livelier than she had earlier in the evening, staring at me with a curious, almost intrigued look on her face. She did not give me her scary warning look, and I wondered if that was a good thing or a bad thing. Either she was finally getting on with her life, or she really didn't care anymore. Or both.

* * *

The next day, I went shopping, feeling special and super excited about having been asked out by someone like Maria and curious about what our evening would hold. I wanted to look nice but had nothing appropriately formal in my closet to wear, and instinct told me that I should not show up in a dress. So, I bought a nice pair of slacks and a matching vest, keeping it neutral, neither too feminine nor masculine, but nice. Definitely nice.

At seven sharp, I entered the community center to find everyone busy with preparations. I walked around the little theater, then made my way backstage, casually roaming, basically getting in the way as people flurried about, getting ready for the show. After a few minutes, when I didn't see Maria, I asked someone who worked there where I could find her.

"Last door on your left," a stagehand pointed, directing me further down the hall.

I quietly knocked and waited only a moment before the woman who had gotten our drinks the night before answered the door. She gave me a friendly nod and stepped to the side, showing me a small room with barely enough space for the two makeup tables and couch it held. There was a mirror along one wall and a wardrobe rack along the other, and Maria, standing next to the wardrobe with her back to me, wearing nothing but her underwear. As I walked in, the woman who opened the door walked out, leaving us alone.

"Hi, Maria."

Maria turned and smiled. "Hello, Shannon. I'm so glad you could come." We met in the middle of the little room and exchanged air kisses, which went much smoother than the first time, as I remembered not to try and kiss her back. She looked me up and down and smiled. "You look nice."

"Thank you." I blushed, more over her proximity and

nakedness than her compliment.

"Did you get a chance to look around a little?"

"Yes, I did. It's very impressive. Very cool. I've never been backstage before."

Maria walked back to the wardrobe and began looking through it, all the while talking about the play and her part in it. She had a beautiful body, and the underwear she wore only accentuated her long legs, perfect ass, slim waist, flat stomach, and lovely breasts. My body was above average, and I was secretly proud of it, but my ass and breasts never looked like that in the underwear I wore. Her panties were made up of a few strips of pink lace, barely covering her lovely parts, and her bra was so sparse, it was clear that her breasts were holding up the bra and not the other way around.

And she smelled delicious, her fragrance spreading throughout the room as she shimmied into her dress, turning this way and that, her hands on her hips one moment, her stomach and waist the next, and then on her breasts as she fit everything perfectly into place.

I stood there watching her get dressed, getting warmer by the second, the light pulse between my legs intensifying, and just like that, I was picturing us having sex on the makeup table.

"Excuse me?" I startled, her alluring voice rousing me from my lascivious thoughts.

"Could you zip me up, please?"

I stepped behind her and slowly zipped her up. She looked over her shoulder at me and smiled, then walked over to the mirror. I took three steps back, returning to my position by the door, and the strangest feeling of masculinity took hold of me. I cleared my throat and adjusted my stance so that it wasn't so—for want of a better word—butch.

"Everyone is planning to go out afterward, but I was thinking we could spend some time together alone. Would you like to have a drink with me at my place after the play? It's not far from here." She turned her head and looked at me, waiting.

"Yes, I would."

"Great, then that's what we'll do." She smiled as she turned back to the mirror, her eyes sparkling as she glanced at me through it. "Enjoy the show. I'll see you out front afterward."

That was my cue. I returned her smile, opened the door, stepped out into the hallway, and closed the door behind me. Oh my God! She was definitely out of my league and way more feminine than I could ever hope to be. I had never felt so butch in all my life. I made my way to my seat, slowly realizing that butch, femme, and everything in between was totally relative. Still, the realization that this woman was out-femming me had me curious to know how I was perceived. Was I butch? Was I femme? What was I?

As I waited for the play to start, I decided it didn't matter. I was what I was, and wherever I fit on the scale of possible identities, I was excited by the idea of experiencing whatever I was with someone like Maria. I had never given my femininity a second thought, and now I was about to get to know my butch side. I could think of no better way to do this than with an ultra-feminine lesbian.

I loved that the gay community was involved in events like this. I had never been to a play before and was glad that my first one was a gay one. The theater quickly filled, and soon I was surrounded by a lively group of gay men, making everything that much more fun. The play was great, and Maria was very good—very funny in fact. There was a lot of audience participation, and I took part in it, totally enjoying myself, already making plans to visit the gay community office to get more information on activities like this. This was a whole other part of being gay that I was missing out on.

I made my way outside, where most, if not all, of the audience had reassembled, visiting together as they waited for the actors to come out. We applauded when they did, the atmosphere festive and somehow exclusive, and I enjoyed my role in it as Maria's date for the evening. She made her way to me through the crowd, speaking a few words to people she knew, shaking hands and smiling. Everyone watched as she walked up to me and took my arm. It was the highlight of my evening thus far, I had to admit. As we sauntered down the sidewalk toward her apartment, she talked to me about the play, telling me how well it went and describing some of the mistakes that were made. I told her that I had not noticed any mistakes, to which she smiled and squeezed my arm, making my heart beat faster.

"What did you think? Did you like it?"

"Yes! It was hilarious. You are very funny."

This pleased her, and she squeezed my arm again. We arrived at her building, and after she let us in, we took the stairs to the second floor. Her apartment was surprisingly big and very nice. There was a small, narrow table in the entryway next to the door, where she neatly placed her purse before removing her wrap. She asked if she could take my jacket, and I handed it to her before stepping into her living room, where two plush cream-colored couches sat cattycorner around a large glass coffee table. There were two windows facing the street, and the streetlights from below illuminated the entire room. On the wall directly to my left, across from the windows, hung a large round mirror. Around the mirror, in three separate rows on each side, hung framed photographs of Maria playing characters in different plays.

As I looked at the photos, Maria came up behind me with a beer in one hand and a glass of white wine in the other. She handed me the beer and began addressing the photos, explaining which play it was and which character she was playing. Then she walked over to one of the couches and sat down. I followed and sat next to her, listening intently as she talked about how she got started in acting and how rewarding it was. She explained how difficult it had been to get the community center to volunteer space for weekly performances and all the politics involved and diplomatic maneuvering it took to get essential signatures and licenses, not to mention everyone's input and the host of other things required to put on a simple community show.

"It was a nightmare!" She dramatically shuddered, then went on to blow-by-blow describe each act of the first show they put on. The more Maria talked, the more I suspected I had probably misunderstood her intentions. Maybe she only wanted to sit and visit. Maybe she wasn't interested in me sexually at all. I sipped my beer and listened, and soon my beer was empty.

"Would you like another?" she asked.

"If you're having another."

Her glass was still half full. "No, I'm finished."

She put her glass on the coffee table, put her hand on my thigh, and looked me directly in the eyes, making her intentions clear. I leaned in to kiss her just as she leaned in to kiss me, and our lips unexpectedly bumped before finally coming together awkwardly. She deepened the kiss, and I moved closer, touching her arm, then her back, then her hip, and then her arm again, never quite sure if I was touching her in the right place, as her responses were quite limited, if not nonexistent, although her hand was still firmly on my thigh. After only a minute or so of making out, she abruptly pulled back, stood up, and held her hand out to me. I took it, and she pulled me off the couch and led me to the bedroom. She had me enter first, and when she didn't follow, I turned and looked at her standing in the doorway.

"Make yourself comfortable. I'll be right back," she said before turning and disappearing into the bathroom.

My novice brain kicked in, and for a moment, I was unsure if she meant for me to undress and get into bed. I shook my head to rid myself of any confusion before it took hold and tried to think logically. Of course she wanted me to undress and get into bed, and the reason I knew this was because the alternative was not possible. The plot thickened, and my head began debating this very question. Why else would she have brought me here? What if she came back and I was still standing here fully clothed? This thought got me moving. I would rather be wrong, naked and in her bed, than be wrong, still standing here fully clothed. I gave myself a mental head-slap as I undressed and climbed into bed, then waited another five minutes before she joined me.

Maria appeared in the bedroom doorway, and... Wow! She wore an off-peach silk negligee that barely covered her curves. I was instantly wet, my clit springing to life. Each step she took teased at what was underneath as she sauntered across the room and hesitated at the edge of the bed. She tilted her head, gave me an undiscernible but decidedly sexy look, and slipped under the sheets.

She propped her head up on her pillow, and I immediately moved up next to her and slowly uncovered her. My eyes ran down the length of her body and back up, pausing at her breasts for a moment before looking up at her beautiful face. I leaned in to get things started with a kiss, only to find her head slightly turned away from me, and instead of prolonging the awkwardness building as seconds passed and she still did not look at me, I decided to start with her breasts instead. I untied the tie holding her negligee together and folded back the two sides, exhaling a breathy moan as I laid her breasts bare. They were the most beautiful breasts I had ever seen in my life. I leaned in and lavished them with attention, sucking, licking, and fondling, my breathing accelerating by the second, my core pulsing like a drum. I looked up at her, eager to see her reaction. No response.

It was obvious by her lack of enthusiasm that I was enjoying this much more than she was, so I decided to add some heat. I slipped my hand between her thighs and ran my fingers up the length of her pussy, finding her only moderately wet. Determined to rectify this, I stroked her more energetically, desperate for any sign that she liked what I was doing. I glanced up at her. No response. In fact, she looked a bit bored. Obviously, something more substantially dramatic was needed. I positioned myself between her thighs and promptly went down on her, latching onto her clit, overwhelming it with quick little licks, hoping to get her attention.

I glanced up at her. Nothing. No heavy breathing, no hip

movement, no nothing, and it looked like she was looking over my head. I raised my head slightly, and sure enough, her eyes moved down and locked onto mine. She smiled and said, "Enter me."

Finally! Some input! I was totally failing at being butch and desperately needed some direction. I slid two fingers inside her, starting slowly, then picking up the pace, and before long, was banging her quite nicely, giving her clit a wonderful workout with the heel of my hand. I looked up at her, and she had the most unusual look on her face, an expression I'd never seen during sex before. She was looking slightly upward to the right, as if she were thinking hard about something.

"The G-spot! Find the G-spot!"

My arm hesitated, and I lost my rhythm.

"Ah...the G-spot?"

"Yes, and then rub it, you know, pressing on it," she explained.

I looked down at her pussy and leaned in closer, attempting to locate what she was referring to.

"Shannon, it's here."

She placed her right hand demonstratively on her lower abdomen, her fingers elegantly splayed across her mound.

"Oh!" I exclaimed, glad for the help. I placed my left hand where hers had been and began sliding my ramrod-straight fingers in and out of her again, slowly finding my rhythm.

"Upward! Upward!"

With my left hand still on her lower abdomen, I angled my fingers upward by lowering my right elbow to the mattress, quickening my thrusts as I struggled to keep my balance. Concentrating on my rhythm and the position of my fingers inside her, I hadn't even realized how hard I was pressing down on her abdomen until she grabbed my arm and snatched my hand away.

"Stop! Stop! Stop!" she ordered as she practically threw my arm back at me. She grabbed her negligee and pressed it to her breasts, looking at me with an expression of disbelief.

I slowly sat back on my heels, an apologetic grimace spreading across my face as I asked the question I already knew the answer to.

"I'm doing it wrong, aren't I?"

"You have no idea what you're doing, do you?"

"I don't know what a G-spot is," I confessed.

"Obviously!" She let out an exasperated breath. "I heard you were quite adept... I mean, I thought that you did this!" I looked at her, confused. "I was told you were very good!"

"Really?" I said, a little gobsmacked as it dawned on me what she was talking about.

"Well, obviously the rumors are greatly exaggerated! I want you to go!" Maria swung her beautiful legs off the side of the bed, stood up, and walked out of the bedroom.

I sat there on my knees and ran my fingers through my hair, wondering if there was any way to repair this. "God, help me," I mumbled, and then climbed out of bed and got dressed. As I walked out of the bedroom and down the hallway, Maria suddenly appeared behind me. I glanced back at her. She was wearing a matching silk robe over her negligee. She looked stunning. We walked through the living room into the foyer, and I turned and faced her. "I'm sorry, Maria."

"Shannon, you are not to say one word about this to anyone. Do you understand me!"

"Yes! Of course."

She handed me my jacket, reached around me, and unlocked the door. I opened the door and walked out into the hallway, cringing when the door slammed shut behind me. As I passed by the front of her building on the way to my truck, I looked up at her windows just as the light in her apartment turned off. Ouch!

During the drive home, I ruminated over the utter fiasco with Maria, trying to control my embarrassment as three important takeaways from my experience slowly formed in my mind. First, I had no idea what I was doing in bed. Second, I had the reputation of someone who slept around and knew what they were doing in bed. And third, I had to find out what a G-spot was, where it was located, and how to activate it.

* * *

The next morning, I woke to the memory of what happened the night before and groaned. I totally sucked at being butch. I spent the rest of the day shaking off feelings of inadequacy and rejection while several questions occupied my mind. Did Maria really accidentally lose her scarf, or did she do it on purpose to create a chance meeting between us? Had I somehow developed a reputation for sleeping around without knowing about it and without sleeping around? How much sleeping around was necessary to get a reputation? Obviously, not much, but then again, Maria had made it sound like I slept with a lot more women than I actually had, so maybe the truth had nothing to do with getting a reputation.

I stayed clear of the club the rest of the week, but on Saturday, stopped by for a drink. As I sat at the bar, keeping to myself, still harboring a boatload of embarrassment about what happened with Maria, a very attractive woman sat down on the barstool next to me. I'd seen this woman around and knew her name, but she frequented other groups, cooler groups, some of the same groups Jordan did. Her name was Bethany, and she was hot, and up until now, had no idea I existed.

Instead of my alarm bells ringing when she introduced herself, I was totally flattered and started to believe that maybe I was not such a loser after all.

She bought me a beer and began telling me all about herself. She had seen me around and knew my name. She was originally from Illinois, had three sisters, worked as an airplane mechanic in the Air Force, and was stationed at Mather AFB. She was currently single due to a recent breakup and, at the moment, was living with friends. She smelled really good, looked amazing, was incredibly charming, and I was mesmerized by her attentiveness. The way she looked at me made me believe that I was the only one she wanted to share her entire life story with. After only an hour of conversation with Bethany, I forgot all about what happened with Maria.

Then, very suddenly, Bethany leaned in and kissed me so passionately, I had to hold onto my barstool to keep from falling off of it. She gave me an awkward moment to recover, then invited me to go home with her. As we headed for the exit, I glanced around the club and locked eyes with Jordan. She just sat there looking at me, with no intention of getting up and challenging the woman who was about to bed me. No scary warning look, no more sad demeanor. Instead, she crossed her arms, tilted her head to the side, and graced me with an amused, curious smile, pissing me off and on my way, more determined than ever to defy her.

* * *

Sex with Bethany was nice, if not a bit transactional, and afterward, I slept very well and woke the next morning to a hot cup of coffee and Bethany sitting next to me on the edge of the bed. We exchanged smiles and flirtatious small talk, and then her expression changed to concern when loud voices came from somewhere in the house. The bedroom door opened, and two women leaned in.

"You need to take care of this," the taller one said.

"I'll be right back," Bethany said to me as she stood up.

She left the room, closing the door behind her, leaving me to listen to the faraway, shrill voice of a very angry woman.

"You forgot this!" the woman yelled as something big hit the floor with a dull thump. "And you took all my tapes! I want them back! Now!"

"Those are my tapes! I made them!" Bethany yelled.

"You made them for me! You gave them to me! They are mine!" the woman yelled back.

"You two need to take this outside," a third woman said.

I got the sinking feeling I was about to have company as

bumping and shuffling noises made their way down the hallway toward the bedroom. I pulled the bedspread up to my chin, sensing what was about to happen. The door swung open, hitting the wall behind it, and a very angry woman stood in the doorway, looking at me.

"This? This is what you *did* last night?" she yelled, looking down the hall to her right, sarcastically laughing. She looked back at me, shaking her head in disgust, almost spitting as she let out a huff of attitude that said, *I am so much better than you!*

Then, without closing the door, she stomped back down the hallway. I jumped out of bed and started dressing. I had everything on but my pants when Bethany appeared in the doorway.

"No! No...wait. This will only take a minute. I'll be right back."

Bethany closed the door, and I put on my pants. Whatever was going on out there, I would need to be fully clothed to deal with it. I slowly opened the bedroom door, stuck my head out, and looked up and down the hallway. There was no sign of Bethany or the angry woman. I walked down the hallway, and as I entered the living room, I stopped in my tracks, surprised to see the two women from earlier, who I assumed owned the house, standing in the middle of the room clutching each other as though they were hostages in a hostage standoff. I gave them a weak smile and pointed in the direction I thought was the front door. "Front door?" Both women nodded.

I proceeded to the front door and hurried out onto the front lawn. Movement on the street to my right caught my eye, and I quickened my pace. It was Bethany, and when she saw me, she started running, catching me before I could get to my truck.

"Where are you going?"

"I thought I would go, you know? It looks like you have something going on this morning..."

"No! That? No, it's nothing. I mean, yeah, I have a

situation, but I thought maybe you could help me with it."

Glancing several times at my truck, she explained that she needed my help moving her things from this house to a new place she'd arranged to stay at only a few miles away.

"Please, Shannon. This is the third woman this year who's thrown me out, and it's usually no problem coming back here. But now Paula keeps *stopping by*. I can't have her showing up here anymore. It's unacceptable. Stephanie and Robin won't put up with it. They've asked me to find another place to stay. And I have. A place where Paula can't find me. It won't take long. I don't have much."

I couldn't say no. We started packing up her stuff and were able to move all of it in one trip, using my truck for her furniture and her car for everything else.

Afterward, Bethany bought me lunch at *McDonald's* and told me the whole terrible, sad story about her and Paula, from the moment they fell in love to the moment Paula threw her out of her apartment, a period of fewer than three weeks.

I felt bad for Bethany but somehow knew this wouldn't be the last time she'd find herself in this situation. As we walked to our vehicles, I gave her a bit of advice. "Get to know the woman you love before you move in with her."

I immediately recognized the irony of our different realities. Bethany started relationships with practically any woman who showed the slightest interest in her, and the only relationship I wanted was with a woman who couldn't be less interested in me if she tried.

Bethany thanked me for my help and for the enjoyable time we spent in bed together the night before, reminding me of a question I wanted to ask. "Do you know anything about a G-spot, you know, where it is, how it works?"

"No. I've never heard of it. What is it?"

"I have no idea."

"Okay, well, sorry I can't be of more help."

"No, don't be. You're not the only one who doesn't know what it is. No one I've asked seems to know anything about it. Thanks, though." I gave her a wave and a smile as I turned toward my truck, wondering if this elusive G-spot really existed or if Maria just made the whole thing up.

Whenever I saw Bethany in the club after that, she'd give me a hello-nod, but that was it. She never sought my company again. I don't know what I was hoping for. I mean, it was a one-night stand for crying out loud. Why was I feeling so weird about it? Why did it matter if she didn't want to see me again? Because I couldn't shake the feeling that she had used me. She knew my name and my rumored reputation, and she knew that I had a truck. She picked me up, not because she thought I was cute and felt attracted to me, but because she needed me to help her move. And I was pretty sure Maria had used me too.

And Jordan? She hadn't even tried to warn me off with one of her scary looks, and it slowly dawned on me why. She totally knew what she was doing. It was diabolical, a conspiracy. She was picking and choosing who she let bed me, hoping to maximize negative outcomes, hoping to discourage me and get me to return to the church. I held her completely responsible for my deteriorating reputation. I had to admit that up until now, my attempt at being a single lesbian in the club scene had been less than stellar. I had made more than a few rookie mistakes, but I could change all that. I was determined to repair my reputation and to show Jordan that I was just as gay as she was and had no intention of ever returning to church.

CHAPTER TWENTY-THREE

I spent the next couple of weeks on my barstool, keeping to myself, quietly celebrating my celibacy. I'd developed an indiscriminate suspicion of any woman who even remotely showed interest in me, rarely taking up a conversation unless the woman was notably attached, and even then, cautious when the slightest flirtatious banter ensued. Being used had left me a bit gun-shy, and I needed a short time-out to get my balance back and priorities straight before climbing back into the dating saddle again.

The perfect opportunity to test my balance came a week later when a woman sat next to me, two stools over, not at all interested in me, talking to Mason about her girlfriend, who was in the military. I was soon swept up in an interesting back-and-forth between the two of them about how difficult it was to have a gay relationship in the military. It surprised me to learn that Mason had been in the military, and I laughed out loud at some of the antics she'd been caught up in trying to hook up with a beautiful recruit she had fallen head over heels for. But my heart ached a little for the woman sitting next to me when she told us her partner was stationed in Hawaii and how much she missed her.

I was actually relieved when she asked me my name. If she didn't know my name, maybe she hadn't heard about my reputation, and she already had a girlfriend. What was the harm in making a new friend? I told her my name, and she told me hers, and Mason went back to work, leaving us to ourselves. Her name was Sianna, Sia for short. "Like, *see ya* later, sweetheart," she teasingly enunciated in her best Bogart. We spent the next couple of hours getting to know each other, and later, when I walked to my truck alone, I felt good. I had made a new friend, and I hadn't slept with her.

We sat together again at the bar the following Saturday evening, hanging out, drinking beer, and sharing insights about our lives. I told her about my background and about my outing, not mentioning Jordan's name, just covering the basic high points and low points.

"Wow, that's intense. How did you survive that?"

"I haven't yet," I realized, "But I'm working on it."

Sia talked about her partner, Valery, and announced that she would be home on leave at the beginning of October, just a week away. It tickled me to see how excited Sia was about seeing Valery again, and from the pictures Sia showed me, she had every right to be. Valery was beautiful. She was mulatto, very feminine, and looked very sexy in her uniform. Sia told me that Valery's mom was white, her dad black, and that Valery was originally from Washington State. She told me they wouldn't be able to visit Valery's family in Washington while Valery was on leave, and then Sia read off a list of activities she was planning to do with Valery instead. She actually had a list she carried in her wallet. I was impressed.

"How do you manage being separated from her like this?"

"She only has six months left on this tour, and she's requested Fort Irwin in Barstow, California as her next duty station, so we're keeping our fingers crossed for that. We write letters and talk on the phone a couple of times a week, but it's not easy. We can't write or talk openly. It's just the way the military is, so we have to be careful. Military relationships are complicated—long-distance ones even more complicated. But we do everything we can to make it work. That's why these visits are so special. I try to plan them so that she is doing all the things she likes to do, not only so that she has fun and goes back to Hawaii relaxed and rested, but also so that she comes back to *me* next time she has leave."

I could certainly relate to secret relationships, Jordan and I had become experts on that front, but Sia's last comment surprised me, reminding me how fragile even the most loving, committed relationship could be. As if on cue, Jordan walked up to the bar and stood just a few feet away from me. I glanced at her, then looked at Sia, who I caught staring at

Jordan. Most women responded to Jordan this way, and I waited patiently, rolling my eyes slightly, knowing that it would take a moment for Sia to get over the rush of seeing such a beautiful woman up close. I couldn't help but wonder how Jordan dealt with all the attention. She didn't seem to notice it, and it occurred to me that I had never seen her romantically connected to a woman during the entire time I'd been coming out to the club. I had suspected some of the women she hung out with of being possible girlfriends, but over time, realized they were just her friends. Jordan could probably have any woman she wanted, but she didn't seem to be interested in having a girlfriend, and I was suddenly thankful for that, thankful that I hadn't had to deal with watching Jordan fall in love with someone else. I didn't know how I would react if I had to watch her kiss someone and was relieved that she was being so discreet about her sexual exploits, which was more than I could say for myself. I almost felt guilty, then reminded myself that Jordan didn't feel that way about me anymore. She didn't want me anymore and didn't care who I kissed.

Jordan turned to go, then hesitated, looking at me. I braced myself, hoping she'd spare me her scary warning glare—then hoping she wouldn't. She surprised me. "Hi."

"Ah... Hi," I sputtered, giving her a weak smile.

She returned my smile, then looked at Sia and nodded.

"Wow. Do you know her?" Sia asked as we both turned and watched Jordan walk away.

"Yeah, I know her."

"What are you waiting for?"

"What do you mean?"

"I think she's into you."

"Oh... I don't think so." And then I blushed.

"And you are obviously into her. You should talk to her. She's hot."

I rubbed my forehead for a moment, wondering if I should tell Sia about Jordan. I decided not to and let my hand fall to my lap as I shook my head and sat up straighter.

Sia watched me carefully, raising a quizzical eyebrow. I'm sure it was obvious to her that I had something to say but had decided not to say it. I couldn't tell Sia that I'd once had the most beautiful girl in the world and had let her slip through my fingers.

* * *

When Sia and I met the following Friday night at the club, she invited me to go with her to pick Valery up from the airport on Saturday.

"I would love for you to meet her."

I agreed, and Sia picked me up the next morning at eleven o'clock. On the drive to the airport, Valery was all Sia talked about. It was very sweet, and I was happy for Sia, but I found myself getting nervous about meeting Valery and concerned about the possibility of becoming a third wheel. I was sure they wanted to be alone after not seeing each other for so long, but Sia was a very considerate person, and I wouldn't have put it past her to invite me to hang out. If she did extend such an invitation, it would be out of politeness, and out of politeness, I would decline. The last thing I wanted was to overstay my welcome.

When we got to the arrival gate, I pulled back and stood near the last row of chairs in the waiting area as passengers exited the airplane, leaving Sia standing alone. Valery appeared a few minutes later wearing her dress uniform—a green skirt and jacket, black tie and pumps—looking even more beautiful than in her pictures. Valery and Sia embraced for a long time. It was nice to watch. Then they turned toward me, Sia pointing in my direction as she spoke to Valery, Valery trying to pick me out of the crowd. Her eyes finally found mine, and she smiled. As we walked up to each other, I started feeling shy and my heart began to race. I was way too nervous and couldn't get a proper hello out of my mouth. Valery saw that I was struggling and extended her hand for me to shake.

"It's nice to finally meet you, Shannon."

"Nice to meet you, too, Valery," I managed, then blushed. Damn.

We headed toward baggage claim, where Valery's duffle bag already sat waiting on the baggage carousel. From there, we made our way through the parking garage to the car. Valery and Sia got into the front seat, I got in the back, and as soon as the doors were closed, they kissed. It was a long, slow, deep, soft, sweet kiss, and I did not look away.

On the drive home, they made polite conversation with me while holding hands and sharing long glances with each other. It was definitely time for me to go, but instead of taking me home, Sia drove to her apartment complex. Valery was probably tired, and Sia was just dropping her off first before taking me home. We all got out of the car, and instead of Valery saying goodbye and telling me how nice it was to meet me, she headed off toward the apartment while Sia grabbed her duffle bag out of the trunk.

"Come up and have dinner with us, Shannon," Sia said as she strode off after Valery, glancing over her shoulder at me as she added, "We're having a little party tonight to celebrate Valery's arrival."

I hesitated, not sure what to do, but then Valery stopped and turned, smiling invitingly as she threw me a big come-on wave. "Shannon, come party with us. It'll be fun."

I hesitated again, but then took off after them, catching up with them at the stairs. I wasn't going to insist they take me home when they'd obviously planned for me to join them, and I did enjoy being around them, and I didn't want to be rude. If Valery wanted me there, I just couldn't say no.

Their apartment was bright and homey. It had an open kitchen with a bar and three barstools, a dining nook off to the side, and a cute little cozy living room. Valery disappeared down the hallway with her duffle bag, and Sia began preparing dinner. I took a seat at the bar.

"Are you hungry?" Sia asked.

"Yeah, actually I am."

Sia pulled a plastic container out of the refrigerator and

held it up. "These are lemon, rosemary-marinated pork chops. Valery's favorite."

There had been a definite positive change in Sia's countenance since we'd left the airport. She was radiant, her facial features softer, brighter, and younger, and her smile was infectious.

"Yum, I love pork chops," I declared, smiling back at her.

Sia laughed, then pulled two beers out of the refrigerator and opened them, giving one to me. "I told Valery about you a few days ago, and she wanted to meet you. She likes you, and we're both very happy that you came to the airport and that you're spending the day with us. I didn't say anything about dinner earlier because I didn't know how Valery would feel about it…whether she would be too tired. I didn't know what she might want to do. I don't think she did either. But then she saw you, and she met you, and she likes you, so you're invited."

"Thank you for inviting me."

As we clinked our bottles together in a silent toast, we made eye contact, holding it for several seconds. Sia smiled, and I smiled back. It was a definite moment, and I blushed. I needed to get a life and a girlfriend. I was completely shy and tongue-tied around Valery, and all Sia had to do was look at me and my heart started pounding like a drum.

Sia began making dinner—peeling potatoes, snapping green beans, and cutting up veggies for the salad—all the while narrating her every move as if she were the host cook on a TV cooking show. It was very funny, and we laughed back and forth as I threw in commentary about her snapping technique and the unwatched pot of potatoes boiling over. Suddenly, a pair of hands grabbed my shoulders from behind, and I jumped.

"Are you two having fun?" Valery asked.

She leaned over my shoulder and looked at me, her face so close to mine, it was all I could do not to pull away from her. She had showered, her fresh herbal bouquet surrounding me, making me dizzy. It was clear how very pretty she was, even without her makeup.

She held my eyes a moment longer, then gave me a soft squeeze before releasing my shoulders. She walked around the bar into the kitchen and wrapped her arms around Sia's waist from behind as Sia snapped beans over the sink. They flirted, smiling and laughing, whispering things to each other, while Sia finished up the beans and put them in a pot of water. Valery put the pot on the stove, and Sia opened a bottle of white wine and poured Valery a glass, both of them moving comfortably around the kitchen together, talking to each other and talking to me, asking me what I thought about blue curtains over the couch or maybe yellow ones, trying to pull me into their cute domestic conversations.

Valery set the table as Sia put the finishing touches on dinner, and after we were all seated, Valery said a prayer. "Dear God, please bless this food. Amen."

It was quiet for a moment, and I peeked up at Valery, her hands folded together, head bent, eyes closed. "Amen," I offered, and Valery looked up at me and smiled.

The pork chops were excellent. I ate two of them. I could have easily eaten a third. After dinner, I helped Sia with the dishes while Valery lounged on the couch watching television.

"I'll finish up, go sit down," Sia said, handing me a glass from the cupboard. "Here, bring Valery a glass of wine and a beer for yourself."

I poured Valery a glass of wine, grabbed a beer from the fridge, and walked into the living room, setting the glass on the coffee table as Valery swung her legs off the couch and sat up.

"Thank you," she said, picking up her glass and holding it up. "Cheers."

I returned the toast, then sat down in a small sofa chair on the other side of the coffee table across from her.

"Why are you single, Shannon? That's what I want to know. You're very attractive. I'm sure the ladies have noticed."

"I date some. I try anyway. It's complicated," I answered, giving her a quick smile as I tried not to blush.

"Shannon has an interesting history," Sia threw in as she walked into the living room with her beer. "She was raised in a religious family like yours... Well, not exactly like yours. Her family wasn't as progressive as yours, so..."

"So, she found a new family," Valery interjected.

"Exactly," I said, liking very much how she seemed to instantly understand my complicated life and, in a nutshell, perfectly sum it up.

Valery raised her glass again, her eyes locking with mine, her smile generous and warm with no trace of pity. "To family."

"To family," I returned.

As Sia made herself comfortable on the couch, leaning back on its arm, propping herself up on a pillow, and stretching her right leg out along the inside cushion, Valery reclined up against her, snuggling in between her legs as she laid her head back on Sia's chest. They were a very attractive couple, and even though they rarely saw one another, they looked completely comfortable with each other. I looked at the television without seeing it, watching Sia instead as she wrapped her arms around Valery and pulled her closer, resting one hand on Valery's stomach, the other on her thigh. I let my body react and pushed away any concern that I might be a third wheel. They invited me here; I would let them tell me when it was time to go.

Soon, I was enjoying their display so much, I did not even pretend to watch television anymore. My arousal hummed through my body, strong and confident, and I was more than just comfortable with it; I savored it, openly staring as they kissed and touched, whispering softly to each other, enjoying being close to one other, and I suspected, enjoying having an audience.

It was like being woken from a trance when Valery suddenly sat up. She swung her legs from the couch and faced me, and I knew something was about to happen, her penetrating stare making me shift in my chair. She turned to Sia, Sia gave her a short, barely noticeable nod, and then she looked back at me, her quirked eyebrow and the subtle twist of her lips telling me a decision had been made. She stood up, pulled Sia up off the couch by her hand, and led her around the coffee table and past my chair.

"Shannon, join us in the bedroom if you want," Valery said.

I turned and watched them disappear down the hallway, waiting a moment to let what I thought I heard—an unmistakable invitation to their bedroom—sink in. And then I stood up and followed them, emerging four hours later a changed woman, wearing nothing but a light green, see-through, negligée wrap and feeling like a sex goddess, unequivocally desired and thoroughly sated, with no doubt left in my mind that I knew exactly what I was doing in bed.

I joined Valery and Sia in the kitchen, taking a seat at the bar, smiling at Sia as she set a beer down in front of me. Valery and Sia's negligee wraps were not see-through at all, Valery's red and Sia's black, both of them silk.

"I love that one. You can see everything," Sia said, winking at me as she took in my outfit.

"I picked it out for her," Valery said, giving me a wink as well.

Valery sipped her wine, looking at me affectionately, almost admirably, if not contemplatively, as if she were studying a painting or some other work of art. Yeah, that's how it felt being looked at by Valery. Sia made omelets as if it were the most important thing she would ever do, and I sat there feeling like this was exactly where I should be, not at all like a third wheel would feel. We moved into the living room, Valery and Sia on the couch and me on the sofa chair, and ate omelets while talking about love, relationships, and life in Hawaii.

Around ten o'clock, Valery stood up, signaling that she was tired and ready to sleep. Sia and I followed her to the bedroom, shed our negligee wraps, and climbed into bed next to her. I was pleased when Valery pulled me into her, holding me from behind. Sia draped her arm over the both of us a moment later, pulling us even closer together. And so, we slept, a spooned threesome.

* * *

I woke to gentle nudging. "Shannon, wake up." I opened my eyes to find Sia kneeling next to the bed. "Don't wake Valery."

Sia stood up and walked out of the room and down the hallway. I carefully slipped out of bed, got dressed, and after a quick jaunt to the bathroom, joined her in the kitchen, planting myself on one of the barstools.

"How do you feel this morning?" Sia asked.

"Good."

"Did you sleep okay?"

"Yes, very. What time is it?"

"It's seven o'clock. Coffee?"

"Yes, please."

"I'm going to take you home," Sia said as she poured my coffee and set it in front of me.

"Okay, great. Thank you." I sipped my coffee in relative silence, hoping everything was okay, finishing just as Sia finished hers, announcing as I stood up, "I'm ready."

Sia grabbed her keys and wallet, and we headed out the door, and as Sia drove me home, she began to explain herself, almost apologizing.

"I didn't mean to rush you... Okay, I meant to rush you a little bit, but not because of anything you did. You are wonderful, and last night was great—more than I hoped for." Sia reached over and took my hand. "I have one week with her every four months, and this was the first twenty-four hours. It was perfect. Thank you, Shannon."

"She loves you, Sia. I can see it. She'll always come back to you."

"I'll do anything to make sure she does."

A moment or two passed before I asked my question. "Did

you know who I was when you first sat next to me at the bar?"

"No. Why do you ask?"

"I need to know. You didn't approach me for this, did you?"

"No! I just came to the club that night to have a beer. We met, you were super nice, and I came back because I enjoyed talking to you." Sia cleared her throat, hesitating. "Okay, there is something I have to tell you. Valery and I have often talked about having a three-way. It's a fantasy we both have, and we decided if we ever found the right person, we'd try it. I told Valery about you, she noticed that I liked you, and said that I should invite you to the airport so that she could meet you. So yeah, I did start thinking about you that way, and I did begin to plan what happened last night. It didn't just happen; I planned it. But I didn't know who you were until I sat down next to you at the bar that first night and got to know you."

Sia looked at me, trying to gauge my reaction, and I looked at her, relieved that this had nothing to do with my reputation, begrudgingly acknowledging as well that it also had nothing to do with Jordan. This one was all me.

"Valery told me that it was the way you looked at her in the airport that made her choose you. Still, I wasn't sure she would go through with it even after you were in our apartment. She was actually nervous until she said the words, 'Join us in the bedroom.' After that, she was unstoppable."

"Yeah, she was. I mean... Wow."

Sia shot me a quick glance. "Did you like it? Did you have fun?"

"Are you kidding me? It was incredible. I never imagined... I mean, it was perfect." We released mutual sighs, then fell silent, allowing another question to pop into my head. "Do you know anything about a G-spot? Where it is, how it works?"

Sia let out a surprised laugh, cocking her head at me as she raised her eyebrows. "Do you remember your second orgasm?"

"How could I forget," I said, blushing a little at how intensely enjoyable that particular orgasm had been.

"That was your G-spot."

"Oh…" I blinked, the mysterious spot suddenly remarkably vivid. "But, how do I…"

"Find it?"

"Yeah, I mean, I don't want to fumble my way around looking for it."

"Oh, looking can be pretty hot, and I think they'll appreciate the effort."

"Yeah, but it would be helpful if I knew what I was looking for."

"You're right. Knowledge is sexy. So, the G-spot. It's located on the ceiling of the vaginal wall as you enter. To look for it, use your finger, touching upward. You're looking for a very small, rough, protruding spot. It's very sensitive, and when you find it, you have the key to that woman's orgasm. I didn't know about it with any of my exes, so Valery is the only one I've ever looked for it with…well, I mean, except for you."

"Was mine easy to find?"

"By your reaction, yeah. It took no time at all."

"I think I remember that exact moment." We both laughed.

"It was one of the first things Valery and I did when we first slept together."

"Finding your G-spots?"

"Yeah. Valery takes lovemaking very seriously. She's very goal-oriented."

"Yes, enjoyably so." I blushed at the memory. "Out of all the people I've asked, you're the only one who's had a halfway decent description of it. Almost clinical actually."

"Valery made me aware of it, but my *clinical* description came from a Cosmo magazine."

"Really? You read Cosmo?"

"And this surprises you after last night?" she smirked, quirking her eyebrow at me.

"No, I guess not." A soft hum escaped my lips and I blushed again. "That thing we did at the end was amazing."

"Yeah, I think that was my favorite."

"And lounging around in a negligee afterward was icing on the cake. I've never worn a negligee before. It made me feel…powerful. Is that weird?"

"No, it's not weird. I feel the same way. And I must say, it suits you."

"It suits you, too."

I gave her hand a quick squeeze, then released it as she pulled into my apartment complex and parked next to my truck. "I have been surprised by many things the last few months, Sia, but you have pleasantly surprised me the most."

Sia grabbed me and pulled me into a hug, laying a kiss on my forehead. I jumped out of her car, stood to the side, and threw her a wave and a smile as she backed out and drove away.

* * *

What happened on Saturday occupied my mind for days. There was something about Sia and Valery's relationship that I found fascinating. They were opposites who complemented each other. Valery looked feminine on the outside but was very dominant in private, and Sia, who appeared soft butch in public, was surprisingly feminine, very domestic, and seductively submissive in private. She would do anything Valery wanted. In public, they looked like your typical butch/femme couple—almost role-playing, it was so plain to see. In private, the roles disappeared. They were just themselves, taking care of each other, loving one another. Meeting them, spending time with them, and getting to know them had so affected me that I could not get them out of my mind. Not just the sex part, but them, how they were together, the intimate closeness they let me see.

That they discussed their fantasies with each other and had agreed to live them out if the opportunity presented itself, completely intrigued me, and the trust and respect it must have taken from admitting they had such a fantasy to making it happen, awed me. I was thrilled to have been allowed to participate in their fantasy, and the thought that I would always be a small part of their lives, a small piece of the memory they would have of each other, was priceless.

CHAPTER TWENTY-FOUR

Over the weeks that followed, a feeling of impatience grew inside me. Something was missing, and I began to ask myself what I wanted from my new life. I had never seriously asked myself that before, never having contemplated much further than church, marriage, children, and couldn't say with any clarity what I expected to accomplish by the time I was thirty, forty, or fifty.

The club scene began looking small and unimportant—more trouble than it was worth, a waste of my time—when in reality, just the opposite was true. Caught up in all the drama, I'd forgotten how crucial clubs were, a safe place to hang out, a place where I could exist without shame or judgment. But the club lifestyle was not viable, at least not for me. I enjoyed spending time at *Club Imagine*, hanging out with other lesbians, but I had also learned a couple of very valuable life lessons, most notably that the sleeping around part of clubbing wasn't really me.

It started as a means of rebelling against Jordan's attempt to control me and snowballed into me picking up a bad reputation. I was interested in a relationship, preferably with Jordan, but the more improbable that seemed, the more I knew it was time to move on. I needed to stop waiting for her to want me again. I needed to clean up my act and my reputation. No more one-night stands. I needed to present myself as serious relationship material to all the other eligible women out there who felt the same way I did about relationships. I needed to be ready in case love ever visited me again.

I started by not hanging out in the club so much and spent more time on my favorite hobby. Cooking. And then I stopped thinking of it as a hobby and started taking it more seriously. I began spending all my evenings after work perfecting my cooking techniques and recipes, and soon, I was the go-to student in class, demonstrating for Chef Allen, roasting, braising, and sautéing, creating delicate sauces and velvety gravies. I even made friends with a couple of my fellow students, and although I never came out to them, I felt comfortable enough around them to invite them to my kitchen and accept invitations to theirs, where we practiced the art of cooking together and generally had a really good time.

I had never had worldly straight friends before, and the experience helped pull me out of the space I'd been occupying the last few months, broadening my world a little bit and reminding me that I was much more than just gay. I slowly began to experience the perfect mix of the parts of my old self that I valued and the parts of my new self that I was just discovering—a perfect balance of everything that made me who I was. I found that these two parts of me and all the other parts of me got along just fine with each other. I wasn't just one thing, I was a bunch of things, and all my things were important, and I wasn't going to ignore them anymore.

* * *

It had been more than a month since I'd been to the club, and I decided to drive out and have a beer, see how my sisters were doing. I pulled into the parking lot, enjoying that familiar mix of nervousness, anticipation, and excitement, feeling unusually confident as I glanced at myself in the rearview mirror, glad that walking into a gay club would never become routine for me.

I strolled in, smiling, happy to see everyone, and headed for my barstool, not noticing the cute little blond blocking my way, trying to get my attention. Brushing by her, I stopped when I heard my name.

"Shannon, wait. I don't think we've met." Talk about oxymoronic. I turned and looked at her. She walked up to me, looking me up and down, waiting for me to make the next move, and when I didn't, she blinked and bashfully smiled, suddenly unsure. "Sally," she introduced.

"Shannon. But of course, you already know that."

She smiled and batted her eyelashes at me, looking sure of herself again, and then, as we stood there silent for a few moments, her look of uncertainty slowly returned.

Suddenly, a hand appeared over her shoulder, attached to a very tall, strapping young woman who looked very upset with me. She gave me the most evil look, then tucked her girlfriend into her arm and guided her away. More than happy to leave them to it, I scanned the room as I made my way to the bar, spotting Jordan sitting at a table near the back, watching me with interest. I came to an abrupt stop when the tall woman returned, suddenly standing right in front of me and way too close for comfort.

"I may lose her, but it won't be to the likes of you," she said, poking me in the chest with her finger.

Rubbing my chest where she poked me, I struggled to stand up straight as my face broke out in a blush. The look of pure disgust on her face totally floored me, leaving me embarrassed as she flounced around to make her exit.

Jordan, meanwhile, had left her chair and was standing next to her table, watching me as if primed to spring into action, prepared to come to my aid in the event of having the crap beaten out of me.

The thought heartened me, and I gave her a small smile. Her body noticeably relaxed, and she sat back down at her table.

I took a stool at the bar, feeling a little exposed, wondering if everyone viewed me as the club player, the cocky womanizer chancing to pick up someone else's girlfriend. I tried telling myself it didn't matter what anyone thought about me, except it did because I was trying to repair my tattered reputation. I had to admit, though, it could have been worse. Everyone saw me *not* take Sally home, so that was something.

Waiting for Mason to bring me a beer, I was surprised when one of Jordan's friends sat next to me. I turned away, grimacing as I rolled my eyes, embarrassed by the thought that she may have witnessed what happened.

Mason set my beer down in front of me with a sympathetic smile, and I smiled back, thanking her, taking a quick sip as I glanced at the woman sitting next to me through the bar mirror in front of me. She had been with Jordan at Gay Pride, San Francisco. She was the one who'd given me that regretful, apologetic look when Jordan made a scene in the bar. Her gaze met mine, and before I could turn away, she smiled.

"Hi. I'm Poppy." I was reluctant to make any more random acquaintances, given the fiasco with Sally's girlfriend, but Poppy's polite acknowledgment of me prompted me to engage her.

"I'm Shannon. You're one of Jordan's friends. You were in San Francisco."

"Yeah. It's nice to finally meet you, Shannon."

"Nice to meet you... Jordan didn't send you over here, did she? I'm fine. Just having a bit of an identity crisis."

"Aren't we all," Poppy said, chuckling. "Be careful if you've got your eye on that one, though." Poppy nodded toward Sally, whose girlfriend seemed to be in another altercation with yet another innocent, unsuspecting woman, a woman who looked even less interested in Sally than I was—if that was possible. "Her girlfriend knows how to fight."

"She's got nothing to worry about from me. Besides my inability to fight, I'm not picking up girls anymore." I'd spoken a little too defensively and shifted uncomfortably on my barstool as my face began to burn. "It's not who I am. It's not what I want." I closed my eyes a moment and took a deep breath, reining myself in as I seemed determined to spill my guts to this woman.

"I'm not here to judge, Shannon."

Then, like an epiphany, I knew exactly who Poppy was, her name suddenly vividly connected to a long-ago memory. She was the woman Jordan bumped into at the grocery store way back when we spent that wonderful week alone at her brother's house. She was responsible for Jordan leaving me!

She was the reason all of this was happening!

"Then why are you here? To rescue me like you did Jordan?" I snarked, letting her know I knew who she was and what she had done.

"I didn't rescue Jordan. Jordan rescued herself," she said, confirming it.

"You told her to leave the church. You told her to leave me. Do you always involve yourself in other people's business?"

"She needed help, and I helped her. You know this, Shannon."

"You think you know me?"

"I know you want the best for Jordan."

I glared at her—the woman had an answer for everything. "Won't Jordan be upset that you're talking to me?"

"Why would she?"

"Because she can't stomach the thought of me being here. She wouldn't approve of you trying to talk me out of going back to the church."

"I'm not trying to talk you out of going back to church. I only encourage you, like I did Jordan, to be yourself and live your own life."

"Good, because I have no intention of going back. At least we agree on that. Maybe you could convince Jordan to stop trying to change my mind," I huffed, my attempt to blame Poppy for everything falling short at every turn.

"I understand why you don't want to go back to the church. What I don't understand is why you married a man. You *are* gay."

I cursed Jordan for giving this woman so much information about me, then sighed in resignation. Jordan couldn't very well share her own story without sharing a little of mine. But all the same, it was irritating that Poppy knew so much about me, and... Dammit! It was none of her business in the first place! And then I cursed Poppy for sounding so rational. Damn her!

"I had no choice," I said, and would have left it at that, but it needed an explanation. "I couldn't stay in the church without getting married and having children. It's a woman's pathway to salvation." Poppy looked skeptical, so I added, "Yeah, I know how it sounds. It's in the Bible. You can look it up."

"No, I believe you. Some of the stuff Jordan told me sounded way out there."

"I also believed that Christian men were special," I continued. "But that turned out to be a myth. And now I'm stuck wondering what else about the church is a myth. I was doing what I believed was right at the time…" I stopped myself before I went into a full-on listing of all my grievances, which would only serve to show how very pathetic I was and how very badly I needed someone to talk to. I didn't want her to see that.

"It must be difficult coming to terms with your life outside the church," Poppy said, sounding very sympathetic. "I know Jordan is still struggling with her beliefs as well. She believes she may be responsible for you not making it to heaven. She thinks that contact with her might entice you further away from the church. I think she's in a battle between her beliefs and her feelings for you."

"She is not the reason I left the church. After she left, I stayed. The church is the reason I left the church."

"I don't understand. Are you saying you don't believe anymore?"

"No. I'm saying that if the men who lead the church aren't all they appear to be, what else is not what it appears to be?"

"Was your husband not what you thought he should be?"

"He hurt me!" I slammed my hand down flat on the bar a little too hard and then cringed, balling my hand into a fist. "He hit me when I wouldn't have sex with him. It defies belief. He is supposed to be special, the closest human to God, and he chose to react to our unique situation, which he was fully aware of before we got married, by beating me. I can't wrap my head around it. He shattered the very basis of my belief system. If he, the guy with the keys to the kingdom, couldn't behave in a godly manner, then what is all of this about?" Another wave of irritation hit me as I seemed unable to stop sharing private information with Poppy. She was like a clever little FBI interrogator with all her indirect, unimposing questions, patient and understanding, tactically silent, getting me to open up and dump my whole crazy life out all over the place. Aargh!

Poppy looked at me for a long time, not saying a word, and I was just about to sarcastically ask, *Cat got your tongue*, when it hit me. She didn't have a snappy comeback because she didn't know about this part. Jordan hadn't told her because Jordan didn't know about my fight with Samuel. Jordan didn't know because her brother, Shawn, didn't know, which of course meant that the church didn't know. My family did not inform the church that Samuel might be a wife-beater, which explained why Jordan was taking the entire blame for my spiritual demise and all the guilt that went with it.

I closed my eyes for a moment, absorbing the meaning of this revelation, almost certain that Jordan would never have pressured me to go back to the church had she known, or at least not back to Samuel. I looked over at her, and a feeling of deep compassion welled up in me. Believing she was the sole reason I left the church must have been torture. There were plenty of scary Bible scriptures threatening fire and brimstone for those who led Christians away from the church.

"I don't know what to say," Poppy finally said. "I'm sorry."

"It's okay. I didn't mean to dump all of that on you. I'm okay, really."

"Yeah, both of you are doing remarkably well given everything you've been through, but still, it must be difficult. I mean, Jordan is doing much better, but she is not living a very full life with all the baggage she carries around."

"It's a fuller life than the measly, fake one I offered her. Believe me, she is in a better place."

"After all she's been through, why would she settle for a

better place? I wouldn't be satisfied with only half of what was possible. She had that in the church with you, and that was destroying her."

I cringed again; her words felt like a slap. "She'll get there. She has you and her friends to help her."

"I don't think that's enough. I think she hangs out here all the time so she can see you. You haven't been around a lot the last month or so, and she has been going nuts, driving the rest of us nuts."

"Well, that must be very unpleasant for you and her other friends, and her girlfriends, or whoever."

"She doesn't have a girlfriend," Poppy said with a small smile.

"Oh…well… You know what I mean, whoever she's dating."

"She doesn't date."

"She doesn't date?"

"No. She's like a nun. When I said she's not living her full life, that's part of what I was referring to. She doesn't date, and she doesn't talk about dating. You are the only woman I've ever heard her talk about."

"Really?"

"Yeah. Women flirt with her, and they ask her out, but she's not interested. Jesus, if I looked like her…" Poppy huffed, shaking her head. "Anyway, yeah, as far as I know, she's never been with anyone but you. Like I said, I think she hangs out here so she can see you."

"Yeah, so she can bully me into going back to church… Although she kind of stopped doing that. She's not giving me her scary warning look anymore, and she even smiled at me a couple of times and said hi to me once."

"Well, that's gotta mean something."

"I have no idea what it means, to be perfectly honest. We don't talk, so I'm a bit blind when it comes to what motivates her. But it doesn't really matter. I'm further along in the process than she realizes. I'm not going back to the church. She has to accept that."

"Maybe she's further along in the process than *you* realize."

"Or maybe she just doesn't care about me anymore."

"I don't believe that. That makes no sense to me. She obviously has feelings for you. It's frustrating to watch. The same feelings that brought you together broke you apart and are keeping you apart. She can't be with you because she loves you. She's willing to give you up forever so that you won't be lost. It's sad really. You risked everything to be together, and now that the two of you *can* be together, you can't be together."

"It's complicated, Poppy."

"It really isn't, Shannon. You need to talk to her."

"She has to talk to me first. That's the price for leaving me."

"Wow…"

"No! Not wow! Everything you've told me about Jordan… And by the way, I'm not sure she'd appreciate you talking about her like this…"

"I don't care," Poppy interrupted. "I don't let people tell me who I can talk to and what I can talk to them about."

I gave Poppy a quick *whatever* glance, suppressing an eye roll. Her unflappable self-assurance was irritatingly admirable. I could definitely use a dose. "Listen, I don't want Jordan to be unhappy, and I hate that she is carrying so much guilt." I took a deep breath and blew it out. "I won't deny it. I love Jordan, and I have to admit, I'm feeling a little hopeful knowing she doesn't date, but I'm still very hurt that she left me. I know she believes she did the right thing, and I even understand her attempts to get me to return to the church given she didn't know all the details about why I left. But I'm gonna need her to explain it to me and show me some respect, the respect she neglected to show me when she walked out without a word. And I need her to listen to my side of the story. And you need to let me tell her about what happened with my husband. I need to explain it to her. I need her to understand it and accept how I chose to deal with it, even if she doesn't agree. This is crucial to any relationship we hope to have with one another, even if, in the end, all that's left is friendship."

"That's a lot to ask. Jordan made life-altering decisions based on assumptions about you, and if you ask me, they were pretty rational assumptions, and now you're asking her to question her assumptions without any input or any guarantees."

"Poppy, if you tell her, you'll send her into a spiral. She'll blame herself for putting me in a situation where I thought my only option was a quick wedding to a guy who body-slammed me because I was a crappy wife. You'll compound her guilt, and that will hurt her. She'll never be able to open up to me."

"If she knew…"

"No! I want her to come to me without knowing. That's what's required. It's a leap of faith. She has to trust me."

Poppy slowly shook her head at me, clearly not agreeing with my decision, and I had to admit, it made me doubt myself a little. I was being stubborn and a little unreasonable. But could I live with Jordan's acceptance if it was predicated on this new piece of information alone? It irritated me to think that she couldn't accept my decision to leave the church unless it was somehow qualified by egregiously pernicious circumstances. I mean, was it too much to ask that she just trust me?

"What are you going to do?" Poppy asked, interrupting my thoughts.

"I'm going to move forward. I'm going to learn how to cook. I'm going to live my life. I'm going to try to find happiness. This is the first time I've been allowed to, and I want to get it right."

Poppy and I spent another hour talking about lighter topics—my ruined reputation and her new girlfriend, Becca—and then Poppy walked me to my truck.

"Listen, here's my number. Call me, and let's do this again." Poppy handed me a piece of paper with her phone number on it. I looked at the paper, then at her, surprised that I liked her so much. She smiled, grabbed my shoulder, and pulled me in for a hug. "It's going to be okay, Shannon."

I got in my truck and drove home, thinking about Jordan and Poppy, wondering about their relationship. Poppy knew a lot about Jordan. They were obviously close. I was thankful that Jordan had Poppy to talk to, someone who understood. Poppy helped Jordan back then when I didn't know how to; she saved Jordan when I was unable to. I decided right then and there that I would try to spend more time with her. She was compassionate and smart. She cared about us, about Jordan and me, and she knew how hard this was.

* * *

Fall faded into winter, and suddenly it was early December and I had completed another semester of cooking classes, this one with Best Menu, Best Entrée, and Best Pasta Dish—a chicken, red pepper, and spinach ravioli filled with a thick cream sauce. It tasted like heaven if I did say so myself. I celebrated with a visit to my favorite hairdressers, Flo, Sherri, and Marg.

"I can't believe you waited six months to have your hair cut again," Flo said. "Your hair grows really fast. You need to have it cut every two months."

Flo cut my hair in her very serious, methodical, professional way. She didn't try to make small talk, and I closed my eyes and tried not to fall asleep. I enjoyed it just as much as the first time but also experienced that bittersweet feeling again of losing something that had been such an emotional, complicated part of my life.

"Let's make an appointment now for February," she said.

I agreed and paid, and they sent me off at the door, waving goodbye. As I walked to my truck, a huge sign in the middle of a neighboring parking lot grabbed my attention, and I paused, taking in the odd sight of a pair of boots hanging from the sign by their laces. The contrast between the gigantic billboard sign and the little pair of black boots was stark, and

I blinked, raising my hand and shielding my eyes from the sun to get a better look. They must have been hanging at least twenty feet up. How could someone have gotten them up there? They would've needed a very long ladder, and why go to all the trouble to hang a perfectly good pair of black boots on a sign? My attention was drawn to the actual words printed on the towering sign as I walked toward it. *Sacramento Military Recruiting Center.* Huh.

A small building suddenly appeared next to the sign as if out of nowhere. It had posters and advertisements plastered all over the front windows with the dominant theme, *Be all you can be, Army*. The message hit me right in the face. I blinked several times, staring at it as if the message were just for me. A shiver ran through my body, and I shook myself, huffing out a breath at the thought that it could all be that simple. I looked up at the sky expecting the earth to shift, but it didn't, and for a moment, I was tempted to feel silly for my reaction to the hanging boots, the big sign, the little building, and the message. But I didn't. Signs, messages, and helpful hints about life came in different forms, and I didn't want to inoculate myself from their power by getting hung up on the way they manifested themselves.

I jumped in my truck and drove home.

* * *

In January, something extraordinary happened that gave me a large dose of hope. I was at the restaurant registering for my next semester of cooking classes when Chef Allen himself came out of the kitchen and greeted me at reception.

"Ms. Callaghan, good evening." He took my hand and held it formally, insisting on addressing all students and staff by their surname. "I could not get a hold of you over the phone and instructed Ms. James to notify me when you arrived to register."

I looked over at Merrell, and she smiled at me as if she'd been caught doing something naughty.

Chef Allen pulled me to the side and released my hand.

"I've nominated you for our on-the-job program."

I actually gasped at his news, which brought a smile to his lips.

"I would be proud if you would consider being my protégée de Choix, my candidate as Chef Assistant for Chef Dillon at *Bonny's Pocket*. It's in downtown Sacramento, and you would only be required to be there on your *off* nights, from six to ten in the evening. I still expect you to register for the new semester, so I will have you on class nights. Tell me now if you are not interested. I can still nominate someone else, but you are my first choice. You are such a wonderful student and an excellent cook..."

"Yes! Yes! Yes, of course. I can't believe it. Thank you, Chef. I would love a shot at this," I blurted, reaching out and grabbing the sleeve of his white shirt.

"Okay. Good. I will know his decision in a couple of weeks, but I'm sure you will be accepted. He has never rejected one of my candidates."

"Thank you, Chef. Thank you for this opportunity."

"Ms. Callaghan, you deserve it. I will leave you to register. I need to return to the kitchen. I will be in touch."

After we said goodbye, I turned to Merrell, a look of open-mouthed shock plastered on my face. "Wow, I totally did not see that coming."

"Congratulations, Shannon!" she squealed, then quickly clapped her hand over her mouth.

"Thank you, Merrell!"

Merrell finalized my registration and told me again how happy she was for me. I walked to my truck in a daze, unable to believe that I could soon be on-the-job learning my dream job, cooking delicious food for people who would actually choose it from a menu, enjoy it, and then pay for it, which for me was the ultimate validation.

I got home and paced through my apartment, letting my mind imagine what this new opportunity could mean, allowing myself to dust off an old dream of owning my own restaurant—nothing big and important, just something homey and comfortable with good food you could sit down to and enjoy, or a good meal you could pick up and take home to your family.

I wanted to tell everyone about my achievement, but there was really no one to tell, no one who could appreciate what it meant to me. Only one name came to mind, Jordan, but I couldn't tell her. Poppy! I dialed her number, a bit nervous. Our conversation at the club was weeks ago, and I never called her. I hoped she would still be the person I believed her to be—interested, intelligent, kind...

"Hello."

"Hi, Poppy. It's me, Shannon."

"Shannon! Hi! I was hoping you'd call. I was thinking about you. I swear, I was just about to ask Jordan for your number."

She was such a nice person. Damn! I should have called her sooner. "Yeah, I just wanted to call and say how much I enjoyed meeting you."

"I enjoyed meeting you, too. I was afraid you would feel too uncomfortable to call me, and I kicked myself for not getting your number. I'm really glad you called."

"I should have called sooner. I've been busy, but I thought about you, and yeah... I should have called to tell you how much our conversation meant to me."

"Well, I'm glad. I like you, Shannon. You're a nice person, and I hope that you can be happy."

"I'm happy. In fact, something just happened that has made me very happy."

"Oh! Do tell!"

I told Poppy about my chef-assistant nomination, and she reacted exactly as I had hoped, congratulating me and asking me a million questions, hinting at a potential dinner invite. I laughed as she charmed me with compliments and promised her I'd have her over for dinner when she had time. She surprised me with an invitation of her own.

"Listen, there's a Gay Pride fair in San Francisco this Sunday, and I was going to meet up with some friends at a club on Saturday night. Why don't you come with me? We could go a little early and do some sightseeing."

"Yeah, I'd love that. What time?"

"I could pick you up Saturday at noon. I just need your address."

I gave Poppy my address and my phone number, and the date was set. I hung up the phone, even more buoyed than before. Both of our conversations had been positive and constructive, both leaving me feeling better about myself and more confident. I began to understand more and more why Jordan felt so drawn to this woman. She was genuine and honest, a breath of fresh air, and seemed to believe in everything connected to happiness, openness, and honesty. I hadn't had a lot of conversations in my life that left me feeling so hopeful, and I couldn't wait until I was in Poppy's company again, not only to bask in her vibe but to reciprocate. Encouragement and acceptance were most potent when given by another woman, and in my opinion, was the most preferred and enjoyable way to receive such needed attention.

CHAPTER TWENTY-FIVE

Poppy picked me up at noon on Saturday, and we were strolling around San Francisco by three-thirty.

"Where do you want to go first?" Poppy asked.

"Let's get something to eat. I'm starving."

We found a small bistro-café selling slices of pizza to go and an empty bench just across the street to sit on. While we ate, we were entertained by a street performer dressed head-to-toe in neon green spandex, juggling bowling pins while balancing on a big rubber ball. It was a mystery to me what kept these guys motivated to spend hours out here performing, and I wondered where their unique skill set would land them in life. I asked Poppy what she thought, and she said she knew a street performer who was a hedge fund manager.

"He did this on weekends and on his days off. He loved it."

"You're kidding."

"I'm not."

I found it hard to believe that business professionals were out masquerading as starving artists and only considered it because it came straight from Poppy's lips, though I did watch the street performer with a whole new perspective, and I had to admit, he definitely looked happy. We finished our lunch, tossed a couple of coins in the street performer's bucket, and headed for the cable cars.

We got off at *Ghirardelli Square*, bought a couple of freshly made chocolate chip cookies at a place called *The Chocolate Experience*, and then made our way to *Fisherman's Wharf*, where we took lots of pictures of the bay before heading over to *Pier 39*. We walked down to the end where the pier met the bay and took some pictures of *Alcatraz* before making our way back. On the way, I spotted a quaint little bookstore—*Premium Books*. Poppy noticed me eyeing the store and asked if I wanted to go in.

"No, I don't want to go in. But I think I know someone who works there."

"You should go in and say hi to her," Poppy offered.

"I will probably do that someday, but not on this visit. And how do you know it's a her?"

"I didn't, but I do now. Who is she?"

"She was a...one-night stand."

"Oh, okay. Understood..."

"No. It's not like that. She was really nice. Special, you know?"

"She must have been if you're thinking about visiting her."

"Her name is Kandis, and she invited me."

"Wow, that is special."

"To be honest, all of my one-night stands were special."

"Yeah, I know what you mean."

We walked from the pier to a gay bar Poppy knew of, and I was pleasantly surprised to find that it was the cool little dive bar Kandis showed me during Gay Pride. We sat at the bar and drank a beer, sharing some of our more memorable one-night-stand stories—Poppy's proving to be way more entertaining than mine—and then drank another beer while we played a game of pool.

After Poppy thoroughly kicked my butt at pool, we decided to get something to eat before going to the club to meet up with her friends. As we made our way through crowded streets filled with people and traffic and noise, passing shops and clubs and restaurants, we spotted a tattoo studio. I stopped in my tracks.

"I have to get a tattoo!"

Poppy grabbed my arm. "Whoa, there. Wait a minute." She stepped in front of me, squaring off as she leaned in and looked me in the eyes, seemingly trying to determine if I was of sound mind—or just drunk. "Are you sure?" she asked, gauging my response to see if I was serious.

"Yes, Poppy, I am. I want a tattoo!"

We went inside, and I spent fifteen minutes looking at all

the pictures of tattoos hanging on the walls but could not find one that I liked.

"Can I help you?" A man appeared at the counter that separated the room I was in from the tattoo room behind him.

"Yes. I want a tattoo, but I don't see one here that I like."

"What did you have in mind?"

I explained what I wanted, and as I did, he sketched it on a piece of paper.

"Like this?" he asked, turning the paper so that I could see his sketch. It was a bird soaring with the letters *JET* underneath it.

"Yes! That's perfect!"

He opened the door separating the two rooms and invited me in. We discussed the size of the tattoo, where I wanted it, and how much the tattoo would cost. He asked me to take a seat and remove my shirt so that the back of my left shoulder was exposed. I didn't feel the least bit shy sitting there in my bra, the entire setup having a distinct doctor-patient vibe. I think the beers helped too.

He strategically positioned himself behind me and began the very painful first strokes of my tattoo. The whole thing lasted an hour, and when he was finished, he handed me a mirror so I could take a look at it. It was perfect—smaller than the palm of my hand, centered on my left shoulder blade. He smeared a Vaseline-like substance on it, slapped a square cellophane cover on it, and told me how to take care of it so it wouldn't get infected or lose its clarity.

"If you follow my instructions to the letter, your tattoo will be healed in a couple of weeks and will look exactly like the picture I drew for you."

I paid him and thanked him, and as we left the tattoo studio, Poppy gave me a dubious look, shaking her head.

"JET? Really?"

"Yeah, JET. It stands for Jordan Elain Tallis."

"I know what it stands for, Shannon, but a tattoo is like…forever."

"I know, and that's what it means to me even if we don't

get a forever. It's not about what she meant to me; it's about everything she means to me now. Please, don't say anything to her, okay?"

"I won't say anything." Poppy smiled, hooked her arm in mine, and led me down the sidewalk. "So, let's grab a quick bite to eat, and then I'll take you to a club that you've never been to before. *Club Echo*. It's nice. I think you'll like it."

We headed out toward a small industrial area near the bay, stopping at a fish sandwich vendor near the wharf on the way, and as we walked and ate our sandwiches, I asked Poppy what kind of club she was taking me to. As she described it to me, I began to fear I wasn't dressed appropriately. I examined her outfit more carefully—a jacket, a long-sleeved T-shirt, stone-washed jeans, and a pair of boxed-toe western boots. She wasn't dressed that much differently than I was but somehow looked way more dressed up than I did—cooler and more sophisticated—and I began to worry that my outfit wasn't going to cut it.

"Are you sure I can get in dressed like this?"

"Yes, I'm sure." She shook her head, letting out a sigh. "Shannon, you don't have to worry about that. You look great."

We took a right on a dark, deserted-looking, wide, multi-lane street with huge storage warehouses on both sides, and about halfway down, a long line of people appeared, waiting to get into one of the larger storage warehouses on the left. We walked along the line of waiting people, and I felt even more underdressed than before. The women in line were dressed in high heels, sexy short dresses, lots of makeup, and perfectly styled hair. And the men were even more gorgeous than the women. At the door, the man whose job it was to let people into the club nodded at Poppy and let us in without waiting, making me feel oddly special yet even more self-conscious.

We walked through the entrance into a foyer, and a loud base beat vibrated from a room just beyond a set of double doors. As we approached, two men in formal garb opened the doors, and a blast of music slammed into me, halting me in place. Poppy smiled, grabbed my hand, and pulled me inside. The room was the size of a baseball field, and along the wall, all the way around, was a beautiful, blue-lighted, continuous bar packed with hundreds of women drinking and socializing. In the center of the room was a large, oval-shaped opening surrounded by a railing trimmed in white light. I had no idea whether the owners intended this *vulvacious* visual, but it was unquestionably feminine and very sexy. There were tables for standing and tables with chairs, but there were also coffee tables surrounded by couches and comfy armchairs, each one an intimate living room hosting a private party. The place was packed. I hoped Poppy's friends saved us a seat.

Poppy led me along the right side of the opening, and I stopped and looked over the railing, astounded at what I saw. It was a huge dance floor jam-packed with people so eclectically arrayed, I was suddenly perfectly dressed.

We walked toward the back wall, and as we approached a corner group of couches and armchairs pulled together around a coffee table, I saw none other than Jordan herself sitting on one of the couches, surrounded by a large group of women.

Jordan stood up, looking surprised but not shocked, nervous as she smoothed her jeans, hopeful as she searched my face for any sign of disinclination, her body language generally positive but still ambiguous as to whether she was expecting me or not. Shaking my head, I glanced at Poppy, who was smiling ear-to-ear, and gave her a look like, *Are you sure this is a good idea?* But she just kept smiling, encouraging me forward, leading me toward Jordan, who had rounded the coffee table and was headed right for me. Jordan gave me a smile before turning to Poppy.

"You brought a friend."

"Yeah, a mutual friend."

Jordan looked at me, hesitated, then pulled me into a wonderful hug. I closed my eyes and let myself relax into her arms, enjoying how familiar it felt, not at all surprised by my body's reaction to being so close to her. And she just kept holding me, and I breathed easier than I had since she left me.

"Hi," she whispered in my ear.

"Hi," I replied, slow and breathy, warm and happy, not wanting her to let go.

Jordan pulled back from me and smiled a brilliant smile, just slightly more brilliant than her sparkling diamond earrings—her sparkling eyes coming in a close third.

"Here, you can sit with me." She gestured toward the couch.

I was very much aware of Jordan's hand on my lower back as she guided me around the coffee table. Her friends nodded at me and scooched over to make room for us, and as we sat, Jordan began introducing me to everyone.

I recognized some of them from *Club Imagine,* but most of them I'd never seen before. Everyone was super nice, and none of them seemed to mind that Jordan and I were acting so familiar. It was obvious that none of these women were girlfriends or former girlfriends of Jordan's. There were no looks of jealousy, just welcoming smiles.

We settled on the couch a bit squished together—Jordan sitting on the very end, my arm pushed up against the front part of her shoulder—and as she arranged herself, trying to give me more room, her arm landed on the back of the couch behind me, allowing my arm to instead rest up against the side of her breast.

She let out a small gasp, prompting me to stare. Had I caught her being affected by our close proximity? She gave me a shy smile, her face blushing, clearly affected, and I was ready to drag her off somewhere and kiss her. I was so turned on my head was spinning. It had all happened so fast. Just a couple of minutes ago, I was hanging out with Poppy, and now I was sitting in Jordan's arms. From one moment to the next, Jordan was so far away, and now, so close I could hardly think straight.

Poppy returned from the bar holding three beers. She

handed one to me and one to Jordan before taking a seat on the edge of the coffee table facing us. I gave her a half-smile, wondering if she had planned all this by herself or if Jordan was in on it too. Jordan's reaction so far suggested that she was not unhappy to see me, but it didn't clear up the question of whether she'd expected me or not, and it really didn't matter to me at the moment, but I would definitely ask Poppy about it later. She was certainly enjoying her surprise and my reaction to it. She leaned forward, laid her hand on my knee, and gave me a smile that said, *Told you so.* She glanced at Jordan, then back at me before raising her beer.

"To forever."

Jordan and I hesitated a moment, unsure about the toast, but then raised our beers too, and many of the other women did as well. "To forever!" voices called out, including our own, making the toast more about everyone and not just about Jordan and me.

We spent the next couple of hours just hanging out, visiting, talking, and laughing. Even some of Jordan's friends talked to me, mostly asking about my hobby, cooking, and what my favorite dishes were, explaining why they didn't know how to cook. It surprised me how many of them couldn't cook but wanted to learn. It seemed they all knew who I was, where I had come from, and how I liked to spend my free time. Jordan told them, of course, which made me feel special, but it was still strange to meet strangers who knew me so well. At one point, Poppy's girlfriend, Becca, showed up, and Poppy introduced us. From her friendly smile and casual wink, I knew she was well-informed about what was going on between Jordan and me. We hit it off right away.

"Hey, let's dance!" Jordan said a few minutes later. I looked at her, a bit hesitant, and she leaned in and whispered in my ear, "Becca loves to dance. Besides, you have to dance down there. You'll regret it if you don't."

So, we all stood—not just Jordan, me, Poppy, and Becca, but also four of their friends—and filed down the stairs to the dance floor, where the music was even louder. The floor was packed, and I couldn't tell who was dancing with whom, all of us dancing back and forth, changing partners, or dancing in groups. We danced for almost an hour, and although I never got to dance with Jordan one-on-one, we seemed to be in constant contact, exchanging glances filled with fun and flirting, generating a tantalizing energy between us that made me want to grab her and kiss her. But then everything about tonight made me want to grab her and kiss her. Whether she was a coconspirator in tonight's *chance* meeting was not important to me anymore. If I could have my old Jordan back for just one night, I could die happy tomorrow.

As we climbed the stairs, laughing and catching our breath, my mind immediately worried that I wouldn't be seated next to Jordan anymore, and I hesitated, a bit unsure as everyone took their seats. I didn't want to presume that I would get to sit next to her, but as she took her seat on the couch, she looked up at me and smiled, patting the cushion beside her, pushing on the shoulder of the woman to her left to scooch over and make some room. I edged in between Jordan's knees and the coffee table, and her hands lightly touched my hips as she guided me through. I was warm from dancing but could still feel the heat of her touch as I sat down next to her.

She repositioned her arm over the back of the couch, smiling at me as she leaned in a little, getting comfortable, her face just inches from mine. I gulped. We were so close, and I wanted her so badly. I could feel a throbbing ache slowly grow between my thighs. She hesitated, looking at me intently, creating a level of intimacy between us that left me breathless. Contrary to what her actions over the last year suggested, I could swear she wanted me.

I tore my eyes from Jordan's and looked over at Poppy, who was sitting in an armchair with Becca sitting on her lap. Poppy looked very pleased with herself, quirking her eyebrow at me. I smiled at her, amused by her cockiness, touched by her kindness and thoughtfulness. Who else would care enough to take the time to set up an unofficial rendezvous between two people who, over the last year, acted like they couldn't stand each other? Poppy would, that's who.

I didn't want to be anywhere but here, sitting next to Jordan, and I hoped this night would never end, but half an hour later it did exactly that. Poppy ordered a round of shots, and we all stood and raised our glasses, hesitating a moment as Poppy raised hers.

"To Love!" she shouted.

"To Love!" everyone repeated.

And then, turning in different directions and facing different people, other toasts were made. Jordan, Poppy, and Becca turned to me, their glasses touching mine.

"To you!" they toasted.

"To you!" I returned.

We continued the toast until all four of us had toasted each other, then threw our heads back and drank our shots in one gulp. I enjoyed a warm hug from Becca, a playful hug from Poppy, and then, with no other way to describe it, a hug full of promise from Jordan, because that's where my heart was and that's what I wanted. A promise of something, anything, whatever she could give me.

It was two in the morning and time to go. Becca linked her arm in mine and we headed for the exit, Jordan and Poppy right behind us talking in soft voices. I was a little nervous about what would happen next as we stepped out onto the sidewalk, all of us suddenly silent. Jordan looked a little nervous herself as she glanced at Poppy and then at me.

"Jordan, it was so nice seeing you again. I wish…we could…you know…" I began, not wanting to lose what we'd gained tonight, wanting to build on it.

"Yeah, it was nice to see you too. I…um. I've been wanting to talk to you."

"Yeah? Talk to me."

"I wanted to apologize for behaving so badly the last few months. I've been working through some stuff, which is no excuse… I just wanted to apologize."

"I understand. It's okay, Jordan. If there is anything I can do to help, please let me know."

"Thank you, Shannon."

Jordan had a pained expression on her face, and I wished I could do something to change that. She gave me a forced smile, and it nearly broke my heart. Tears threatening, I looked away, glancing at Poppy, who was standing across the street with Becca, waiting for me.

"I guess I should go. They're waiting."

Jordan looked over at Poppy, then back at me, and nodded. She was standing so close, it would have taken no effort at all to lean forward and kiss her. But that was impossible, there was no way she wanted me to—I mean, what was I thinking—and I took a step back instead. Jordan blinked, and her hand shot out and grabbed my arm. She hesitated, then pulled me into a hug, a hug that was probably meant as a friendly goodbye hug, but one that left me so aroused, I moaned before I could stop myself.

As she released me, her hand lingered on my arm a moment before letting go, and I stepped back, offering her the best smile I could before turning and walking away. Poppy shot Jordan a confused look as they met me in the street, Becca throwing her arm around my shoulder as we all turned and walked away from *Club Echo* and Jordan.

"Shannon! Wait!"

Coming to an abrupt halt, I hesitated a moment before turning, blinking back tears as I struggled to appear strong and casual and relaxed, or whatever it was that looked like I wouldn't break to pieces if Jordan didn't say what I needed her to say.

"Shannon, could I take you home? I mean, I'm staying with a friend tonight. I won't be driving to Sacramento until tomorrow morning. But if you want, you can come too. There's plenty of room, and then tomorrow maybe we could grab some breakfast on the way home...and talk."

"Okay. Yeah. I'd like that." My voice was clear and sure, and I was so glad it had not failed me. I blew out a quick breath and looked at Poppy and Becca. Poppy was smiling broadly, and Becca had tears in her eyes. "Is that okay, Poppy?"

"It's perfect, Shannon." Poppy let out a small chuckle and added, "Call me."

"I will. Thank you, Poppy."

"Are you staying at Ally's tonight?" Poppy asked Jordan.

"Yeah."

"Tell her I said hi."

"Will do. You guys be careful."

There were quick hugs all around, and then Poppy and Becca walked away arm in arm, leaving us standing there in the middle of the street, alone. I turned and looked at Jordan, and she smiled, her pained expression gone, replaced with hope. Her leap of faith was in my hands now.

* * *

Jordan and I walked in silence for a few minutes, my thoughts reviewing the day, pleasantly surprised when Jordan suddenly took my hand. She blew out a quick breath before turning and looking at me, giving me a questioning smile. When I smiled back, her smile doubled in size. I was holding hands with Jordan in public. I looked down at us and then out at the city we were in, marveling at how far we had come.

"Who's Ally?" I asked, curious to know where she was taking me.

"She's a good friend of mine. She lives here in the city. It's not far."

It wasn't far, and before long, we were standing in front of an older, red-brick building five stories high. Jordan pulled out a key and unlocked the front door, letting us into a dimly lit entranceway. We took the stairs up to the third floor and stopped in front of one of the apartments. "Shhh," Jordan said, holding her finger to her lips.

She unlocked the door, and we stepped into a large room, the only light coming in through the front windows. I could hear people moving, breathing softly, and as my eyes adjusted, I could just make out the shapes of a dozen or so people lying on the floor, sleeping. A voice whispering came from my right, and I jumped.

"You ladies can sleep in the corner by the window. There's a pillow and a blanket on the chair." I felt a touch on my arm. "Hi Shannon, I'm Ally."

"Hi, Ally," I whispered, not really surprised she knew my name.

Jordan took my hand and led me through the obstacle course of bodies, zig-zagging us toward the far corner of the room. Jordan began making our bed on the floor as I stood there looking out the window at the night.

"Okay, lay here," Jordan whispered, touching my arm. I knelt down and let her guide me onto the makeshift bed. My head found the pillow, and she settled in behind me, covering us with the blanket, her arm holding me, pulling me closer. A second or two passed before Jordan's hips shifted and pushed into me. She tsked, mumbled an apology, pushed into me again, then let out a deep sigh. "Sorry."

I was totally aroused, and the only thing keeping me from turning and kissing her were the dozen or so other people in the room. Instead, I snuggled my ass gently into her lap and whispered, "It's okay."

Her arm tightened around me for a moment and then relaxed, and before I knew it, I was asleep, only to wake a moment later, it seemed, with Jordan kneeling next to me, shaking me gently. "Wake up." I sat up and could see by morning's first light pouring in through the windows that the living room was indeed filled with sleeping women, of every shape, size, and color. Jordan handed me a very small cup of coffee. "Espresso. It's strong. Drink. We have to go."

I drank my coffee while tidying up our sleeping corner, piling the blanket, pillow, and mat on a chair, and then made my way through the sleeping bodies toward the front door as Jordan and Ally entered the room from the kitchen.

"Good morning, Shannon," Ally whispered as we met at the door. She took my cup, then surprised me with a hug.

I held on to her for a moment, feeling touched and super emotional, and whispered back, "Thank you, Ally."

Jordan gave Ally a quick nod in farewell as she opened the door, and Ally returned the nod, sending us on our way. We quietly headed downstairs to the street, where the neighborhood was still fast asleep. Jordan's Chevy was parked two blocks over, and once she got it started, we made our way out of the city. Except for stolen glances, which spoke volumes, we were quiet the first half-hour of our trip—navigating the city, even at this hour, required a bit of concentration—Jordan not speaking until we hit the freeway and the first signs for gas, food, and lodging appeared.

"You hungry? You want to stop and get something to eat?" Jordan asked.

"Yeah, if you do," I replied, hoping she wasn't just asking to be nice but actually wanted to sit with me at breakfast so we could talk.

"Yeah, I could eat something."

We found a *Denny's* and shared a knowing smile as she maneuvered into a parking spot. I remembered our first breakfast out together so long ago and could feel every piece of it again, like the perfect déjà vu. We were shown to our table, and, as if nothing had changed, Jordan was inundated with looks and stares. Our waitress acted like Jordan was a movie star or something, dropping her order pad twice as she attempted to recite every possible extra Jordan might find appetizing with her pancakes. I sat there and watched, amused, remembering all the women Jordan had had this effect on in the past, and could not help but think how much more beautiful she was now. She seemed not to notice all the attention, sitting patiently, smiling charmingly, listening to the waitress go on and on.

The waitress finally asked for my order, suggesting not one extra, then turned and left us with a sigh and a smile. I raised my brow at Jordan and shook my head, and she laughed, igniting a rush of heat through my body. I blew out a quick breath and started laughing too, thrilled that I was still so intensely receptive to her.

"How do you know Ally?" I asked, hoping to get us talking.

"I met her this past summer on one of my first visits to San Francisco, partying in the clubs, a little bit drunk, and in no condition to drive all the way back to Sacramento. Ally saw me and talked me into staying with her for the night. At first, I thought she was coming on to me, but she assured me she wasn't, and I needed a place to stay, so I took her up on her offer. When I got to her apartment, there was a long line of women waiting to get inside. Ally just wanted to keep me from driving home drunk. I slept in the same corner as we did. I'll never forget it. The next morning, I was so relieved I didn't try to drive home the night before. Ally does this for women visiting the city. She charges about twenty bucks a night, a bargain in a city like San Francisco; everybody out by nine in the morning, no entry until after eleven at night, and only sleeping allowed." Jordan smiled and shrugged her shoulders. "And we've been friends ever since. She really helped me, you know? She's not a big talker, but she's an excellent listener."

"Do you visit San Francisco a lot?"

"I do. I like it here. I fit in, and the people are great. I mean, I like *Club Imagine*…"

"Where you can keep an eye on me and plan your next attempt at making me return to the church?" I quickly interjected, suddenly impatient to get to the point. I wanted to talk about us.

Jordan shook her head at herself, looking a bit embarrassed. "I'm sorry. I've been acting like an idiot."

"Yeah, you have," I shot back, but immediately softened. She looked really sorry, and I wasn't without fault—I had certainly done some idiotic things myself over the last year. "But I'm glad you were there. It was the only way I could see you, although your presence had me hanging out there more often than I probably should have. And…well, I didn't always behave perfectly either." I looked down at my plate, readying myself, knowing I had to address my promiscuous behavior before I could tackle the rest. "I know you're aware, I mean, I know you saw…" I cleared my throat, hating that I was blushing. "Jordan, I made some mistakes. I got a little carried away, but I learned pretty fast that that's not what I want."

"I heard the rumors. Some of them were quite amusing. I have to ask… Did you really sleep with over thirty women?"

The look of surprise on my face made Jordan laugh. "I did not sleep with thirty women!" I stated, indignant, and then began laughing too. "Thirty women? How did they even come up with that number?"

"Rumors are like that. The facts they're based on are liberally exaggerated, and the rest is made up"

"There *were* women, Jordan, but only six of them. That's all. And I swear, it's not what you think, and I don't do that anymore. It's important that you believe me."

"I do believe you. There is no way anyone could convince me that you were doing some of the things they said you were doing. I mean, the Shannon I knew didn't even know what a clitoris was until I showed her."

She was getting a jab in, teasing me, and I was glad of that, overcome with gratitude that she was being so gracious, her teasing reference to a time long ago when we were first learning about ourselves, discovering each other, making the topic easier to address and her all the more endearing.

"I'm sorry, Jordan."

"Shannon, I don't blame you. We weren't together anymore, which was my fault." Jordan straightened in her chair, and I thought maybe she had more to say about my improprieties, but she just sat there looking at me, her expression turning somber. "Poppy told me about your conversation with her."

"God dang it, Poppy," I muttered under my breath. "She promised me she would not tell you about that."

"You really thought she'd keep that to herself. It would have been friendship malpractice. She had to tell me, and I'm glad she did." Jordan grimaced a bit, then let out a sigh. "She told me what happened with Samuel and made me aware of something I should have already known. You would have never just up and left the church after having married some idiot just so you could stay in. I don't know what I was thinking. I was so full of myself. I should have known that something happened."

"You couldn't have known…"

"I should have…"

"Jordan, you couldn't have known that a Christian man would behave that way. You had every right to think I was in good hands. That's how we were raised. That's what we were taught. Your assumption that I just up and left him was reasonable given our situation."

"I know what you're saying, but still…" She closed her eyes for a moment, her brows furrowing. "Damn it! This is all my fault. The whole thing. I should have talked to you right from the very beginning about what was going on with me." She shook her head, her expression one of frustration and regret. "None of this would have happened had I not left you like that. I thought I was doing the right thing. I knew I couldn't be happy in the church. I knew I had to leave, but I did not want to pull you out with me. I was afraid you would follow me and later regret it. I couldn't let you ruin your life. I couldn't be responsible for your soul, so I left you alone to fend for yourself, and I'm sorry."

"The *whole thing* is not your fault, Jordan. I could have followed you when you left, even though you told me not to. But I didn't. I chose to stay in the church. It was my decision, not yours."

Eyes brimmed with tears, Jordan covered her face with her hands, letting out a grunty growling noise followed by a couple of expletives, one of them the F-word. "I'm so sorry he touched you like that." She removed her hands from her face and clutched them together, fist to palm. "If I ever see him again…"

"It's done, Jordan. Don't think that way." I picked up my

napkin and wiped my eyes, sniffing loudly and blowing my nose, wanting so much to stop the continuous hurt we let everyone around us create. "Think of it as a blessing. If he had been half the man I expected a Christian man to be, I would have stayed."

"So, I have Samuel to thank?"

"It sounds crazy, but yeah. Had he not been such an asshole, I probably would have stayed." I let out a shiver at that possibility. "But I did leave, thank God. If I had stayed, I would have been miserable and made everyone around me just as miserable. I would never have been happy, not even content, and that's not fair to me or anyone who loves me. I only have this one life, and I don't want to spend one more moment of it with anyone who doesn't care about me."

"I care about you, Shannon. I love you, and I am glad that you left him."

"I love you, Jordan."

"You still love me?"

I quickly wiped the tears from my eyes, sniffing as I reached over and picked up her hand. "I am madly in love with you, Jordan, and nothing and no one can change that."

Jordan squeezed my hand, and our fingers intertwined, and all at once, the way forward was unhindered, inviting us to grab hold. There were no more obstacles, the church's grip sliding away, letting us breathe and speak and feel without fear.

CHAPTER TWENTY-SIX

I went into the bathroom, removed my clothes, and peeled the cellophane plastic cover from the back of my shoulder. I took a good look at my tattoo in the mirror, wondering what Jordan would think when she saw it, and then took a quick shower, careful not to get it wet. After I got dressed, I made coffee, mulling over the incredible morning I'd just had with Jordan.

On the drive back to Sacramento, we were careful to keep the conversation light after such an emotional breakfast. Not until Jordan pulled into my apartment complex to drop me off did we talk about what was next, deciding in the end that we should not rush things. Actually, this was Jordan's idea, and I respected it and patiently listened to her explain the benefits of taking it slow while every fiber of my being wanted to invite her up and into my bed.

She asked me to meet her at the club the following Saturday, a whole week away. A whole week? She wanted to date me, explaining that we needed time to get used to each other again, which was sweet but maddening, and while I understood the necessity of taking it slow after all we'd been through, the decision to take separate cars to our first date had me wondering what message she wanted to send to everyone who would undoubtedly notice that we were hanging out together. Did she not want anyone to know that we were on a date?

She defended taking separate cars by explaining it as a sort of buffer, something that would keep us from acting too rash, and I realized she was trying to keep us from falling into bed together. I tried to act like I was totally on board while wondering if this signaled that she wasn't altogether comfortable with us. After all, it had been more than a year since we'd been together, and during that time, I'd picked up a reputation for being a bit of a slut.

And then she said something that gave me a glimmer of

hope, telling me that she would wait for me at the entrance of the club, explaining that she wanted to walk in with me and show everyone that I was dating her now and no longer available for whatever their imaginations could conjure up and spread throughout our shared community. She was right. There was probably no better way to get the word out that I was off the market than to show up on a Saturday night with Jordan.

Our first date set, we sat in her car another few minutes, holding hands and looking into each other's eyes like two love-sick teenagers. I really wanted her to kiss me, but the tender way she kissed my hand when we said goodbye was just as sweet, if not more so, intensifying the anticipation I felt when I thought about our future first kiss.

The week crawled by, and with each passing day, I grew more and more anxious. I hadn't heard from Chef Allen about my training position with *Bonny's Pocket* yet, and my new culinary classes didn't start until January, so I had plenty of time to worry about our date, working myself into a frenzy about everything that could go wrong. This was our moment and I would leave nothing to chance. I even went out and bought a new outfit for the occasion. I wanted to look every bit the part when I let everyone know that I was the one who'd been able to catch the eye of the mysterious Ms. Tallis, someone everyone wanted but no one could have because she was in love with me! Ha!

By Saturday afternoon, having thoroughly overthought everything, dismissing Jordan's lofty words of encouragement as conciliant sweet talk, I was a nervous wreck. I had dated in public before, observed and judged as I stepped out on the arm of over fifteen different men over a period of eight years—each one my potential savior, each one a reminder that I was super gay—making me a virtual expert on uncomfortable debuts. This debut promised to be a whole other level of uncomfortable. I was the club fumbling-floozie, and Jordan was the club sweetheart-hottie, and when people saw us together, they were going to judge, questioning my worthiness, possibly making Jordan question it too. I was in a near panic at the possibility and considered rescheduling our date to a different venue.

But I couldn't. We had to make an appearance there, the sooner the better, my fears be damned. This was our community, our place of fellowship. This was my final debut and I was finally in love with the person I was walking in with. This was potentially the start of our new life together, and I had to get it right. I completely changed strategies. No flaunting and no showing off. Hell, I'd be lucky to get through the evening without Jordan realizing she'd made a grave error in judgment. I ditched my new outfit and opted for jeans, a sweater, and western boots—something comfortable, something me. I didn't want to hide who I was. I *was* the club floozie, dammit, and I didn't care what anyone thought or whether they approved, and I could only hope that Jordan didn't either.

As I walked out of my apartment and jumped into my truck, I was still nervous about our public appearance together, but it was nothing compared to the excitement I felt about seeing Jordan again. When I drove into the *Club Imagine* parking lot and saw her already standing outside near the entrance waiting for me, I embraced my nervousness, enjoying my butterflies, hoping she could hardly wait to see me too. After checking my makeup, I jumped out of the truck and walked as confidently as I could toward the building. Jordan met me halfway.

"Hi." Jordan took my hand, leaned in, and kissed me on the cheek.

"Hi. You look beautiful," I greeted her.

"*You* look beautiful," she said, smiling. Jordan glanced at the entrance, then back at me. "You ready?"

I gave her a nod, squeezed her hand, and then we were walking through the doors. The reaction we got was way more than I'd feared. The fact that we were holding hands got everyone's attention, and a loud hush rolled through the room, starting at the front and ending way in back. Everyone, including women on the dance floor, stopped what they were doing and gawked at us.

My heart pounded and my knees shook as I looked around the room, feeling wobbly and awkward and totally spotlighted as we slowly walked past the bar. I glanced at Mason and gave her a weak smile, hoping she had my back. She did not disappoint. She was obviously surprised but gave me a thumbs-up and a smile of her own. I let out a quick breath and let Jordan, who seemed completely unfazed, lead me through the room, where we received similar gestures of support and approval. "It's about time" was the most common verbal refrain tossed in our direction, but there were also nice comments from women I didn't even know. "Well, I'll be damned" … "No fucking way" … "Another one bites the dust," just to name a few.

We finally reached our table, where Poppy, Becca, Ricky, and Stef sat waiting for us with smiles and raised eyebrows, obviously surprised by all the attention we were getting. We took our seats, and everyone in the room went back to what they'd been doing before we'd arrived, satisfied with the bit of entertainment we provided.

Jordan gave me a wink, and I smiled and took a deep breath, glad that the hardest part was over. I said hello to Becca, Ricky, and Stef, then leaned into Poppy and whispered, "Where were you all week? I tried to call you."

"I had to work graveyard. Why? Did you want to ask me something?" Poppy gave me a cheeky grin, quirking her eyebrow at me.

"Yeah, I did, smart alec," I said, jabbing Poppy in the ribs with my elbow. "First, did Jordan know you were bringing me to the club last weekend? I mean, was she in on that?"

"No, she wasn't," came Poppy's quick reply. "That was all me. And second?"

"And second"—I hesitated, giving her a cheeky grin of my own— "I thought we agreed you weren't going to tell her about our conversation and about what happened with Samuel."

"Are you really complaining?"

I narrowed my eyes at her, admitting to myself that without Poppy's help, our reunion could have taken much longer. Still... "No. I'm not complaining, and I'll thank you later, but just so I understand, when you say you won't tell, what does that mean? Just for future reference."

"I never said I wouldn't tell. You asked me not to, and I thought about it and decided I should. I couldn't watch her blame herself anymore, and I couldn't watch you sleeping around just to spite her." Poppy chuckled at the surprised expression on my face.

"So, you knew all along why I was sleeping around?"

"Yeah. You're not really the player type," she said, looking almost apologetic. "Shannon, I don't always do what I'm told. It's not that I didn't respect your wishes, I just didn't agree with them... Just for future reference."

I stared at her, marveling at her astute perception, her kind heart, and how, with all the people we'd met since this whole thing began, we were lucky enough to have met her and have her as a friend. "Okay. Good to know." I laid my hand on her knee and gave it an appreciative squeeze.

"It looks like your first conversation went well," Poppy said.

"Better than I expected, actually. We're taking it slow. We're dating."

Poppy tilted her head and nodded slowly. "Dating. Good. I'm happy for you, Shannon. I'm happy for both of you."

I pressed my lips together and tried not to tear up. "Thank you, Poppy."

Ricky walked toward the table holding several bottles of beer, followed by Mason, who was carrying three wine glasses and a carafe of white wine. After everything was put on the table and distributed, Mason scurried around to where Jordan was sitting and whispered something in her ear. She threw me a smile and a wave, then hurried back to the bar. I had never seen Mason deliver drinks to a table before. I had never seen her on this side of the bar before and was about to comment on this when Jordan leaned into me and relayed what Mason had whispered in her ear.

"The first round is on Mason."

"Wow, that's nice of her. Did she mention what the occasion was?"

"Love," Jordan replied.

I opened my mouth, then closed it, touched by such a simple gesture, caught off guard by how much it meant to me.

"Can't decide how you feel about that, huh?" she asked.

"It just hits me sometimes, you know, to have people rooting for us with so many people out there rooting against us."

"Yeah. Being accepted for who you are never gets old. These ladies can be very opinionated when it comes to who's dating who, and they're not shy about expressing themselves, but they all agree that love is love."

Our table nodded their drinks at us in a silent toast, and then Jordan asked me to dance. The thought of being in her arms again excited me, and I practically jumped up out of my seat. She grabbed my hand and led me to the dance floor, looking sure of herself and very sexy as she placed her hands on my hips. I slid my hands around her shoulders, and we stood there swaying, looking into each other's eyes.

"You know how to dance," Jordan said, using the same words I had used way back when we first danced together.

"A little, I'm learning," I replied, letting her know I remembered.

"Are you still nervous?"

"Are you saying you could tell I was nervous when we walked in here?"

"Yeah, I could tell."

"How?"

"The way you squeezed my hand like a vise."

"Sorry. I was a little nervous, but I'm not nervous anymore."

"Good."

"And thank you for doing this, for suggesting we have our first date here. It means a lot to me that you wanted to be here with me."

"Why wouldn't I want to be here with you?"

"You know, I'm the slut or the player or whatever. What *will* people say?"

"They'll probably say, 'Damn! I missed my chance,' because your player days, my dear, are over."

"That's very funny, Jordan, very sweet, but do you really not worry what people will think?"

"I'm not worried. Let them think what they want. I want to be here with you. I want everyone to see that we're together. You are beautiful, and any one of these women would be lucky to have you. And they know it."

We held each other close through the entire dance, her words making their way into my heart, giving me confidence. I couldn't wait any longer. I would ask her to go home with me when she walked me to my truck. I would find out if she thought I was worthy. I would find out if she understood how lucky we were to have this second chance and whether she believed like I did that there was not a second to lose in starting our life together.

As the music faded and a new song began, Jordan took my hand and kissed it before leading me back to the table, where we spent a wonderful evening talking, laughing, and just hanging out, everyone enjoying being accepted for who they were.

Around ten o'clock, Barbara, Maggie, Michelle, and Denise walked in. Michelle was the first to notice me, smiling questioningly, her expression curious about who I was sitting with. I smiled back at her just as Jordan draped her arm over the back of my chair. Michelle's mouth dropped open in response. She grabbed hold of Maggie and swung her around, pointing at us as she whispered something in her ear. Maggie's eyes practically popped out of her head. Maggie reached over and grabbed Denise, and the three of them stood there staring at us while Barbra, completely unaware, was busy organizing seating. I smiled and waved them over. They slowly approached the table, a little shy but curious about my new friends, one in particular.

"Hi," they all said at once.

"Hi, you guys. Grab some chairs and sit. There's plenty of room."

Ricky jumped to her feet and ran over to where Barbara had rounded up four chairs at the end of one of the nearby tables.

"Hey!" Barbara called out, turning to Ricky as she dragged two of the chairs to our table. "Those are my chairs..." Barbara stopped mid-sentence and squinted in our direction. She walked over to us as Ricky made a second trip to get Barbara's other two chairs. "Hey you guys, what's going on? I found a place..." And then even Barbara saw what was going on. "Hi, Shannon," she greeted, her eyes ping-ponging back and forth between me and Jordan.

"Come on, you guys, sit," I said. I made introductions, and slowly our celebration took on a new level of fun.

Getting to know new people who didn't necessarily hang out together proved to be very entertaining. There were new things to talk about and new stories to tell, and between Michelle and Ricky's constant joking around, we were laughing so hard, I feared someone would tip over their drink.

Poppy and Becca said goodnight first, then Stef made her exit, giving Jordan a kiss on the cheek and me a wink and a smile. Ricky left next, slipping Michelle her number before circling the table and stopping next to Jordan, whispering something in her ear before planting a quick kiss on my cheek. Barbara and Maggie left after that, and then Jordan leaned over and brushed her lips against my ear, sending such an intense shot of desire through me, I barely heard what she said.

"You ready? Let's go."

I gave her a nod, then looked over at Denise and Michelle. "Hey, you guys, we're gonna go."

We exchanged quick hugs as we said goodbye, and then

Jordan took my hand and led me to the bar to pay our tab.

"Don't be strangers, you two," Mason said as she tallied our drinks.

She went on to explain how new couples tended to disappear off the face of the earth during the first few months of their courtship. My eyes squeezed shut and I reached up and pinched the bridge of my nose as my face began to heat up. We had just survived our first public date and now Mason had us in a relationship, her ill-timed comments a potential threat to any chance I had of getting Jordan to accept the invitation I was about to extend her. Mason added an innuendo-laced eyebrow wiggle, and I nearly dragged Jordan out of there. Jordan had been clear about her desire to just date for now, giving us time to get reacquainted. The last thing I needed was for her to freak out over Mason's inappropriate ribbing and entrench herself even further into this ridiculous notion. I needed to reacquaint myself with her, now!

As they talked, I studied Jordan's facial expressions for any clue to her state of mind, realizing that if Jordan didn't accept my invitation, it had nothing to do with Mason. If Jordan turned me down, it was because Jordan wasn't ready. And that was okay.

Suddenly, they were finished talking, and it wasn't okay anymore. I needed her to come home with me! I took a deep breath as she led me toward the truck, feeling desperate as I thought about what I could say to change her mind. She was telling me something about Mason, but I was hardly listening to her. There was only one thing that mattered to me.

"Mason thinks she embarrassed you. You weren't embarrassed about her calling us a couple, were you? I mean…"

"Come home with me!" I blurted, cutting her off mid-sentence, then winced, sure I'd ruined everything with my inability to wait patiently for her to want me again. "Sorry. I didn't mean it that way."

"How'd you mean it?" Jordan stepped closer and put her

hands on my waist.

"I meant it like… Okay, yeah, I meant it that way. But I didn't mean to say it. It just popped out. Sorry. I know you need time, and I respect that. I can give you whatever time you need. I completely understand your hesitancy…"

And then she was kissing me, and I didn't know up from down or right from left as the most delicious warmth spread through my body. I moaned when her gorgeous tongue touched mine, grabbing onto her shoulders when she pulled me closer, practically crawling up her body as she leaned into me, her breasts caressing, her hips pressing…

"I'll drive," she said, releasing my lips in a breathless gasp.

"Huh?" My eyes fluttered open, and I looked down at her hand as she held it out to me. It took me a moment to realize that she was saying yes, and another moment to realize what she wanted from me. I quickly dug my keys out of my purse and handed them to her.

"Get in," she said, her tone urgent, almost gruff. I turned and stepped away from her, only to be pulled back into her arms for another kiss. "Please…" she amended, her voice wonderfully husky. "I meant, *please*, get in."

"Jordan…" I reached up and touched her cheek. "Use whatever tone you want, just tell me you'll come home and make love to me."

"Let's go home."

"Okay." I hurried around to the other side of the truck, hoping she didn't leave the love-making part out on purpose.

We drove through the night, oddly not touching, just breathing hard and glancing at each other. I remembered our first time together, how much I wanted her, ready to risk everything to have her. And this time was no different. If I didn't have her soon, I felt like I was going to die. A dilemma, because that's exactly what would happen if I touched her right now. I wouldn't be able to stop myself from crawling on top of her, practically guaranteeing a twenty-car pileup on the I-80 freeway.

It was unseemly and a little ridiculous, but I couldn't risk it. My whole body was throbbing intensely, the rippling effect coursing from the tips of my nipples to the depth of my core. My panties were ruined, and I feared my jeans were as well. I wanted to be civilized and cool, cuddle up to Jordan and hold her hand, but such lofty behavior was not possible right now, and I knew it. So, it was my duty to show the only restraint I could manage and not touch her while she was driving. I could hold her hand and cuddle her on our next ride when she was back in my life again, where she belonged.

She parked in my parking spot, and I smiled, glad she remembered which one it was. I waited near the stairs as she locked up the truck, then took her hand, meaning to lead her up. But she hurried ahead of me, leading me instead. She pulled a single key from her pocket and unlocked the door, and a sensation of pure joy filled my heart. She was home, and she still had her key!

She pulled me inside, practically swinging me around in her enthusiasm before releasing me. I came to a stop in the middle of the living room as she turned to close and lock the door. She whipped back around, then hesitated, looking at me for a sign. All I could hear was our breathing, all I could see were her eyes telling me she wanted me, and all I knew was that if she didn't get over here right now and kiss me, I was going to explode. I whimpered her name, and she was on me a half-second later, her hands everywhere on my body, her mouth greedy and rough on my neck, making me pant and moan and beg. And then she kissed me, and she was mine.

She walked me backward toward the couch, totally taking control of the situation, negating all my careful planning. I'd been so confident that not having had sex in over a year would make her putty in my hands. No chance! She clearly had plans of her own. In no time at all, she had my boots, pants, and panties off, had me on the couch with my legs spread wide, and was down on her knees eating me out like she was starving to death, leaving me gasping for air and my head spinning. My body was so tightly strung, it arched in response to her mouth's first touch, reveling in her ravenous assault, arching again when her fingers thrust inside, panting and moaning, quivering and quaking as my orgasm fast approached. How she had such complete control of my body, my mind, and my heart was a beautiful puzzle I never wanted to solve. As my orgasm engulfed me, I released a cry extolling her name, "I love you, Jordan!" She then took me to bed and insatiably made up for every moment we'd been apart, breathlessly declaring, over and over, that she would never leave me again.

* * *

I woke up suddenly, delighted to find Jordan draped over me, irresistibly naked. It was wonderful, and I just stared at her, trying not to move, not wanting to wake her and end this beautiful moment. As a collage of memories from the previous night flicked through my mind, from '*Let's go home*' to '*I'll never leave you again,*' I knew that we were about to embark on the next part of our journey, the one that began three and a half years ago when I first caught sight of her sitting under that tree in the park.

I wiggled out from underneath Jordan, careful not to wake her, and went into the kitchen to put on some coffee. I returned to the bedroom and watched Jordan sleep for another minute or two before slipping into a pair of sweatpants and a T-shirt. After a quick trip to the bathroom, I walked back into the kitchen, and as I poured myself a cup of coffee, a knock sounded at the front door. I glanced at the clock and wondered who could be knocking at my door at one o'clock on a Sunday afternoon. I set my cup down, walked to the door, and opened it.

Shit! "What are you doing here!" The words strangled in my throat as my body recoiled in a sickening wave of disgust.

"You don't look well, Shannon," Samuel observed with an air of ice-cold indifference. "Should I come back?" His tone was threatening.

I took a step back.

"Nice haircut. Very feminine."

"What do you want?" My eyes were fixed hawk-like on my aggressor, ready for any indication that he was about to strike.

"I want you out of my life and completely unconnected to my name, and I want you to rot in hell for what you put me through."

I heard Jordan before I saw her. Her breathing was so very familiar to me that when I heard it racing toward me, I knew she was going to hurt him. Arm outstretched, she pushed past me in a flash of movement, ramming Samuel in the chest with such colossal force, he fell backward, smashing into the walkway railing. Powering forward with all her strength, her hand slid up his chest and wrapped itself around his neck, bending him back over the railing at an impossible angle. I was suddenly afraid she would kill him.

"You fucking piece of trash!" she yelled in his face as she bent over him.

He tried to gain his footing, but he was no match for Jordan. She wasn't quite as tall as he was, but he was skinny; she probably outweighed him by fifteen pounds. "You like to hit women! Hit me! Give me a reason to kick your ass!"

He let out a growl, struggling against her, and a wave of satisfaction hit me seeing him totally emasculated, thrashing and flailing so pathetically.

With one hand still wrapped around Samuel's neck, Jordan notched it up a gear. She reached down with her other hand and cupped Samuel's package as she cooed at him mockingly. Then, grabbing harder, she took complete control of him. She yanked him forward by his crotch, swung him around, and delivered a powerful blow to his chest with both of her hands, sending him reeling backward, dumping him on his ass, and putting him firmly in his place!

"Jordan! Jordan!" I grabbed her and pulled her back, keeping my hand on her chest as I stepped in front of her and looked down at Samuel.

He scrambled to his feet, leaning slightly forward,

breathing heavily, his face red, his hand on his crotch, checking for damage. "You need to put her on a leash!" he spat at me.

My hand whipped out without the slightest hesitation and struck him hard across the face.

He grabbed his jaw, letting out a cry of pain as his head jerked to the side, looking stunned as he slowly turned and gaped at his hand and the blood that stained it. I had busted his lip. Better late than never.

"Leave now, or I will call the police," I warned. "And if I ever hear that you have hurt another woman, I will tell everyone what you did to me. I will drag your precious name through the mud."

"No one will believe you," he growled.

"It doesn't matter. The accusation alone will destroy your career. Mark my words, Samuel, I have eyes and ears in the church. I will know, and I will make your life hell."

He let out a very unconvincing, quivering, high-pitched huff, turned, and limped away.

I turned to Jordan, gesturing her toward the door. I did not want to give Samuel the satisfaction of seeing us up here as if we had nothing better to do than waste one second of our lives watching him as he disappeared from our lives forever.

I closed the door behind us, locked it, then turned to Jordan. "Are you okay?"

"Yeah, I'm okay."

"Jordan, what was that?"

"That was me hating the thought that my actions might have led you to that monster, hating that he made you feel you didn't deserve him, hating that he believed he had the right to hit you. That was me making it clear that if he ever shows up here again, I will finish what I started."

"Okay. But..."

"And that right hook you gave him will forever burn this moment into his brain. He won't be able to get it up for the next decade, at least. You took all his power away from him, Shannon. And you know what? I'm going to call Shawn and tell him what happened. I want him to keep an eye on Samuel. Maybe with the right people knowing about this, we can keep women out of his way. God, what a horrible man."

"Jordan, let's not get involved in this…"

"No! You threatened him, and I'm following up. That's all."

"I was just trying to scare him. I don't want him coming back."

"Shannon, let me do this, okay? Shawn and Elena are good people. We can trust them. They have been super supportive of me this past year. I was surprised when they kept reaching out to me. I mean, I felt so ashamed and worried that I had ruined their name. But they kept calling me, talking to me, and asking me questions. They can help with this. Let me talk to them."

"Okay. Then I will let you handle this, but please do not be vindictive. It will reflect badly on us. You Know? Hateful and bitter is not who we are. I don't want people to see us that way."

"Okay."

"Having said that…" My voice broke, and tears filled my eyes. "Thank you for what you did out there." Before I could crumble, Jordan took me into her arms and held me. "I'm so sorry. I should have followed you immediately. I should never have let him into my life."

"Shannon. It's over. I'm here now."

Jordan took me to bed and erased every memory of Samuel from my body, replacing it with her own unique tapestry, marking me forever her own. During her very personal and enjoyable exorcist, baptizing me in her love, she discovered a tattoo on the back of my shoulder, delighting her to no end to find that I had already marked my body hers—forever.

CHAPTER TWENTY-SEVEN

We remained in bed through the afternoon and into the evening, wrapped around each other in the throes of glorious ecstasy, from one moment of sexual gratification to the next, in love and desperately needing to show the other how much. By the end of it, we lay breathlessly worn out, a little sore, and completely famished. We discussed dinner plans and decided to order a large pizza and eat it in bed, just like old times. I went into the kitchen and rifled through the junk drawer, looking for a pizza delivery menu, and as I turned, half-reading the menu and half-reaching for the phone, a large brown envelope lying on the kitchen table caught my eye.

"What's this?" I yelled to Jordan.

"What's what?" she yelled back.

"There's an envelope on the table." Jordan got out of bed, and as she walked down the hallway, my breath caught at her beauty. It took me a moment to remember what I had asked her. "Um...an envelope..."

"Oh. Yeah. Samuel dropped that on his way *out*. It's addressed to you and has a stamp on it. He never got around to mentioning the reason for his visit, but I'm guessing it was to deliver *that* to you personally and generally terrorize you, and if you weren't home, he was prepared to drop it in a mailbox. It was lying on the ground outside the door. Sorry, I forgot about it." Jordan reached for me, pulled me into her arms, and ran her lips and tongue down the length of my neck. "You distracted me."

I let out a deep moan as I held onto her, astonished at how quickly she could make me warm. Did we have time to do it again before our pizza arrived? I was ready to find out. I tipped my head back as she worked her way around the base of my neck.

"Let's see what it is," Jordan said as she leaned away from me.

"See what what is?" I complained as my eyes fluttered open, wondering what she was talking about and why she wasn't kissing my neck anymore.

"Your envelope... From Samuel." She grabbed the envelope off the table, then laid a lovely kiss on my mouth. "Order pizza. I'll wait in bed."

She walked back down the hallway—butt-naked, envelope in hand—and I grabbed the phone and dialed the pizza place. As the telephone rang through the line, I took a slow breath, letting out a quiet hum, amazed at the effect she had on me, jumping when a voice shot into my ear.

"*Domino's Pizza.* Delivery or pickup."

"Delivery please." I placed our order, then hurried back to the bedroom. "And? What's in the envelope?"

"The envelope?" she asked, as if she had no idea what I was talking about.

"Yeah, the envelope."

"Oh. I didn't open it."

I let out a small laugh, amused that she was being so coy. "Well, open it."

"Well, I didn't know. I thought maybe you'd want to open it yourself."

I crawled on top of her and kissed her full on the mouth, sucking on her bottom lip for a moment before releasing it with a smack. "You can open my envelope any time you want."

"Really?" Jordan purred.

"Yeah, really. What's mine is yours," I purred back.

I kissed her again, then rolled off her and grabbed the envelope, hesitating when I suddenly remembered that Samuel had been here before carrying an envelope just like this one. "He was here before, about six months ago, and I think he was here to deliver this." I handed the envelope to Jordan as she sat up against the headboard. I cozied up next to her, making myself comfortable, watching her rip the envelope open. "I can't understand why he didn't just mail it to me. It makes me think he's been here more than just that one time." I shivered at the thought. "He really wanted to deliver it personally. I'm just glad you were here when he finally did."

"Me too. The guy is dangerous. He's a menace. But don't worry, he won't be back." Jordan pulled a thin stack of papers out of the envelope—not more than four or five sheets—and silently read them while I watched. I would never grow tired of watching her. "He's petitioning for annulment based on fraudulent misrepresentation."

"Really?" I sidled up closer and quickly read the highlights. "Thank God. I kind of forgot that we were technically still married."

"Yeah. It says here you don't even need to show up in court. Just sign and initial these marked spots and send it to this address." Jordan looked at me and smiled. "Then you're a free woman again."

"Wow. Let's do this now. Or do you think I should get a lawyer?"

"Um... Let's read it through carefully, and if something looks off, we can think about contacting a lawyer. But if there is any way possible to not get a lawyer involved in this, we should do that. You know, annulments are not that uncommon, and it's not like you've broken any laws or anything. He's asking for an annulment, and you're giving him one."

I read through the annulment papers carefully, then Jordan read through them again. It all seemed very straightforward, in fact, so too-good-to-be-true, I read through them one more time just to make sure.

The pizza came, delaying my signing ceremony, but after we ate, it was the first thing I did, leaving several oily pizza-sauce smudges on the document in the process. I threw it in an envelope, addressed and stamped it, and laid it on the kitchen table for tomorrow's mail pickup. I wanted it on Samuel's lawyer's desk as soon as possible, hoping to send them the message that I wanted this annulment yesterday.

We made love, then lay in each other's arms, thoroughly

enjoying this simple but very affirming activity for the first time without any real care in the world. Jordan reminded me that her car was still parked in the parking lot of *Club Imagine,* and I told her I'd drive her out to the city in the morning to pick it up. Problem solved. We were silent for a few minutes, and then I asked the question that had been at the back of my mind the whole day.

"Move back in with me." Jordan didn't answer, but she didn't seem surprised by my request. "Do you not want to? Is it too soon? Do you have your own apartment? Where do you live now?" Jordan pulled me closer, and I snuggled into her, trying to wait patiently for the information that would help me strategize an argument for why we should live together as soon as possible. But I couldn't wait. "We've been apart too long. This last year has been a huge test, and we passed it. Let's not wait any longer. I want to start my life with you." Jordan remained quiet, and I let out a sigh. "Okay. What would it take for you to consider it? Tell me what I need to do, and I'll do it. I mean, how much time do you need before you know if you're ready for this…"

"I want us to live together," Jordan interrupted my monologue. "I just don't want us to live *here.* Everyone knows where you live, and soon they'll know that I live here too. I don't want them in our lives anymore."

I climbed up on top of Jordan, straddling her, and looked down into her eyes. "You want to move, get our own place? I can do that." Jordan half-smiled as she looked away. "What? Tell me."

"I live with Poppy."

"Really. Wow. Just you and Poppy?"

"No. It's a house, and there are two other women who live there."

"Okay… I mean… You're not involved with these women, are you?"

"No! Of course not…"

"Then I don't understand the problem."

"I don't want to leave Poppy and my other housemates

hanging. It's a big, four-bedroom house, and it's very affordable for everyone when there are four occupants. If I just up and leave, they'll have to pick up the slack, and I don't want to put them in that position. So, my suggestion is, I give my notice to Poppy, we wait until she's found a replacement renter, and then we look for a new place. Is that okay? Can you do that?"

"I can do that."

"I love you, Shannon." Jordan's hands slid down my back and over my ass, caressing my cheeks, the tips of her fingers playing at the edge of my pussy, aching close to where I needed her. "Are you sure you want me back?"

"I've never been so sure of anything in my life, Jordan. I love you, and I want you back forever. And I want forever to start right now."

"So, we're official? We're doing this?"

"Yes. We're doing this. I've always wanted to be official with you. I know it's been hard, but whatever comes up, whatever happens, it could never be as difficult as what's happened to us so far. We can do this."

And as if to signal that all was decided, Jordan slid her fingers through my wet folds, smiling as my face contorted into an expression of desire and love. I spread myself wider, giving her more access, her touch perfect, her love sublime. I came as our eyes locked, our foreheads pressed together, with no doubt in my mind—if there had ever been—that this was exactly what I wanted, forever.

* * *

Finding an apartment wouldn't be difficult, several of what we had in mind were available throughout the Sacramento area—we just needed a one-bedroom this time. The real challenge was finding Poppy a new renter. In the meantime, Jordan spent every night in my bed, making up for lost time. It was as if we had never been apart, starting where we left off, knowing what made each other hot and crazy, knowing where all the secret erotic zones were.

It was also brand new. We were hungry for each other, especially Jordan, who had been celibate for the last year. She seemed to think she had something to prove, pleasantly surprised that I had some new moves of my own but also worried that I would compare her to my past lovers and find her lacking in some way. Just the opposite was true. Her efforts to prove herself took our lovemaking to new heights, satisfying me every night while finding new erotic zones I had no idea existed, leaving me begging for more, and most importantly, wiping clean any memory I had of any other woman who had ever touched me.

A call from a very excited Chef Allen letting me know I had been accepted as Chef Dillon's assistant-in-training at *Bonny's Pocket*, narrowed our apartment search. Jordan's Job was in the city, and my culinary classes and apprenticeship were in the city, so our apartment would be in the city, leaving me with a thirty-minute commute to my day job. But that wasn't a hardship. Jordan had done all the commuting last time we lived together and was happy to continue doing so until we found a new place. I was actually excited about the move. The idea of living in the city was like putting up a wall between myself and my past life.

In March, a student from Cal State University answered the notice we'd posted on campus about the *community living space* Poppy offered. She was a communications and politics major, young, gay, and very adventurous. She was flirtatious and a lot of fun, and I was sure the veteran residents of Poppy's commune had no problem coming to an agreement on her rental application.

We moved into our new place in April, I finished my last culinary class in July, was hired by Chef Dillon as a part-time Chef's Assistant in October, and by February—technically our one-year anniversary, but as far as I was concerned, and Jordan agreed, our four year and nine-month anniversary—there was nothing I could conceive of that could make the fairytale I was living any more complete. I was working a job and a half, and Jordan was so supportive. All the insecurity and complaint she'd had in the past didn't exist anymore. We spent all our free time together, bolstering our confidence in each other and our relationship. We decided to come out to people at work and then to the world, always holding hands in public to remind us of where we had come from, all that we'd been through together, and especially to show that we were not going back and would never hide who we were again.

We had joint checking and savings accounts with sizable balances, our apartment lease had both our names on it, and we took out a life insurance policy that covered the other in case something happened. We even exchanged vows and rings in an open ceremony at our place of worship, *Club Imagine*, with Mason officiating and anyone wanting to celebrate with us welcome to witness our declaration of love.

I was so in love with Jordan and our life together—more official and complete than I could ever imagine two lesbians in a relationship in my lifetime ever being. And then in May, on our official five-year anniversary, Jordan challenged all my assumptions, questioning whether our love had explored all the possibilities this life had to offer.

* * *

We had celebrated our anniversary before, but never in public, always at home in the safety of our secret world, and although I'd always enjoyed our quiet celebrations on the couch eating pizza, this anniversary was different. We weren't a secret anymore. This, our fifth year together, was our first year as an officially committed, open and out, lesbian couple. Jordan made reservations at the *Cliff House* in Folsom for a table for two near the window overlooking the American River.

Excited and determined to dress up for the occasion, I dug through my closet looking for an outfit that would show Jordan how much I loved that we were celebrating our anniversary in public. After pulling out every formal dress I owned, then discarding them one by one as either too conservative, outdated, or both, I packed them all up in a big *Hefty* plastic bag and drove them to the nearest *Salvation Army*. Then I went shopping.

Never having worn a worldly dress before, I was frustrated when I couldn't find anything quite my style after only an hour browsing shops in the mall. I was a total rookie when it came to such dresses and was near giving up as I fingered through the racks mumbling to myself, attracting the attention of a woman standing nearby. She made eye contact with me as she approached, asking me if she could help. Feeling defensive, I attempted to brush her off and act like I knew what I was doing, but she wouldn't go away, always hovering nearby, giving me a smile. I was beginning to think she was coming on to me when I noticed her nametag, *Lana, Lana's Boutique*. She not only worked there but owned the place. I gave myself a mental head-slap and turned to her, relieved when she smiled and again asked me if she could help.

"I need a dress for dinner tonight, and I have no idea what I'm doing."

Lana asked me a few seemingly innocent questions about the details of my planned evening, and an hour later, I walked out the door with a simple red dress—sleeveless, lower neckline than I was used to, just above the knee in length—and some fancy, sexy, matching underwear. She almost sold me the perfect pair of pumps, but I assured her that I had seven pairs of identical pumps of varying colors at the bottom of my closet, one of which was sure to match my dress.

I hurried through the parking lot to my truck, already doubting my purchase, knowing that this dress was a thousand times better than any dress I'd ever owned, taking comfort in the knowledge that Lana was an expert and knew what she was doing—because I certainly didn't. I had to trust Lana. She owned a successful boutique.

I had just gotten out of the shower and was standing in front of the bathroom mirror blow-drying my hair when Jordan walked in behind me, startling me. I immediately relaxed when her arms slipped around my waist. She snuggled herself into my neck, kissing me, and I turned in her arms, wrapping mine around her shoulders, suddenly feeling very confident about my wardrobe choice. It didn't matter what I wore. It would be fine. Jordan loved me. That's all that mattered.

Still, I got a kick from the look on Jordan's face when she got out of the shower and saw me in my dress for the first time. I had to admit, I looked all grown up, very feminine, and a little bit sexy. It felt wonderful.

"Can you zip me, please?" I asked, looking over my shoulder at her as she walked toward me from the bathroom.

"Wow. You look beautiful, Shannon," she said as she slowly zipped me up.

"Thank you. I went shopping today." I turned and looked at her, naked except for the towel draped over her shoulder. "Hurry up, we'll be late." My instruction to speed things up was unconvincing as I quickly licked my lips and looked her up and down, my eyes coming to rest on her breasts. Damn, the woman was hot! I looked up to find eyes dark and smoldering and glued to mine. I blew out a quick breath, let out a light chuckle, and shook my head. "No. We'll be late. After."

The corner of Jordan's mouth curled upward, her eyes squinting adorably as she turned and walked back to the bathroom.

Looking forward to *after*, thoughts of her slowly removing this dress from my body played out in my mind as I walked into the living room, sat on the couch, and waited for her to finish dressing.

Fifteen minutes later, she stepped into the living room and did a twirl, showing me sexy black slacks, gray pumps, and a tailored gray silk blouse. She looked happy, confident, and very sexy. She was breathtakingly beautiful, and for a moment, I considered canceling dinner and just staying in for the night.

We took the truck, and as soon as we hit the first red light,

Jordan's hand was on my knee, slowly moving up and under my dress. The light turned green, and her hand was gone. I smoothed out my dress, letting out a slow breath, catching a sly smile on her lips as she put the truck in gear and made her way through the intersection. I again considered canceling our plans for the evening and having her turn around and take us home, but the focus tonight was a celebration of everything about us, not just her ability to get me hot with a single look or touch. I smiled. She would no doubt have me molten hot by the time dinner was through, and I very much looked forward to the drive home and *after*.

Our table was perfectly placed in the corner next to a window with a spectacular view of the river. The lighting was soft with candles on every table, the atmosphere romantic, and our waiter seemed to understand that we were a couple. He was respectful and treated us like any other couple on a romantic date. It made all the difference. We ordered red wine and the special, porterhouse steak with asparagus and roasted baby red potatoes. It was delicious, and after the waiter removed our plates, we sat there sipping the last of our wine, comfortably silent, just staring at each other.

Something moved at the edge of the table, and a square flat box, not much bigger than the palm of my hand, appeared next to Jordan's wine glass.

"Is that for me?" I asked, my body springing to attention as I sat up straight in my chair, my smile beaming with anticipation.

Jordan chuckled at my reaction. "Yes. Happy anniversary."

"Happy anniversary, Jordan."

"Please, open it."

I picked up the box and lifted the lid, unveiling a gold locket bracelet. I stared at it for several seconds before looking up at Jordan. "It's beautiful, Jordan. Thank you. I love you."

"I love you, Shannon."

I carefully pulled the bracelet out of the box and studied

the etching along the band and the locket itself. The locket was about one-by-one inch, and I could tell by the clasp on the side that it was expensive. It popped open with a confident *click*, and I smiled. One side of the locket was empty, and the other side contained a picture of me and Jordan that I couldn't quite place, our heads close together, looking blissfully happy.

"Remember that group picture at the club last summer?" she prompted. "The one that Ricky took."

"Oh yeah, of course," I remembered.

I liked that we were in the same picture together rather than her on one side of the locket and me on the other, leaving me to fill the other side at a later time. I smiled and looked up at her, ready to tell her how perfect it was.

"Are you happy?" she asked, her face etched with a pensive expression.

I reached out and touched her hand. "Yes, baby, I'm happy. I've never been happier. Are you happy?"

"Yes. I'm very happy." She took in a deep breath. "There is something I want to ask you."

"Ask me. You know I'd do anything for you. I love you."

"Okay." Jordan took another deep breath. "I want to have a child with you."

My eyes blinked and my brows furrowed, sure that I had misunderstood her. "Did you just say you want a child?"

"Yes. I want to have a child. I think a part of me has always wanted to have a child."

"How do I not know this about you?"

"Well, we've probably never talked about it because we were always expected to get married to a man someday and have children. It was inevitable, a foregone conclusion, so I never thought that much more about it…until recently. Over the last few months, I have been examining for the first time how I personally feel about having children, and I am absolutely certain that I want to have one with you."

"Okay…" I was surprised, shocked really, and said the first thing that popped into my head. "You're sure you want to have a child…with me?"

"Yes, I'm sure. And of course with you." She released a mildly exasperated sigh, smiling a little as she shook her head. "Growing up in the church, the whole idea of getting married and having children was a stressful and unpleasant thought. I know you had similar feelings. We never talked about how we felt about having children because we assumed we already knew how we felt. But now I want to talk about it. How do you feel about having children?"

She looked at me, waiting. I didn't know what to say since I had never thought about the possibility of having children outside the bonds of the church and traditional matrimony. "You don't like children?" she asked when I hesitated.

"No. I love children," I quickly responded. "The pressure and stress I felt about having them has nothing to do with children, per se. It was that they were undeniably connected to getting married to a man, and because I was gay, that became a major problem in my life. And that's not all. It was about taking this one thing that was unique to me, that belonged to me, and giving a man control over it. It was like getting pregnant and having children for someone else. And there is something about fertility dictating a woman's salvation that is so off-putting. It was like my entire worth was connected to having babies. I have to admit, since I left the church, having a baby has been the furthest thing from my mind."

"I know exactly what you mean, but with all that stuff no longer an issue, I've been able to really look at this and decide how I feel about it. I want to have a child with you for no other reason than that I love you." Jordan looked down at my locket, and my eyes followed, suddenly understanding why our picture was on one side and the other side was empty. "Will you have a baby with me, Shannon?"

My heart thumped hard in my chest, my breathing steady and deep. If there was any lingering doubt in my mind that Jordan was serious about us, this request just zapped it into a million pieces. I nodded my head, and a moment later, I said the words, "Yes, Jordan. I would love to have a baby with you."

Jordan reached over, took the bracelet out of my hand, and closed the locket, looking up at me as she held it by both ends. I held my hand out to her, and she secured the bracelet around my wrist, kissing my hand and holding it a moment before giving me one of her smiles. "Let's go home."

* * *

All we talked about from that moment forward was the baby. Obviously, Jordan had given having a baby a lot of thought. She explained the world of baby-making as she understood it, using terms I'd never heard before, like artificial insemination, in vitro fertilization, fertility treatments, fertility drugs, fertility clinics, and something called the turkey baster method that I could totally visualize and hoped we wouldn't opt for. She said that there was no reason to believe she was infertile, but still, she needed to have a physical by an OBGYN to determine if there were any problems that could keep her from getting pregnant.

"So, you would like to carry the baby," I asked.

We were sitting at the kitchen table together on Sunday morning, a week after she'd popped the baby-question, the stack of baby books she'd collected over the last few months sitting on the table in front of us. Jordan was an avid reader—always reading something when I wasn't sitting directly on top of her—but for the life of me, the idea that she'd been reading baby books this whole time never occurred to me. I was pretty busy with a full-time job and a cooking gig on the side, but still, I felt a twinge of guilt and slightly embarrassed that I'd never noticed before.

"Yes. I mean, if *you* want to carry, we can talk about that, but I just thought, because it was my request, I would carry the baby. And actually, I would like to." I slowly looked her up and down, trying to visualize her pregnant. "What do you think?" she asked.

"I think you would look very sexy pregnant," I said,

grinning at her.

Our baby-talk moment turned into a make-out session, which turned into two lovely hours in bed. I fell asleep in her arms and woke up alone later that afternoon. I found her back at the kitchen table, one of her baby books cracked open in front of her as she scribbled notes on a pad of paper. She looked up at me and smiled.

"Come here," she said softly, holding out her hands to me. I sat on her lap, and she went over her checklist and notes with me. She was very sweet, and as I listened to her explain the difference between the first and second trimesters from the perspective of fetal development, I realized how much she wanted this and what a great mom she would be.

The following day, Jordan made an appointment for a reproductive physical with an OBGYN. There were some basic tests, which all came back normal, classifying her as reproductively healthy. Fertility treatments would only be necessary if several attempts at becoming pregnant failed. She was given a packet showing her how to monitor her cycle and calculate her period of ovulation, her most fertile time, the optimal time to become inseminated, maximizing her chance of becoming pregnant.

"What is your preferred method of impregnation?" I asked Friday morning, a day after she got her test results back.

"Artificial insemination."

"Um... Which one is that again?"

"It's where sperm is injected into the vagina. It travels through the cervix into the uterus to the fallopian tube, where the egg is fertilized."

"Oh, right..." I said, impressed anew by her knowledge of the female body.

"I think I explained it to you, or at least mentioned it."

"No, you did explain it. I remember. What I can't remember is the part about where we would get the sperm."

"You can get sperm from a donor bank, but I already have a donor in mind. Of course, I wanted to talk to you about everything first before I officially asked him."

"Who is he?"

"It's Jeff from work."

"Jeff, your work wife?"

"My work *spouse* and one of my best friends."

"And you think he would help us?"

"Yeah, I do. I'm almost positive he would."

"How can you be so sure?"

"Because we've talked about it."

"You've talked about getting pregnant?"

"Yeah, we talk about a lot of gay issues. About relationships and having a family. These are not strange issues to discuss with a good friend, whether you're gay or not."

"No, of course not... And you've talked to him about this? I mean, not just about having a family, but that you've considered him as a donor?"

"Yeah, well, we've talked hypothetically, but he's been pretty clear that he would be honored to donate to a lesbian couple. I'm pretty sure he would help us. Actually, in my enthusiasm, I may have brought the subject up more than once over the last month. I think he's getting suspicious. Listen, he's a super person. I want you to meet him and get to know him. I was thinking we should have him over for dinner one night soon."

"So, you're ready to do this?"

"We both have to be ready." Jordan took my hand and kissed it. She was so excitedly animated, her expression filled with hope, I could see how happy this made her. "Baby, my checkup was perfect, and my tests came back good. I'm healthy. If we're doing this, finding a donor is the next step, and if Jeff is the one, he will go through the same types of tests I did, including an HIV test."

"And you really think he's the guy for us?"

"I know he is. He's a great guy, totally sweet, comes from a great family, he's very good-looking, and he's smart."

"Okay then, yeah. I mean, you're right. What are we waiting for? If we're going to do this, then let's do it. Invite him over, tonight even, if he's free. I want to meet him as soon as possible." I leaned forward and kissed her softly on the mouth. "I love you, Jordan, and I want to have a baby with you."

* * *

As luck would have it, Jeff was free that very evening, and he was everything Jordan said he would be. Tall, blond, good-looking, very sweet, super smart, and totally gay. When Jordan popped the donor-question at dinner, Jeff squealed like a girl, jumped up from the table, and enveloped us both in a wildly jubilant hug. "I knew it! I knew it!"

After dinner, while helping me clear the table and wash the dishes, we talked, and the more he told me about himself, the more I liked him.

"Do you have any nieces or nephews?" I asked after he told me a little about his mom and dad and his brothers and sisters.

"I have two nieces and four nephews, and they all call me Uncle Jeff."

"That's amazing. You are so close to your family," I said, shaking my head at how different Jeff's family was from mine.

"I am very lucky to have such a tolerant and accepting family. Raising three boys and three girls, my parents didn't have time to worry about my sexual orientation." He laughed, bumping shoulders with me as I handed him another plate to dry. "I know it's more than that. My parents love me no matter what, and they want me to be happy. They want all of us to be happy." Jeff gave me a sympathetic smile and added, "Jordan told me about what happened to you. I'm sorry."

"No. Don't be. I mean, what happened with my parents is sad. It pains me that they didn't inform the church about my husband, but I'm not even sure they knew the whole truth. And their reaction to me being gay, they really didn't have a choice. I often wonder how they would have reacted had we not been in the church. But we were, and you know what, I'm thankful I turned out to be a lesbian. I'd still be in the church if I were straight. I never would have left. Being a lesbian saved my life. It's been difficult, but I think Jordan and I have dealt with everything pretty well."

"That is an understatement if I've ever heard one. I've never met anyone who has so beat the odds. You two are my heroines, and I am honored to be a part of your incredible journey."

"Thank you, Jeff," I said, touched by Jeff's slightly dramatic yet sincere words, amused that Jordan still felt it necessary to tell everybody about every step of our incredible journey.

Jeff immediately grabbed me around the shoulder and pulled me into a one-armed hug. "Oh, sweetheart, this is going to be so great! You and Jordan are going to be the most awesome parents. If there is one thing the world needs more of, it's awesome parents."

"You're right about that, Jeff. Having good parents is so important. You know, my parents were pretty awesome for the most part. I'm not mad at them. I understand their world, and I know they did what they thought was right, and I'm fine, Jordan's fine, and everything worked out okay."

"Shannon, you are a better person than I am. I would never forgive my parents if they treated me the way your parents treated you. The way I see it, the most important responsibility parents have is to love and support their children no matter what."

I had no response to that. Jeff was right, and when you're right, you're right.

* * *

We sat together in the living room, talking well past midnight, asking and answering questions, deciding how we wanted to do this.

Jordan had certainly done her homework. She handed Jeff a to-do list that needed to be completed by the end of the week and then went over the whole process from where, when, and how Jeff would donate to the insemination procedure itself. It was all very interesting, and I was again impressed with how organized Jordan was and how fluently she spoke about not only getting pregnant and being pregnant but about the wonder she felt at the prospect of giving birth to another human being. She went on at length about her desire to become a mother, sharing in more detail how much it meant to her to have a child that would never be under the control of the church or answer to any man. And if the child were a girl, how much more sweet that would be.

"She will not have been conceived for any reason other than because you and I wanted her to be here with us. She will know that being a girl is just as important as being a boy. It will be as natural to her as breathing, the idea that no man is more important than any other person on this earth just because he is a man."

"Well...except for Jeff," I said, trying to deliver a humorous, mini-homage to Jeff, realizing it sounded more like I was contradicting Jordan. "I mean, in this situation..." I tried to correct, my mouth clapping shut, much too late. I'd firmly stuck my foot in it and potentially opened a whole new can of worms. I looked at Jeff, then at Jordan. "Should we talk about after we're pregnant? You know, after we have the baby?"

Jordan looked at Jeff, then at me. "You're right, Shannon. What Jeff is doing for us is uniquely male and makes him uniquely important." She turned to Jeff. "We can't do this without you, and we are thrilled that you've agreed to help us."

Jeff smiled and said, "I need you both to know, I fully understand my role in this amazing process. I won't expect or assume to have any contact with the baby unless you want me to."

"I want him to," I quickly responded, turning to Jordan. "Don't you?"

"Absolutely," she wholeheartedly agreed.

Jeff put his hand flat on his chest, looked up at the ceiling, and dramatically declared, "Oh my God!" I grabbed his other hand and squeezed it, smiling broadly at his unbridled enthusiasm. He looked at me, and there were tears in his eyes. "I would love to be your baby's Uncle Jeff!"

"I would like that too!"

"Me too. Okay. Good," Jordan agreed, can of worms averted. She took my free hand, reached for Jeff's other hand, and we sat there in a circle holding hands. "I think this was a good first meeting. Jeff, when your test results come back, let us know, and we'll have another meeting to discuss when we will actually do this."

"In the meantime," I jumped in, "I would like to spend more time with you, Jeff. I've heard so many wonderful things about you from Jordan over the last year, and after meeting you tonight, there's no doubt that all of them are true. But I would like to get to know you better myself, one-on-one. Can you free up your schedule the next couple of weeks?"

"Absolutely. I want to know you better, too. We are going to be great friends, Shannon." Jeff stood up and stretched. "I'm going to take off now. It's getting pretty late. I will see you tomorrow at work," he said, pointing at Jordan. "And Shannon," he said, turning to me. "Thank you for dinner, it was delicious."

"You're welcome, Jeff. Thank you."

We walked him to the door, where he gave me air kisses and a lovely hug, and then Jordan walked him to his car.

While I waited for her to return, I went over the evening in my mind and could feel my confidence grow. I was suddenly completely sure about what we were doing. The uncertainty of picking the right candidate was gone. Jeff was the right candidate, the right man for the job, and for the first time, there wasn't an ounce of nervousness left in me. I was ecstatic. I was going to be a mother. I thought I had forfeited my chance at having children, and I had made peace with that, but Jordan had made my chance possible again. She was prepared to give me everything if I would just step up and take the leap with her into a life that I never believed I could have. I remembered back when I had been satisfied to keep us in the shadows so that I could have her, but she kept showing me that such a life was not enough for us. And from one leap of faith to the next, I followed her, and now we were having a baby.

The door opened, and Jordan walked in, her eyes immediately locking with mine. I smiled, shaking my head, tears filling my eyes, happier than I had ever been in my life. She returned my smile and let out a quiet "Yay!" sweeping me up into her arms. "We're going to have a baby!"

EPILOGUE
ONE YEAR LATER

On our six-year anniversary, even though she was eight months pregnant, as big as a baby beluga whale—her words, not mine—and not crazy about going anywhere that required dressing up, Jordan insisted we celebrate with a night out at the *Cliff House* again. Her belief system had evolved over the last year, definitely leaning karmic, so that everything we did meant something important for the baby, including how we spent our anniversary celebration. She had the whole evening planned out, from reserving the same table we had last year to eating the same meal. We didn't drink wine, and this time I gave her the anniversary present, but other than that, the stage was set for a very positive, meaningful, cosmic night out, including our *after*-dinner plans. Being pregnant had made Jordan even more romantic, not to mention more emotional and more sensual. She loved pregnant sex, and I loved giving her pregnant orgasms. It made us closer and stronger, soothed and relaxed us, and was sure to be the highlight of our anniversary celebration.

She looked gorgeous, her face aglow in candlelight, displaying a level of contentment and confidence that made me proud to be sitting across the table from her. Her features over the last year had changed, ascending to a new level of beauty that continuously left me breathless. Like right now, her eyes glimmered with excitement, her smile radiant as she told me she had finally decided on our baby's name. I knew the list by heart and had watched it narrow down to three names over the last eight months and was curious to know what the final name would be. But then Jordan refused to tell me her choice.

"Why won't you tell me? I'm dying to know," I pleaded.
"Because you won't tell me *your* choice," she countered.
"I want you to choose."

"I will choose, but I want to hear your name first. I know you have one. I know you weren't satisfied with the names on the list. Tell me your name for our daughter."

"No. I'm afraid you'll choose my name because I want it and not because you really like it."

"I promise I'll tell you if I don't like your name," she appeased.

I almost let the name slip from my mouth, but her sudden strained expression told me she wouldn't keep her promise. She would never tell me if she didn't like my baby-name because she knew it would hurt my feelings, and she would rather die than hurt my feelings. She would choose my baby-name even if she thought it was a crappy name just so I wouldn't feel bad, and I couldn't have that.

"Shannon, honey, please..." She hesitated as a look of consternation furrowed her brow, and I thought maybe I had irritated her too much, but then the worrying look passed. She took a deep breath, and a nervous smile ghosted her lips.

"Babe, we both know you would never tell me if you didn't like my baby-name. It really doesn't matter to me which name we choose," I explained, not wanting to irritate her further.

"It matters to me..." she began, then froze, her face grimacing with pain. "Shannon!" She looked down at her stomach as she pushed her chair away from the table.

I was at her side in a second, my shoe slipping on something wet next to her chair, instantly recognizing her changing demeanor over the last couple of minutes for what it was. She was in pain, something was wrong, and now her water had broke and it wasn't supposed to yet! Shit!

Jordan turned in her chair and leaned toward me, her hands on her stomach, her eyes wide and scared, her lips in the perfect shape of an O. I got down on my knees, grabbed hold of her thighs, and looked up at her as her eyes squeezed shut. Her hand slipped around her stomach, down and under, and when it reemerged, it had blood on it. I swiveled on my knees, threw my hand out to get someone's attention, and slammed it into the leg of our waiter, who had probably come over to see what all the commotion was about. I grabbed onto his pants leg and looked up at him.

"Call 911!" I said, pushing at his leg to get him moving. "Somebody help me!" I added, calling out to the eerily quiet restaurant.

Everyone moved at once. We had Jordan on the floor in seconds, stranger's coats and restaurant cushions underneath her to support her and make her comfortable. The manager brought us a really nice blanket from his car to cover her with, and then we waited for the ambulance to arrive. Kneeling next to her, holding her hand, telling her not to worry, I was surprised when I was suddenly pushed aside as EMTs took over.

I wrung my hands as they stabilized her, scurried in place as they lifted her onto a gurney, and shuffled alongside her as they rolled her out the front door, ignoring the men who were trying to help her, yelling at me to get out of the way. The legs of the gurney folded up with a snap, and as they slid her inside the ambulance, I reached forward and grabbed her hand in a desperate attempt to touch her before she left me, receiving an elbow to the chest from one of the EMTs in the process.

"Jordan! Jordan! I'll meet you at the hospital!"

Jordan's eyes popped open, and she looked at me.

"Hey, baby. Everything's going to be okay," I tried to reassure her.

"Her name!" Jordan demanded, practically shouting.

I blinked, not understanding what she wanted.

"I need to know the baby's name!" She cried out, making the EMTs hesitate.

"Abigail! Her name is Abigail!"

Jordan gave me a weak smile and closed her eyes. Her hand slipped from mine as the gurney slid away and locked into place. The ambulance doors closed, and then she was gone. I ran back into the restaurant to grab our coats and purses and hesitated at the sight of our waiter and a busboy cleaning our table and the area around it. The manager stepped up next to me and touched my arm, and I turned, letting out a quick breath.

"I need to pay the check," I said as I pulled my wallet from my purse. When he insisted our meal was on the house, I pushed a couple of twenties into his hand and asked him to give it to our waiter. I thanked him, then ran to my truck as three words repeated themselves in my head like a mantra. Hold on, Jordan!

* * *

As I made my way through the hospital's emergency entrance, I came to an abrupt stop in front of a row of payphones on the wall to my left. Had I not seen them, I probably would have forgotten all about Jeff. I snatched the receiver from the closest payphone, fed it some quarters, and dialed Jeff's number, scanning the huge waiting area for any sign of Jordan as I waited for Jeff to pick up. She wasn't there, which meant they had her somewhere else. Whatever was wrong, it was serious. I turned back to the phone when Jeff's answering machine came to life, informing me that he was not in at the moment.

"Jeff! It's me, Shannon. Jordan's in the hospital. Kaiser. Come as soon as you can!"

I returned the receiver to its cradle, then made my way to the reception desk, trying to make eye contact with the three nurses standing behind it. The place was chaos, but the general demeanor behind the desk was brusque and businesslike, and within a few minutes, I was standing in front of a nurse who looked like she hadn't slept in a year.

"Hi. I'm looking for a patient who was just brought into emergency. Her name is Jordan Tallis."

"Middle name?" the nurse asked as she entered Jordan's name into her computer.

"Elain."

She shook her head. "We don't have anyone here by that name."

A second nurse walked over and placed a file on top of the computer keyboard, and I could see from where I stood Jordan's name clearly printed on the tab.

"Was this one just brought in?" the first nurse asked the second nurse.

"Yeah, but she's already gone."

My eyes widened, and I gasped. "What? What do you mean, gone! She's not..."

The second nurse looked at me, shaking her head, and the first nurse, who had opened Jordan's file and was reading it, raised her hand, putting a stop to what was quickly becoming a misunderstanding. "She's not here anymore... Sorry... I mean, she's on her way to surgery."

I let out the breath I hadn't realized I was holding and asked the nurse where surgery was.

"Fifth floor," she said, pointing toward the elevators.

I looked over at the elevators just as one of them opened and took off running. "Please, hold the elevator!" I shouted as the doors began to close. I skidded to a stop in front of the elevator, slipped my arm in between the doors, and they instantly slid back open. I quickly stepped inside and punched button number five several times, hoping that no one else needed a lift. The doors hesitated for an insanely long period of time before they slowly began to close. I let out a relieved breath when they finally did, then endured the slowest elevator ride of my life to the fifth floor. The stairs would have been less stressful and a lot faster.

The atmosphere on the fifth floor was much more subdued. It was quiet, and only a few people were sitting in the waiting area. The reception desk was smaller than the one in emergency, and behind it sat the only nurse on duty. When she didn't immediately look at me, I cleared my throat.

"Excuse me. I'm looking for a patient. Jordan Elain Tallis."

"Your name and relationship?" the nurse asked without looking at me.

"Shannon Callaghan. Friend. She's my partner."

This got the nurse's attention, and she graced me with a quick glance as she began tapping on the keyboard of her computer. "We don't have a patient here by that name," she said, finally looking up at me.

I immediately understood the problem. Jordan had just arrived and was whisked away so fast, her paperwork couldn't keep up with her. "She was just brought into emergency, and they said she was here. Could you please try again?"

The nurse looked at me from over the rim of her glasses, then looked down at her computer monitor. She entered Jordan's name again, slowly, taking her time, and I waited, trying to remain calm.

"Okay. She's here. She's about to go into surgery."

"Can I see her?"

"No. She's about to go into surgery," she repeated, sounding a little irritated with me.

"Is she going to be okay? Can you tell me anything?"

"I can't discuss the condition of this patient with you."

"Is the baby okay?"

"I'm sorry. Only family members are privy to patient information."

"Do you know when she'll be out of surgery?"

"I can't share that information with you."

"Do you know the name of her doctor?"

I looked at her long and hard, willing her to tell me what she knew, but she did not waver, her silence making it crystal clear the conversation was over. I took a quick look around the waiting area, and when I saw no payphones, I jumped back in the elevator, took it back down to the first floor, and called Shawn.

"Shawn! It's me, Shannon. Jordan's at Kaiser. She's in surgery on the fifth floor. I'll be in the waiting area..."

"We're on our way!" Shawn shouted, cutting me off.

"Okay!" I shouted back, grimacing as I hung up the phone. I really needed to calm down.

I took the elevator back up to the fifth floor, took a seat in the waiting area, and tried not to stress out about Shawn and Elena's impending arrival. I hadn't seen them since I left the church, and to be honest, I wasn't looking forward to it. But I needed a family member here, fast.

Jordan often talked with them on the phone and kept them abreast of our situation—they knew that Jordan and I were together as a couple and that we were going to have a baby together—but except for family gatherings, she rarely saw them socially. She seemed happy with the arrangement, and I was happy with it too.

After finally convincing Jordan that she was not responsible for me leaving the church, I was reluctant to share with her that I still struggled with guilt. Anything remotely connected to the church—including any talk of Shawn and Elean—triggered me, and I'd spend days trying to clear my mind of guilt's toxic effect. I was glad Jordan had a relationship with Shawn and Elena and equally glad she never insisted I have one with them. I liked our relationship just the way it was—indirect but official enough—and that's how I wanted to keep it.

Knowing that I would have to see them soon made me uneasy. As I nervously wrung my hands, I noticed traces of dried blood on them. My dress was stained with blood as well, and the knees of my stockings were soiled with Jordan's amniotic fluid. I was a mess. I stood up and searched for a bathroom, finding one just past the elevators. I washed my hands, staring at myself in the mirror, worried almost to the point of panic that Jordan and Abigail were in trouble. If I lost them, I would not survive it.

I took a deep breath and let it out slowly, thinking of Shawn and Elena again. This was hardly the time or place for conversations about sin and guilt and heaven and hell. They wouldn't dare. Christians were notoriously self-righteous and were even known to be a little acrimonious, and although I didn't necessarily expect such behavior from Shawn and Elena, especially in this situation, one could never be too prepared for it. I steeled myself, resolved to treat them with respect regardless of how they treated me. As I dried my hands, I practiced in my head what I could say to them to steer us away from any guilt-provoking, awkward conversations.

I left the bathroom and stopped dead in my tracks when I saw Shawn and Elena exit the elevator and head for the waiting area. I was strongly inclined to run and hide, but before I could, Elena turned and saw me, her arms already up and out as she hurried toward me. The sight of her—*so* Elena—made my eyes tear up and my chin quiver. Damn her! I blinked my tears away and stood tall, trying to act like a strong and proud lesbian, but when she threw her arms around me, I totally collapsed into them and started bawling. Shawn's arms were around me next, and I closed my eyes tight, wanting to delay the moment I'd have to look him in the eye until I could get myself under control. Shawn handed me a tissue, and I wiped my eyes and blew my nose. Elena rubbed my back, and Shawn asked me what happened.

"We were at a restaurant, and her water broke. She was in pain, and she was bleeding. The ambulance brought her here to emergency, but by the time I got here, they had already taken her to surgery. I don't know what's wrong or why she needs surgery. She was conscious when they put her in the ambulance, so I'm assuming she gave consent. If not, it must be pretty serious for them to proceed without it. I don't have her doctor's phone number with me. He's out of town this week. Jordan wasn't due for another month."

Shawn and Elena waited patiently for me to continue.

"They won't tell me anything because I'm not her family."

Shawn turned and walked toward the reception desk. Elena took my arm, and we followed him.

"Excuse me. My name is Shawn Tallis, and my sister, Jordan Tallis, is in surgery right now. Could you please tell me what her condition is and why she's in surgery?"

"I need to see your ID, Mr. Tallis." After scrutinizing Shawn's ID, the nurse pulled up Jordan's file on her computer. "Jordan Elain Tallis is having an emergency C-section due to complications. The surgeon is Dr. Mack. I'll let the Doctor know you're here. I know she'll want to talk to you, but it won't be for another hour at least."

Shawn thanked the nurse, then turned and pulled me into a hug. "It's going to be okay. I'll go get us some coffee. Let's sit down and wait." He pulled back a bit and looked down at me, giving me a comforting smile. "Welcome to the family, Shannon."

I nodded at him, swallowing hard, unable to speak as Elena wrapped her arm around my shoulder and pulled me into a group hug with them. I don't know what Shawn and Elena went through when Jordan left the church, and I don't know how they handled Jordan's outing, but one thing was sure, they weren't holding any grudges.

* * *

Around half an hour later, Jeff arrived, and at first, I didn't recognize him. All traces of the slightly effeminate Jeff I knew were gone. He wore a dark brown suit, his tie was loosened, and the first button of his shirt was undone, giving him that no-nonsense, hard-working businessman look. I had only ever seen him in loud shirts and designer jeans, eyeliner, eye shadow, and hair all done up and styled. There was no makeup this evening, and he had somehow managed to tame his hair into a very generic hairdo, making him look like anyone out on the street and totally not gay. I knew he was in middle management at *UPS*, but I had never given any thought to his work persona before. He was the picture of heterosexuality. I stood up and greeted him in the middle of the waiting room with a big hug.

"Are they okay?" he asked.

"I don't know. They're still in surgery."

I turned to Shawn and Elena and introduced Jeff to them.

"This is Jeff Black, Abigail's father."

Jeff shook Shawn's hand, then Elena's, and then turned to me with raised eyebrows. "Abigail? I didn't see that name on the list."

"Yeah, well, it was a late entry." I looked at Shawn and Elena. "We decided to name the baby Abigail."

"It's a beautiful name," Elena said, smiling at me, rubbing my arm, generally trying to soothe me. I was really glad she was there. She led me back to our chairs while Shawn updated Jeff, and then we all waited together—an eternity it seemed—for any news of Jordan and Abigail.

* * *

It was almost ten o'clock when a tall woman in green scrubs appeared around the corner at the other end of the main hallway. She stopped when two other women in scrubs caught up with her from behind. They talked in hushed voices for a moment, and then the other two hurried away.

The tall woman in scrubs continued down the hallway, her swagger so irrefutable, it looked like she owned the place. She stopped at reception, the nurse pointed in our direction, and she turned and immediately made eye contact with me. I stood up, my heart pounding hard in my chest, and took a couple of steps forward, barely noticing Jeff, Shawn, and Elena beside me.

The first thing I noticed about Dr. Mack, besides her white-blond hair and brilliant blue eyes, was that she was smiling. I smiled back at her, knowing instantly that Jordan and Abigail were okay, pure relief washing over me as happy tears filled my eyes. Jeff's arm made its way around my waist and squeezed, and I looked up at him, his smile just as big as mine, noticing a third thing about Dr. Mack. She was Australian, and her accent was wonderful.

"Shawn Tallis?" she asked Jeff.

"I'm Shawn Tallis," Shawn answered.

"You're Jordan's brother, the family member?" Dr. Mack asked as she looked over at Shawn.

"Yes."

"Do you mind?" she asked, gesturing to me.

"No. Of course not. Please," Shawn gestured back.

Dr. Mack turned to me, introduced herself, and again smiled. "The operation was a success," she said, her voice soft and reassuring. "Jordan is in recovery right now, and she'll be able to have visitors soon. I'll have the nurse let you know when she's awake."

I nodded my head in response and sniffed loudly.

"Abigail is doing very well. She is resting in the NICU. She'll need to spend a week or so in what we call an incubator. She's just under a month premature, and she'll need a little help getting up to weight, and we want to monitor her lungs and heart to make sure she's not having any problems there. But she is very strong, and I am not expecting any difficulties for her. She was breech, and a vaginal birth was no longer the safest route. An emergency cesarean section was the only option. Jordan was conscious on arrival in emergency and gave permission to deliver Abigail by whichever method was needed. She told me that you are her partner and Abigail's mother and should be considered her preferred contact person in any case."

I reached out and touched Dr. Mack's arm, and before I could stop myself, took two steps forward and laid my head on her chest, squeezing her arm with one hand and grabbing the back of her scrub-shirt with the other. I was pretty sure this was not proper hospital etiquette, but Dr. Mack seemed willing to let it slide.

"Thank you," I said, sniffing as I pulled back and wiped my nose. Dr. Mack laid her hand on my shoulder, and Jeff laid his hand on my other shoulder. Shawn and Elena were next, and before I knew it, I was enmeshed in another group hug. I could get used to this.

There were handshakes and pats on the back, and, of course, Shawn got all emotional and started crying. It was perfect. And then Dr. Mack took me aside and handed me her card.

"As soon as Abigail is released, I want you to contact my office and make an appointment for afterbirth care. We'll strategize all things Abigail."

"Do you do this for all your patients?" I asked, already loving Dr. Mack's bedside manner compared to Abigail's *former* obstetrician.

"No. But Jordan asked me to. She didn't know what was going to happen. I'm sure she thought she might not survive the operation, and I was there, and she needed to tell the person in front of her to take care of you and help you."

"I'm sure it was more than that, Dr. Mack. Thank you for saving Jordan and Abigail. I'll never forget it. And we will call and make an appointment with your office. We are definitely changing doctors." I reached out and grabbed Dr. Mack's hand. "Thank you for treating us with respect."

"Shannon, I know how it is. Believe me. They discriminate under the guise of protecting patients' privacy, and it's shameful. I'm sorry I can't do more."

"You've done so much. Thank you."

"You're welcome. I look forward to meeting with you and your new family in the coming weeks."

Dr. Mack walked back down the hallway, and after she disappeared around the corner, I looked at her card. *Caroline Mack, MD. Resident Obstetrician.* I felt a touch on my back, and I turned to find Shawn smiling at me, eyes filled with tears.

"Uncle Shawn," I said, pulling him in for a hug.

"I know. I'm so happy," he said, sniffing. Shawn was such a big, tough guy, my rock of support an hour ago, and now he was crying. He was so emotional. Men.

A nurse came and took us to see Abigail. After changing into protective gowns, caps, shoe covers, gloves, and masks, we found Abigail rooming with a handful of other preemie babies, lying on her stomach in a plastic incubator, surrounded by beeping machines. She was small, but not as small as I thought she would be, and except for the tube in her nose and the drip connecting her to an IV, she looked as normal as any baby I'd ever seen, and I'd seen a lot of babies during my years in the church.

She was beautiful, and I wanted to pick her up and hold

her. Instead, we all stood around her incubator box and peeked inside, cooing at her, letting her know how much we loved her, and telling her that everything was going to be okay. The nurse said I could touch her, but only with my gloved hand. I slipped my hand through the opening in the box and patted her little butt, rubbed her little back, and touched her little head, marveling at the thick black hair covering it. When I slipped my finger under her hand, she grabbed on and held it, strong and sure. We all took a breath and let out an "Awww." It was an awesome moment, and my heart practically leapt out of my chest. The nurse told us it was time to go but that we could visit her again later, so we said goodbye to Abigail and told her we'd be back soon.

Walking down the hallway toward the waiting area, high as a kite and oblivious to everything around me, pictures of Abigail flooded my mind as the absolute certainty that I loved her above all else filled my heart. We had just taken our seats when a nurse came over and told us that Jordan was awake and ready for visitors, but only for a few minutes and only two at a time. I let Shawn and Elena go first, and Jeff held my hand while we waited.

"She looks so beautiful and much bigger than I expected. Five pounds, two ounces is small, but she's tall. Did you notice that?" he asked.

"Yeah, her chart said she's almost twenty inches long. I'll have to look it up in one of Jordan's books, but she definitely looked bigger than I thought she would. And the grip she gave me was amazing. Maybe they'll let us hold her when we visit again. You have to touch her, Jeff. She's solid and strong. She's really there, you know?"

"Yeah. Wow. I'm so proud of you guys."

"Jordan did all the work. And you... Between you and Jordan, Abigail has some really awesome genes."

Shawn and Elena appeared at the end of the hallway, and I stood up, eager to know how Jordan was. "How is she?" I called out before they even reached the waiting area.

"She's fine. She looks great. She's so happy," Shawn said,

sniffing loudly and wiping his eyes.

Jeff put his arm around Shawn's shoulder to comfort him, and Shawn let him. I couldn't help but smile as I watched Abigail's Uncle Shawn and Uncle Jeff hold each other. It was definitely something I never thought I would see in my lifetime, but then this past year had been full of so many things I never thought I would ever see, and I was suddenly extra thankful that Jordan and I had not given up on each other.

"You guys go in. We'll wait here for you," Elena said, giving my arm a squeeze. I nodded, grabbed Jeff's hand, and headed down the hallway toward Jordan's room.

I slowly opened Jordan's door and peeked inside. There was a nurse at her bedside helping her fill out some paperwork. Jeff hovered over my shoulder, and I turned and gave him a questioning look. He nodded his head, and we walked in. The nurse looked up at us, but she quickly faded from my view. All I could see was Jordan, her smile pulling me across the room. Her hands were already out to me as I reached her bed, and I wrapped myself in her arms.

"Hey, baby," she whispered sweetly.

"Hi," I breathed into her neck. "I love you."

"I know you do."

Her arms slipped away, too weak to hold on to me for very long. I didn't want to let go. I wanted to kiss her. I wanted to tell her all about Abigail. I straightened and took hold of her hand, looking down at her beautiful face. She looked totally exhausted.

"...and you just need to sign here," the nurse said.

Jeff stood on the other side of the room, bent over a table, signing a document. He handed the nurse back her pen, and she left the room, leaving us alone.

"Elena said you guys got to see her. How does she look?" Jordan asked me.

"She's so beautiful, Jordan, really, it's amazing, she looks just like you, she has tons of hair, and she's so big, she weighs over five pounds, and she's almost twenty inches long, it's unbelievable, I love you so much…" I took a breath, and Jordan chuckled at me before turning and looking at Jeff as he took her other hand.

"Are you okay with the birth certificate?" she asked him.

"It's perfect."

I looked at Jeff, then at Jordan. "Was that the birth certificate?"

"Yeah. I named her. I hope you don't mind that I didn't ask you first."

"No. I told you. Whatever you want to name her is perfect…"

"I named her Abigail."

"Oh…okay…good." I stood there grinning like a goof, surprised, overjoyed, and a little confused all at once. "What a relief. I've been telling everyone her name is Abigail. It would have been a little confusing if you'd decided to name her something else."

Jordan laughed and squeezed my hand. "We never discussed Abigail's full name."

"Oh," I said, finally understanding what she meant. "What did you name her?"

"Abigail Tallis Callaghan. Jeff's name is on the birth certificate as Abigail's birth father, and my name as her birth mother. I've given her my family name for her middle name, and your family name will be her family name. I wanted your name on her birth certificate too."

I closed my eyes for a moment, pressing my lips together, trying not to lose it. "Wow. I like that." My voice broke, and I cleared my throat, chuckling to myself. "She will curse us when she has to learn how to spell it, then learn how to write it, and then later when she has to sign her name on everything."

Jordan laughed and squeezed my hand. "I can live with that." And then, as if just remembering something, her eyes widened. "Oh, did you meet Dr. Mack?"

"Yeah. She's awesome."

"Right? We're so lucky she was here. I'm so glad our

doctor was on vacation. I want Dr. Mack to help us with Abigail. I asked her to be Abigail's godmother."

"Jordan, we're not Catholic, and besides, she's probably been asked by a million people to be their kid's godmother. If she can't, don't be disappointed."

"She already said yes."

"What kind of conversation did you have with her?" I asked, surprised at how quickly and thoroughly Jordan had made Dr. Mack a part of our family.

"I thought I was in trouble. I didn't know if I was going to make it, and I wanted you to have someone I trusted and had talked to. She was unbelievable. She listened to me and held my hand until I went under. I want her in our lives."

"I want her in our lives too." A nurse popped her head in the door and told us it was time to go, as Jordan needed her rest. Jeff gave Jordan a kiss on the forehead and left, but when I said goodbye, Jordan wouldn't let me go. She held my hand tight to her chest, and I remembered Abigail's strong grip. "Abigail is strong, just like her mom," I said, smiling proudly at Jordan.

"She sure is," Jordan replied, looking me right in the eye, squeezing my hand tighter. "Kiss me, Shannon."

I got carried away and gave her a bigger kiss than I had intended, but she was all smiles when I finished.

"You're going to be a great mom," she said. "I will always love you for taking this leap of faith with me. For giving me this life. You've always believed in us, even when I didn't. All the things you did to keep us together. My God, Shannon, it was impossible, and crazy, and hard." She took a deep breath and slowly let it out. "Thank you."

She was probably high on painkillers and wouldn't remember that she said all these beautiful things to me. But I would never forget.

"I've loved you from the moment I first saw you, Jordan. There is no way I was going to miss out on any of our leaps of faith together, and none of them would have even been possible without the very first one."

"And which one was that?"

"The leap of faith you took when you loved me back."

"I remember that exact moment," she said, smiling. "And it was more like falling than leaping as I recall. But there was a lot of faith. I knew when I first saw you that whatever happened in my life, I wanted you in it. I love you, Shannon."

"I know you do, Jordan. I love you, too."

Printed in Great Britain
by Amazon